PRAISE FOR
A RIVER OF GOLDEN BONES

"I inhaled this novel. *A River of Golden Bones* by A.K. Mulford is a gorgeously written queer fairy tale–fantasy conjured with the bones of wicked worldbuilding and laced with decadent spice. Get ready to devour this wolfish tale."
—Charissa Weaks, bestselling author of *The Witch Collector*

"A beautiful journey of self-discovery and queer identity, filled with heart-stopping romance and page-turning adventure. *A River of Golden Bones* is a must-read for fantasy and romance readers alike. I couldn't put it down!"
—Cait Jacobs, author of *Medievally Blonde*

"The relationship between Calla and these performers becomes the most compelling part of the book, giving rise to questions about gender and the difference between a protector and a tyrant. Defeating evil is important, sure—but the real thrill is finding people who make you want to be your fullest self. It's lovely, life-affirming stuff."
—*Washington Post*

"I was taken by the expert dismantling of the gender binary amidst a quest that is sexy, romantic, and heroic all at once."
—Book Riot

"A steamy romance between Calla and Grae unfolds amid battles against monsters and dark magic, intertwined with Calla's fight against patriarchy and oppression and her burgeoning acceptance of her own genderqueerness. This series is off to an exciting start."
—*Publishers Weekly*

"It's one of those books that just sucks you in and makes you want to keep reading into the night."
—Smexy Books

"I've been waiting for this one for a long time, and I'm happy to say that it was one of the most moving books I've read in quite a while. . . . Really, really beautifully done!"

—The Book Review Crew

"If you've been looking for a queer adult fantasy to sink your teeth into, this is the one! . . . If you love shapeshifters, stories about overcoming odds and re-examining our beliefs, and politics, this is for you. It's a series I know I'll be keeping up with."

—Utopia State of Mind

"An incredible book. From the depth of the characters to the beautifully described scenery. The sense of mild humor even when things are tough and the overarching sense of loyalty. This is a found family book and it shows in their interactions. I didn't want this book to end, and now that it has, I can't wait to read the next one."

—Nonbinary Knight Reads and Reviews

"*A River of Golden Bones* by A. K. Mulford is a romantasy full of wolves, malicious power and the path to acceptance. I'm completely in love with this first book in The Golden Court series. . . . This is a book you need in your life."

—Immersed in Books

"I just want to hug this book!!! I loved it so much for the comforting characters and the author's smooth storytelling. . . . Most meaningful to me is the author's incredibly kind and understanding way of expressing Calla's gender and the very real fears that go along with self-discovery. This not only made me feel seen but just so comforted by these characters."

—Laughing Loving and Books

A
SKY
OF
EMERALD
STARS

A
SKY
OF
EMERALD
STARS

BOOK TWO OF THE GOLDEN COURT

A.K. MULFORD

HARPER Voyager
An Imprint of HarperCollinsPublishers

A SKY OF EMERALD STARS. Copyright © 2024 by A.K. Mulford. All rights reserved. Printed in the United States of America. No part of this book may be used or reproduced in any manner whatsoever without written permission except in the case of brief quotations embodied in critical articles and reviews. For information, address HarperCollins Publishers, 195 Broadway, New York, NY 10007.

HarperCollins books may be purchased for educational, business, or sales promotional use. For information, please email the Special Markets Department at SPsales@harpercollins.com.

Harper Voyager and design are trademarks of HarperCollins Publishers LLC.

FIRST EDITION

Designed by Jackie Alvarado

Map design by Nick Springer / Springer Cartographies LLC

Library of Congress Cataloging-in-Publication Data has been applied for.

ISBN 978-0-06-329147-8

24 25 26 27 28 LBC 5 4 3 2 1

To my writer friends, I am so grateful to have you in my corner cheering me on, sharing highs and lows, and helping me find my own way!

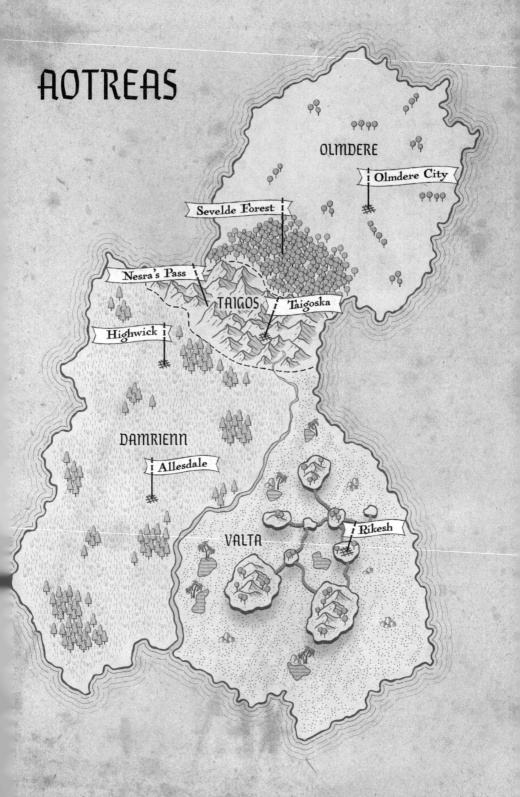

AOTREAS

OLMDERE

Olmdere City

Sevelde Forest

Nesra's Pass

TAIGOS

Taigoska

Highwick

DAMRIENN

Allesdale

VALTA

Rikesh

Map by Nick Springer, copyright © MMXXIII Springer Cartographics LLC

A
Sky
of
Emerald
Stars

SADIE

GOLDEN LEAVES DANCED PAST THE WINDOW OF THE LITTLE cottage. Olmdere seemed to hang in a state of perpetual autumn. In Highwick, it would still be summer, and—though I wouldn't admit it to anyone—I missed the bloom of flowers, the scent of silver stones baking in the sunshine, the iced drinks and bounty of summer fruits, all while lazing in the shade of the forest and swimming in the streams. It was a brutal place sometimes, but not all of it had been evil. Not all of my childhood as a high-ranked member of the Silver Wolf pack had been bad. But everything I'd known—*evil or not*—had been ripped away from me now, and I was sure I'd never go back.

It felt like I was falling through midair and the ground never rose to meet me. I didn't belong to my former pack anymore. And as horrible as that was, even worse was the thought that I didn't feel like I belonged here, either.

"So you've decided on sulking forever then?" Maez asked through a mouthful of lentil stew.

"I'm not sulking," I muttered in a voice that would be definitively classified as "sulky."

Briar pulled a skillet of corn bread from the fire and placed it on the stone windowsill to cool. "You're avoiding my twin, Sadie," she said, glancing over her shoulder at me. "And your Queen."

"Your twin and my Queen are one and the same," I said bitterly. "Stop being so dramatic."

I assessed Briar's red hair braided back off her face, her bright blue eyes, and long lean frame. She didn't look much like her twin, Calla, now the Queen of the Golden Court. Now *my* Queen, too, as everyone seemed to feel the need to remind me.

It still felt odd. I thought I'd be a member of the Silver Wolf pack for the rest of my life. I was one of the royal guards—the elite. I was meant to live and die protecting the Silver Wolf throne . . . and I had accepted that.

Now, I wasn't a member of any pack at all, but rather a *court*, one comprised of both human and Wolf. It was a good change, and yet it still left me reeling. Was it possible to miss something even if it was wrong?

Everything felt tight as a bowstring. Every day we waited for King Nero to attack and the war he promised to begin in earnest, but there was nothing but silence from the Damrienn border.

When a Wolf is silent, that means it's hunting.

So we all idled by in a tension-filled routine. Planning. Waiting. Rebuilding.

Briar cleared her throat, and I spotted the silent conversation whizzing between her and Maez. Her eyes widened as she jutted her chin in my direction and mouthed something I couldn't quite make out.

"If I'm ruining your mating bliss, just say so," I grumbled, pushing to a stand.

Maez shot to her feet across from me. "Sit," she commanded as if I was still a puppy. She picked up her spoon again and resumed eating. "I know you came here for more than my mate's famous corn bread. Talk."

I sighed, lifting a hand to rub across my face and then thinking better of it in case I got spice in my eyes. Then these two would think I was crying and that's the last thing I fucking needed. I wasn't a Wolf who got her heart broken by anyone—let alone a human. I was a warrior and now one of Queen Marriel's official guards . . . well, I *would* be if I spent any time at the castle actually performing my duties instead of drinking every Olmderian tavern dry, definitely not thinking about a human.

My hair and clothes still reeked of ale from the night spent at the tavern . . . several nights, weeks even, if I was being honest. I'd spent the rest of my time since Sawyn's death at Maez and Briar's cottage, not because I particularly liked cottages or the puppy eyes they constantly made at each other, but because the palace reminded me of the battle and a certain tall musician who occupied even more of my dark thoughts than the pack I'd lost.

"You can't avoid the castle forever," Maez said, already knowing my line of thought.

"I know it's become a sore spot between me and Calla," I muttered. "It's just been . . . a lot."

"Does she know that?" Briar asked pointedly, tossing a dish towel over her shoulder and untying her apron. She was the picture of rural bliss, looking even more regal in this little cottage than she did in a castle. More, she looked happy.

"Maybe it's a one-sided sore spot," I muttered, pulling out the knife from my thigh belt and flicking it back and forth.

Maez's hand shot out and covered my own, pinning my wrist to the table and ceasing my knife fidgeting. "Look," she said. "We all think Navin is a piece of shit."

"Mm-hmm," Briar agreed as she sauntered over with a pitcher of lemonade.

"*But*," Maez continued. "He's a piece of shit that you're going to have to get over *without* stabbing someone . . . or my mate's carefully selected new table."

I yanked my wrist away and sheathed my knife, knowing I was moping and hating myself for it. "Nothing ever even happened between us," I said tightly. "A few chaste kisses and nothing more. I'm acting like such a bloody fool and I hate it, but I can't settle into this life here. Everything about it chafes. I just . . . I don't know."

"A human would've never satisfied you," Maez continued. "You would've dropped him like day-old bread after one roll in the sheets. You like the tough ones, Sads—a human who wears daisies embroidered on his lapel is never going to work out."

"Yeah. You're right." I blew my bangs out of my eyes from the corner of my mouth. I really needed to trim them but couldn't summon the fucks to give to do so. "There weren't exactly a lot of places for us to sneak off to on a moving wagon, and the one night I thought we'd have together we got captured by Silver Wolves . . . and then his face got smashed in." The memory of that horror flooded through me, and I was once again reminded that Navin was not as strong as the Wolves. I shoved up from the table into a stand, feeling a little more in control. "You're right." I said it with more confidence this time. "He and I were a bad idea from the start. There's no way we could've lasted." My shoulders shook with bitter laughter. "He was never strong enough for me."

"Yes," Briar said as Maez slapped the table and shouted, "Damn straight." I thanked the sweet moon for my friends and their unerring—if not overzealous—support.

Their words were finally sticking. Navin was a sad little human who chose to protect his Rook brother over me in battle. Of course he'd chosen his own kind, just like I would choose mine now.

Yep, I absolutely believe all of that.

"Thank you." I whirled with newfound bravado, reaching for the door.

"Anytime," Briar said, and Maez added, "Well, not *anytime*. Maybe let's plan a time for you to drop by next—Ow!" Without looking, I knew Briar had smacked her by the sound. I wondered how many intimate moments I'd interrupted over the last few months.

As I opened the door, I found my brother, Hector, with his fist raised, poised to knock. *Looks like I wasn't the only one interrupting the newly reunited mates.*

"What are you doing here?" I asked.

Hector shook his head at my attire, a constant disapproving frown on his face. He wore his new royal armor: black battle leathers with plated gold accents. He looked both royal and lethal, a deadly combination of elegance and strength. I, however, was out of uniform, favoring plain brown trousers and a tunic that came down to mid-thigh that hid the plethora of weapons I wore underneath.

"The Queen has summoned you," he said sharply in that scolding brotherly voice he used whenever I'd pissed him off. Why did my only sibling and I *both* have to take up the family business of fighting for a living? Why couldn't he have been a baker or something?

"Great," I muttered, shooting over my shoulder to Briar and Maez, "I'm being summoned."

"Yes—queens can do that," Hector said.

"Oof," Maez said.

"Good luck," Briar added.

I couldn't dance around it anymore. Calla would make me face them. They'd probably strip me of my title and kick me out. I had been ignoring my responsibilities to Calla for long enough, losing myself in taverns and gambling halls, trying to forget all the ways I'd betrayed myself. Maybe this was a good thing, then. Be done with the farce and focus on getting really, truly, stupidly drunk.

Hector stepped to the side to let me pass. I skirted around him, not wanting to look him in the eyes. His very presence felt like one giant "I told you so," and I didn't need him gloating over the pain in my chest that I refused to name.

I stormed off down the cottage path, lined with autumnal flowers in burgundies and marigolds that Briar had so carefully curated like she was a whimsical fucking faery. I fought the urge to stomp through the beds like the grumpy storm cloud I was. Time to face the consequences of my actions. Time for the punishment I'd been waiting on this last month as I frittered away my coins on a mission to find the bottom of every bottle of Olmderian wine. Time to lose this newfound family I'd done nothing to deserve.

With Hector at my back like my own bloody executioner, I made my way back through the forest and toward the city, dreaming of slitting Navin's throat for making me feel this way . . . and then slitting my own for having such a thought.

I TRIED TO WAYLAY HECTOR WITH THE PROMISE OF DRINKS ON me at his favorite local tavern of choice, but he was having none of it. My big brother marched me through the forest on the outskirts of Olmdere City, and I walked tethered to him like a horse with an invisible lead rope.

His silence was practically saying, *At least* one *of us can honor our duties.*

I could not let such a lack of statement go unchallenged. "So how's *your* human?" I muttered, storming through the deep leaves with an ever-quickening pace.

"She's not my anything," Hector said tightly. "Not yet at least."

"But you want her to be," I prodded with the deft ability of a sibling who knew *exactly* how to get under her brother's skin. "You've grown close since her sister's passing."

Mina had stayed behind when Galen den' Mora rolled out of Olmdere, both to grieve the death of her twin, Malou, and to help Calla with the reconstruction. She now sat on the queen's council and advised Calla on all sorts of issues. I'd been too busy with my own pursuits to notice my brother's closeness to her before. But since her sister died at the hands of Sawyn, Hector, of all people, seemed to be there the most to pick up the pieces.

"Bringing up her sister's passing is low even for you," Hector said. "You act as if I'm only comforting her to gain something."

"Aren't you?"

Hector grabbed me by the shoulder and spun me around.

"First off, screw you for ever thinking that of me. Second, *enough* of this, Sadie," he growled, a hint of his Wolf coming out as he spoke. Two humans walking down the forest path in the other direction gave us a wide berth. "You've always been a bitch, but now you're just downright cruel."

"Keep pursuing her, and you'll find I'm relatively mild in comparison to what you'll get from others," I said, instinctively grabbing one of the knives from my thigh belt and flicking it back and forth. Sweet Moon, I wished I could stab it into someone right now, preferably a tall bronze-eyed musician.

"I'm not a sk—" He caught himself before he said it, but we both knew the words about to tumble out of his mouth: "skin chaser."

It was an insult slung at Wolves who cavorted with humans. Now, as members of a Wolf-human court instead of a pack, those words didn't apply here, and yet I still couldn't shake them. Whether I wanted it or not, the shadow of everything I was raised to believe loomed over me. Losing those beliefs wasn't as easy as shedding a too-tight coat. Layer upon layer and I still found myself wincing at the insult skin chaser.

I certainly didn't want my brother to have to go through that, too.

Still, I couldn't just *say* that to him—I *was* a bitch, after all. So I pulled out of Hector's grip and kept walking, hating how he and I both still acted more like Silver Wolves than Golden Courtiers. "No talking about your human," I said more to myself than my brother. "Touchy subject. Got it. Not that it will matter after Calla banishes me for ignoring my duties."

"Look." Hector cut in front of me again. "I know this has been hard. All of it. But I'm here, for what it's worth, and I will always have your back."

"Aw, don't," I said, giving him a smack on the shoulder and clearing my throat. "Rauxtides don't do feelings."

He chuckled. "True."

We wound our way through the forest as views of Olmdere

City peeked through the autumnal foliage. A long row of white boats sat nestled on the eastern shores of the lake for the night. Only two punters were still working, sitting on the bow of one boat playing cards. During the day, the boats ferried people all around the city: to the northern end with rolling gardens and cottages, the eastern quarter with its theaters and restaurants, the southern streets that were packed with workshops and trade stalls, and the western markets where you could buy just about anything your heart desired.

Despite my prickly state, I still appreciated the capital of the Golden Court every time I walked through it: the gold-flecked red stones, the towering domed architecture, the old dusty bricks, and the sound of the river rushing through the city never too far away.

My neck craned further as the castle rose above the last stretch of woodland between us and the city. The striking gold-flecked stone that comprised most of the city was also used in the castle construction, but with much more gold embellishments and detailing. It was clear the Gold Wolves of old were as rich as thieves, having made good use of the gold mines of Sevelde—much to the humans' peril. But that was part of what Calla was trying to change. Tearing down the castle wasn't going to change that, though—not that it would be easy to do anything to the castle: the stones were expertly cut and arranged, forming intricate patterns that caught the light and seemed to glow more in the fading sun.

"Do you think the sight will ever stop filling us with awe?" Hector asked as if he'd heard my thoughts.

The castle of our birthplace, Damrienn, was enormous and formidable, but it was also sharp and cold, nothing like the warmth that seemed to seep from this castle, open and welcoming. Still, part of me yearned for that coldness and for the unquestionable sense of belonging that came with it.

"This, this is our home now, Sadie," Hector added, and it made my already tight lips curve downward.

"Home," I echoed. It certainly didn't feel that way. I had no clue what home was meant to feel like, in fact. Maybe the feeling was just a made-up faery story.

Our family's townhouse in the city of Damrienn never felt like home, nor did this giant castle, despite Calla's best efforts to make it feel like ours. Briar and Maez's cottage felt *homey* but didn't feel like mine. Goddess, even that roving wagon had felt more right compared to the intricate adornments of castle life, but that wasn't it, either. I would have taken a seat in the wagon in a heartbeat rather than be here, though. I was done playing the games of kings and queens. I couldn't just sit on my hands and politic for the rest of my life. I wanted to move, wanted to roam, wanted to *fight*.

We plunged back into the forest, taking the last little deer trail toward the boats as the sun set. As if summoned from my thoughts alone, a structure caught my eye. I squinted into the shadows, seeing the arched roof of a giant wagon through the trees, and my heart met my throat. The last thing I wanted was to be anywhere near it. Near *him*. I would have gladly ignored it, thinking I might have actually conjured it in my mind. Maybe I'd finally *lost* my mind, and I was about to thank all the wine I'd drank the last month . . .

But then I smelled it.

Hector stiffened beside me. "Blood," he said, sniffing the air and confirming my fears.

I started running toward the wagon, my mind racing to catch up to my feet. As we darted through the thick undergrowth, a body appeared on the narrow path. His long frame, tattered velvet clothes, and scent like old song sheets and resin . . . With that scent, the memories hit me harder than I'd ever remembered them.

"Navin!" I screamed, darting the last stretch of forest. My knees squelched into the muddy ground as I dropped in front of Navin, all my anger replaced by ice-cold dread. He was so caked in mud and dried blood that I didn't recognize him at first, only his telltale scent shot through me like a poisoned arrow: Navin. He was here. In Olmdere.

Hurt.

Relief coursed through me as Navin lifted a shaking hand, and I thanked all the Gods that he was alive. I'd hate him later, wish him death again, once I was certain he was alive. I didn't care about the hypocrisy. Right now, I just needed him to be alive.

Navin's hands slid under his chest and he tried to push himself to a seated position, but he collapsed back to the forest floor. My eyes scanned over his body, searching for the wound.

"Ora," Navin panted. "They're gone. Taken—taken by . . ."

"What?" Hector barked, rushing over to Navin's other side. "Who? Who took Ora?"

"Wolves," he groaned.

Hector perked up, alert, looking around. Sniffing. He paused a moment, but then shook his head.

The Wolves were gone.

Not that I cared. "Where are you hurt?" I begged, searching for the slash marks in his clothes, trying to discern where the blood was coming from.

A small wooden instrument that looked like a tapered flute still remained clutched in one of his hands. Navin swayed up onto his knees, his shaking grime-covered hands dropping the flute and reaching out to me. He cupped my cheeks and leaned his forehead against my own, taking a deep breath like a Wolf scenting the air. I hated that my eyes pinpricked with tears, but I couldn't stop it. Nothing about how I felt about him had ever been in my control. The same relief bracketed his expression before his eyes clenched closed. His body trembled as he whispered, "Sadie," and collapsed.

I caught Navin's long torso in my arms, slowing his fall as I teetered over with him.

"We need to get him to a healer," I barked.

"What does it mean?" Hector asked, frowning down at Navin. "Do you think the Silver Wolves took Ora to retaliate somehow?"

"Hector," I snapped as I slung one of Navin's arms over my shoulder. Navin groaned, barely clinging to consciousness. "Help me."

My brother, seeming to remember himself, burst into action and helped me lift Navin to his feet. "The boats are just through there," he said. "We'll take him to Calla."

"Fucking Moon." I let out a shaking breath.

Hector kept his gaze focused on the shoreline. The boatman saw us and leapt from the gunnel of his boat to help us get Navin inside. "If the Silver Wolves really took Ora, Calla's going to start a war to get them back," Hector muttered.

"Good," I said. "It's about damn time."

CALLA

I DIPPED MY HAND INTO THE TURQUOISE WATER OF THE LAKE, so clear I could see the silt all the way at the bottom. Light filtered in through holes in the cave, making the golden treasure all around me glitter. Little iridescent fish danced around my hands, darting in and out of the craggy rocks below the surface.

I perched on the steps that led into the lake below the palace. Above me, holes in the ceiling tunneled upward to where I knew the dungeons sat. Only the gentle lap of water sounded, and yet I could still hear the screams, still remembered the feeling of biting into the ostekke's tentacle, still gripped with the feeling that I'd come all this way only to die in the dungeons of my own palace.

I swirled my hand in the water as that day replayed over and over behind my eyes.

I'd killed my aunt . . . and she'd killed me.

Loosening the laces of my tunic, I traced a hand down the golden bolts of lightning bursting from my chest. Vellia's light magic had stitched me back together, leaving this gilded mark that felt like skin but weighed so heavy on my soul. If I even still had a soul . . .

Dying wishes were made as a trade: a faery's gift of magic in exchange for them taking one's soul to its final resting place.

Did that mean I was soulless? I'd already made my wish. Would my soul be reaped when I died again or was it already gone?

Everything felt jumbled and restless inside of me. I mourned for Malou and for all those who died trying to bring peace to Olmdere and for all those who suffered for so many years under Sawyn. I needed to make it right for them. I needed to bring this court back from the brink. I needed to make the second chance I was given count for something.

I needed to make it so that all this gold didn't seem like it was still covered in blood and shadows.

"I thought I'd find you down here," Grae said, his boots clicking down the steps. He perched beside me and dropped a kiss to my collarbone where the tip of one lightning bolt ended. "It is too early for such contemplation," he murmured against my skin, smoothing away the tightness in my shoulders.

"I can't stop thinking . . ."

His warm breath skittered across my neck. "Come back to bed and I'll help with that." When I let out a long sigh, he clearly knew my mind was still too far away, mate or no, and he threaded his fingers through my hand and squeezed. "Sawyn is gone, along with her ostekke."

"How many of them do you think are left in the world?" I mused, lifting my hand from the water and wiping it on my trouser leg.

Grae shrugged. "I don't think anyone will be volunteering to venture through the lakes of Lower Valta to count them." He stared out at the treasures mounded upon the shores. Mountains of gold hugged the corners where the palace walls met the lake rock. "I hope not many."

I let out a soft laugh. "Me too." I hovered my hand over the lake water again, and Grae did the same with his own free hand. "How quickly this place came back to life without Sawyn's dark magic."

"And through the leadership of a certain Gold Wolf," Grae reminded, squeezing our joined hands.

I pursed my lips, staring down at the little fish darting back and forth. "I don't—"

"You do," Grae cut in before I could even get started, already knowing all the doubts in my heart. "Seeds have been sown, villages have been rebuilt, families have been reunited . . ."

"It will be many seasons, if not *years*, before those crops produce enough to sustain our court," I said. "Decades before the towns are back to their old populations, generations before those families don't fear that everyone they love will be taken from them again."

Grae released our hold and gently cupped my cheeks with both hands, making me meet his endless umber eyes. "You cannot contain everyone's suffering in your heart alone," he said for what felt like the hundredth time. Still, we both knew I needed to hear it again. "You cannot carry the burden of every single citizen's grief. You can only take another step forward each day. Breathing life back into this court will be the slowest sunrise, not the brightest lightning strike," he said, dropping one hand to trace his fingers across my scars. I thought of Sawyn's emerald bursts of lightning, the ones that flashed in the sky the night I found out Grae was my mate, that same emerald magic that claimed my life. "But the sun will rise on the Golden Court, little fox. Trust in that."

A tight knot formed in my throat and I nodded. I wished I could leash the sun and hoist it into the sky faster, but Grae was right, it *was* rising, the court was healing, I just needed to give it time.

"We should be turning our eyes south anyway," I murmured.

"Ah," Grae said, gesturing to my soldierly attire. "I should have guessed."

"Damrienn has still made no moves," I said. "Not a single peep from across their borders. It makes me feel like we're walking a tightrope just waiting for a strong wind to blow us over."

"Or a juvleck to yank us down," Grae said, and we both

shuddered, remembering the monster from the gold mines of Sevelde.

"It feels like preparing to battle a shadow," I muttered. "Will they attack through the treacherous waters of our coasts? Will they attack through our border with Taigos? Or will it be something far more insidious—will they attack us from within? And if Damrienn attacks, what do we do then? We have no pack and a fledgling army to fight them."

"That army is growing every day," Grae assured me. "Hector and Maez are already working hard to assemble a new retinue. They're retraining the old palace guards and recruiting more soldiers. The smiths' forges are always lit making new weapons. The tanners' purses are heavy with gold making new battle leathers. All of Olmdere is coming together for their future."

"And Sadie? Will she forever require a royal summons to stand by my side?" I asked, hopeful that my friend was beginning to come back into the fold. Grae let out a long-suffering sigh, which told me everything I needed to know. I wondered if Sadie just needed more time or if she didn't want to be my royal guard at all anymore.

"She needs someone to scruff her and drag her back in," Grae growled. "You're being too lenient with her. It's been long enough since Navin left. This is self-indulgent."

I chuckled.

"What?"

"When have these feelings ever made sense?" I asked with an arch of my brow. "When have we ever followed a perfect timeline? Maez and Hector focus too hard on their work, Sadie too little. We're all finding ways to cope." I glanced down at the turquoise water just beyond my boots. "We're all mourning the loss of what we thought our lives would be. Even I miss that certainty in my own strange way."

The day before had been a sword and dagger day, one where I wanted to look and feel like the assassin I'd trained to be.

Today I was a ruler, a fighter. Perhaps tomorrow I'd feel like a queen. And that was just about what I *did*, not who I *was*. No, I was only beginning to unravel the freedom of my true gender: merem—with the river. Yet unlike the still, silent waters before me, I moved in and out of womanhood, dipping my toes in all forms of expression. I existed between and beyond, some days one, some days all, and some days none. I slowly absolved myself of the need to find my box and stay in it. I was merem. I flowed.

It just wasn't in any way *easy*.

Perhaps it was naive to think peeling back the layers of who I was would only unearth positive things. Revealing my identity to others had been both freeing and frightening, and still I wondered every day that I claimed that name if the world would actually accept me. Every single interaction I had, I questioned it. Every time I spoke the word "merem" aloud, I wondered if the person listening would understand me: a Wolf with human words, a Wolf who wanted to be *more*.

Grae dropped his chin onto my shoulder. My mate at least embraced every part of me, made me feel safe to not make sense, sometimes even to myself. He granted me the reprieve from absolutism, let me quietly figure out all I wanted to be. He moved with me in lockstep, subconsciously knowing my push and pull, following where I guided like a partner in a dance. He and I waltzed through this revelation with more ease than any Wolves would have, gliding from a rigid world of males and females into the bright spectrum of colors we never knew existed. Just like this burgeoning court, everything within us was being brought back to life, both of us healing from our lifelong wounds.

Grae dropped one last kiss to my temple and stood. "Alas, I didn't just come down here to bring you back to bed."

I glanced up at him and took his offered hand. "What now?" Was it another court meeting? Were there more people at my doorstep needing aid? Mapmakers? Builders? Farmers?

"The painter is to arrive this morning," Grae said hesitantly, already bracing for my response.

"Oh no," I groaned, hustling up the steps. "Do I really need to be added to another portraiture? Can't we just point to one of the Gold Wolves already up there and *say* that it's me?"

Grae laughed. "And your human portrait for the fresco?" My stomping footsteps echoed up the stairwell. "You're willing to ride off into near certain death for your people, but sitting for a portrait is one step too far?"

"Of course! One is exciting, the other is mind-numbing tediousness."

Grae's hand slid from the small of my back to my ass and squeezed. "Do this and then afterward we'll do something more fun." He smiled. "If you feel numb after . . . I'll remind every inch of your body what it is to feel."

I blushed but couldn't let him leave with the upper hand. "Only if 'something more fun' involves far less clothing and that little bottle of aromatic oils I gifted you for your birthday," I said, reaching back and squeezing his thigh. He let out a little growl, and I smiled with all the smugness of a cat toying with a mouse. Grae didn't get to torture me without me returning the favor.

His arms wrapped around me, holding me to him as we awkwardly moved up the steps in unison and I let out a chuckle. "This better be the fastest artist in Aotreas," he grumbled, his hands roving my body as we hit the second spiraling stairwell. "Or your portrait will be in the nude."

We heard the iron grate of the entry screech open, far on the other side of the palace. As we walked up the twisting stone steps, we heard an accompanying shout from one of the guards. Both Grae and I instantly reached for our weapons as the door above us was thrown open.

"Your Majesty!"

SADIE

I COULDN'T TAKE MY EYES OFF HIM. EACH OF HIS BELABORED breaths made me flinch as if it were my lungs being shredded. I squirmed on the plush velvet chair, raking my nails across the armrest with one hand and tossing my knife around with the other. Navin's limp body was sprawled across the chaise longue beside my chair, the two of us tucked into the corner while my friends conferred around the grand council table.

A horde of healers had worked on him and left . . . that had been three hours ago. *Three hours* he'd been unconscious, not a single groan or snore. I kept my eyes pinned to the rise and fall of his rib cage. I despised him, hated him even, but he couldn't die. I wouldn't let him.

Across from us, Calla, Hector, Grae, and Maez all stared down at maps scattered across the table, plotting ways to infiltrate Highwick and the dungeons below.

"We don't even know if Ora was taken by Nero or just some rogue Silver Wolves," Briar called from where she sat at a table next to Mina, who was anxiously rapping her fingers along her leg in a steady percussive rhythm. The table was laden with bowls of food and cups of tea that rattled at each drum of Mina's fingers.

Briar stood and offered a bowl of candied almonds out to her twin, prompting them to eat.

"The Silver Wolves do nothing without Nero's command," Hector countered. He slid a golden paperweight carved like a howling wolf across the largest map, moving it from the peninsula of Olmdere, across the snowy mountains of Taigos, and settling it atop the rolling pine forests of Damrienn.

"All he said was *Wolves*," I added, turning my gaze back on Navin. "He didn't say which pack. It could've been a scuffle at the Valtan border for all we know."

Briar's hand landed on Calla's shoulder. "Right. So let the poor chap wake before you go declaring war on an entire kingdom."

"That kingdom has *already* declared war on us," Calla reminded, grumpily snatching the bowl from their twin. As Calla tossed a handful of almonds in their mouth, Briar pressed her lips together to hide her grin. Briar knew how to twist a person's arm just as well as her sibling knew how to wield a sword. "We are just waiting for Nero to launch his first attack. This might have been it."

"But, again, we don't know that. So let's focus on rescuing your friend first," Maez said, poring over the war maps again. She slid the golden wolf paperweight back up to the autumnal forests of Olmdere.

It was only then I remembered that Maez had barely met Ora. The leader of Galen den' Mora had become like family to us on our travels with them, but Maez had been locked in this very castle the entire time.

"We could dress like humans, go in through the servants' passage," Hector offered.

"I could set the southern hall on fire, and we could go in while everyone was evacuating," Maez added. "We could dress as laundresses. No one would look at us twi—"

"No," Grae interrupted, shaking his head. "My—*Nero* will have guards checking everyone coming in and out now. A random fire would only make him more suspicious. He'd probably rather let half the castle burn than let anyone in now."

I flicked my knife back and forth faster, needing to do something with my hands. It felt strange to hear Grae call his father by his name. Not "my father," or "pack leader," or "*king*," just Nero. I wondered if it still hurt him every time he spoke of his father—now his enemy. I'm sure it did. It hurt me to think of, too. Grae wasn't the only one who lost his pack. Hector, Maez, and I had to leave our whole families behind, and this was yet another painful reminder.

"We need more people," Maez said, tapping the snow-white tundra on the map.

"What do you have in mind?" Calla asked.

"We need to call upon your new friend Queen Ingrid. Maybe she'd be willing to send some Ice Wolves along with us or even garner an invite from Nero, and we could hide amongst her retinue. Either way, we're going to need Taigos on our side if it really comes to war, so we might as well start that conversation now."

"We'll need more than just Taigos," Hector said, smoothing his palm over the sand-covered kingdom of Lower Valta and down to the floating mountains that the Onyx Wolves called home. "We'll need everyone. Valta, too. No one can match the Silver Wolf army alone."

It hurt to hear my brother say it—something that used to fill us both with such pride. We were once part of that unstoppable army. Now, we were trying to figure out how to defeat them.

Navin twitched beside me, and I bolted up from my slouched position, leaning my forearms on my knees as I watched his eyelids flicker open. I was about to tell everyone that he was waking, but held it in. For some strange, selfish reason, I wanted him to see me first.

Sure enough, his eyes opened and flickered straight to me as if he knew I would be sat right there. His lips curved up in a soft smile for a split second that made whatever mended parts of me shatter all over again. Then, as if remembering what had transpired between us, his expression guttered and his face morphed into cold and serious once more.

"He's up," I called to the group, hating the feeling that coursed through me. What had I wanted him to do? There was no answer. Nothing he could've done would've made me ache any less. Too many feelings knotted together to pick them apart.

The group rushed over as Navin sat up with a groan and dropped his head into his hands. The healers had discerned that he'd sustained no life-threatening injuries—a few nicks and bruises, maybe a couple broken ribs, but the exhaustion and dehydration were probably what had caused him to pass out. It looked to me like he'd been kicked while he was down, judging by the purpling bruises down his spine and torso. A dark little part of me was satisfied with that. Good. Let him feel exactly as I did.

Calla perched on the lounge next to him and rubbed a hand down his back, asking, "What happened? Who took Ora?"

"Esh," Navin cursed as he let out a shuddering breath. "Wolf soldiers."

The whole room paused, waiting for him to say which kingdom.

"Soldiers from *where*?" Calla asked slowly, clarifying, and I too wondered if Navin perhaps had suffered one too many kicks to the head. "Damrienn?"

"Yes," he panted, each breath making him wince. He waved a finger in a semicircle across his chest, making the shape of the crescent moon that the Silver Wolves wore on their chest plates. "There were three of them. Wearing King Nero's royal sigil. One was missing an eye."

Instantly, Hector and I locked gazes. Our uncle—Aubron—it had to be. I only had one guess who the other two Silver Wolves were. My father and his two brothers were littermates and always together. The fact that Nero sent three of his oldest friends to kidnap Ora did not bode well for any of us. Usually lower-ranked henchmen were tasked with "human troubles" as he liked to put it, which meant either Nero knew that Ora was special to us, or my father and uncles had fallen *far* out of the King's good graces.

Navin's grunt of pain snapped my attention back to him. Curse the fickle moon, I felt that pain as if it were my own body broken beneath my father's boots. There would be no shifting for Navin, though, no magical healing that our change brought on. He'd have to heal at the snail's pace of humans. I did not envy him that.

Maez's lip curled as she surveyed Navin. "So this is Nero's plan? Goad Calla into crossing into Damrienn by kidnapping Ora?"

"Why else would Nero take Ora, if not to provoke Calla?" Grae snapped, pacing back and forth down the table's length. "That's what he does. He pushes you into making rash decisions. He uses one person to torture another."

I ground my teeth at that, remembering the ways Nero used Grae's mother to keep Grae in line. He did that with many of my own family, too. There was one thing Nero was a master at and that was manipulating his pack through fear—a fear that at one point in my life felt a lot like loyalty.

"I don't know what they'd want with Ora." Navin looked pointedly at the floor and merely shrugged his shoulders. It was a strangely cagey action coming from someone as earnest as him. Maez and I exchanged glances. She clearly thought he was lying, too.

"What do you know that you aren't telling us?" I pushed, making those bronze eyes lift to meet mine. I hated the way that eye contact made my whole body buzz, as if he could see right to the very core of me.

"I don't know what the Silver Wolves want with Ora," he repeated a little more firmly. That only made me warier. Besides Maez, the rest of the room seemed to believe him, but I knew Navin was holding something back. Still, I tucked my desire to interrogate him aside for later.

"So what's our plan?" Maez asked after staring hard at

Navin for a few more seconds. "Whatever his reason for taking Ora, Nero is making moves."

"Now," Calla said, looking around the room. "Whatever we're doing, we need to do it now. Starting with calling in every ally and favor we have." She looked at Grae. "We should go to Taigos. Convince Ingrid to help us with the rescue mission and secure her support for whatever Nero has planned next."

Grae nodded in agreement.

"We need a representative of our court to go to Valta, too," Calla said. "Secure King Luo's allegiance if this all escalates."

"I can take whoever wants to go," Navin murmured. "I was planning on taking Galen den' Mora to Rikesh next for the wine festival."

"The wagon? The oxen?" Calla asked. "Are they okay?"

"Fine." Navin slid his gaze to Mina and said, "I could use a few more musicians on my travels, though."

Mina's brows lifted, a silent conversation seeming to pass between the two of them. Whatever was going on with Navin's evasiveness, Mina seemed to know, too.

"I think I'd rather stay close to my Queen," Mina signed, making Navin's frown deepen.

"Navin, you can't go as my ambassador without any backup," Calla insisted. "I don't want to make Galen den' Mora a target."

"Let me go," he pushed. "Galen den' Mora will be far less suspicious than Wolves traveling on their own, and safer, especially now," he added pointedly. "No one can breech the steps of Galen den' Mora without one of us welcoming them in. It is stormproof, fireproof. We could ride through a battlefield and be safe in there."

Maez let out a low whistle. "That's a pretty strong dying wish." She rubbed her chin and stared back at the map of Aotreas. "At least one person with fighting skills should go with you."

"And Luo will be more likely to listen to Wolves rather than humans," Mina signed, giving Navin a knowing look.

Calla nodded. "Sadie will go with you."

"What?" My eyes bugged as I whirled. "You can't be serious. Why don't you send Maez? Then she can communicate any news from her travels with Briar?"

Maez let out a soft growl at the suggestion she be split up from her mate. But my logic was sound. Mates could communicate in Wolf form, even from hundreds of miles apart. Yet Calla was already shaking their head and I looked at them in disbelief. They just looked back, and it was clear they were being stubborn to punish me.

I almost said as much before Calla pinned me with a look. "Can I speak with you in the hall?"

My shoulders bunched around my ears, my knife tight in my grip as I stood. Maez patted me on the shoulder and I snapped in the air between us, threatening to bite her mocking hand. I knew Calla would admonish me for abandoning my duties, but *this*, this was beyond cruel.

"Thank you, Your Majesty," Navin said to Calla. "I promise I can help fix this."

I didn't know if he meant the relationship with Valta or *our* relationship, but it made me fume. Maybe he truly was kicked too many times in the head if he thought me traveling with him was a good idea. I had no interest in his apologies or amends, but I did have quite a few ideas of what I could do with the weapons under my now-bloodied tunic. If Navin wasn't on the brink of death, he'd have the good sense to be afraid.

I stormed through the doorway, pushing past Calla and muttering, "I can't believe he's *thanking* you, oh gracious one."

Calla didn't follow straightaway. Instead, they paused behind me and turned back to Navin.

"I may look like a benevolent queen right now, Navin," Calla said, giving him one last piercing look. I leaned back in through the doorway to see his good eye widen at the menace in Calla's voice and my lips curved. "But I was first and foremost trained as a warrior. If you hurt *any* of my court again, I will gut you myself." Calla then marched through the door, leaving him speechless.

CALLA

I STALKED INTO THE HALL AFTER SADIE WHILE THE OTHERS continued their questioning of Navin and made plans. The muscles in her jaw popped as she folded her lean, muscular arms over her chest, looking like a petulant child being scolded by a tutor. I lifted my chin. She could mope all she liked, but it was time for her and me to have a reckoning. If she wasn't going to climb out of the pit she'd fallen in of her own volition, I'd drag her out by the tail with my teeth.

"This is ridiculous." She sounded more like a hissing cat than a Wolf. "This doesn't seem like a fair punishment for a few weeks shirking my responsibilities. I'm sorry I had a couple of nights out, but this is just plain evil . . . Your Majesty," she added hastily as she spotted the two guards at the end of the corridor.

The guards stood at attention, their heads facing straight ahead, but their eyes darted to the side, watching me. All it took was a nod of my head to the eavesdropping guards and they left.

I waited until we had our privacy before folding my arms in a mirrored posture to Sadie's own and leaning against the far wall. "A 'couple' of nights?"

She had the presence of mind to at least look chagrined.

Softer, I asked, "You think I'm punishing you?"

"It sure feels like it," she groused as my eyebrows lifted in amusement. I still had a flair of her same stubbornness, but none that rivaled her own. Grae had tempered a lot of it in me, and right now, I knew I had to be that counterbalance for her as she scowled at me and asked, "If not punishment, then what?"

I studied her face—the half-moons under her eyes, her tattered clothes, the stink of ale in her mussed hair. "I'm saving you, Sadie."

"*Saving* me?" she echoed dubiously. "From what?"

"From this," I said, gesturing from the red velvet carpet below our feet all the way up to the frescoed ceilings. "The others might think you've been sulking because of Navin, but that's not the only reason, is it?"

She looked away, unable to meet the force of my stare, and I knew the arrowhead of my words struck true. I empathized with just how unsettled she felt. Deep in my bones, I felt it as well. But my way forward was here, leading my people, muddling ahead even if I faltered. Sadie needed adventure, needed conflict—my eyes dropped—needed someone to threaten with her blades at the very least.

She needed to not be a house pet, which was clearly how she thought of her current assignment.

Sadie toyed with her knife like a cat's tail flicking in anger. "I have no idea what you're talking about."

Fast as a striking ostekke, I plucked the knife from her hand. "Don't you, Stabby?"

I looked from the knife in my grip to Sadie's balled fists, the nickname clearly grating on her last vestiges of decorum. Dispossessed of her weapon, she started pacing along the hall, needing to move, if not her hands, then her feet. She reached inside the leather lining of her vest and pulled out a smaller blade secretly sheathed down the center laces.

I pinched the bridge of my nose in frustration. "Of course."

"Just thought I'd get you another blade to stab me in the back with," she said, flipping the knife over to offer me the hilt.

"You're a soldier through and through, Sadie," I said with an exasperated shake of my head. "That is why this life is intolerable to you. You can't keep moping around council chambers and running off to Briar's cottage and drinking all of the taverns out of their best ale—" She opened her mouth to deny the claim, but I held up my hand. "My people talk and rumors of your quest to drink every tavern dry have now grown infamous. And even though it reflects poorly on me, I allowed it, because I thought you'd come through the other side of this, but you seem intent to keep up your rakishness forever."

"It wasn't that much ale." She twirled her tiny knife in one hand, windmilling it through her fingertips with practiced ease. "Humans just can't hold their drinks next to Wolves—that's all."

"From how you smell, I'd say you can't hold it too well, either—you've got ale spilled all over you."

She looked at me, and I pointed to my nose. "Wolf."

She slumped a bit.

"You're bored," I said. "And it's making you reckless. Yes, I'm sure Navin's betrayal played some part in all of this, too, probably a bigger part than you're letting on." Her knife hand stumbled, a break in its rhythm, as I passed back her first knife. "You're strong—maybe too strong. But you also are unwilling to admit that life in the Golden Court is grating on you."

"I wouldn't say grating," she hedged.

"Be honest with me," I implored, grabbing her wrist to still her flicking hand. "If you had to choose between sitting on my council or going on a diplomatic mission with someone you hate and doing some subtle investigation—"

Her dark eyes shot up to meet mine. "So you think he's hiding something, too, huh?"

I ignored that. "Which would you pick?"

"Interrogation," she muttered. "Obviously."

"*Subtle investigation*," I reminded. "I need you to handle this delicately. Whatever Navin is keeping from us, I'm sure he has legitimate reasons." Sadie clicked her tongue and dramatically rolled her eyes. Despite her being years older than me, she seemed so young in that moment, so adrift. "But legitimate or no, we need to know why Nero has Ora and you're the only person I trust to handle this. It can't *just* be to irk me." That made her puff up a little bit. "You know Navin better than anyone. Can you uncover his secrets? Or do you want to go back to the tavern and destroy everything you once were?"

Sadie looked at me sharply.

"Yes—I said it. You are not a palace guard, but nor are you a lush. *Yet.* I don't think that's who you want to be, either." I was trying to be softer, but I couldn't hold back all the iron in my voice.

She pursed her lips. "Something strange is going on," she said, not really responding to what I'd just said, but that was okay— she was thinking rather than just reacting, and that was more than she'd done in weeks. "I don't find it coincidence that on the precipice of war, someone important to you has been abducted, nor that their closest friend and traveling companion seems to be unwilling to say why."

"I need Ora back and safe. They are family to me. And I need answers that I trust you will be able to acquire." Sadie's eyes sparked. That mischievous twinkle made me even more certain that this is what she needed—a little freedom, more adventure, and to face the wounds she still harbored from Navin. Maybe when she returned from Valta she could settle into this new life more easily. Or at least give me time to figure out how best to use her. No matter what, she needed a bigger purpose, and whether she liked it or not, I was determined to give her one. "I need you to bring King Luo on to Olmdere's side. Promise him unending gold and treasure and trade. Use whatever means you deem necessary. I want an Onyx Wolf pack at our back when we meet Damrienn on the battlefield."

Her grin widened at the mention of a battlefield. "I don't think I could say no to that even if I wanted to."

"And you don't want to," I said. "We'll give Navin the night to rest here, but I expect Galen den' Mora to be rolling out toward Rikesh at dawn, and I expect you to be on it."

She sheathed her blades and inclined her head at me. "Yes, Your Majesty."

I chuckled, pulling her out of her awkward curtsy and into a fierce hug—a hug that reminded her that we were more than Queen and subject, we were friends, we were family.

"Thank you, Sadie." As we hugged, I hastily added, "And you're not allowed to stab Navin."

"Fine." She groaned and pulled out of the hug, practically skipping down the hall with a gleeful wave. "But you said nothing about nose-breaking."

SADIE

I AWOKE TO A BOOT TOEING MY SHOULDER AND A FAMILIAR voice saying, "Come on, Sads, let's go."

I squinted up into the face of Maez. The pounding in my head made me already regret the decision to have one last hurrah—spending all night out at a little hole-in-the-wall frequented by farriers and smiths. Maez towered above me, backlit by the peach-tinted morning light. I blinked in confusion, staring up at her attire. She wore her black and golden fighting leathers, knee-high riding boots, a dagger on one hip, and a sword on the other.

"Wh-what are you doing?" I asked as she adjusted the giant fawn skin pack on her shoulders.

She shrugged. "I'm coming with you."

"What?"

"I'm coming with you," she said again slower as if I were a small child . . . or very drunk, which I was still balancing on the edge of. "It was agreed upon last night while you were off—" She waved a hand over my body as she wrinkled her nose. "How did you even end up in this park? Calla would've told you directly, but you made it very hard to *find* you."

"Great," I muttered, sending out a silent word of thanks into the morning air that at least Calla didn't send Hector to tell me off again. Having my judgmental older brother hovering over me this entire trip would've done me in.

"Oh, come on," Maez tutted, stretching her arms to the sky and taking a deep breath. Her leathers groaned as her broad muscles stretched her uniform. "It'll be fun. I'm a way better travel companion than Hector, right?"

I sat up, rubbing my pounding temples. "You read my mind."

"It'll be just like when we were pups in military training," she said, offering down her hand and easily hoisting me up to my feet. ". . . Except we'll be traveling in a wagon and there'll probably be less brawling."

"So nothing like our training." It took more effort to stand without toppling over than I would've liked, but I managed to stay upright.

"Whatever we're doing," she said with a wink. "It's always more fun with me around, though, isn't it?"

I chuckled, sizing her up. I was tall but Maez stood a whole head taller than me. When we were little, we were the same height, and I never forgave her for when she shot up past me.

I understood, too, why Calla would want to send Maez for such an important task besides her connection to Briar. She had a stocky, muscular build that no matter how much I trained I couldn't rival. She was incredible in close combat and grappling, but I was the blade master of our group. I could hit someone straight in the heart from across a crowded room, and a bandolier of knives was much easier to hide than Maez's hulking sword.

Maez was also much more adept at political charming than I was. She was similar to her mate in that regard. Though Briar approached in a more regal, poised way, Maez easily became one of the lads wherever she went. It didn't hurt that she was Nero's niece and raised high in the Silver Wolf pack ranking. She was born with enough swagger to convince King Luo to support our cause, too, unlike myself who was generally far too abrasive to win anyone's allegiance. I always believed whether people liked me or not was their problem . . . which was probably why Calla sent Maez along, too.

I swept my braid over my shoulder and glanced downriver through the blossoming orange gardens to where a lone figure stood, and I understood I was mistaken about one thing: Maez wasn't coming because she could communicate with Briar over long distances. No, because that would only make sense if Briar wasn't waiting with a pack leaning against her shins, her mouth tight and nose crinkled at my sorry state.

"Briar should stay behind," I said in protest. "She doesn't know how to fight, and despite her diplomatic prowess, this trip could be dangerous. She's more protected if she stays with Calla."

"Navin doesn't know how to fight, either," Maez countered. "But he's going."

"He isn't important." I frowned down at my mud-stained boots, remembering that wet, stormy night when he and I were captured by the Silver Wolves. "Briar is one of the only Gold Wolves still alive. If a single person identifies her on this trip, they will be climbing all over each other to abduct her. She is leverage to whoever has her. She—"

"Briar isn't coming." Maez cut me off with a wave of her hands. "I was just making a point."

"But she . . ." I gestured to her. "She has her pack with her."

"That is *your* pack," Maez said dryly.

I narrowed my eyes at the pack leaning against Briar's shins, recognizing the scuff and hastily sewn patches pockmarking the exterior.

"Oh. Right." I dusted off my clothes and ruffled my bangs so the hair sat evenly across my forehead again. I hooked my thumb at Maez. "You're okay leaving your mate behind for this trip?"

"Okay? No, I'm not okay." Maez's hackles raised at that comment. "I'm furious, and part of that fury is aimed at you, so maybe be a little nicer to me, all right?" She took a deep breath. "But I agree with you that she is safer here. It is too dangerous for her to come. And it would be good to have a way to communicate between our two parties," she said, confirming my original thought—it felt good to know I hadn't completely pickled my brain. "As much as it will hurt to be away from her, having something happen to her would hurt me far more."

I pretended to dry heave at the sentiment . . . which then caused actual bile to rise up my throat, and I was reminded of the many, *many* pints I had drank the night before.

"Dear Moonlight, you're a mess," Maez muttered; she grabbed me by the shoulder and steered me downhill. "Let's go, grumpy little Wolf. Time to be a soldier."

GALEN DEN' MORA SAT IN A MEADOW AT THE EDGE OF THE CITY, blanketed in the fading shades of summer. Burnt orange- and caramel-colored flowers dotted the tall grasses, their tiny seedbeds bursting and scattering to the wind. Two giant oxen grazed, their copper-red hair swishing in the gentle breeze. It was a beautiful, idyllic sight . . . until I threw up into the nearest shrub, which happened to be covered in stinging nettles. The stale sourdough bread I nibbled on did nothing to calm my curdling stomach.

"Maybe I should offer to drive the wagon," Maez grumbled as we stalked through the grasses. "I'd rather be covered in juvleck goo than ride with you."

"There's a bathing chamber on board," I said, wiping my mouth with the back of my hand. My arms wheeled as I tilted to the side, forcing me to stop and adjust my heavy pack again. *Did they put frying pans in this thing?* "I'll have a wash and be fine."

"There's a bathing chamber?" Maez asked incredulously.

"You're going to like this place."

"I certainly will, especially once you avail yourself."

The massive wagon was easily two stories tall, an intricate network of seating areas and bunks inside, not a single inch of the place gone to waste. The outside had bars of musical notes wrapping around it, words scrawled in every language of Aotreas, and ribbonlike pennants waved from the edges of the vaulted canvas.

It was a beautiful space, quirky and artistic, much like the musicians who called it home.

Navin climbed down from the back of the wagon and paused, his eyes locking with mine. His face was purpled with bruises, one eye still so bloodshot his pupil looked to be floating in a sea of crimson. The normal elegance with which he held his body was pinched and angled to one side, probably from his bruised ribs. I trailed my eyes from his russet leather boots to his matching leather suspenders that held up his stiff olive green trousers and up to his knitted cap. He wore a billowy cream shirt and a velvet azure jacket with a high neck and musical notes embroidered around the cuffs. I shook my head. Why had I ever thought I could understand a human musician? I looked at Maez's midnight fighting leathers and my disheveled garb, still tinged with menace from my bandolier of knives. I was a killer and a Wolf; nothing about me matched anything about him. Even if we'd had a chance to see where things could've taken us with a bit more time . . . there would've never been a happy ending between someone like me and someone as gentle and soft as him.

Navin gave Maez a warm greeting, gesturing out his hand to the wagon for her to enter. Maez only gave him a perfunctory nod in return, probably out of loyalty to me.

I wandered over, taking my time. As I neared, I thought of a million things I wanted to say—I also thought about grabbing one of my many knives and cutting out his eyes—but instead I just moved to walk past him.

He didn't let me, though.

His hand reached out and gently touched my elbow, barely a graze at first, and then a little more confidently those long fingers wrapped around my arm, imploring me to stay. I laughed in disbelief. As if he could ever stop *me* with his delicate artist's hands.

It took nothing to pull out of his grip, and yet I lingered.

"I'm sorry, Sadie," he whispered as I squinted at the horizon. I made a study of the dragonflies zipping through the meadow and the diaphanous cobalt clouds that promised rain over the ocean—anything but him. "I had to protect my brother. There are reasons I can't explain . . ."

That piqued my interest. More secrets. I wondered if this secret was related to what Navin knew about Ora's capture. Was it all interconnected? How much was Navin keeping from us? He was more a stranger to me than I'd even realized. Most of the people traveling with Galen den' Mora seemed to be people trying to either reinvent themselves or hide from the world. I realized my question from the night before wasn't so pressing. I shouldn't be asking what was Navin hiding, but what was Navin hiding *from*?

Tilting my face back into the bracing wind, I vowed I would get my answers from him, whether through persuasion or through the knives on my belt. I would know all his secrets by the time this trip was over.

It felt good in some strange way to know Navin was keeping secrets from us all. At least I hadn't been the only one who misjudged him. Maybe Hector's hatred of the man had been more shrewd than the brotherly overprotection and wolfish bigotry that I dismissed it as being. It made my hatred of Navin now feel even more justified, too, and I quietly prayed that he turned out to be an even worse person that we first thought . . . it might be enough for me to keep on hating him forever.

Muffled on the wind, I could hear Maez's awed exclamations as she explored the inside of Galen den' Mora.

"Your wounds seem extensive," I said tightly, still staring straight ahead as I broke our silence. "Does it hurt every time you breathe?"

From my periphery, I spotted the bob of Navin's throat. "Yes."

"Good."

"Sadie—" He reached for me again, but I climbed up the steps without another word.

Navin didn't protest further or follow me into the wagon, instead turning to go gather the oxen and begin our journey south.

At least I knew his loyalties were pulled in as many directions as my own. I hoped all of it was as senseless and confusing for him as it was for me. Maybe one day I could parse apart why I felt anything at all.

Patience. A little voice whispered in my head. First, I needed to bend him, twist him until the point of breaking so that all his well-kept secrets would come spilling out when I applied enough pressure. Maybe then I'd finally feel settled back into myself enough to understand that nonsensical pull or why he and I ever fell into each other's orbit.

SADIE

AS I SHOWERED THE GRIME AND STENCH OFF ME, I WATCHED through the grating below my feet as the cobblestone road morphed to a forest trail. Soon, we'd be passing through the Sevelde Forest. It was a beautiful, haunting sight—a forest filled with golden trees of every hue from honey to dandelion to amber. I thought of Navin driving through this place. On the trip here, I'd sat beside him on the couch, holding his hand, his grip tightening in mine with every turn of the wagon's wheels.

There would not be a repeat of that today.

I kept looking out the grate. Below the Sevelde Forest lay the gold mines of Olmdere, which had been the only way in or out of the kingdom during Sawyn's reign. Navin had escaped the blight and famine through the mines underneath us. His father, who had fled with him, never made it out the other side.

I twisted the spigot that controlled the water canister above my head. The sound of the wagon wheels crunching leaves and the clinking rattle of the uneven terrain filled the echoey metal bathing chamber. *Chamber* was a bit of a misnomer. It was more like a tiny nook with a giant water canister that you needed to crouch under and grated iron flooring. Still, little warm touches filled the space. There were fluffy towels waiting on the shelf, along with hooks to hang washing. The whole place was warm from the metal firebox that sat right above it, ensuring the water at least wasn't freezing and quickly drying people's washing. One of Ora's dresses still hung from the drying hooks, and it made my stomach sour again—an eerie reminder that they'd been abducted, the reasons still a mystery. Did Nero know how close Calla and Ora had become? Or was Ora important in other ways? What purpose did Nero have with the leader of Galen den' Mora?

I grabbed the fresh clothing that Briar had packed for me and pulled it on. Steadying myself against the wall, I struggled to keep from toppling over as I yanked on my trousers over my still damp thighs. The wagon rocked and I toppled backward, landing flat on my ass. I slicked my wet hair off my face with a growl when I heard another sound . . .

Humming.

Navin was humming a tune to himself as he drove the wagon. It was easier to hear with the open grate below me. The sound echoed up into the cavernous space. He hummed a sad, slow song and I recognized the tune: "Sa Sortienna"—above the golden trees. It was an Olmderian miner's song for their loves back home. My fingers twitched with the urge to go to the front of the wagon and hold Navin's hand again, even though I knew I shouldn't want to. He'd raised his weapons against me to defend his Rook brother. I'd never forgive him for choosing one of Sawyn's lackeys over me—brother or no. Whatever his reasons were, they'd never be good enough, and yet . . . we were rolling over the final resting place of his father and his humming haunted me.

I decided sitting there listening to him hum was a cruel form of torture. I stood up, yanked my trousers the rest of the way up, and climbed the ladder back into the wagon.

I found Maez in the kitchen, searching every drawer and pantry as if mapping out the place. She opened one drawer and lifted a sprig of dried lavender, opened another and lifted up a handful of loose buttons.

"This place feels like a fever dream," she murmured, shaking her head as she craned her neck up to the stovepipe that rose out through the canvas ceiling.

I dropped into one of the kitchen chairs. "It certainly has a magic all its own."

Maez opened the oven and let out a surprised grunt as she pulled out a now-cool tray of sourdough bread. How many days had that loaf been in there as Navin raced to the capital for Calla's aid?

"Perfect." Maez lay the tray straight on the table between us. "Breakfast. Now I thought I saw . . . ah!" She grabbed a ceramic bowl of butter and a single knife and dropped into the chair across from me.

I stared up at the ribbons hanging above the kitchen table, little embroidered badges hanging down the strands.

"Ora hand stitched these for different people who traveled with Galen den' Mora," I said, trailing my fingers across a badge with a raindrop on it.

"Did you ever get one?"

I pinched one of the far ribbons between two fingers, turning the strand for Maez to inspect. "I'll give you two guesses which is mine."

Maez grunted and pointed to the crescent moon and knife. "That's so cool! I want one."

"We've got to save Ora first."

Tearing off a chunk of the bread, Maez said, "I didn't really get much time with them after Sawyn's demise before they rode off again, but being here in this place, I feel like I know them a lot better now." She buttered a piece of bread and passed it to me. "I understand now why Calla was so adamant to get them back now, too."

"It feels like we're heading in the wrong direction." I took a bite of bread and let out a low hum. It was far more delicious than the loaves at the bakery. "We should be going to Damrienn to rescue Ora, not Valta to rub elbows with the Onyx Wolf King."

A little twang went through me as I thought about Ora—about how this bread was probably meant for them and Navin, about their clothing still drying on the hook, about their life just snatched from them and for what? A prisoner of war? A symbol of the burgeoning Golden Court?

"Having King Luo's support will help Ora," Maez said. "And all of us."

"Ora is one of the best people I know," I replied. "Though I don't know a lot of good people."

"Mostly Wolf ruffians, eh?" Maez chuckled. "So what does Nero want with a traveling musician? Navin made it sound like these were capital soldiers who took Ora, not just some random pack members?" She crooked a finger at her eye. "The one with the missing eye . . . you think that's—"

"My uncle," I said with a definitive nod. "I'll give you one guess who the other two are."

"Shit," Maez muttered, shuddering at the thought of the three of them. "Why would Nero send them on a foot soldier's errand?"

"That is the question I've been asking myself, too," I said through a mouthful of bread.

Just hearing our former king's name on Maez's lips sent a chill down my spine. I'd lived my whole life in fear of disobeying him. He was not one to listen to reason and his will was law. He destroyed many families in ways I was ashamed to admit I was only beginning to understand as unjust . . . and in some cases complicit.

"A political pawn maybe?" Maez mused. "It's no secret that Ora was close with the Golden Court Queen . . . but was this Nero's declaration of war between the Silver and Gold Wolves? Kidnapping a human? I'd thought he'd do something . . . bigger."

"No idea."

"If there is a war . . ." Maez cocked her head and gazed up at the badges swinging above us. "Do you think King Luo will actually put his army into the fight with us?"

"He must. That is our task now," I replied. "We need the Onyx Wolves. We can't take no for an answer."

"If Calla can get the Ice Wolves in line, then maybe Luo will feel forced to side with the bigger army."

I swallowed. "It would certainly help. But the same goes for getting the Ice Wolves to join. We have to go in as if he's the most important ally to us. Because we're going to need everyone, every single possible friend, if we have any hope of beating the Silver Wolves in a war."

"That thought used to fill me with pride." Maez's voice tinged with shame as she clasped her hands together, voicing the same thoughts I'd been ruminating over for weeks. "To be a part of the mighty Silver Wolf army."

"Me too," I said more quietly, remembering my thoughts from the other night. "We'll be fighting our own families. Friends we've known since pups. I . . . I will defend Calla's court with everything I have . . . but Gods, I wish I wouldn't have to."

Maez pursed her lips. "I think having a Gold Wolf mate makes it easier in some ways," she mused. "I would destroy every friendship and home I've ever known to protect Briar."

I toyed with the piece of bread in my hands before taking another bite. I wished I had that conviction. I wished I didn't feel this tumultuous upheaval of everything I'd ever known.

Maez tapped a finger on the table. "There's more Navin isn't telling us."

I hadn't missed what I'd seen from her last night, then. I let out a breath through clenched teeth. "Yep."

Leaning her forearms on the table, Maez said, "Sadie." She waited for me to look up at her before she spoke again. "You're going to have to get these answers from him." I hated the way she said it, even if I knew she was right. "I know you two were once . . . close." I dropped the bread and pulled out one of my knives as she continued, "I think you might need to be close again. Get him to trust you. Get him to tell you what he's hiding. If it could help us prevent an outright war . . ."

I flicked my knife back and forth. "I could just stab him in the side, and I bet he'd spill whatever we wanted to know."

Maez narrowed her eyes at me. "Think smarter."

"I'm thinking like a *soldier*," I countered.

"Think smarter," she said again, and I almost laughed. Almost. "We need him to help us get to Rikesh undetected," Maez pushed. "We need this ruse. If Nero knows we're making a move for the Onyx Wolves, it might force his hand faster than we can prepare. So much is at stake. We're on the brink of war, I can feel it, and . . ." She sighed and shook her head. "If you can't handle it—"

"I can handle it," I gritted out, knowing she was goading me but still falling for it anyway.

"Excellent." Maez handed me a chunk of buttered bread. "Now go convince him you're sorry so we can figure out what he's hiding. You're a spy for your Queen now."

"Ugh." My lip curled as I grabbed the piece of bread from her and stood. "Why can't I just stab him again?" I groaned and stomped to the front of the wagon.

"Not everything can be solved by stabbing."

I vehemently disagreed, but kept my mouth shut for now.

THIS WAS FOR THE MISSION, I TOLD MYSELF FOR THE HUNDREDTH time as I parted the heavy velvet curtain and climbed through the tiny window onto the driver's seat. Navin's humming stopped briefly as he glanced at me and then he carried on.

"Brought you something to eat," I said, offering him out the bread. "Wh—" I glanced down and realized he wasn't holding the reins. Instead, he sat with his ankle crossed over his knee and a green linen-bound book in his hands.

"Thank you," he said, setting the book aside and taking the bread.

He continued to hum mindlessly as he ate. Very strange.

I wasn't sure if it was a nervous compulsion or what. Perhaps it was his way of coping with passing through this haunted place. It was said that thousands of people died trying to escape Olmdere during Sawyn's reign. I could almost feel their souls still lingering heavy in the air.

The golden trees stretched out in the distance in front of us, the farmland dipping away to the wide expanse of molten ore.

I clambered the rest of the way through the window and sat beside Navin. "Don't you need to be driving?" I asked, tipping my head to the slack reins.

"It's a straight shot. There's only one road through the Sevelde Forest," he said through a mouthful of bread. "Besides, they know where we're going," he added with a jut of his chin at the oxen.

"Then why are you out here?"

"To give you some space." He chewed thoughtfully for a while before adding, "I know Calla forced you to come."

"Right." The stilted silence stretched out between us again. *Come on, Sadie, say something useful. Figure out what's going on.* "I . . . I've been thinking about it and . . . I'm glad I came, though."

Navin's eyes widened slightly, the faintest flicker of excitement—*hope* even—at my words before he schooled his expression again. We rolled on for several more heartbeats before he said, "I'm sorry I ruined everything between us."

There was never anything between us.

That is what I wanted to say, at least. To let him know I'd keep pushing him away forever. I had a bit of excitement in his human world, just morbid curiosity, and now it was over. Instead, I said, "For reasons that you can't tell me?"

"I . . ." He glanced up at the golden canopy that now stretched above us, the forest hanging in a perpetual autumnal glow. "My brother had . . . secrets," he said very carefully, and I tried not to study him too closely. *How do I act casual?* I crossed my ankle over my knee and took in the gilded foliage. "Secrets I needed to make sure he didn't share. Something I wouldn't have the answers to if you rammed him through with your blade."

I considered his words. "So it wasn't done out of brotherly love?"

"Esh no." Navin let out a bitter laugh. "I can't deny somewhere deep down I still love my brother. Maybe something in all those childhood memories makes me hang on to him even though he betrayed our family by siding with that sorceress." He dusted his flour-covered hand down the thick fabric of his trouser leg and then stole a glance my way. Those brown eyes that swirled like molten bronze held a magic all their own. Every time I looked into them, it felt like falling under a spell. "But I didn't save him out of love," he said, holding my gaze. "I wasn't *choosing* him."

I couldn't take it. I couldn't handle all the things unspoken that passed between our eyes. I severed that spell and stared back out at the speckled sunlight through the honeyed canopy.

"Did he do it?" I asked.

"Hmm?"

"Did he share the secrets you were hoping he'd keep?"

Navin paused for a long time before replying, "No, he didn't. And it makes it a lot harder to hate him now."

What were these secrets? And why was it so important that Navin's brother not share them? I knew he wouldn't tell me if I just asked outright. Already he'd told me more than I'd expected. Guilt was a powerful tool. Maybe he felt a little heartbreak, too.

"This secret," I hedged, holding up my hands when Navin tried to interject. "You don't have to tell me what it is. But does this secret with your brother also have something to do with Ora?"

He stared straight ahead and I already knew the answer: yes.

Shit. This was bigger than a family secret then. This would be no small thing if the Silver Wolf pack knew about it. Something was happening right under my nose, but I couldn't catch the scent of it yet.

"Keep your secrets," I said quietly. "As long as they don't impact me, it doesn't matter. But will you promise to tell me whatever I *need* to know to keep Maez and me safe on this trip?"

"All you need to know is that Ora knows something very important," Navin said. "I don't know how much the Silver Wolves know, if they know anything at all. But if those Wolves can get Ora to talk . . . it could set the whole world on fire."

"Fuck." I sucked in a sharp breath, jostling my knee anxiously up and down. What in the Gods' names could Ora know that would be so world destroying? "Nero is probably torturing information out of Ora right now."

Navin shook his head. "Ora has ways of protecting their mind if not their body."

I glanced at Navin from his knitted cap to his pointy boots. "Who *are* you?"

He let out a rough laugh, making his broad shoulders shake. "I'm a musician." I scrutinized him for a long time before he asked, "Who are you, Sadie Rauxtide?"

"A Wolf, once Silver now Gold, a member of the Golden Court, a soldier, a killer," I added pointedly.

A skin chaser, I thought in my mind. *A person too rough and too heartless for a gentle soul like you.*

"Thank you for telling me about this," I said with a nod, rising to stand.

Navin stared back out at the rolling golden forest that completely consumed the wagon now. "Thank you for coming with me." His voice had grown hollow, and I wondered if he was reliving what horrible memories transpired in the mines below us. Could he still taste that fear? Was he thinking of his father's body still down there somewhere, unburied, but continually mourned?

"If the oxen can lead themselves . . ." I paused at the curtain. "Why don't you come inside?"

"I think I need the fresh air right now," he whispered.

I sighed, turning around and dropping back onto the bench beside him. I reached out and threaded his hand in my own, just as I had done during the ride over. He squeezed my hand in silent acknowledgment and then went back to humming.

"I think I need some fresh air, too."

SADIE

I LISTENED TO NAVIN HUM TUNE AFTER TUNE AS WE ROLLED through the Sevelde Forest. Holding his hand was like holding a flame to candle wax: I wanted it to burn me, but it only made me melt more into his side. I couldn't deny the comfort of his warm grip on my own. *Just a physical comfort*, I assured myself as I wrapped another layer of thorns around my heart. It didn't matter how my body responded so long as it helped me uncover his secrets.

If Navin was aware of the ebb and flow of my incongruous thoughts, he didn't show it. Even at rest when he wasn't performing, he couldn't seem to stop himself from carrying a tune. It was only when the golden trees were far behind us that Navin finally fell silent.

When we rolled into the sleepy border town of Durid, we only had to pay one crover for the border tithe. It was strange not having Sawyn's Rooks posted every few stretches along the trail. They had bullied us out of quite a lot of money on the ride to Olmdere before Sawyn's demise. I wondered for not the first time what would come of the former Rooks like Navin's brother.

When Calla was saved by their dying wish, I saw the way the light patched them back together, as if an entire sun was consumed into them, their scars like rivers of gold across their body. The Rooks' swords clattered to the ground instantly at the sight, knowing that even the Gods themselves wanted Calla to protect Olmdere.

There was not a whisper of dissent, not a single murmur of uprising amongst the remaining Rooks. It was strange . . . and wholly unsatisfying. Humans who one second I'd been driving my blade into were all at once cowering on their knees, begging our forgiveness. It would've felt better for some of them to rebel, some of them to rise up, to fight. At least then I'd know they had a backbone. But no, the Rooks all sided with Sawyn out of fear. I thought it would've been easier slicing my knife across a few more throats, making some examples with public hangings . . . which is why I was a soldier and not a ruler. Still, I liked the way people avoided me in the streets, worried that I'd take my vengeance out on them for their traitorous past.

That past seemed too close to me now as we rolled through the outstretches of Durid and parked the wagon a short walk from the town proper. This was the location . . . the one only so many weeks ago Navin had taken me by the hand and dragged me through the muddy streets to find a *quiet place* for the two of us—the one and only time he'd ever even kissed me. Sweet Moon, this wasn't me at all to think such things.

I wasn't a shining moonbeam. I was a thundercloud.

I sounded like such a puppy, reliving a kiss . . . But that kiss was brutally interrupted by King Nero's inner circle of Silver Wolves. I'd watched as they nearly beat the life out of Navin. The fear still gripped me even now.

Humans were so fragile—too delicate and breakable to withstand Wolf brutality. *I* had shifted, and my wounds had healed while I watched Navin take weeks and weeks to recover. He'd take weeks and weeks from the injuries he sustained now, too.

Hector had been right. Ugh. I hated thinking about my older brother being right about anything, but it was true. I should've stayed away from Navin those many moons ago.

Wolves and humans couldn't be together . . . not that I wanted to be with Navin anymore, with all his secrets and lies, anyway.

When we parked, Navin squeezed my hand and finally released my grip. I'd forgotten we were still holding hands long past the Sevelde Forest. It'd felt so natural to be hand in hand with him, and yet *nothing* was natural about it at all.

"Thank you," he murmured to me before hopping down from the seat with practiced ease.

He unhitched the oxen from the wagon and took them off to a distant pasture to graze. I sat on the driver's bench, my legs numb and tingling as I watched the back of his head fade into the distance. He moved so confidently around these parts, clearly having traveled through Durid several times before. I wondered if Galen den' Mora played in this little town even before Sawyn opened the borders. It seemed the eccentric wagon traveled to every corner of Aotreas.

"So?" Maez's voice made me jolt. I hadn't noticed she'd pulled apart the velvet curtain and was peeking up at me through the window. "What did you learn?"

Oh, right. Espionage. I let out a long sigh, finding my knives again. I was pretending to care about someone I actually once *did* care about and might *still* care about—a little—but *shouldn't* care about at all . . . Great. Nothing confusing about that.

"He said his brother had secrets and that he couldn't let him die without knowing if he'd shared them."

"Damn," Maez said, watching as Navin's figure dipped over the distant hill. "So if you killed his brother now, he wouldn't mind?"

I cut Maez a look. "I still think he'd *mind* if I killed his brother." I flicked my blade back and forth. "But perhaps not as much as he would've before he knew his brother didn't spill these mysterious secrets."

"Secrets he wanted him to take to the grave. Wow," Maez said. "I'm actually impressed the sweet, lanky musician could be so cold."

I clenched my jaw, wishing I had something to stab. "There's more."

"More than the suspicious, secret-keeping brother. Intriguing." She grabbed my elbow and tugged on it. "You climb in. There's no way I'm fitting through that window without looking like a drunken mountain goat."

"A very cool, tough drunken mountain goat," I said, and she rolled her eyes, half dragging me back into the warmth of the wagon.

It was only once I felt the fire she'd lit that I realized how cold it had become outside. Despite it being the tail end of summertime, we'd climbed high enough into the mountains that the air was brisk. Another few days of nearly vertical ride and treacherous paths and we'd be in the snowy landscapes of the Ice Wolf kingdom.

I rubbed my hands together as I wandered to the sunken seating area and dropped into one of the patchwork couches.

"It's Ora," I said.

Maez sidled over, flopped onto the couch across from me, and kicked her feet up on the low table between us. Her boots sat along the grating at the back door, and she wore only her woolen socks, making the way she anxiously shook her foot even more noticeable. "What about Ora?"

"Apparently they have a secret that could destroy the world," I said mildly.

"Fuck." Maez scrubbed a hand down her face. "Of course they do."

"What could Ora possibly know that's so catastrophic?"

Maez's foot shook faster as she folded her arms across her chest. "If Ora has been taken by the Silver Wolves, I'd bet a thousand gritas that those bastards have already tortured every secret out of them."

I shook my head. "Navin said Ora has a way of keeping their mind protected."

"Mind magic, you think? What kind of human possesses such power?" Maez shuddered. "That's so creepy."

"We speak into each other's Wolf minds through magic," I reminded her, but she ignored me.

"So the Silver Wolves are hacking poor Ora up for answers to some secret that Navin won't tell you . . ." She stared up at the ceiling. "What could it be?"

"I'm still unsure the Silver Wolves even know Ora possesses such secrets." I shrugged. "It's just as likely Nero did it to piss off Calla."

"I wouldn't put it past him," Maez muttered. "But we still need to know exactly how serious this threat is."

"Ora has traveled all around the continent; I imagine they've acquired all sorts of secrets during their travels," I said. "They can be in a roomful of Wolves and be unseen, just a performer, just window dressing. They probably hear all sorts of drunken whispers at parties and events."

"But one so important?" Maez pulled her feet off the table and rested her elbows on her knees, jiggling one leg up and down. "One the Silver Wolves would take Ora to get? Or at least one that Navin fears they'd stumble upon?" She let out a frustrated sigh. "And Navin won't tell you what it is?"

"No."

"Then you need to get closer to him," she said. "I know you don't want to—"

"It's fine," I muttered. "You should keep searching this place. Maybe there're secrets hiding within the nooks and crannies of the wagon. I'll deal with Navin."

She was right. He was already opening up to me more than he seemed like he wanted to, which meant he would be willing to divulge more the closer I got to him. And any guilt I might feel for that was mitigated by the fact that I absolutely didn't care for him in any way whatsoever.

"We need to know what we're walking into," Maez said. "If

he was willing to tell you this much . . . why couldn't he tell you what this secret was?"

"I don't know." I held Maez's dark gaze. "But whatever this world-changing secret is, he must know it, too. And his brother."

"I need to shift soon. I'll update Briar on what little we know so far." She tipped her chin toward me. "You need to get these answers out of him."

My hand slid to my belt of knives. "Oh, I intend to."

Maez clicked her tongue. "Not that way."

"You mean you think I should seduce the answers out of him," I grumbled.

"Yes."

"Really?"

"If you have to. Definitely that over the knives."

"But I *know* how to use knives. I have no idea how to do . . . *that*," I groaned. "I am not the fluttering eyelashes kind of Wolf. I'm the tear out your throat with my teeth kind of Wolf. If you wanted someone for seduction, you should've picked better."

"There was a time, not that long ago, when it seemed like you both mutually wanted to get in each other's pants," Maez goaded. "I know things have soured between you two, but some of that attraction must still be there."

"Nope."

"So that's why you held his hand for hours?"

I glared at her. "You were *spying* on us?"

"The hand-holding worked," she said with a mischievous smile. "Now if you'd only Wolf up and start holding some other parts, maybe we'd get some answers out of him."

"You are seriously foul."

"And you are seriously naive." She rolled her eyes. "Don't you want to know what he's hiding from us?"

"Yes," I gritted out.

"Then find a way to get him to willingly let down his defenses," she said. "If he can guard his mind like Ora can, then there will be no prying answers out of him with the tip of your blade. The tip of your tongue, on the other hand . . ."

I scowled at her, knowing that she was right. I had a new court to protect, a new family that could be hurt by Navin's secrets . . . I'd put my pride aside and get closer to the human. Whatever this secret was, I needed to know it, too.

Maez stood and turned an ear toward the sky. "He's coming back."

I nodded and we switched into a conversation about the proper way to cook gloftas as Navin climbed the wagon steps. Whatever I had thought this diplomatic mission to be was slowly unraveling before my eyes.

SADIE

WE RODE THROUGH THE NIGHT BEFORE FINALLY STOPPING AT dawn in a little snowy town just outside the capital of Taigoska. We wouldn't be traveling to the capital this visit—too much attention, too much danger. Navin had spent most of the trip in the driver's seat despite the oxen being able to guide themselves, with us two Wolves staying out of sight. Maez and I took turns sleeping in the narrow bunks scattered throughout the upper shelves of Galen den' Mora. There was no reason to sleep in shifts, but our soldierly instincts got the better of us. Still, I had one of the best sleeps I'd had in months.

By the time I woke up, we'd passed the spires of the Ice Wolf castle and turned toward the Firestorm Peaks that bordered Valta. I'd never ridden that way, never been to the kingdom of Valta even. Everything in me told me we should be heading west toward Damrienn, not east toward Valta. It hit me anew that I may never see the pine forests of my homeland again.

We stopped in a little human town that popped up in the middle of the frozen tundra. After Navin found a stable for the oxen—which *technically* they didn't need being magical oxen—he announced a little too cavalierly that he was venturing into town to buy some supplies.

Maez and I exchanged glances.

"Might want to bring back some food," Maez called from where she stirred a pot of blackened goo.

I grimaced at the bubbling pot. I nearly chipped my tooth on her attempt at baking the night before. There was no apparent reason why Maez had decided to take up the culinary arts on this trip, but I suspected it was her way of missing Briar. Her mate— and kitchen goddess—was sorely missed by me as well. I could certainly go for some of Briar's beef stew right now.

Navin gave a salute. "I think that's for the best." He waved us a hearty farewell, which was normal for his overly friendly disposition, but *still* ever so slightly exaggerated.

Maez chucked the pot into the metal basin with a scowl, waiting a beat to make sure Navin was well and truly gone, before turning to me and asking, "We're following him, aren't we?"

I grabbed my cloak from the back of the kitchen chair. "Yep."

"Good," she said, throwing her tea towel on the bench. "I think this place is going to stink of burnt sallaneva for a while."

"Will you *please* find a less disgusting way to miss your mate," I said with a mock gag.

She threw her apron on the bench, too, the sight of her comical, standing there caked in flour and armed to the teeth in her battle leathers. "Maybe knitting?"

I rolled my eyes and snatched my fur hat. Maez bundled up beside me.

"Be quick," I said.

Now it was her turn to roll her eyes. "He won't have gotten far on those human legs," she said with a chuckle.

"His human legs are very long."

"And"—she looked at me pointedly—"there is a thick layer of snow on the ground that will make it incredibly easy to follow his footsteps." I reached for my knife belt in annoyance, needing something to do with my hands. "Okay, okay," she said, walking to the grating at the back of the wagon and yanking on her snow boots. "No need to get the blades out. Jumping juvlecks, this human has your fur all ruffled, huh?"

I debated for a split second about socking her in the jaw, but then thought better of it. She'd have to shift to hide the inevitable welt and then that would create more questions. No, I'd save the maiming for another time.

It didn't dawn on me that hitting my friend was the wrong thing to do, period.

I hastily tied my laces and stomped out into the snow, walking the easy-to-follow trail of Navin's large boot prints. My gait was wobbly at first, already so used to the rocking motion of Galen den' Mora that it felt strange to be back on solid ground. The air was so cold that steaming whorls of breath clouded around our faces as we walked. At least the biting gales had died down and now there was only a gentle dusting of snow falling from the skies. I pulled the cloak tighter around me, wishing I was wearing my fur instead of a coat. My skin was so unprotected and delicate, the cold easily seeping into my bones as we trudged through the snow.

How did humans do it?

We slowed our pace as we wandered into the little village. Pulling our hoods up, we linked arms, looking for all intents and purposes like a couple out for a midmorning stroll about town. We zigzagged down two more streets before we turned another corner and I halted abruptly, yanking Maez back. We'd caught up to Navin. He wandered down the silent street, humming to himself all the while.

"What is he doing at this end of town?" Maez asked, nodding to the streets in the opposite direction. "All the taverns and markets smell like they're that way."

I bobbed my chin in agreement, unlinking our arms. "This part of town seems dead."

"Perhaps he deals in some nefarious trades on the side," Maez whispered. "Maybe that's his secret. A person constantly traveling from one kingdom to the next would be the perfect smuggler."

I considered it for a second before shaking my head. "That

can't be it," I said. "Smuggling goods isn't enough to *set the whole world on fire* as he put it."

Maez shrugged. I peeked around the corner again as Navin turned down an alleyway up ahead. As soon as he disappeared, we followed, tailing him to the next corner. When we reached the alley and peeked down, Navin's humming abruptly halted.

"Shit," I whispered, yanking my head back.

My heart pounded in my ears, waiting, waiting. But then Navin's humming resumed and he carried on. We continued our pursuit. At the other end of the alley was an old town square. A bell tolled and the square erupted into applause and laughter as a wedding party poured out of the human love temple. As the crowd entered the square, Navin strolled casually into the throng.

"Great," Maez muttered as we tried to keep our eyes on him in the crowd.

We shoved through the merry well-wishers, finding the road diverted into two around the temple. Navin was nowhere to be seen, nor any footprints in the snow down either path.

I glanced at Maez. "Split up?"

She nodded. "Meet you back at the wagon in one hour."

I darted down the left-hand side, moving quickly through the lingering crowd and back into the quiet of the side street. The human temple was a long rectangular building constructed of sandstone and ice. I hugged close to the wall. It ran all the way down toward a giant snowbank, a dead end to the right. If Navin had come down this way, he must've gone left. I tiptoed up to the corner, my hands twitching for my knives. I peeked around and saw nothing but a wall of icicles hanging from the building's roof.

I was distracted, assessing the wall for holes, the snow dampening my senses, when a hand reached out and grabbed me by the back of my cloak.

As I was yanked backward, I snagged a thick icicle in my grip, spinning my attacker by the arm and slamming them into the temple wall. I had the distinct impression the towering figure was letting me maneuver them backward, not even putting up a fight, but moving just as I willed them to. Bodies weren't that compliant; even those without fighting skill instinctively should've resisted. I held the tip of the icicle to the cloaked figure's throat with one hand, releasing my grip on them with the other to yank back their hood.

A pair of bronze eyes stared back at me, drained of their normal mirth for a flash before that crooked smile returned.

"I would think you followed me out of concern for my safety," Navin said with a grin, "if you weren't two seconds from impaling me with an ice dagger."

"What the . . . ?" I looked to my left and right, then up to the roof, which was also covered in a deep layer of snow, no footprints to be found. How the fuck did he get behind me? More, *how* did he sneak up on me, a Wolf?

I cleared my throat. "What are you doing out here?"

He kept his head flattened to the wall, only moving his widening eyes to the icicle in my grip. I scowled and threw it into the snow. The bloody thing was burning my hand anyway. Navin pointedly rubbed his throat with his pointer finger before reaching into the inner pockets of his cloak.

He produced a bundle of fabric and unwrapped it. The smell of freshly baked meat pies wafted out. "I made a detour from my shopping to get these," he said. "Saba makes the best pies in town." He cocked his head, his eyes warm and eager. "Were you looking for me? Did you want to come with me to the markets?"

How? How! How did he have time to go buy these pies—we were right behind him this whole time. What sort of magic did he possess to whip these hot pies out of thin air? I tried not to scan around the space. Was there some secret shop below the love temple? Was there a stand in the square that we completely missed?

A more ominous thought unspooled from my mind: maybe this secret wasn't about someone, *something* else, maybe it was about *him*. His friendliness now seemed tinted with malice, my skepticism sharply cresting within me. That flicker behind his mask, that look in his eyes, what lurked beneath? I'd sniff him out, dig up what I couldn't yet see.

"Oh, um," I said, trying to appear flustered and not look like I was solving this mystery. "Yes. I need some . . . rope."

He arched his brow. "Rope?"

"Yes," I hedged. Why the fuck had I picked rope? "It's a common item to carry in our packs in case of emergencies." I tried to hide my cringe of embarrassment. I sounded like a complete fool.

Maez rounded the corner, skidding to a stop when she saw Navin and the meat pies he proffered out. She turned her stumble into a swagger. "Navin!" she called in a jolly tone. "Oh, good, we found you. We thought we might accompany you to the markets. I'm in need of some . . ." She glanced at me and I grimaced at her. "Salve," she said with a confident nod, trying to sell the lie. "This thin Taigosi air is making my lips chapped."

Fuck that was good. My lips *were* kind of chapped from the cold air. Why didn't I think of that instead of *rope*?

"Excellent." Navin smiled at her and then at me. "Shall we eat and walk?" He offered each of us a pie, acting ever the host and not the least like the stealthy liar I was beginning to suspect him of being. "These will be your new favorites."

We each took a pie as we strolled out of the dead-end road. Our boots crunched through the snow, the fresh powder whining as it compressed beneath our soles. Wisps of chimney smoke rose up toward the overcast sky, and the smell of mulled wine and roast meat cut through the crisp air.

When I took a bite of the flaking buttery pastry, I moaned. Maez echoed my noise with her own.

"Sweet Moon," she crooned. "If I didn't already have a mate, I would swear myself to these pies."

I snorted, bits of pastry flying out of my pressed lips.

"I told you," Navin said to me as he nudged Maez with his elbow.

We strolled side by side, making appreciative grunts and hums as we devoured our pies. Navin started humming a merry tune to himself again, and I couldn't help for a moment but feel like we were just three friends wandering the streets of the little town. Then I remembered the speed with which Navin grabbed me, the way he *let me* overpower him, the stealth with which he snuck up on me, and the skill with which he covered for it.

Everything I thought I knew about the man was crumbling to ash between my fingertips. What more was he hiding? What more could he do? And would he use these secret skills *against* me and Maez? I'd foolishly once thought he was a gentle soul . . .

Now I was beginning to wonder if we were even *safe* with him.

All the ease of the moment drained away. I knew then for certain that there was more to Navin than just the traveling musician I'd met moons ago, and my hackles rose as I readied for whatever I was about to discover.

SADIE

NAVIN AND I WANDERED THE QUIET SNOWY ROADS, HOLDING mugs of steaming tea in our hands. I blew on the cup, enjoying the warmth bouncing back at me. I considered Navin with new eyes as we meandered through the village, scrutinizing everything from the way he positioned his body against the sudden gales of frigid cross-breeze to the depth of his steady gait. Even that sweetly awkward smile he gave me now seemed limned with malice. Was it all a ruse? He became more of a mystery to me with each turn around the frozen courtyards and tumbledown townhouses.

Maez had broken off from us, easily falling into friendly conversation with every stallholder in the markets. She found her salve, and I acquired my embarrassingly random length of rope that I tucked deep into my cloak pocket. Navin and I had walked on, silently agreeing to take in more of the town side by side.

The little township seemed frozen both literally and in time. It looked half-abandoned, too, unloved shutters hanging from hinges, locks rusted shut, drifts of snow shoveled against disintegrating pinewood doors. Townsfolk must have moved to the nearby capital of Taigoska, where there were more work and more amenities. Even in the human quarter of the city, I remembered how much it was bustling with life and activity. There would be no art galleries and restaurants in a sleepy little village like this, no shows or concerts, no adventures to be had.

I didn't blame the humans for wanting to leave this humdrum existence. It reminded me a little of the stagnancy I'd felt in Olmdere, though I'd never admit it aloud.

I slid a glance at Navin. No musicians would be paid enough to stop here either . . . and why would they when they could stay in the capital only a stone's throw west where they would be paid handsomely for their performances? Yet Navin knew the place well—well enough to sneak up on me. The soldier in me bristled. No one snuck up on me. I added Navin's furtiveness and familiarity with the town to my ever-growing list of suspicions about who—and what—Navin really was.

"How old were you?" I asked, my ringing voice too loud in the snow-mantled quiet. "When you fled Olmdere? How old were you?"

Navin's shoulders tensed but he didn't break his stride. "Fifteen," he said with all the casualness of a sharpened knife.

"So young." I blew out a long, steaming breath that curled into my hair. "How old was your brother?"

"Seventeen."

"Sawyn recruited Rooks young then," I said. "Makes sense. If I was a teenager with the world crumbling down around me, I'd want someone to put a sword in my hand, too."

"Or at least food," Navin said, and I nodded, a little ashamed that hadn't dawned on me as a motive for his brother. I forgot humans couldn't just shift and go hunting for some bunnies. I'd never feared an empty belly with the forest always just beyond my window, my keen sense always ready and scenting for prey. Yet another way I didn't understand humans at all.

Navin's footsteps faltered as he peeked at me and then back to his mug. "I hate that I can understand why he did it."

I nodded and sipped my drink, enjoying the pleasant warmth

that trailed from my mouth to my wool-cloaked chest. "This family secret—"

"Sadie." Navin took a step in front of me, blocking my path forward. The steam from his tea swirled up into his shadowed hood. "I can't tell you about this. I wish I could, but it's much bigger than me, and—and I can't."

I wore an impassive mask even as I cringed inwardly. I was blatantly digging and now he knew it.

"Okay," I said, knowing if I pushed any harder, he'd pull even more away from me.

"Okay?" He sounded surprised.

I shrugged, feigning nonchalance. "I don't really need to know. I was just curious."

He narrowed his eyes at me for a beat. I needed to be a more convincing liar. I sidestepped around him and kept walking. "So how long until we get to Nesra's Pass?"

"We're not going down Nesra's Pass." He fell into an easy stride beside me again, seemingly relieved at the pivot of conversation. "We're cutting straight down from Taigos to Valta."

I looked side to side, trying to remember every map of the continent I'd ever seen, but I could recollect no such passage. "But . . . Nesra's Pass is the only way down through the mountains?"

"It's the only *Wolf* way down through the mountains," Navin said as a rueful smile whispered across his face. "There are other ways down from the Ice Wolf kingdom."

My mouth twisted in thought. "You seem to know a lot about these secret roads." I watched his face carefully as I spoke, trying to find any tell, hoping that something I said would give it away, but he merely shrugged. I yearned to set him off-balance, for him to give me something to fear or hate or even begrudgingly respect, some flash of truth and redemption for all he'd done. Worst of all, this stranger before me had rung every alarm bell within me, and Gods help me, I *liked* it—a thrill after my stagnancy in Olmdere—a riddle I needed to solve. What truths were brewing beneath the surface of this conversation? What deceptions lay just beyond these pleasantries?

"It's the life of any traveler," Navin said breezily. "Ora would line up all of our events. They were constantly sending pigeons and letters to this lord or that—solstices, coronations, town festivals, barn raisings, you name it. We play for Wolf and human alike. We've always been constantly on the move for as long as I've been a part of the troupe. You learn how to get to places the fastest course possible."

"And why haven't the Wolves ever learned about this traversal?"

"Why would they?" Navin didn't immediately continue as we looped the township, returning to the tea cart that sat at the edge of the markets. We delivered back our empty mugs to the weathered old tea lady with a nod of thanks and kept rambling back toward the wagon.

We crunched through the ice-crusted snow for another minute before Navin said, "The towns along the Valtan border are all human ones on both sides. The capitals are nowhere near there, nor are any resources of economical value. Wolves travel across the Stoneater River to get to Rikesh. What business would they have traveling this way?"

"I don't know," I mused, perturbed that there was a whole section of the continent I knew little about. "You'd think the Wolf kings would know every inch of their own lands."

"Not better than the humans who *inhabit* every inch of their lands," Navin observed, his voice tinged in bitterness. "Wolves keep to themselves and their forests and their capital cities . . . except when it comes to collecting taxes and crop tithes, of course."

Here we were again at the point of impasse. He was a human. I was a Wolf. We would never fully understand each other's lives. I knew Wolves had mistreated humans in the years since they banished the monsters and were placed on their thrones . . . but Wolves were not wholly evil as some humans thought. Long ago humans landed on our Wolf shores, and we'd guarded them from the harsh new world. We were once the humans' saviors, protectors, *Gods* to them. What had happened along the way to change that? Where did it all go so wrong?

"So we are heading toward a secret road to Valta?" I tried to carry on the conversation, but it felt uneasy now with all the unspoken truths floating between us.

"It's a commonly used farming route to deliver goods to Taigoska from Lower Valta," Navin said. "It's a secret only to Wolves through their own sheer ignorance."

I grabbed him by the elbow right as he whirled toward me, those bronze eyes heated. I glowered back at him.

"I get it," I said. "I get that you hate Wolves for all they've done to your people. There's no need to dance around this anymore. I suppose men both Wolf and human alike are the same in one regard: you never say what you fucking mean." My grip on his elbow tightened. "Do us both a favor and speak plainly: you hate them. And if you hate them, you have to hate me."

I released him and took a single step before his hand shot out, his large legs easily outmaneuvering me and caging me in against the crumbling temple wall on the outskirts of town.

I could've ducked under his arms. I could've pulled out my knife. I could've tipped the balance of power once more in my favor . . . but I didn't. I let him stand there, towering over me, leaning into me. A white-hot thrill ran down my spine, imagining what it would be like if he could truly overpower me.

"I never said I hated you." His words were tight and barely restrained, the venomous warning of a scream.

There he was. The real him.

"But you hate everything that I am!" I shouted back, pushing further, not letting his closeness cow me. "Tell me, did you pursue me out of morbid curiosity? Was it a form of self-loathing? Was I some sort of oddity for you to explore? Some vile taboo conquest you could—"

His lips silenced me. His mouth collided with mine in a

scorching kiss, and I instinctively rose up on my tiptoes to meet him. My fingers twisted in his cloak and tugged him closer as his tongue plundered my mouth. How could he keep pulling me in like this? What spell did he hold over me that so easily had my heart racing and my limbs buzzing?

Our kiss was more fevered and urgent than the one we'd shared many weeks ago. His teeth scraped over my bottom lip, sucking it into his mouth. The low hum he let out sounded like the last resonant note of a song. Then he pulled away, leaving me toppling forward, lips parted and breathless. I barely caught my footing, my body bending toward him with a fevered magnetism.

Navin took another step back, steam swirling around from our panting breaths, the distance making my cheeks heat in a furious blush. I swallowed the shame of that kiss, composing my expression into nothing but steel as I met Navin's darkening gaze.

"I only knew I wanted you. That's all," he murmured. "Just you, Sadie."

Just me.

He said it like I could *just* be a human for him. As if I existed outside of anything else—no culture or kingdom or space—just me in isolation. But I didn't exist like some faery floating in the ether. I was a product of all that I was raised to be. I was a product of my people, good or bad, evil or righteous, and whether I chose to carry on that legacy or not it still irrefutably existed within my blood. There were parts to me that I couldn't deny, parts I didn't *want* to deny. Navin needed to pretend I was a human to want me at all.

I held his stare, letting the primal ferocity of my kind leak into my expression as I said, "Who *I am* is a Wolf."

Then I ducked under his arm and moved with my true speed. He reached for me, but I quickly sidestepped him, reminding him that I was faster and stronger than I seemed, too. We would only play these games when *I* allowed it. Let him never forget I was not some human girl that he could tower over and kiss if I didn't want him to do exactly that.

As I raced over the frozen tundra, my thoughts became a tangled web. I wanted his secrets—*needed them*—for Calla, for Olmdere—but I couldn't do it this way. I couldn't open myself up to this man and guard myself from him at the same time. It had to be one or the other.

I found Maez whistling merrily as she milled about the wagon.

She raised her hand in a half wave. "Hey, I—"

"I can't do this, Maez," I said, my throat constricting. "Not like this."

She spun on her heel and followed after me. "Okay," she said in a calming voice, her swift change in tone denoting how much she sensed my jumbled mess of feelings. "Okay, Sads, we'll find another way."

CALLA

I HUNG HALFWAY OUT THE WINDOW, WATCHING THE GOLDEN leaves dance down upon our convoy of mounted guards and carriages. It had taken three days to send word to Taigoska and assemble our traveling party. Three days we didn't have.

Hector, Briar, and Mina had taken the front carriage, Grae and I behind. Four human guards rode ahead and in the rear. We were a formidable presence rolling through the small rebuilding villages of Olmdere, so it wasn't surprising to see many citizens taking to the streets to wave; I returned each of their smiles and greetings long after my arm was numb and my lower back was aching. It was all a show. They saw this as a sign of our strength, or a return to what used to be. Yet, despite the gleaming carriages and gilded cavalry, I knew this little force wouldn't be enough if the Silver Wolf pack somehow made it into Taigos. Four Wolves and five humans? Less a force and more a farce. Even with the hundreds of Ice Wolves at our side, the Silver Wolf pack was unparalleled in their fighting skill. I was trained by Vellia to be at their level, but there was only one of me. Grae and a few other Wolves had that training as well, but it wasn't enough. I waved and smiled even as I was loath to admit that I'd need twice as many Wolf allies to win any real fight.

Grae hooked his finger into my belt loop and tugged me back inside, a golden leaf dancing through the window after me.

"One inch farther and I'd be hoisting you in by your ankles," he said with a chuckle.

I picked up the leaf and twirled it by the stem. "We didn't get to truly appreciate its beauty last time."

He tensed. "Last time we were almost eaten by a juvleck."

"Do they live in groups?" I wondered, staring down at the carpet of honey and marigold. "Do you think there are many more down there?"

"So long as they don't come up here, we shall never need to know."

"Whoa!" the driver called, and the carriage rolled to a stop.

I stuck my head out the window again, spying a group of a dozen humans huddled by the side of the road.

"Gods," I breathed, throwing open the door as Grae called my name—probably to remind me that, as Queen, I shouldn't be the first one to run into an unknown situation, but we both knew that wasn't me—and hustled after. "What happened?" I stared from one dirt-covered face to another. I knew the look in their eyes too well—haunted. Too wide, too wary. Many were covered in bloody bandages; others had tear streaks carved through the mud on their cheeks.

When their eyes landed on me, they all began dropping into bows. I suddenly felt a strange shame in my fine attire—my beautiful riding jacket, polished boots, and golden crown. Guards moved farther and farther in front of me, and I shoved between them. I got their motive, but what exactly were they defending me from? These clearly traumatized people?

"Rise," I implored them. "Please. Someone, tell me what happened." One of the elders at the front stepped forward. "What is your name?"

"Elyra, Your Majesty. I am the"—she paused and looked around before saying—"oricsia of the town of Eastbrook." She bowed again.

I inclined my chin to her and placed my finger to my forehead in honored greeting. "Oricsia" was a human word that loosely meant grandmother, but implied much more. Many of the human villages were matriarchal. Oricsia meant Elyra was a village elder, a leader and guardian, a cherished one amongst her town.

"You've come from Eastbrook?" I tossed the town name around. "But that's in—"

"Damrienn," Grae said, moving to stand beside me. The group bowed again to him, and I couldn't help but note how they inched farther backward.

My stomach dropped. Somehow instinctively I knew, but it still twisted in my gut to hear it. "What happened?"

"The Silver Wolves," Elyra said, pulling her shawl tighter around herself. "They sent the Silent Blades to attack our village."

"Attack?" I choked out. "Who are these Silent Blades?" I looked to Grae but he shook his head, as confused as I was.

"Much has changed since the fall of Sawyn," Elyra said, clearing her throat when her voice wobbled.

"I haven't heard a thing from Damrienn since Sawyn's demise," I said, shaking my head. "Nor has Taigos, if Queen Ingrid's letters are to be believed."

"You wouldn't have heard of what's been happening. They've stopped all trade," Elyra said. "Only Wolves are permitted to travel the realm now."

"What has Nero done?" Grae's voice dripped with venom because he already knew. He of all people was aware of what his father was capable of.

"The King said it was the humans who corrupted you." Elyra met my gaze. "King Nero told us were it not for those human musicians, you never would've taken the word 'merem,' never welcomed humans to sit on your unlawful court, never permitted Wolves and humans to"—her cupped hand waved through the air—"*be* together." My stomach tied into a knot as a hot flush crept up my cheeks. Nero knew about Sadie and Navin then, or at the very least suspected human-Wolf relations within my borders. Elyra's rheumy eyes bore a flash of sympathy as she added, "Nero said it was the humans that encouraged you to betray your pack."

Fury rose in me at that. It was *Nero* who betrayed me and my sister. Briar and I had been willing to give our *lives* over to him and his pack, and all he did was threaten us and use us for our court's gold. Corrupted by humans? More like enlightened. It was only once I met Ora that I realized that belonging to a family wasn't done out of fear.

"I knew he'd do something like this," Grae snarled. "It was only a matter of time before his hatred finally made him snap."

The humans trembled, shifting farther away, and I put a hand on my mate's chest and gently—but firmly—pushed him back behind me. These people were already too afraid of his anger whether it was justified or not.

I searched their fearful faces. "Nero has punished you all for *my* leaving?"

Elyra bobbed her chin, the wrinkles around her mouth deepening with a frown. "He tore down our temples." I gasped, unable to hide my horror. In only a few moons, he'd managed to destroy his kingdom so much? "He told us we are only allowed to pray to the Wolf Gods now, only to use the Wolf words. He said he allowed human customs to stray too far from his leadership and that he'd shepherd us back to Wolf morality. I'm no longer allowed to call myself oricsia." Her solemn eyes met mine. "You'd no longer be able to call yourself merem." That sentence slammed into me like a kick to the gut. Because I had claimed a word, claimed *who I truly was*, he'd taken it away from everyone else, too. "Anyone caught not obeying Wolf laws is being rooted out by the Silent Blades."

That name again. "Who are these Silent Blades?"

"It's what we call his spies," Elyra said. "They are Silver Wolves who police the human villages, hiding as humans until they find a reason to proclaim a town disobedient. There's not a single town where the Silent Blades have not found someone guilty of *disobeying* their King."

"No," I whispered, my words coming out as shaky as Elyra's own now. "How could he do that to you?" The words stung coming out of my mouth and yet nothing about Nero's true potential for evil surprised me. He was angry I'd taken back *my* court from him—and therefore *stolen* the gold he felt belonged to him—believing that because I didn't have a cock between my legs that I should forfeit the entire region to *him*. But I hadn't, and in doing so I'd embarrassed him. And for that slight, he was taking it out on the most vulnerable. It astounded me still how many lives one man could unflinchingly destroy just for his lust for more gold.

"There's more, Your Majesty," Elyra continued, beckoning forward a fearful human who seemed the same age as me. "It's all right, mezmevia." The woman—Elyra's granddaughter judging by the word the elder used—had a blanket wrapped around the crown of her head that draped down her body so that only her eyes peeked out. She had piercing hazel eyes that watched me warily as her grandmother wrapped an arm around her shoulder. "You can show them. It's okay."

The woman dropped the blanket to her shoulders revealing a blistering brand that covered her face from her jaw all the way up to her lower eyelid. The sight of the scabbed and weeping red paw print on her cheek made bile rise up my throat and fire fill my veins.

"What is the meaning of this?" My hackles rose as I stared at the brand. So much anger filled me that I had to force my Wolf not to take control, no easy task. The pull coiled deep in my belly, my bones aching to shift, my mind begging for the fury and vengeance that only my Wolf form could bring. I would gut Nero for what he'd done to these innocents . . . but he wasn't here, and there was no one nearby for me to eviscerate.

With a deep breath, I found my center and stayed in my current form.

"They are marking humans for encouraging skin chasing," Elyra said.

"What?" I gaped back at the old woman. "But . . ." The thoughts tumbled through me. Only Wolves were punished, sometimes brutally, for "sullying" themselves with humans. It was a Wolf punishment based on a pack rule, not a human one. And Wolves could shift, Wolves could *heal*. This human would be scarred for the rest of her days. Another poisoned word snagged in my mind. "*Encouraging?*" I swallowed, barely able to ask as I stared at the mark. "What happened before they placed that brand on your cheek?"

"I think you already know," Elyra said tightly, holding the girl closer to her side. "They've taken everything from us. From our beliefs, from our homes . . . from our bodies."

I searched the hollow faces of the group. "Where is the rest of Eastbrook?"

"We are all that's left of Eastbrook."

My eyes welled before Elyra could even finish her sentence. She continued, "We fled on our fishing boats, tried to sail around the border, but the Olmderian shores are too treacherous to breech. A storm washed us ashore at the foothill of the Storm-crest Ranges. We've been seeking refuge in your court ever since, Your Majesty."

I blinked back tears, trying to hold my resolve for the people in front of me. They didn't need my pity, they needed my protection, and I swore then and there that I'd be the instrument for their vengeance, too.

"You will be safe in Olmdere," I vowed to the group. "I promise this to you." I stepped aside. "Take my carriage back to the city. You need to see the royal healers at once."

"Calla," Grae murmured, but I held up a hand.

"You will take that carriage, too." I gestured to the other

carriage and saw Hector, Mina, and Briar huddled together behind the wall of royal guards, their faces matching the horror I felt in my body. Hector's arm was around Mina's waist, tucking her into his side as she cried. "I will send my best guards to ride with you," I assured them.

"Thank you, Your Majesty," Elyra said with a bob of her chin.

"You will be safe in my court," I said again and knew I couldn't say it enough times for them to believe it. I knew it would take a long time, perhaps the rest of their lives, before they ever felt safe again. "You are home now." Elyra's eyes misted, clearly holding on to the last bit of strength that had guided her people this far. She reached out and clasped my hands with her own. "I'm sorry I've brought this evil to your village."

Elyra shook her head. "None of our kind thinks this is your doing," she said. "We whisper of the Queen who lives beyond the golden trees." She craned her neck up and smiled at the tapestry of gilded leaves above us, lifting her crooked fingers in supplication. "A ruler who believes humans and Wolves should live as one. Where our lives are weighted just as much as your own." Her eyes dropped to the peak of gold skin lifting above my collar. "A queen who died to make this a place of peace."

A tear slid freely down my cheek now. I knew eventually the remaining humans of Damrienn wouldn't be saying such things. Soon they would blame me for all their pain. Soon the Silver Wolves would torture and scare them into hating the Golden Court. I thought of Ora again, wishing I could turn back to Olmdere with this group but knowing I needed to keep moving ahead to Taigos. I needed to end this even more urgently than I had before.

"I will return to the Golden Court soon," I assured the harried faces staring back at me. "Until then, you will be guests of the crown and treated as such. Olmdere welcomes you."

They bowed to me, and I flagged down one of my guards, giving him coins and instructions along with a heavy-handed threat that if anything should happen to these people, he would be held personally responsible.

Grae leaned his shoulder into me, his voice a low whisper. "And how are we meant to get to Durid tonight?"

I glanced at him. "Mina can ride with the remaining guards. The rest of us run on four paws." Hector and Briar nodded at me in unison. "I need the wind in my fur. I need to howl at the moon. I need to imagine our pack slaughtering Nero for what he's done. Let's go."

SADIE

THE WAGON TILTED PRECARIOUSLY TO ONE SIDE, TURNED, AND then tilted the other way as we switched down the back road toward Valta. Maez and I were both turning green as we sat on the couches getting tossed to and fro. Nesra's Pass was a long, steep ascent, but at least it was steady. This road was a short, sharp nightmare.

When the wagon finally leveled out, it took me a second to feel like we weren't still moving. My stomach roiled and my hands shook.

"Fuck that road and its grandmother," Maez snarled.

"Never again," I groaned, clutching my gut.

Navin knocked on the wagon door. The stairs were lifted and locked for the rocky journey, and they rattled with each pound of his fists. "I'm heading into town for some food," he called. "Come find me at Jevara Vanesh when you're ready."

Jevara Vanesh. It meant "the roasting pig" in Valtan, a restaurant or inn I presumed.

I wondered if Navin had more secret errands in this place. If we tailed him, where would he go? More, did he have the wherewithal to *know* he was being tailed? I intended to further my line of inquiry over our meal. It seemed like the farther we traveled, the more evasive he became, or maybe I was finally being more astute now that I wasn't looking at him with puppy dog eyes.

As I took more queasy breaths and fanned myself, I noticed that the air in the wagon was starting to turn more humid. The sweat on my brow wasn't only from nausea but also the heat. Maez's short hair curled at the temples, her face flushed. We'd dropped so far in altitude over the course of the day, the Valtan weather had started to seep into the cracks of the wagon.

I pulled back one of the windows above my head and a wall of heat blasted at me. "Ugh," I grumbled, looking back and forth between Maez and my clothing of thick furs and leathers. Maez and I exchanged glances as we both started disrobing and went searching through the trunks of abandoned clothes for something lighter to wear.

When we stepped down off the wagon, I stifled a gasp as I craned my neck up toward the sky. In the far distance were mountains floating amongst the clouds. The bottoms of the mountains were diamond-shaped rocks—the darkest iridescent black, like ravens' wings. Far below the floating mountains were circles of shade and turquoise pools of water. I'd heard of nomadic groups that would spend each day following the trail of shade from the mountains' shadows. I believed it. It would be the only way to survive in such an unwelcoming environment. Unlike the lush, pastoral landscapes in the sky.

The floating mountains were called Upper Valta, where all the Onyx Wolf pack lived. The biggest mountain at the center of the cluster was the capital of Rikesh. I gaped, unbelieving that anyone could reside in the sky like that. Yet people clearly lived there, noting the long rope bridges that tied the floating mountains together. My already sore stomach twisted at the thought of riding across them with nothing but open air beneath us.

I lowered my gaze to the desert that stretched out on the ground below. It seemed like a wasteland of deep golden sand. No cities popped up in the distance, no other signs of life except for those from above. The teeming verdant green and sharp onyx stone of the mountains above sat in stark contrast to the rolling sand dunes below. Behind us was what appeared to be the only low-dwelling village in all Lower Valta.

The town was built near vertically into the sandstone cliff-side. Little darkened square windows cut into the stone and criss-crossed pathways led up to the higher buildings. Donkeys pulled carts up and down the narrow roads as people darted to and fro between the shade of the buildings. There was no greenery apart from the plants that sprung up from a lean waterfall that poured from the cliffside down onto the top of the township, like a miniature oasis amongst a sea of sand and beige.

The few people who moved from building to building all wore broad hats and lightweight, pale clothing to keep cool from the scorching sun.

"So glad Briar packed my fur hat and woolen cloak," I muttered, "considering we're going to be in the scorching heat for most of this trip."

Maez let out a half snarl beside me at the derogatory mention of her mate. "You'd have frozen your tail off in Taigos, you ungrateful fool."

She fanned out the billowing white shirt she wore over her half vest and fitted linen trousers. Her weapons belt was still strapped to her waist, but it was the only thick material in her otherwise desert-appropriate attire. I, on the other hand, wore similarly light fabric . . . but over the top of my fighting leathers. I wasn't going to risk being stabbed just to keep cool. My bandoliers of knives were all hidden within my clothing now. For all intents and purposes, I was dressed like a human civilian, far more stealthy than Maez's weapons belt, though I knew I might boil alive for the choice.

"Come on," Maez said, elbowing me and taking a step out of the shade of the wagon and into the sunlight. "Before we shrivel up, I need to eat something greasy."

The first step into the sunshine felt like stepping too close to a fire, and I fought the urge to retreat into the shade. Behind us, four giant posts poked up from the earth, a shade sail hanging above it. Navin had parked the wagon under the sail alongside many other wagons and carts. There were feeding troughs and water—a makeshift barn. But a wooden barn would've probably been impossibly hot and equally easy to catch aflame. One spark and the whole thing would burst into an inferno. This place seemed teetering on the precipice of a firestorm.

I forced myself forward as the sun seared every inch of my exposed skin and I grimaced at the brightness. The sand was baking in the sun's heat, and I felt like I was being cooked alive from both above and below. If the makeshift barn had been even a few more paces away from the shelter of the township, I might've collapsed from heat exhaustion right then and there.

Wearing my hidden leathers was a bad fucking idea. The regret mounted with each step through the burning sand, yet I didn't dare turn back when the shade of town was so close. I had half a mind to strip naked right in the middle of the desert but realized that might be far more suspicious than wearing a sword on my hip.

When we reached the arched doorway to the township, we entered a corridor that tunneled into the hillside and traveled up through the shadowed town. The relief of the shade was so great I wanted to let out a moan.

"How does *anyone* live in this fucking town?" Maez groaned, wiping the back of her sweaty neck.

An old man carrying a tray of glass vials stopped short and frowned at her.

Maez grimaced. "Apologies," she said in her best Valtan accent.

The man blustered off, shaking his head and muttering something about Damrienn.

"He knows where we're from," Maez whispered to me.

"What did you expect?" I waved to her bright red face and

my sweat-soaked tunic. "We look like we've just been dunked in the ocean. All of the people around us look fine with the heat," I said as Maez desperately fanned herself. "At least we pass for humans of Damrienn."

"For now," Maez muttered. "Any more of this heat and I might go completely feral."

"Bad idea," I said. "We're not built for these climates. You'd combust in your furs."

"Good point."

We wandered farther down the main corridor, passing a cart of fans made from woven palm leaves. My eyes darted left and right, studying each passage, searching for a lanky musician who was far more than he seemed. Would this town hold any more clues that could help decipher his true nature?

"Here," I said, plucking two off the cart and passing the woman a crover.

She eyed it suspiciously, turning the foreign coin over twice to make sure it was real. Then she nodded and kept walking.

We frantically fanned ourselves as we kept walking and Maez started loudly talking about our family's farm and visiting cousins in Valta. It wasn't the worst ruse, but she was certainly overselling it.

"How about we just be quiet humans," I muttered out of the corner of my mouth.

"Why yes, cousin!" Maez said loudly and laughed at the family passing in the other direction. I elbowed her hard in the ribs. "How my cousin loves to jest," she tittered.

"By all the fucking Gods," I spat and stormed off ahead of her.

Off the main vein of the town were narrower corridors, some bustling with people, others quiet. With Maez hot on my tail, I followed the Valtan signs up and up toward the top of the town, following the words *Jevara Vanesh*, along with the symbol of a plate and spoon drawn next to it.

My stomach rumbled more with each step upward, the smell of roasted meats and spiced nuts drifting down the tunnel. When we finally turned from the main hallway into the restaurant, all my relief disappeared.

Navin sat in a far corner booth, wide-eyed, with a knife pressed to his throat.

And the person holding that knife?

My father.

CALLA

THE SLEEPY TOWN OF DURID SAT SILENT AS I PROPPED MY elbows on the windowsill. My eyes lingered on one spot—that interruption in the houses, that ashen scar on the earth. Illuminated by the swollen moon, I could see the blackened mark where the mill once stood, the final burial ground for the two Wolves who chased Grae and me inside. If running away from Highwick was the spark, killing members of the Silver Wolf pack was the blaze.

In some twisted ways I understood Nero's anger, but his retaliation against the humans was unfathomable. Grae and I alone should bear his wrath. It didn't matter those Silver Wolves were trying to *capture* us, didn't matter that returning with them would've been tantamount to a death sentence. In the mind of a Wolf, we betrayed our pack and we deserved everything that came next. But the humans hadn't betrayed Nero, and he should thus be treating them as an alpha would: as members of the pack that needed his protection.

Not his teeth.

I smelled Grae's scent a split second before his arms wrapped around me and his chin dropped onto my shoulder. He let out a long, slow sigh and pulled me from over the window ledge and tighter against his chest, anchoring me from my storming emotions.

"You need to stop leaning out open windows, love," he murmured, "before you make my heart explode."

"It's a two-story drop," I said with a whisper of a laugh. I waggled my hand at him, displaying the heavy amber ring on my finger. "Besides, I am protected."

He toyed with the ring, centering the protection stone that consumed my left hand. It had once been a necklace that Grae had gifted me when we were young. Now, it was my wedding band, a reminder of his love and protection.

Grae let out a frustrated sigh, but it had no bite to it. "A few blows might miss, a few arrows stray, a few assailants more easily felled," he said. "But it's not a miracle. And toppling out a window is a cruel thing to do to your mate, protection stone or no."

I felt his smile against my shoulder and my cheeks mindlessly lifted in mirror to his own. "How careless of me to not be thinking of your delicate heart." I stretched my hands across the window again, and Grae's grip on me tightened, keeping me from breeching the sill into open air.

The entire top floor of the inn was dedicated to me, my court, and my guards. I was probably the first queen who'd ever stayed there, but without our transportation, we decided to rest in the border town before riding out to the Taigosi capital in the morning once the carriages returned. It would be a long day, normally broken up even further, but after what I had seen, I knew I needed to speak to Queen Ingrid straightaway. The sight of that human's burned face flashed through my mind again, spiking my panic anew.

"Your pulse is racing." Grae dropped a kiss to my neck. "I only have one guess why."

I swallowed, sticky guilt clinging to my skin, unable to be scrubbed away no matter how I tried. "If I hadn't—"

Grae's arms tightened. "No," he murmured, his bottom lip skimming my pulse. "This was not your fault, little fox."

"I brought this upon them," I said, my voice shaking with horror. "People died because of me. If I hadn't fled—"

"If you hadn't fled, Maez would still be trapped in that tower, Briar would still be under a sleeping curse, and your court, your *people*, would still be ruled by an evil sorceress." Grae brushed a featherlight kiss to my temple, his hands splaying across my rib cage and down to my belly. "This is what my father does. He punishes you by hurting others." His voice trailed off and I knew he was thinking of his mother. "He is using you as a reason to solidify the control and power he's always craved. He'd take the entire continent if he thought he could get away with it."

"Surely Ingrid will join us in rising up to fight him, right? She knows how it feels to defy controlling men," I whispered. "Gods, I pray that Valta will rally to our cause, too."

"Sadie and Maez will convince King Luo of it," Grae said, but his reassurance lacked the conviction I needed.

"I don't know," I hedged. "Luo seems nearly as backward as your father. He will take whichever side stands to benefit him the most."

"We have mines filled with gold."

"That will never be mined again," I reminded him. I was never sending another soul below the Sevelde Forest.

"Luo doesn't need to know that," Grae countered. "You forget I was schooled in Rikesh. I know Luo well, and he is more strategic than purely malevolent."

"Not exactly a rousing vote of confidence."

Grae chuckled. "We offer him power, gold, and prestige, and he will align with us," Grae said. "Besides, he always liked me better than my father."

"Maybe we should've sent you."

Grae shook his head and skimmed his lips back down my neck. "You are needed here," he murmured, his hot breath making my skin prickle with gooseflesh. His hand drifted lower from my hip to my thigh. "And I am needed wherever you are."

I let out a little delicious hum as his hands fisted in my night-dress and he began slowly, tortuously lifting up the hem. When his hand delved under the fabric, his calloused fingers trailed up my inner thigh again, moving higher and higher in taunting circles.

"My mind should be in a thousand other places right now," I panted, dropping my head back onto his shoulder.

"Those thoughts can only do so much," Grae whispered into my ear. "You cannot save everyone from worry alone. We are heading to Taigoska to take action, but if you are so exhausted and broken down with concern, you won't be able to help anyone."

"It feels selfish to take care of myself right now," I said, gasping as his finger trailed higher.

"Maybe it is," Grae said, parting my flesh and coating his fingers in my wet heat. "Maybe you need to be selfish enough to keep yourself whole. If you chip off a piece of yourself to every moment of suffering, without taking the time to put yourself back together again, there will be none of you left to help fix this broken world. And we *will* fix this, little fox," he said, swirling his finger around my throbbing clit and making me moan. His calming words coalesced with the pull of lust, making me melt farther into my body and away from my mind. "We will save Damrienn, just as we have saved Olmdere. We won't stop fighting until Aotreas knows peace for humans and Wolves alike."

"I—" The words fell out of my brain as Grae pushed two fingers inside me. My breath hitched as I relished the feeling of him massaging his rough fingers over my inner walls.

"If it helps, think of it as *me* being selfish. Let me take your worries away." Grae pressed the heel of his hand against my aching bud as his fingers moved in and out. "Let me be the calm in your storm. Please?"

I swallowed, barely able to nod as he kept working me,

building me higher and higher. I felt the outline of his erection against my backside, and I ground against him, eliciting a low rumble of pleasure from him. I turned to face Grae, his fingers still inside me. His lips captured my own, his tongue tasting me as his hand moved.

I pulled back and he released me as I commanded, "Take your clothes off."

He stepped away from me, a smug smile curling his lips, a satisfaction in his eyes that he had won this battle with my fraught doubts. He put his wet fingers into his mouth, smiling as he tasted me, before they moved down to his belt buckle as I sauntered over to the bed, unbuttoning my nightdress. It skimmed down my body and fell to my feet, leaving me bare. Grae's umber eyes heated as they roved my naked body.

"Do you remember how desperate you were for me to fuck you the last time we were in this town?" he asked as he hauled his tunic over his head. My eyes feasted on his broad chest and chiseled torso.

"I would've had you take me on those rainy ruins if it meant having you," I said, my eyes dropping to his cock as it sprang free from his trousers. I inched up on the bed and spread my legs, giving him a full view of my glistening core that I knew would snap any thoughts left in his brain. The snarl that escaped Grae's lips was pure wolfish desire.

He stepped out of his trousers pooled around his feet and prowled forward. Each inch he crawled up over me filled me with carnal delight, the anticipation making me writhe underneath him as he lowered his mouth to my peaked nipple and sucked.

A deep moan pulled from my lips as he swirled his tongue around one peak and then the other. My hands threaded into his hair, and I yanked, pulling his mouth up to my own. His tongue dipped into my mouth as he guided the head of his cock to my slick entrance.

Grae's thumb slid under my chin, and he tilted my face so he could stare deep into my eyes as he pushed into me. I'd never get over this. This feeling of free-falling into his endless gaze. Our bodies joining. Our souls colliding.

I saw it all in his hooded stare as he filled me to the hilt—my mate. Every inch of him claimed every inch of me. My fingernails scratched down his back and kneaded into his ass as he rolled his hips in and out. The friction sent lightning through my veins, white-hot desire sizzling out to my very fingertips.

Grae moved faster, dropping his head into my shoulder and testing the flesh of my neck with his teeth. He trailed his love bites up to my earlobe as he thrust into me. I hooked my ankles over the small of his back, angling myself to take him deeper. My chest heaved, everything feeling heavier and lighter in me all at once as I danced higher and higher to the edge of release. Relief and pleasure warred for pride of place in my mind, finally free of the burdens of the day and tumbling into bliss.

As my moans turned breathless, Grae's movements lost all control as he drove into me in a frantic rhythm.

"Yes." The words barely escaped my lips as I clawed up his back. "Make me come."

Grae's lips found my own again, a desperate groan on his tongue as it licked back into my mouth. The fingers of one hand rolled my nipple while the others clenched my hip, pinning me to the mattress as he pounded into me harder. My eyes rolled back, my sounds becoming more frenzied. He worked my body with such skill as if he could feel every ounce of my ecstasy he unspooled from me, drawing each pleasure out until I had no choice but to combust.

With one final thrust, I shattered. Grae absorbed my hoarse cries of pleasure with his mouth, battling my clenching core as he spilled over the edge of his climax and rode me through the last echoes of my release.

When our breathing had steadied, he rolled to his side and

gathered me into his chest, kissing me deeply. Sleep danced with pleasure as my sated body finally relaxed. I knew the feeling would be fleeting, knew I'd wake to new anxieties, new horrors. But just for a moment I indulged in the feeling of being safe and whole in my mate's arms.

SADIE

"FATHER." I CAREFULLY HELD UP MY HANDS IN PLACATION and wandered into the restaurant. The tables were all vacant apart from the corner booth. The squat, bald-headed bartender stood frozen behind the bar, his cheeks tinted scarlet, seemingly paralyzed by fear.

"Sadie." My father said my name like he'd caught me sneaking sweets at a full moon service. He tipped his chin toward the booth, a silent command to sit.

My father scrubbed his fingers down his weathered face that had always bent toward a frown. His broad, stocky build was crammed into the center of the bench by the two Wolves who sat on either side of him—his brothers, Aubron and Pilus—all three of them close friends to King Nero.

"Lord Rauxtide," Maez said awkwardly beside me as the two of us walked tentatively forward. "Pilus." She nodded to the lanky older man. "Aubron, looking handsome as ever," she added with a wink.

Aubron had a long black beard that was braided to a point and a completely bald head. A wide scar snaked down his eye socket from where King Nero had cut it out. I remembered that day like it was yesterday. I saw it behind my eyelids still. I was seven years old, and Aubron had been pulled up onto the dais by the King's guard and accused of spying. Accused by *who* we never knew. Accused of *what* we never knew, either. Now, I understood that King Nero didn't need to have a true reason to show his dominance. No one would ever question him . . . except Calla. Calla was the very first Wolf to dare to go against Nero. But then, we thought, *This must be justice. He must deserve this.*

Now I had my doubts.

Maez dropped onto the bench across from my father and uncles and I slid in beside her. Navin stared straight ahead as if he were afraid to even shift his gaze lest he be stabbed by my father's blade. I wondered if he was reliving the last attack when Ora was kidnapped. He seemed still enough to know that a knife to his throat from this trio was no idle threat.

"So," Maez asked, propping her elbows on the table as if we were all just catching up for a pack dinner. "What brings you to Valta?"

I went to elbow Maez and she pulled away from me. She always did this, always dug our graves a little deeper when we were already in precarious situations. What I really wanted to know was why they took Ora in the first place and if now they intended to take Navin, too.

"What do you think I'm doing in Valta?" my father rasped in his scratchy, lethal voice. "I've come to fetch my wayward daughter and get her out of our current predicament."

"Predicament?" I balked, hating the flash of relief that he wasn't here for Navin.

My father's dark eyes found mine, a curl on his scarred lip. "You are a skin chaser and a traitor, Sadie. You and your brother have brought so much shame to our family's name," he said. I tried not to flinch, clenching my fists so tight below the table that my nails were drawing blood. "We were nearly cut out of the pack entirely."

My eyes flared at that. I hadn't expected King Nero to retaliate against my family for Hector's and my betrayal. My father and uncles were some of Nero's closest advisers . . . but then I looked at Aubron's scar again and realized I shouldn't have been surprised.

"Father," I said tightly, stealing a glance at Navin who still held perfectly still. He didn't look frightened so much as frozen, like he was in such a deep state of meditation that he was no longer aware of where he was. "Will you put your knife down at least? The human knows better than to run from a pack of Wolves."

I'd hoped insinuating that my father and I were still part of the same pack might win me some favors, and judging by my father's arched curious brow at the words "the human," I'd say I was succeeding. Navin finally reacted then, cutting a glance across the room to the barman. It was such a subtle move, barely a nod. Still, it was jarring to see the completely vacant look in his eyes. I wondered if he was trying to tell his fellow human to run. I wondered, too, if he was using the same sort of magic that Ora used to evade spilling secrets.

That he seemed to use back in that snowy mountain village.

Should I even be defending him? Who was I even protecting?

I resisted the urge to snarl like a Wolf guarding its kill. Deceptions or no, Navin was *mine* to deal with as I willed. And for all my distrust, I didn't want him to die at my father's hands.

"So you mean to bring us back?" I asked my father, my shoulders easing as he lowered his knife from Navin's throat.

"Just you," Pilus said, spitting on the table. "Maez can rot in the Valtan sun with your Wolf-loving boyfriend for all we care. If she steps one foot in Damrienn she'll be skinned alive, her furs worn as a nice winter stole."

"You paint such a lovely picture, Pilly," Maez said, her hand drifting to her weapons belt. "But I think I'll opt for rotting in the Valtan sun." Maez shrugged. "You know I've always liked this tune."

It was only then I realized that the barman had taken out a

lastar and started plucking its strings. He looked petrified and yet he still strummed. Was that what Navin was instructing him to do? Play a song?

What the actual fuck?

"I can't go back to Damrienn," I said tightly.

My father's smile widened. "That's good, because you *won't* be going back to Damrienn."

My brows knitted in confusion. "Then where?"

"Rikesh."

"Rikesh?"

"Congratulations, Sadie," my father said, slapping the table. "I've arranged for your hand in marriage to Prince Tadei of Rikesh."

Bile rose up my throat as all the blood drained from my face. *"What?"*

Two patrons tried to walk into the restaurant and the barman shouted, "We're closed." The humans quickly scattered out the door. And still the barman kept playing his tune, the tempo increasing now to the pace of a jig.

My father leaned into the table, smiling wickedly at me. "You will be Luo's little brother's bride. You'll be a princess. More, you'll be an ally to Damrienn."

So this was their bargaining chip to bring Luo to their side of the war? A Silver Wolf princess?

Me?

My face flushed further and I couldn't blame the heat. "No."

"No isn't an option for you anymore, little one," Aubron said.

"What would your betrothed think?" Pilus taunted. "You'd deny a prince?"

"Tadei has been shirked by plenty of bitches already," Maez said with a chuckle. "I'm sure he'd understand one more. I swear he must have a haunted fella to have so many brides reject him."

My uncles snarled in unison at her. I had no idea why so many marriages to the Onyx King and his little brother fell through, when, like me, none of those brides really had a choice. But they had, and I wasn't about to test seeing if I could become another one. Gods forbid he actually try to hold on to me. Maybe one more rejection would make him finally snap.

"You *will* marry him and bring the Onyx Wolves back into play for the coming war," my father insisted, confirming my suspicions. They knew a war was brewing, too. But that also meant the Onyx Wolves weren't already on their side.

"Oh, so I'm a trade for his armies?" I asked, noting how Navin stiffened from my periphery.

"Something like that," Pilus said.

"And here I thought you'd come because you cared for me."

"We care for you inasmuch as it keeps you—and our family—alive," Pilus said.

I was about to respond when Maez interjected, "Funny how Tadei gets older and older, but the age of his brides stays the same. How old is the prince now? Surely into his fifth decade at least, hmm?"

"Silence," Aubron spat. He pointed a gnarled finger at Maez. "We are taking Sadie to Rikesh and delivering her to her prince whether you like it or not."

"And then we're returning with an army that will destroy your little Gold Wolf friends," Pilus added.

"You are putting *a lot* of value in Sadie's honeypot, I must say," Maez said. I gaped at her. "What?" She turned back to my uncles. "They know how sex works. I'm sure they've even had it a time or two." More growls from my uncles. "The real thing I want to know from you"—she pointed her finger back in Aubron's face in mirror to his action, ignoring their bristling at her insult—"is how did you know we were here?"

Aubron's snarl turned into a smile as he leaned into the table. "We aren't the only ones seeking your bounty."

My vision sharpened, my Wolf desperate to break free as panic coursed through me. "Bounty?"

"King Luo has put quite a lot of gritas on anyone who finds his brother's bride and brings her safely home," Pilus said.

"What?" The word barely came out as a rasp.

"He's not the only one who put a bounty out." Aubron laughed maniacally and slapped Maez's hand away. "Nero has announced the marriage of his new heir, Evres, to a certain Crimson Princess."

That . . . was a mistake. Threaten me, and Maez would come to my defense. Threaten Briar . . .

Fast as a snow snake, Maez's dagger embedded into the wood of the table. My uncles pulled their knives and held them out at her in response. "She already has a mate," Maez seethed. "No one can break that Wolf law."

"You're no longer a Wolf," Pilus purred. "You're a traitor. We don't recognize shit from you."

"Briar will make an excellent match to Evres," my father said with a dark chuckle. "A Damrienn Queen just like she was raised to be."

Maez yanked her blade from the wood and was about to lunge when a loud crash sounded from behind the bar. A glass seemed to fall from the bar of its own volition and shattered across the tiled floor. As all the heads turned to the sound, Maez rose suddenly, flipping the table into my uncles. Navin darted from the booth just in time to avoid the wood smacking into him. Before my father and uncles could rise, Maez nailed my father's foot to the bench with another knife. He let out a baying howl, shifting instantly into a snarling Silver Wolf.

"Run!"

SADIE

WE BOLTED DOWN THE HALLWAY, DARTING THROUGH THE SPARSE crowd in the dark, cavernous space.

"This way!" Navin shouted, twisting to his right and running down a smaller corridor.

We followed him easily, practically nipping at his heels to get him to run faster. If the sound of stomping boots was to be believed, my uncles stayed in their human forms even as my father howled behind us. We zigzagged through the labyrinth of tunnels, each one getting darker and smaller. Our panting breaths echoed off the sandstone along with the heavy stomp of our boots. The ceiling sloped down, lower and lower, until we had to crouch.

My father and uncles kept right on our tails.

"Grab the rope!" Navin called, and I lifted my head from my crouch to see the open tunnel ended in nothing but air, a lean rope hanging down in front of it.

"Shit," Maez growled as Navin leapt, grabbing the rope and hooking it around his hands and feet.

He quickly rappelled downward and Maez jumped, grabbing the rope above him. My stomach lurched, but the feeling of my uncle's hand reaching for the back of my neck made my skin prickle. I couldn't go with my father and uncles. I couldn't turn and face the life they had planned for me. And so I leapt.

The rope burned into my palms as I grabbed it. My legs flailed in the open air before I could finally loop them around. Far, far below was the sand-covered ground. A fissure in the rock ahead peeked into the sunshine and I could spy Galen den' Mora still sat under the shade.

Could we make it to the wagon before the Wolves followed?

I slid down the rope, grimacing as my palms burned against the scratchy rope. I watched as Navin and then Maez hit the sand. Maez immediately pulled out her sword and shouted, "Let go, Sadie!" I hesitated for a split second, and she barked, "Jump, damn it!"

I let go, free-falling as she sliced the counterweight rope where it was tied down. As I fell, the rope that had once been in my hands slipped free, shooting upward. I collapsed onto the sand in a heap and quickly rolled back up to stare at the cavern from where we emerged.

We'd descended even farther than I had imagined, the adrenaline making the drop quick. I stared up at my father's human face as he scowled at the loose rope. There'd be no following us down this way. But they could double back and still get us.

"Go!" I shouted, dusting myself off as I stood and started running toward the crevice in the rock.

"Sadie!" my father bellowed, making my muscles tense with traitorous fear. "I will find you! You *will* redeem us!"

We reached the fissure in the rock and raced out into the beating sunshine. I fled, running for my freedom as the scorching sun zapped my energy. My father's and uncles' shouts chased after me every burning step, long after I could actually hear them. The stretch of sand was farther from the wagon here, and my stomach soured as my running quickly turned to fast walking. I thought I might collapse if I didn't get cool. How quickly the sun exhausted us here.

Bile rose up my throat and I vomited nothing but stomach acid onto the sand. I was vaguely aware of hands urging me forward as my leathers cooked me.

When I hit the shade of the back steps, I nearly collapsed onto them.

"Breathe. Breathe," Navin said through his own panting breaths.

"We have to go! Now!" I shouted, trying to frantically stand and my legs giving out from under me. A strange panic gripped me. I felt hot and cold all at once, my vision spotting with black.

Navin caught me easily and lowered me back to the steps. "You need to get inside," he said. "Take these bloody leathers off and cool down before you make yourself sick."

"My father—"

"Your father will be trapped in those tunnels for a very long time," Navin assured me. "The barman will see to it they don't follow us. Sadie?"

I felt a tap at my cheek. I blinked with unseeing eyes, barely able to hear over the ringing in my ears. Is this what heat sickness felt like? Could it come on so quick? Or was this purely from panic?

Navin ordered something to Maez that I couldn't quite comprehend. "On it," she said, darting to the front of the wagon.

"Sadie, take a deep breath for me."

"I . . ." My torso swayed and my head lolled back.

Navin let out a growl that sounded impressively lupine as he caught me, hoisting me up with his long, lithe arms. He carried me into the belly of Galen den' Mora and dropped me onto the couch. His hands swiftly worked over me, first yanking off my boots and chucking them toward the door.

"Esh! Wool socks?" he asked incredulously as he peeled them off my feet and tossed them aside. "Are you trying to kill yourself?"

The cool air swirled around my feet. I placed a hand to my clammy forehead and realized my whole body was shaking, my heart still pounding like I was running full tilt. Navin's hands lifted to my trousers and unbuckled my belt.

"Wh—" I tried to sit up, but a wave of dizziness and nausea

came over me. I was able to snatch a clay vase from the shelf just before my empty stomach rebelled again and I began hurling into the pot.

I barely noticed as Navin yanked my linen trousers off and discarded them. "Seriously?" he snapped, and I was certain he was staring at my skintight fighting leathers underneath and belts of weapons banded around my thighs.

The wagon rocked and swayed, the wheels turning and rattling over the sand dunes. We were moving again? Everything felt distant, like a strange dream. Was Maez driving the oxen?

Navin unlaced my shirt, revealing the leather vest underneath, and he groaned his frustration again. His hands hovered above my chest, about to unbuckle the vest and lay me bare to him when Maez stumbled back through the kitchen. "I've got it from here," she said, climbing down the steps and shoving Navin out of the way. A wet washcloth landed on my forehead. "You go make those oxen move faster."

Navin lingered over me for a second. He was blurry and out of focus, but I could see the concern and hesitation in his eyes.

"Go, Navin," Maez snapped, pointing at the curtain. "She needs to shift. So if you don't want to get *eaten*, go sit out front with the oxen."

"*Shift*." He echoed the word as if he'd forgotten what I was. Maybe he wanted me to be human so badly that he'd forced my Wolf nature from his mind.

In truth, in my panic, I'd forgotten the power of shifting, too. Navin gave me one last quick glance and hustled back toward the front of the wagon, yanking the velvet curtain closed behind him as he went.

Maez snapped her fingers in front of my face. "Okay, Sads, let's go. Wolf time."

"I can't shift in a fucking wagon," I snarled, my Wolf already pulling to the surface, desperate to heal me.

"I won't let you break anything . . . or *eat* anyone if that's what you're so worried about," Maez said as she unbuckled my vest so I wouldn't shred it with the change. "This is just a quick shift, just like we've trained for. Heal and then return."

I took another breath, my pulse still far too fast, my ears still ringing. I nodded and screwed my eyes shut. My Wolf was all too eager to emerge, the survival instinct kicking in. I felt the heightening pain as my muscles twisted, my bones crunched, and then with a pop, there was nothing but sweet relief.

I stood on all four paws, my silver tail swishing. I still panted from the heat, but my heart had slowed and my breathing was steadier. My sight and hearing were perfect once more. I heard every whine of the wagon wheel, every snorting breath of the oxen, every hummed note of Navin at the front of the wagon. I smelled the sunshine baking off the sand and the sweat-slicked socks now discarded around my paws. I stretched, padding back and forth along the couch, shaking the vestiges of clothing off.

"Feels better, doesn't it?" Maez said with a smirk, folding her arms across her chest.

I snapped at her, not liking this human form so close in my space. I heard the whoosh of her blood in her veins, smelled her earthen musk and minty soap she used to bathe across her skin, my eyes honed to all her vulnerable flesh. I was trained to never view humans as prey . . . but with one so close, it was hard to control the hunting instinct. My mind was still foggy, my judgment not as clear as it normally would be. It felt like teetering on a dream. I prowled a step closer and sniffed Maez's skin.

"Don't you bite at me, bitch," Maez growled, asserting more Wolf into her voice. Only then did my judgment snap back into place. I recognized that she wasn't in fact human and pulled back. "Good. Now shift back before you piss on the couch."

I bared my teeth at her again. I was about to will the change when the curtain pulled back with Navin saying, "Did y—" He froze, staring at me. Time stood still. This wasn't the quiet meditative stillness of before. Now, the way he looked at me was so charged I could feel it buzzing through the air. I could *smell* his fear wafting off him like a too strong perfume.

"Navin, get the fuck out of here," Maez said, leaping toward the curtain.

But he didn't. Instead, Navin's eyes hooked with mine. I saw it all there: the concoction of shock and fear. My lip curled in a low growl.

"Sadie," Maez warned, stepping in between me and the human.

Navin stumbled back, pulling the curtain again.

In a blink, I shifted and crumpled onto the couch, wincing at the sharp pain of the sudden change. And not just the physical one. It felt like a tearing that Navin would no longer be able to deny what I was. Not with the truth of it staring him in the face. My body was healed but my soul was a jumbled knot of warring emotions. He'd seen me. Seen me in my rawest, truest form. Seen the *beast* that I am.

And he'd been paralyzed with fear.

SADIE

I'D NEVER BEEN MORE GRATEFUL FOR A SUNSET. AS THE SUN dipped from the sky, a surprising chill filled the desert as temperatures plummeted. We rode southward throughout the rest of the evening toward the bridge that led up to the lowest of the floating islands. We rounded behind a jagged rock formation, hiding the wagon from the main road. Even when Navin parked next to a mound of craggy desert rocks and came inside, he didn't look at me.

"We're breaking for an hour," he said, "then we're on the road again. We need to get most of the way before sunrise if we don't want a repeat of this morning." He grabbed his lute off the shelf and returned to his bunk. A moment later we heard the deep woody notes of Navin's music.

Maez and I exchanged glances as shame filled me. *A repeat of this morning . . .* and he didn't mean my father's surprise attack. I still didn't understand how they knew where to find me. And now, I had no clue which way to turn. My father was somewhere behind us, my *betrothed* was ahead, and everywhere around us was unforgiving, uninhabitable desert. I couldn't exactly show my face in Rikesh with a bounty out for me, could I? But turning back might put us directly in my father's path again.

Turning west would take us to Damrienn, which we definitely couldn't do . . . And what of our mission for the Golden Court? Was there any hope we could still pull the Onyx Wolves into the fray? Or at least convince them not to raise arms against us?

"You look like your brain is about to catch fire," Maez muttered, and my feet abruptly stopped.

I hadn't realized I'd been pacing back and forth. A silent conversation passed between my friend and me. She knew me so well I swore she could hear the questions racing in my head.

The space was suddenly too confining, making my skin itch. Flicking my knife back and forth wouldn't be enough to settle me. I couldn't just sit there and stew about my father and my arranged marriage and every which way I was entirely fucked. Nor could I just listen to Navin playing his music, ignoring me, clearly spooked by seeing me in my Wolf form.

"I'm going for a walk," I announced to no one in particular. I headed to the piles of shoes and yanked on my boots. When I'd shifted back into my human form, I'd put on light linen trousers and a matching sleeveless tunic. The pale cream outfit was the complete antithesis of how I preferred to dress, normally opting for thick black leather, but after feeling the panic of my body shutting down, I wasn't going to risk it. Luckily, I fit into the clothes left behind by Mina and Malou, and the Rikeshi twins had always worn light billowy fabrics even in the depths of Taigos. Galen den' Mora had stashes of random clothing hidden all around the place and I was grateful for the chaotic caching of supplies.

Maez muttered something, reaching for her boots.

I help up a hand to her. "I can go on my own. I don't need an escort."

"Your father and uncles could be right behind us."

"My father would rather die than be parted from the dagger Nero gifted him for his fiftieth," I countered, "which means they won't be abandoning their weapons and shifting to chase after us. And these oxen are the only magical creature that can traverse the scorching heat without rest that *I* know of. So unless there's a magical flying pony that you're not telling me about, my father and uncles are far behind us."

My logic didn't seem to persuade Maez. "I still don't really think wandering off in a foreign landscape is such a good idea."

I threw my hands up, exasperated. "I'll be fine."

"Sweet Moon, would you stop being so stubborn?" Maez snapped. "You practically combusted today! Besides, I'm going to contact Briar. She needs to know about this run-in with your father." Maez's nostrils flared, her throat bobbing as she added, "And to tell her about the Evres situation."

"You're going to tell her?"

"I don't keep *anything* from my mate." Maez's dark eyes narrowed at me. "Just don't go far from the wagon. I don't want to have to rescue your tail again."

I released an angry breath. "I hadn't had breakfast and I wasn't prepared for the heat and I hadn't dressed for a chase through the tunnels of town, okay?" I wrapped my thin cream scarf around my nose and mouth, protecting me from the sand that was getting kicked up in the wind. "And yes, maybe I was also a little rattled about the fact that my father had brokered a marriage for me to Prince fucking Tadei!" The music faltered for a second, played off as a trilling note, but I heard the musical stumble and knew Navin was listening to me.

"Which doesn't mean you should do something foolhardy now."

"I can't—I can't stay in here! I was almost trapped into a marriage. I won't be trapped—"

"You know we'd never let him take you," Maez said quietly, shaking her head. "Calla would wage another war just to get you back. You are a member of the Golden Court. You are no one's to marry off to. The Silver Wolves are not your pack anymore. We are our own pack. Our own *family*. A better one."

I felt the belonging in those words, the family we'd fought so hard to become and the promise of murderous wrath if anyone should lay their hands on me. But I didn't want any war started on my behalf. I couldn't be the reason more people died. It was why I would never want to be a queen. I never wanted to shoulder the responsibility of sending others into battle even if I'd gladly go to battle for my own Queen.

"We're in the middle of the desert," I said, ignoring Maez's words. "There's no one around for miles. And the sun isn't blistering in the sky. I'll be fine."

I lingered on the steps for a second, waiting for Maez to stop me, but she just clicked her tongue and wandered back to the kitchen, probably in search of something not burnt or rock-hard to eat.

I listened to the sound of Navin's music resuming as I walked across the dark sand and up into the jagged hills.

The moon was so bright in these parts that it cast the whole landscape in her eerie silver glow. The constellations, too, were brighter and more numerous than I'd ever seen before, the sky milky with brilliant white patches.

I climbed to the top of the rock formation and sat, staring out at the vastness of the nighttime sky and the desert stretching out before us. A scorpion scuttled from one rock to the next, the only sign of life in this place. I wrapped my scarf around me, turning away from the sudden gritty gust of wind. It appeared out of nowhere and then everything was calm and still again. My skin prickled against the chill, surprised by how cool the desert nights were.

I spotted Maez's silhouette on the horizon as she ran out into the stretch of desert to shift and contact Briar. It would be an awful message to relay. I hoped at least Calla was getting somewhere with the Ice Wolves.

I heard the lute finish its final notes and then moments later footsteps approaching. Even without the telltale silence, I knew it was Navin who was hiking up the hill after me. He had long, confident strides, the loose rubble crunching under his feet.

"Here." I felt the warmth of a cloak wrap around my back

and realized it was my own. I didn't know if I liked the idea that he'd climbed up here to bring it to me, but despite myself I pulled it around me. "The nights can get chilly down here."

I frowned as he perched on the rock beside me and stared up at the moon. "First you reprimand me for dressing too warmly and now for not enough."

"Do you think me bringing you your cloak is a reprimand?" he asked to the stars. "These parts can be treacherous, the temperatures extreme. You couldn't have known."

"But you were angry with me," I said, hating the way my voice went up an octave.

"I wasn't angry," he said carefully. "I was terrified."

Part of me broke at that. "I knew you'd be terrified of me."

"What?"

"When you saw my Wolf, I knew, I—"

Navin's hand reached over and turned my chin to face him. I pulled out of his touch, not wanting to see his disgust, but when I met his eyes, they were wide and honest. "I wasn't terrified of you." His brow furrowed and he shook his head. "I was terrified *for* you. First, I thought those men might take you. Then I thought I was going to watch you die from heat sickness right before my eyes."

"But . . ." I stood, needing to put some distance between us. I backed up, leaning against the peak of sandstone behind me. "When you saw my Wolf . . . you were afraid."

"Afraid? No." His cheek dimpled, the flicker of a smile. "I was awed by you," he said, rising to a stand. "You were— *are*—the most magnificent creature I'd ever seen, and I couldn't bear it, Sadie."

"Bear what?"

He took another step toward me. "To think of all the things you deserve and all the ways I failed you."

I opened my mouth but had no idea what to say to that. What else was there to say? Navin took another careful step until he was standing toe-to-toe with me. I wanted to tell him that he hadn't failed me, but I was still too hurt by his actions during the battle with Sawyn to say it honestly. And I had the strong sense he would spot the lie a mile away.

"This was never a good idea anyway," I murmured, keeping my gaze fixed to our touching boots.

"It wasn't?" Navin cocked his head. "Why not?"

I snorted and met his storming gaze. "You *know* why."

"I'll admit I have some very good reasons why this would be a bad idea, reasons that have nothing to do with you being a Wolf. But I'm curious to know yours." It took everything in me not to push him on what his "good reasons" were. He arched his brow. "Is your only reason because I'm human?"

And the massive secret you won't tell me and caused you to betray me. But I was done with that for now. I pushed off the rock, craning my neck up to hold his stare, my chest meeting his abdomen. "Because I am too strong for you."

"Aren't you the one who nearly died of heat sickness this morning?"

"That was one time," I gritted out. "And once I shifted, I was fine. Can you do that? Heal yourself?"

"No."

"No. But it's more. I'm talking about in a fight. I'm talking about combat. I'm talking about my ability to withstand a lot more than your human body can."

His smile widened, flashing his white teeth. The mask he usually wore began slipping, revealing a different person underneath.

"You think I'm a delicate soul, don't you?" He tucked a stray strand of hair behind my ear and the sensation made my skin tingle. "You think I couldn't handle you?" His head lowered infinitesimally, his eyes flicking down to my lips and back up. "You think I couldn't give you what you want?"

My lips parted, breathless, shocked at his question. He traced my bottom lip with his thumb and hummed. I swallowed the burning knot in my throat and stepped out of his touch.

"That's exactly what I think," I panted. "You don't know what it means to be with me."

"I could learn," he taunted as he stepped into me again.

"I could kill you with both hands tied behind my back," I said tightly. "What could you do to stop me? Play me a song?"

His eyes were alight with mischief as his hands rested on the stone on either side of me. "Songs are more powerful than you think, Wolf," he said. "But let's test out your theory, shall we?"

He reached for me so slowly I wasn't sure where his hand was going. Finally, it dipped to the pocket of my cloak and pulled out a thick cord of rope. The rope I had bought in the markets—my terrible cover. I had forgotten it was still there.

"What are you doing?"

"Hold out your hands," he said.

I swallowed, intrigued. He looped the rope around one of my wrists and then spun me to grab the other. He tied my hands together and tugged on the rope until it bit into my skin, then he spun me back around to face him. I glanced up at his parted lips as he stared down at me.

"Go on," he said. "Kill me with your hands tied behind your back."

He waited there, leaning into me. Far too smug that this thin piece of rope had somehow paralyzed me. But I liked this game, whatever this was. I liked that he had this little modicum of control over me. I liked the idea that we could somehow even the playing field between us.

"I don't want to kill you," I whispered.

"Then what do you want to do with me?" he murmured. "Better yet, what is it you want me to do with you?"

The question made me lick my lips. I knew I should be afraid of this man beneath the mask, or at least wary of him, but he captivated me, too. And maybe I just needed something good, something purely physical to sate the thrill of this new person.

Fuck it.

I stretched up on my toes and kissed him. Navin didn't let

me lower back down, his arms banded around me and pulled me against his chest, his lips meeting mine in a slow, tantalizing kiss. His tongue traced my bottom lip, and he pulled it between his lips, testing it with his teeth before releasing it to plunder my mouth. Each lick of his tongue sent lightning straight to my core. I moaned and his hands dropped lower to my ass, pulling my hips against his thigh.

One of the oxen lowed, a deep whining sound that echoed up through the hills. A sound like a gasp echoed up after it. We broke our kiss and I twisted to see a Wolf shadow bolting across the desert. Maez shifted in a single bound and leapt onto the driver's bench of Galen den' Mora. Her voice echoed up to us. "What the fuck is that thing?"

Navin and I turned in the direction she was pointing. A black shadow skittered low over the horizon. It looked bigger than a horse with black spindly legs and a barbed double scorpion tail.

"Get back to the wagon!" Navin shouted, grabbing my arm to tug me downhill.

"Wait," I said, grunting and yanking my wrists apart, snapping the rope, which fell to the ground. "Better."

Navin's mouth fell open as he stared at my act of strength, realization dawning on him that I was just playing along before.

"Save the gaping for later," I shouted, pulling him after me down the rubble of stones. "Let's get the fuck out of here."

CALLA

WHEN WE ARRIVED AT THE OUTSKIRTS OF TAIGOSKA, A CONVOY of royal sleighs was waiting to take us to the palace. We swept silently through the Wolf part of town. The frozen streets were pristine, and the silver townhouses were devoid of any color, so different from the vibrant human quarter that I'd gotten to know so well months ago. The memory of those humans we met on the road still consumed my every waking thought.

Grae's warm hand covered my jiggling knee, and I frowned down at where we joined. I hadn't realized I'd been bouncing it.

"Maybe I should speak with Queen Ingrid first," Briar offered.

I glanced between her, Hector, and Mina who sat on the bench across from us. Mina nervously thrummed her fingers against the silver armrest. Hector pressed his knee into hers in silent comfort. I knew Mina was eager to get Ora back, but I also knew the sight of those humans had spooked her as much as it did me. Whatever it was she was thinking about it, she didn't let on, though.

"I should be the one negotiating with Ingrid," I said to my twin. Briar pursed her lips at me, her slender brow arching. "You disagree?"

"I think if I wanted to know the best battle tactics or rescue plans, I'd ask you first," she quibbled. The criticism was clear, if unsaid.

"This *is* a rescue plan."

She shook her head. "This is kissing royal Wolf ass to *help* you with your rescue plan." She brushed a strand of her red hair behind her ear. "I've been training for this my whole life. You learned to convince others with force and me with flattery."

She had a point there. While I was off training and sparring, Briar had been practicing her curtsies and how to endear people to her. She was beautiful, poised, strategic, and lethal when she needed to be—similar in demeanor to Ingrid herself in many ways.

"We'll work together on Ingrid," I conceded, knowing it would be foolish not to play to my sister's strengths. I glanced at Hector who sat with his arms folded over his broad chest and his shoulders bunched around his ears. He looked one second away from stabbing someone—clearly a familial trait. "Remember you are all here representing the Golden Court," I reminded him. His shoulders dropped ever so slightly as he scowled out the window.

"What if Ingrid says no? What then?" he asked. "How long until Nero's Silent Blades are filling the streets much like Sawyn's Rooks once did? She's always been neutral to these things even with a sorceress at her border. So forgive me if I doubt she'll side with you now."

"She won't say no," I insisted, trying—and failing—to keep my voice even. "She can't. Letting Nero grow stronger will hurt her, too—she must know that. If Nero is forcing—*destroying*—Damrienn to follow the old Wolf laws, then Ingrid's very throne is in jeopardy. Nero believes there should only be Wolf *Kings*; if he didn't, he couldn't dispute my claim to my throne, either." Grae's grip on my knee tightened. "We need to remind Ingrid that the future of her crown lies with which side she chooses."

The sleighs rode in through the silver gates, swirling in the shape of sharp rambling thorns. We passed down a road of detailed ice sculptures illuminated by hundreds of miniature glowing lanterns.

I blew out a long breath. "Certainly different than the last time we were here."

Mina nodded in agreement, her wide eyes taking in the winter gardens from the frozen fountains to the evergreen topiaries to the snowbirds that fed on winter berries.

I craned my neck up, watching the tall spires and jagged, frozen rooftops of the palace. It was incredible. The bottom half was made of white stone and the top constructed of what seemed to be pure ice. Warm firelight glowed through the carved-out windows, illuminating the crystals hanging in arches over the towering doorway.

We came to a stop directly in front of a retinue of guards and servants who all bowed simultaneously when our sleigh door opened. I couldn't help but notice that Queen Ingrid wasn't there to receive us. Was that normal royal protocol? Maybe I was just reading too much into it. I darted a look at Grae and he subtly shook his head. He didn't know either and seemed just as on edge. Everything felt on tenterhooks. I needed Ingrid's help and I needed it now.

I glanced at my twin as she glided out of the sleigh, ever the regal princess, and I was once again reminded how much better at this she was than me. Even though Briar didn't want to be a queen, she was so much more suited to it. I knew many people in our court and beyond wondered why I was the one to assume the throne and not Briar. I was my own person now, but still, those old wounds were hard to heal and it was hard to compare myself to my sister without feeling lacking.

Grae stepped into my line of sight and found my hand, giving it a squeeze.

"At least Briar's here," I whispered to him, feeling like a fraud once again.

Grae stepped in so close to me he could barely be heard even to my ears as he rumbled, "You *died* for your court, Calla. You are the most deserving ruler in all of Aotreas."

I swallowed the lump in my throat. I didn't know how he knew exactly what I was thinking, but he'd done it so many times now that I couldn't really be surprised. When those old nagging thoughts started to rise to the surface, Grae snapped me back into reality again. Sometimes all I needed was that little reminder. I wasn't Briar. I was my own sort of ruler. I knew who I was; now I just needed to figure out how to share that with the rest of the world.

We followed the guards in through the palace, the sweeping vaulted ceilings making the space echo against the hard ice and stone. It was incredible, otherworldly, all icicles and crystals. Diamonds dripped from giant chandeliers, crystal candelabras stood on white marble pedestals, a silver carpet glittered beneath our feet with not a single stain or footprint on the entire thing as it led deeper and deeper into the space.

Despite the perpetual cloud cover, the palace was incredibly bright, if not a little cold. This was a completely different perspective than the one I received the last time I was there with Galen den' Mora, when we were forced to change in a room that was worse than a farmyard barn.

We twisted up the glass staircases, the ground below our feet moving farther and farther out of view, and I squeezed my hands tighter behind my back to not grab on to Grae. We were climbing so high. Each clink of my shoes on the glass made me flinch. What if it cracked and we plummeted to that perfect silver carpet below?

Finally, we landed back on solid white stone, and we processed down another shimmering carpet to what I could only presume was the guest wing.

"Your Majesty," the first guard said, bowing at an archway painted with the moon phases. A maid held the door open to a fantastical-looking silver-and-white suite.

"Your Highness." Another guard showed Briar to the room across from ours and then Hector to the room to my left.

"And you can follow me," the guard said to Mina, his voice tinged with disdain.

I immediately intervened, stepping up to Mina's side with such ferocity that the guard took a step backward. Good. He should think twice before messing with a member of the Golden Court.

"All of my courtiers will stay on this floor with me," I insisted, staring daggers at the guard who at least had the good sense to look a little embarrassed.

The guard beside him cleared his throat and took a step forward. He had sky blue eyes, white-blond hair, and skin paler than milk that covered his sharp features. "There are no other available rooms on this floor," he said.

I cocked my head at him. He didn't seem to back down the same way the other guard did. He was clearly high-ranking within the pack. I assessed his uniform. He wore more badges and insignia than the other guards, his cape made of finer material, his boots bearing not a single scuff mark.

"What's your name?"

"Klaus," Grae answered for him, clearly already knowing the prick based on the venom in his voice.

Klaus flourished another bow. "I'm the Queen's second cousin."

"Of course you are," I muttered under my breath. I pointed at the last door across from Hector's room. "Who is staying in that room?"

Klaus cleared his throat. "No one currently, but—"

Mina tapped on my arm. "It's fine," she signed.

"It is absolutely not fine," I signed back.

Klaus just glanced between us, confused. Clearly he didn't know the language of signs.

"Mina will stay there," I said to him. "Bring her things."

I turned to the more sheepish of the two guards and asked, "Where is Queen Ingrid? We have urgent matters we'd like to discuss with her."

Klaus leaned in front of the other guard and answered for him. "The Queen wanted you to get settled in first." His smile was predatory, his canines glinting. "And I presume you'll want to get changed?"

I stared down at my outfit. I wore black leather trousers, shined black boots, and a golden tunic that hit me just above the knee. My fur-lined jacket was intricately embroidered and detailed in golden lace. My hair was braided up and a golden crown sat atop my head, my neck dripping in golden jewelry and my fingers covered in gemstones.

I arched a brow at Klaus. "What is that supposed to mean?"

His smile widened. "I can send up some dresses if you desire. Perhaps something more regal—"

Grae let out a feral growl and stormed up to Klaus until they were chest to chest. Despite them being the same height, Grae was twice as broad with muscle and clearly the dominant fighter from his skilled stance. Klaus had the audacity to wink at Grae anyway, daring him to make a move. In a flash Grae grabbed Klaus by the back of the neck and twisted him to face me.

"Say the Golden Court Queen isn't regal," he snarled, his voice promising the violence I knew he could deliver so well. He shook Klaus by the neck and Klaus winced. "Go on."

"Grae," I snapped, giving him my best cutting look. Despite his anger, Grae instantly released Klaus.

Grae's fingers twitched at the hilt of his sword as he said, "The Golden Court Queen wears what the Queen wishes."

Briar breezed over and intervened as Klaus rubbed the back of his neck.

"Apologies, Klaus," she said in her flirty, high-pitched voice as she sauntered over to him and placed a concerned hand on his shoulder. Klaus blinked at her once and then, as if under her spell, he melted under her touch. His scowl morphed into an intrigued smile. "You know how we Wolves can be when cooped up in a sleigh for too long." She laughed as if she'd just told a joke and he smiled along with her. "I'm sure after a good run, we'll all be feeling much more settled. Thank you so much for all of your help."

Klaus flashed her a puppy dog smile, all his bite disappearing. "My pleasure, Your Highness." He lifted her hand and kissed the back of it as Briar demurred; then he gave us one more much less threatening glance before swaggering off with the rest of the guards and maids in tow.

Once we heard their footsteps clinking far enough into the distance down the glass steps, we all let out a collective sigh.

"You are too good at that," Hector said to Briar with a snort.

"You need to teach me your ways," Mina signed with a smile.

"He knows you have a mate," Grae started. "If Maez were here . . ."

Briar pinned him with a look. "If Maez were here, she would say to use every tactic to our advantage and trust me to handle myself when it comes to any hound that comes sniffing my way. Let me handle the puppies like Klaus." She turned back to her room and said over her shoulder, "You said we came here for allies. Starting a war against the Queen's second cousin will do us no favors in the actual war that Nero is bringing to our doorsteps."

Grae opened his mouth to protest but my hand landed on his forearm. "She's right," I said. "Let him misunderstand me for now." I hated the words even as I said them. Maybe there would be a time and place for me to be myself with these Wolves, but I wouldn't risk their allegiance for it. I didn't know if that made me a better or worse person; all I knew was there was too much at stake. "Tolerating him and his jabs right now is for the greater good. And they don't hurt me."

"But they do," he murmured so only I could hear. His eyes were full of concern, and I reached out to touch his face.

"Only so much, though, love."

"I should've slaughtered him for questioning you," Grae growled. "He's lucky I didn't reach down his throat and pull out his spine."

Hector snorted and said to Mina, "Mates."

She nodded in agreement as she turned to the last doorway and entered her room.

As each of the members of the Golden Court disappeared into their accommodations, I leaned in closer and murmured into Grae's ear. "You can defend my honor another time."

"I'll *take* your honor another time."

His smile broadened, the cavalier, wild side of him bleeding through.

"I'll take you up on that," I said, any memory of the insult melting away in his warmth.

SADIE

SAND RAINED DOWN ON US AS THE GIANT BEAST RUSHED FOR-
ward. I shielded my eyes with one hand, keeping them averted
as I shoved Navin toward the wagon. The air whipped around
me, and a long, thick leg speared into the sand in front of me.
Skidding to a halt, I narrowly avoided crashing into it. Undulat-
ing like fish scale armor, the creature's leg rattled as it moved.
I crawled backward on all fours as another leg appeared, then
another. I wanted to crane my neck up and look the beast in
the eyes, but its massive body was creating a whirlwind of sand.
Another rattling leg shot toward me. It seemed made of one plate
of hard black skin atop another, making an unsettling sound like
the tail of a rattlesnake.

"Sadie! Move!" Maez barked from the wagon.

I scuttled backward again right as a giant stinger slammed to
the ground between my legs. Holy fucking Gods. What was this
creature with quivering legs and a scorpion's tail? Another stinger
smashed into the sand beside the first. Two. *Two* fucking tails.

I rolled onto my belly and crawled toward the wagon, feeling
the air swirling and grit caking my skin.

"Almost there, almost there," Navin chanted as he stooped
from the driver's bench and offered out his hand. "Don't look
back."

I opened my mouth to speak but another leg landed right in front of my face, the force of the step throwing sand into my mouth. Scrambling to my feet, I darted around the leg and up onto the driver's bench. I wedged between Maez and Navin as he slapped Opus's rear and the wagon jolted to life. But oxen were not known for their speed, and every other breath, I stood up on the driver's bench to get a good look behind us at the monster that had almost impaled me with its stinger. I could barely make out the shape of its towering, spindly legs in the darkness, but those dozen glowing gray eyes shone like a beacon and moved over the horizon with preternatural speed.

"What *is* that thing?"

"A crishenem." Navin grabbed a handful of my tunic and yanked me back down. "And you staring at it is not helping. It tracks the moonlight reflecting from your eyes."

"Hey Nav," Maez said. "Next time we're traveling through the desert at night, it'd be nice if you gave us a fucking heads-up that there are giant scorpion monsters here!"

"I've never seen one so close to the trail before," he said too calmly for the near-death experience we'd just had . . . still *were* having if that beast decided to attack again.

Maez and I leaned back to look at each other from behind Navin. We clearly both had the same suspicion: Why would he have seen one in the first place? How did an Olmderian human— well traveled or no—have so much knowledge about Valtan monsters? There was no need for traveling musicians this far from the path. When would Galen den' Mora have ever parked in the middle of nowhere? Yet Navin seemed to navigate this detour from the path to Rikesh with far too much ease . . .

"That thing has like fifty fucking eyes, Maez," I groaned, shaking out my hands, my limbs feeling like a bunch of tiny beetles were crawling up and down them. "If it is still behind us in another minute, I'm going to Wolf out."

"No Wolfing out," Navin said tightly. "You'll only provoke it more."

"This is what my people do," I reminded him. "My ancestors rid the world of monsters . . . well, most of them. They must've battled this creature before, too."

Navin clicked his tongue, spurring the oxen on. "Not this one, they haven't."

"And *how* would you know that?"

"I just do," Navin said tightly, keeping his eyes focused on the road ahead. "Besides, it was entire Wolf packs, *hundreds* of Wolves, that took down the monsters of old. Not two."

"Bit of a history buff there, aren't you, Nav?" Maez asked.

Navin shushed her. "I'm trying to focus."

"You can focus on the road all you like; it won't make us go any faster."

I stood to peek at the monster again, and Navin yanked me back down before I could catch sight of it. "I told you: if we ignore it, it'll leave us alone," he said.

"How do you know that?"

"I just know. Trust me," he gritted out. Maez and I exchanged suspicious glances again. "Just stop looking at it."

"Okay, fine," I hissed. "I'm going back into the wagon."

Navin's grip on my tunic tightened. "So you can peek out the back window flaps?" he asked incredulously. "Nope, you're staying right here until we reach the aerial road."

I folded my arms tightly across my chest. "And how long until we reach the first aerial road?"

"Four hours, more or less."

"Gods," Maez groaned, dropping her head into her hands. "And will this beast be following us like the worst fucking puppy all the way?"

"Maybe," Navin said. "Or maybe it'll get bored."

"Bored?" Maez balked. I grimaced as she scrubbed a hand down her face.

Navin's hand reached over and dropped onto my thigh, giving it a squeeze in acknowledgment. "We'll hide out on the first island, Sankai-ed, for a few days. Restock our supplies. Make sure those

Silver Wolves aren't following us." He shot me a sidelong glance. "Then we are coming back down, cutting out to the shoreline, and getting on the first boat back to Olmdere."

"But King Luo," I protested. "Our mission."

"Our mission was fucked from the second we ran into your father," Maez said.

"Agreed," Navin echoed.

"No." It took all my strength to keep my voice quiet, but the last thing I needed was for that crishenem to charge us. "I will stay hidden in the wagon, but you still need to go, Maez. You were the one Calla wanted to broker this alliance anyway. We need the Onyx Wolves. Promise Luo whatever it takes. Gold. Land. My hand in marriage—" Navin and Maez started to protest at the same time but I carried on, "My hand in marriage *after* we win the war."

"Not happening." Navin's voice turned into a guttural rumble.

"You think Luo won't see through those false promises?" Maez added. "He thinks he can have you *now*, Sadie. Nero has promised you to him."

"But we have the gold," I said. "Nero doesn't."

Maez snorted. "The Onyx Wolves aren't exactly lacking in wealth."

"Then you will have to convince him that ours is the winning side, and should he wish to remain king after this war, then he will stand with us."

"You want me to *threaten* him?" Maez shook her head at the stars. "He'll just throw me off the mountainside. Things have changed since we ran into your family."

"They haven't changed," I seethed. "We can't return to Olmdere without this alliance. The Golden Court depends on Luo's armies. We could lose everything."

Maez didn't reply to me for a long beat before finally murmuring, "Let's just get to Sankai-ed and we'll come up with a new plan from there, okay?"

I knew her "new plan" was just to convince me she was right, but I relented. As long as we were moving in the same direction, I was okay to wait.

"What did Briar say about your news?"

Maez wrapped her cloak tighter around her. "I didn't get a chance to reach her." She fidgeted in her seat. "I'd only just shifted when I caught that beast's scent. I was still trying to reach her when I spotted it and ran."

"We can try again in Sankai-ed," I said softly. I knew it was little condolence. This was not a conversation Maez was looking forward to having.

"Delightful," she muttered.

Navin moved closer to me on the bench until his knee was pressing mine, but he didn't say another word.

We rode for another hour in silence with no disturbance from the crishenem. My skin still rippled in gooseflesh every time I thought of it lurking behind us, but true to Navin's word, there was no further incidence. Maybe it was just a curious beast— a giant, poison-tailed, spindle-legged, freaky kind of curious beast.

Before long, the weight of the day and the weight of my head finally caught up to me. I tried to keep my eyes fixed on the rolling horizon, but everything kept blurring as sleep tugged on me. I must have nodded off a few times before Navin reached over and pulled my head onto his shoulder. I glanced up and realized Maez was already slumped against the wagon wall, her mouth agape, and drool trailing down her cheek. I let out a soft chuckle and let Navin's shoulder take the weight of my suddenly too-heavy head. He wrapped his arm around me and I leaned into him more. I wasn't sure if I had faded into the land of the dreaming or not, but I swore I imagined Navin kissing me on the hair before I drifted off.

SADIE

MY HEAD BOUNCED OFF NAVIN'S SHOULDER, ROUSING ME FROM my deep sleep. The sight before us made me suck in a breath, my hands shooting out. His arm hugged me tighter to his side. All around me was sky, only the rickety wooden bridge in front of us leading up into the clouds proving that we weren't flying . . . or falling.

"It's all right," he said. "You're safe."

Thick braided rope was woven on either side of the bridge, making a spiderwebby barrier. But if one of Galen den' Mora's wheels—which were inches from the edge—tipped over one side, I doubted those ropes would do anything to save us.

As the sleep ebbed from my eyes, I leaned over the bench seat, looking straight down to the sand below . . . which I realized was only a couple feet below us still. I swallowed, suddenly feeling foolish for my panic when I could still practically step onto solid ground.

I shuffled away from Navin's tight grip. "Where's Maez?" I asked, noting the empty seat beside Navin as I stretched my stiff neck from side to side.

"Tea?" Maez asked; two hands offering out cups appeared through the curtain.

I looked down to the cup. It looked and smelled hair-raisingly strong. How could Maez even mess up a cup of tea?

Still, I took my mug with a muttered "Thanks," and Navin did the same.

He grimaced as he sipped from the mug, and I let out a chuckle. He leaned his shoulder into me as if I was giving away a secret.

"I guess that crushtem—"

"Crishenem," Navin corrected.

"Whatever. That scorpion creature disappeared in the night," Maez said, pulling the curtain across to sit in the window bench. She took a sip of her tea and tried to subtly spit it back into her mug, but Navin and I both noticed, which made trying not to laugh even harder.

"They're nocturnal creatures," Navin said. "Most of the creatures in Lower Valta are. The sun is too strong to wake and hunt during the day."

That was for damn sure. The sun had only just peeked above the horizon and already sweat was beginning to bead on my skin. I unclasped my cloak that Navin had wrapped around me the night before, and the memory of that kiss flooded back through me again. Curse the Moon, it was so much better than the first chaste kiss we'd shared so long ago. This one had felt so much more real and raw. Navin seemed more confident, powerful even, not the boyish musician but something else entirely. What more layers were secretly hiding there in those depths?

That thought once again brought me up short, because there *were* secrets in there, ones he swore he could never tell me.

It was frustrating how that closed part of him hurt me.

Maez craned her neck up to the sky. "How long until we reach Sankai-ed?"

I was thankful for the reminder of our destination as something to focus on. The first of the floating mountains sat low to the land and was the only mountain that wasn't covered in lush green, probably because it still got too much arid heat from the desert below. It floated so close to the land that I wondered if the castle of Damrienn would've fit underneath. I imagined the tops of its needle-like spires scratching the sandstone belly of the midnight rocks beneath the islands.

"An hour, I'd say," Navin said. "The bridges between the mountains are slow going to keep them flat enough for wagons to pass."

"But we just descended that harebrained road from Taigos?" Maez grumped.

"Not all wagons are built like Galen den' Mora," Navin countered.

"How long until we get to Rikesh?"

"If we were going to Rikesh," he said pointedly, clearly not forgetting our argument from the night before, "it would be another day, at least."

"Great," I said. Plenty more time to get sun sickness.

"I've been thinking," Maez hedged, sliding a look to me. "*If I was going to carry on to Rikesh, I think that maybe you should stay back in one of the lower mountains with Navin.*"

I whirled at her, surprised that she'd even considered continuing on to Rikesh but grateful nevertheless. I knew Maez was torn between her loyalty to me and her court. She and I had been best friends our entire lives, had been raised since pups together, went through military training together. But we both knew the right decision for Olmdere was that Maez do whatever she could to get Luo on our side.

Still, I wouldn't leave her to travel through Upper Valta alone. What if she was attacked? What if relations with the Onyx Wolves soured? What if she needed our help? "I promise I'll stay in the wagon in Rikesh, but I'm not staying behind."

"This wagon isn't the disguise it once was," Maez pushed again. "Your father knows you're riding with Galen den' Mora."

"The wagon is protected from any invasions," Navin said.

"Even if they can't attack the wagon," Maez countered,

"how long until they starve us out of it if they know we're inside?" Navin's frown deepened. "Exactly. Going straight to Rikesh would be like delivering Sadie directly into the hands of her would-be betrothed."

"Only if I get caught," I gritted out. "Which I won't."

"If stubbornness were a goddess, Sadie," Maez snorted, "I would worship you. But you know as well as I, you can never have complete control over your fate. And it doesn't help that there's an apparent bounty on your head. If anyone around here knew who you are, they'd be jumping all over each other to drag you to their prince."

"Which is why leaving me behind is a stupid idea," I countered. "At least together, I have you, a strong, capable warrior, to defend me."

"Your flattery is noted." She rolled her eyes. "As if you're not also a strong, capable warrior."

"So we're agreed then," I said with a smug smile. "We're all going to Rikesh."

"What do you think, Nav?" Maez asked, leaning her elbow out the window. "Should we make Sadie lie low in the wagon when we roll into Rikesh? Or leave her behind?"

"I think neither of us could stop her from doing what she wants," he said, and the compliment made me sit a little straighter. "And despite many people wishing to cash in on her bounty, Rikeshi people are not known to leave their mountain, which means none of them will know what they're looking for. Even if rumors that Sadie is here circulate, they're as likely to grab you, Maez, as they are to grab her. And I doubt Sadie's family would share that she's traveling with Galen den' Mora anyway."

"Why not?"

"Because not only does it sully their name for her to be riding with humans"—I let out a little snarl at that—"but they will want to get hold of her first and not let that bounty slip out of their hands."

I grinned mischievously back at Maez, loving how she

scowled at Navin's point. "See?" I chided. "As long as we act human enough, we will be fine."

"Speaking of," Navin said. "I recommend you wear Mina and Malou's clothes for the rest of the journey, too, Maez." He kept speaking, but I noticed the way his words hitched at the mention of Malou. Her death was still so recent, and I knew he still ached with her loss. I couldn't imagine losing someone that close to me, the closest kind of family like Maez or Hector. The thought alone made me inch closer to Navin. "While the lighter clothes you brought are suitable, they don't *look* Rikeshi. We're going to want to blend in if we have any hopes of maintaining anonymity."

"Those clothes barely fit me," Maez growled. "The trousers hit me mid-shin."

"Roll them so they sit above the knee," Navin said. "That is also a common style."

I could feel Maez's countenance darkening from behind me that she was being forced to wear the more sparkly, feminine clothing, and I chuckled. I couldn't wait to tell Briar.

"Esh," Navin muttered, and I lifted my head to see what he was staring at on the horizon . . . but I saw nothing.

"What is it?" I tried and failed to see anything of import.

"A sandstorm is coming," he said.

I squinted into the distance, seeing what looked like just a whirl of sand in the air. It looked harmless and far away. "Won't we be in Sankai-ed by then?"

"No. Shit." He shook the reins, spurring the oxen on, but they moved at an only slightly faster pace than before. "It's going to hit us head-on."

The dot on the horizon grew, morphing before my eyes into a giant wall that was rushing toward us. The sky darkened and the winds picked up.

"Get inside the wagon!" Navin shouted above the now-roaring wind. "Now!"

The weather shifted so suddenly, the calm sunny day changing into a full-on storm in a matter of seconds. Gritty sand whipped through the air, burning my skin, and I knew it would be nothing compared to the dark cloud rushing toward us. My two long braids flailed wildly behind me, my tunic flying up to my neck, filling like a sail. Navin practically shoved me through the window, Maez dragging me inside by my arms.

"Fucking Moon," she shouted to be heard above the roar of wind and scratch of sand against the wagon. Still, somehow the oxen kept moving, kept walking their steady, unbothered pace, somehow protected as we all scrambled for our lives.

"Esh," Navin barked again as he gripped the window ledge, unable to pull himself through with the force of the storm.

He hooked one elbow over the groaning wood, and I grabbed his other wrist. Propping my feet on either side of the wall, I leaned back with all my force, trying to hoist him through the window. I screamed as his legs flew out from behind him.

"Hang on!" I shouted as Maez grabbed his other arm, trying to anchor him.

The winds wailed and whipped, the force of their power not coming in a steady stream but violent stops and starts. One second I thought I'd lose my grip on Navin, the other second another elbow was hooked on the window. A sudden gale blasted into us again, sand pelting directly into my eyes. Maez and I screamed in unison, and I knew she'd been hit by it, too. Tears streamed down my face, my eyes clenched and burning.

"Hang on!" I shouted again, unseeing as the winds picked up even more speed, rocking the wagon onto two wheels.

The force suddenly shifted again, and with a mighty crack, the windowsill splintered and I was yanked out by the force of its power. Still clutching Navin's arm blindly, I screamed, my mouth instantly filling with sand. My stomach lurched as I was vaulted upward, and then I plummeted, my heart jumping into my throat as I kept falling and falling and falling . . .

CALLA

AFTER AN ENTIRE DAY SPENT TWIDDLING OUR THUMBS, FINALLY, *finally*, we were summoned to afternoon tea with Queen Ingrid.

We wandered through the cold, austere palace, twisting and twining our way until I was completely lost.

Grae seemed to know where he was going, though, even asking the maid, "Greenhouses today?"

"Yes, Your Majesty," she mumbled, keeping her head bowed.

"I can lead the way," he said. "You're dismissed."

The servant's whole body slumped like he'd just saved her life, and she murmured, "Thank you, Your Majesty," before rushing away.

"What was that about?" I asked as we followed Grae down a long, white hallway.

"Ingrid can get a bit *temperamental* with her staff," he said.

I cleared my throat. She'd seemed cold but friendly enough when we'd met before. Now, I wondered if I'd misjudged her. Was it wrong of me to have such high hopes for her support? Or perhaps, like her second cousin, she was different to humans and Wolves.

When we turned the final corner, I gasped. Suddenly, we were confronted by the riot of green and vibrant rainbow hues of the greenhouse. Tropical plants and lush flowers blossomed through the space. When Grae opened the door, the heat blasted through, sweat instantly beading on my brow at the humidity.

"This place is incredible," Hector said, craning his neck up to stare at the giant palms shading us from above.

"How?" Briar exclaimed, staring at the rays of sunlight that beamed from the rafters. "What sorcery is this?"

"Faery magic," a sharp voice said, and we turned the corner to find Queen Ingrid sitting at a white iron table in the center of her little oasis. Two guards, one of them Klaus, stood at attention behind her. Klaus gave a little half wink to Briar as she came into view, and I had to bite back a snarl. He seemed determined to ignore that my sister had a mate. For her part, she somehow both ignored and acknowledged that wink so that he didn't feel dismissed, and I tried not to marvel at the magic of my sister's courtly etiquette.

"Graemon," Queen Ingrid said with a surprising amount of affection as she stretched her arms out to Grae and kissed him on both cheeks.

I couldn't help but note that she greeted him first. Traditionally, kings were always greeted first . . . but I was the sovereign of Olmdere, just as Ingrid was of Taigos. I didn't know if it was pointed or simply out of habit, but I didn't like the way Ingrid turned to my mate first instead of me. Finally, after a long embrace, the Ice Wolf Queen turned to me.

"Calla," Ingrid said with equal laud, greeting me as if we were old friends. "Please do sit."

There were four seats left at the table, and I was about to open my mouth to demand another chair for Mina when she waved me down.

"I'd prefer to play than converse anyway," she signed, nodding down to her violin case that she clutched in her hand.

"Are you sure?" I signed back.

"Music will help lighten the mood."

I snorted at that. "It certainly would."

She bobbed her chin and started getting set up.

"And you must be the Crimson Princess herself," Ingrid said, leaning into Briar and giving her hand a squeeze. She acted as if she hadn't noticed the exchange between Mina and myself at all. "I can't believe we are only just now meeting. I feel like I've known you your whole life."

Briar's smile was forced but only I would know it. She had such a practiced ease about her.

"It's an absolute pleasure to make your acquaintance, Your Majesty," she said with a curtsy.

Hector was already scarfing down the finger food as we sat, and I kicked him under the table. Now was the time to act like a courtier, not a Wolf. He kept eating but slowed down ever so slightly.

Briar and Ingrid carried on chatting for several minutes as the rest of us listened to Mina's violin in tense silence. Briar fell into the role of Ingrid's best friend as if it took nothing to crack through the Queen's icy exterior. The music helped calm my nerves a bit as I tried to politely sip my tea. I knew if Sadie and Maez were here they'd be laughing at me. There's no way the two of them could've handled a tea party in the Taigoska palace gardens. When Briar had heard from Maez last, they were still in Taigos, too. That had been days ago, and I wondered if their trip was still going on uneventfully.

I worried, too, about Navin. I thought he was my friend. I thought he and I had grown close over our travels together. But it was clear now that there were many secrets he was hanging on to. Secrets that he and Ora shared and I wondered how much I really knew about my friends at all. Did I know them well enough to start a war to get them back? What secrets were so important that the world would burn if Ora didn't keep them? Whether out of friendship or strategy, I felt bolstered once again in the decision to rescue the head of Galen den' Mora.

I caught Briar's gaze and held it for a split second, which was enough to tell her everything she needed to know. Our twin communication was still strong.

"As lovely as this impromptu visit has been," she said, "there's a reason we're here beyond a social call."

"I figured as much," Ingrid said. "Given the haste with which you came." She looked at me, her eyebrow arching, before turning to Grae and asking, "So what happened?"

"Our friend has been kidnapped by King Nero," Briar said.

"Friend?"

"A member of the Golden Court and my council," I said.

Ingrid let out a smug laugh. "I'm guessing that means that this person is a human?"

"They are," I said. "They were ambushed in Nesra's Pass."

"Nesra's Pass is Damrienn territory," she said. "Nero has every right to deal with humans in his court as he sees fit."

The music seemed to pick up tempo as Ingrid spoke.

"So you know," Grae said, leaning his elbows on the table.

"Know what?" Ingrid asked even though it was clear from her frown that she knew exactly what we were talking about.

"What Nero is doing to the humans in Damrienn," Grae said.

"I've heard rumors," she said with a shrug. "My guards tell me of an abnormal volume of humans crossing our borders, but—"

"He's slaughtering people," I snarled.

Ingrid kept her gaze locked with Grae's. "Maybe Nero got a little overzealous, but I honestly don't believe it's as bad as they've said."

"Where are these humans?" I asked. "Why don't we go see them and ask them for ourselves?"

"They're being taken care of." Ingrid finally turned toward me, her mouth pinched. "I treat my humans well here. We are on the same side, Calla Marriel." She took a sip of her tea and set it back on the saucer so delicately I didn't even hear a clink. "Two women who chose to rule."

I pressed my lips together into a thin line. I wouldn't correct her. For one thing, I didn't choose to rule; I was *chosen*. More, I wasn't a woman at all. Which allowed an uneasy thought to coil in my stomach: if Ingrid knew I was merem, would she still help us? I didn't know why she wouldn't, but that uncertainty gnawed at me. Maybe it would be too much, too different, from the Wolf world she knew. Maybe I'd lose the support my people so desperately needed. I decided to shove my barbed retort down. If saving Olmdere meant needing to bend my truth for just a little while, I had to do it.

"What your father is doing is wrong," Ingrid said to Grae and my shoulders sagged a little with relief. For a second, I thought she might defend his actions. "He's always been a power-hungry bastard, Graemon, you and I both know that."

"We can't let him get away with it," I pushed.

She turned her blue eyes on me. "And you want me to do *what* about it exactly?"

Briar cleared her throat and leaned in, cutting off our line of sight. "We would handle the rescue mission mostly ourselves," Briar said. "But we could use a few more Wolves to help us since we are all so . . . *familiar* to Nero."

"You're his son," Ingrid balked at Grae, leaning around Briar. "Surely you know how to reason with him."

"If we go alone, Nero will kill us," I insisted.

"But you're so willing to let *my* pack die for you?" Ingrid whirled on me. "You are acting more queenly every day, Calla— I'll give you that." My lip curled and Briar placed her hand on my knee under the table as the Queen continued. "Giving you soldiers to steal back a *human* of all things. That is bold, indeed."

"We all know that if Nero carries on this way, that it will end poorly for Taigos, too," Briar said lightly.

"Do we now?"

"King Nero and King Luo have always been on good terms," Briar said.

A flash of fear crossed Ingrid's face at the mention of Luo, her once betrothed. The fact she had denied his marriage and decided to rule Taigos alone was against everything Wolves believed. Technically, according to Wolf laws, Taigos should belong to Valta now since Taigos didn't have a direct male heir. I glanced at Klaus. Perhaps he would've become a defunct king of the Ice Wolf Kingdom, though the land would officially belong to Ingrid's husband.

"You think Nero is working with Luo?" she asked, her voice growing more serious.

"I think if a war is coming, the Silver Wolves will look to their Onyx Wolf friends for support, yes," Briar said sympathetically. "And now that Nero is doubling down on Wolf law, it might not be long before Luo tries again to stake claim to your kingdom."

"I will not allow it!" Ingrid shouted, her fists pounding the table and making the cutlery clang together. The sudden outburst was at such stark contrast to her usual calm. Finally, we saw a flash of fear in her otherwise cool countenance.

Briar, to her credit, moved slowly and softly as if calming a skittish animal as she placed her hand over Ingrid's. "Olmdere won't allow it, either. But with Silver Wolves attacking one border and Onyx Wolves at the other, you're going to need a friend who supports your claim."

"Have the monthly carts of food and goods to help your kingdom not been enough to win that friendship?" Ingrid asked.

"You have been most generous," Briar said, skirting around answering. "And we will continue to support you as the true Queen of Taigos with all of our gold and natural resources," she vowed. "But now more than ever, we need each other."

Ingrid's hands shook as she pulled them from Briar's. She took a steeling breath and the tremors were gone. The thought of being sold off like a prized horse to Luo truly had her spooked.

"Agreed," she said. "I still haven't made up this mind about a rescue mission, though." She eyed me. "Sending Ice Wolves into Nero's kingdom could mean the start of a war, one neither of us is prepared to win yet."

"You don't have to decide right now," Briar said, and I

squeezed her leg roughly under the table which she pointedly ignored.

"I'll think about it." Ingrid stared at the table, seemingly noting the movement. "I'll have a decision for you by the end of the week."

"The end—"

"That's all we ask," Briar said, bowing her head. "Thank you, Your Majesty."

Ingrid inclined her head in return, rising to stand. "Come. Let me give you a tour of the gardens."

She and Briar took the lead. My hands still balled into fists at my side as I stood. We couldn't just frolic around the ice palace pretending a storm wasn't brewing over both our kingdoms . . . but if playing royals was the way to win over Ingrid then it was our only choice.

SADIE

I AWOKE IN THE SAND . . . NAKED.

The dune above me was so tall that it cast a shadow over me. Without that shadow, I'd probably have been cooked alive. I wiped the sand from my eyes and spit onto the ground. The saliva immediately vanished, sucked into the arid ground. I dusted my skin off and searched for my clothes, but I couldn't find a single shred.

It hit me all at once: the sandstorm.

We'd fallen. I craned my neck up. Beyond the sand dune was a peak of Sankai-ed, the road directly above me caked in a thick layer of sand still. I swore the dune had grown up to meet the road, burying half of it in the ground during the storm.

I stood, brushing off my bare legs and searching for any signs of life. Galen den' Mora was nowhere to be seen, nor were Maez and Navin. I prayed they both somehow made it through the storm. Maez was hopefully safe within the wagon . . . but the way Navin and I flew off, free-falling . . .

How did I survive? My Wolf form must have taken over to protect me. My clothes torn away in the storm. I didn't have a scratch on me, my skin unblemished, my body healed of any fall apart from the stinging of my eyes, which still had bits of grit in them.

I stood and trudged downhill, my bare feet sinking deep into the hot sand. I cared not one whit that I was naked, not when no one was around for miles, not when the shock of the fall still coursed through me. Still, I longed for my knives. More, I longed for water as my body drained of all its moisture, so quickly zapped when I stepped beyond the shadow of the dune.

"Fuck," I snarled and backpedaled into the shade again. "I guess I'll be walking that bridge into the sky butt naked . . . and at night."

I plonked back down into the shade. I'd have to wait until sunset if I didn't want to die in this heat. I lay back down, suddenly deliriously exhausted. Staring up at the now-blue sky, my vision twisted and blurred as fissures of heat rose up around me.

Somewhere in the endless desert, Navin would be buried under a mountain of sand. An Olmderian man with a Valtan complexion. A musician. A secret keeper. Someone who had struggled and lost and found a way to carry on despite the harsh twists life kept throwing at him. This. This shouldn't be the way his life ended. He would probably be strumming his lute in some tavern right now were it not for me. Somewhere deep down I knew I'd be the death of him. I couldn't help but feel I brought this fate to him.

I shouldn't care. He shouldn't mean anything to me at all. We never truly had anything, just a handful of "maybes" and "one days" that we both knew would never come to pass. Still, as I lay in that baking sand, all I could think of was the way those bronze eyes seemed to always see straight through my every defense, the feel of his hand in mine, the taste of his lips . . .

My nose tingled and I sniffed as my eyes welled. A traitorous tear trailed down my cheek and I wiped it away. I should be preserving the water left in me. There's only so much that shifting could heal, and if I didn't get water in the next day, I'd probably die. But I was trapped here in this pool of shadow and so I conserved my energy as best I could.

Another puffy white cloud blew past, and I tried to think of any way that Navin could've survived. Maybe the wind whisked him around and back into Galen den' Mora? Maybe his body got snagged in the netting on either side of the bridge? Maybe he found something to hang on to? Maybe the Gods could spare him somehow?

I sniffed. I had let his hand go. At some point we got torn apart, but I should've hung on, should've been stronger. Even when I lost consciousness, I should've done more. I ached. The weight of loss pressing me down like a two-ton boulder. Thinking of the complicated man, of the secrets he kept, of the ways he protected me, cared for me, *cherished me* at one point even . . . he'd been sweet and beautiful and surprisingly cunning when he wanted to be. If only we'd had a little more time.

I grieved him in my mind, remembering every detail as my eyelids grew heavy. My mind twisted and warped, blurring the lines into lucid dreaming as the heat consumed me.

SOMETHING LEAPT ONTO MY CHEST, AND I JOLTED AWAKE, ARMS flailing to fight off whatever creature pounced on me. But when I looked to my belly it was only a white shirt. My brows pinched as I looked up and there, silhouetted in the late evening sky, stood Navin. Patches of his skin looked red and raw, but he was mostly unscathed, standing there only in his trousers slung low over his hips, his lean muscled torso on full display, and a curving smile on his lips.

"How in the Gods' names . . ." I gaped up at him with a shake of my head. I couldn't believe it. "You're alive."

His eyes twinkled with mischief. "So are you."

"Barely."

I suddenly realized that twinkle of mischief was due in part to the fact I sat there naked, holding his shirt to my chest, but I didn't care. I didn't bother putting it on as I leapt to my feet and threw my arms around him.

He caught me, rocking back on one foot at the weight of

my jump. One of his hands cupped my ass while the other came around to my back, and he buried his head into my neck and breathed me in.

"I'm sorry," I whispered against his skin, relishing in the feel of him pressed against me with nothing between us.

His hand trailed down my back as he slowly lowered me to the ground. "For what?"

"I don't know," I said. "Everything? I'm sorry for hating you. I'm sorry for not trusting you. I'm . . ." I looked up into his storming eyes as the last peek of sun dipped below the horizon. "I'm sorry for letting go."

"I'm sorry for letting go, too," he murmured, not tearing his gaze from mine as I stooped, grabbed his shirt, and pulled it over my head. The billowing garment landed mid-calf and I was reminded once again of how tall Navin was. He looked out to the darkening horizon. "We should start moving before more beasts come out. The crishenem aren't the only creatures who roam the desert at night." I turned in the direction of the road to Sankai-ed and his hand landed on my arm. "Not that way. It's too far on foot and too dangerous at night. I know a closer place."

I turned in a complete circle staring out at nothing but the rolling deserts of Lower Valta. "Closer?"

"Trust me," he said, tugging me a step before releasing me.

He set out at a quick gait downhill, which was now blissfully covered in shadow. The sand was still warm underfoot, but it didn't burn into the pads of my feet like it had earlier in the day. Sweet Moon, I'd almost died . . . again.

"How did you survive?" I shook my head as I stalked up beside Navin, aiming in the direction of the next dune over. "How are you not more injured? What did you do as you were falling?"

He shrugged. "I sang."

I narrowed my eyes at him. "You're going to have to explain that to me further at some point."

He let out a long sigh and scratched at the stubble across his jaw. "I'm afraid I'll have to now." We walked for another few minutes before he abruptly stopped and turned to me. "For what it's worth," he said, "I'm sorry I didn't trust you, too."

I cocked my head. "What didn't you trust me with?"

"You'll see," he said, still not moving. His sad eyes dipped to my lips. I saw it all there: regret, relief, *longing*. The way his gaze lingered on my mouth . . . I suddenly felt more hungry for him than a cooked dinner. He let out a soft little breath and smiled.

"What?"

"I like it when I turn you on," he murmured.

"What?" I gaped at him. "What makes you think I'm turned on?"

He slowly lifted a hand and skimmed a thumb over my peaked nipple, only his thin shirt separating the two of us. I pressed my lips together as his thumb swirled over it again, coaxing it even harder. When he dropped his hand again, every part of me felt heavy and rushing with blood. My heartbeat drummed in my ears. "You're not turned on?" he asked in that soft bedroom voice that made me press my bare thighs together.

I cleared my throat and tried to put on my best scowl. "My nipples are just naturally pointy."

His lips curved up wickedly. "Mm-hmm."

"It's a Wolf thing," I said, turning and walking again.

He chuckled. "Liar."

I turned to offer him another biting retort when I spotted a shadow on the distant dunes. All the blood drained from my face as I lifted a finger and pointed. "Shit."

A crishenem.

"Run!" Navin grabbed my arm and dragged me as his long legs raced across the sand. The creature let out a whining hiss and the wind whipped with the sound of its slashing tails.

"Run?" I shouted. "Run where?"

I heard the chittering clicks as the monster skittered down the sand dune to chase after us.

"There!" Navin pointed. "Up ahead, the bend in the air, do you see it?"

It took me a second of panicked wide-eyed searching before I spotted it. But the sand dune in front of us had a dark gray lightning bolt seemingly cutting through it. At first it seemed like just another warped wave of heat rising up off the desert . . . but it was nighttime and there were no heat waves. I realized then that I'd seen a similar seam of warped air before when we went to collect Calla and Briar from that faery. Shit. It was a magical glamour.

We dashed toward that seam, the sound of the monster behind us growing louder with every step. It felt so close I thought at any second it would pierce me with its stinger, just as we leapt over the threshold.

When we crossed through the bent air, we whirled, watching as the monster screeched and hissed, stabbing at the wall of air like an impenetrable wall of steel.

Navin's chest rose and fell in heavy gasps. "It won't be able to cross the glamour. We're safe here."

I turned and looked to a giant sandstone building shaped like a heptagon. It had fortified walls with archways and parapets dotting every corner. Beautiful intricately painted clay tiles covered the seven archways.

"What is this place?" I whispered, awed by the monumental size of the building.

"This was Yasva's dying wish," Navin said.

Dying wishes were powerful magic. It was Calla's dying wish that had saved her kingdom, and in doing so, her life. Galen den' Mora itself was a dying wish. So many of the greatest monuments and magics of all time were created through the power of a dying wish.

I glanced at Navin. "I've never heard of Yasva."

"Nor should you," a voice called from the archway.

There, leaning against the wall, was a tall, broad man with a thick Olmderian accent. His dark coils were cropped short to his head and his large eyes were a bright hazel. The white and gold of his tunic caught the sparkle of moonlight along with his golden buttons and the capped epaulets on his shoulders. His attire was part military, part regal, and more Gods-like than any painting I'd ever seen. He stood stock-still, his chin lifted, a confidence that bordered on arrogance crossing his face as he looked me over, wearing only the shirt of the man next to me.

His eyes slid to Navin. "You're looking well, Navin Mourad."

"Rasil," Navin said carefully. "I didn't know you'd be here. I . . . I had to bring her here."

Rasil's eyes narrowed as he toyed with a thin metal tube hanging from his neck. "Did you now?"

"Please," Navin implored. "Just let me explain."

"You *dare* to bring a Wolf to our doorstep." Rasil's voice remained steady, pleasant even, but his eyes were tinged with menace.

"Please just let me explain—"

"What is your name?" Rasil cut in, turning his gaze to me as I shifted under his scrutiny.

I straightened my shoulders, trying to not be cowed by the power of this person before me. "Sadie Rauxtide," I gritted out.

Rasil clasped his hands behind his back as he slowly descended the marble steps. The sand around his feet seemed to ripple as he pursed his lips and considered me. "Rauxtide." He tossed the word around in his mouth. "A Silver Wolf then? The worst sort you could bring here."

I blinked at him and then looked at Navin. "What is this? What is happening?"

"Oh!" Rasil let out a delighted laugh and looked to the stars blinking to life above us. "You haven't told her?"

"There was no time. Rasil, please, just let me talk to her," Navin said, but stood transfixed as Rasil wandered across the sand to us and offered out his hand to me.

Before I could yank my hand away, he lifted the thin metal tube to his lips and blew. A piercing shrill note rang out and my mind snapped in two, my knees buckling like cutting a puppet's strings. I heard Navin shout my name before I hit the ground.

The stranger towered over me as my eyes rolled back. "I am Rasil Anweaver." His hand remained holding mine as he stared down at me. My vision spotted as I desperately tried to remain conscious. That ringing sound now pounded in my head and pulled me under. "Head Guardian of the Songkeepers." His grip tightened even further until the point of pain.

"And Navin's husband."

CALLA

THE MOONLIGHT IN MY FUR MADE ALL MY FEARS FEEL FURTHER away. I sniffed the brisk air, smelling the snow hares and ebarvens winding through the pine forest. I loved running through the powder of freshly fallen snow, the howl of the hundreds of Ice Wolves surrounding me, and Grae hot on my heels as I zipped through the darkness.

I was reminded once again of the sheer immensity of the Ice Wolf pack. They were so large that despite their more lax training, they'd still be a considerable force against Damrienn. We needed this, needed Taigos on our side. Running with the pack would surely help. It was the way Wolves bonded; hunting together made us all feel closer.

And closer was what we needed, as Ingrid still was playing coy, not giving us a decision one way or another. Inviting us on this run was at least a sign of good faith.

"Slow down, little fox," Grae spoke into my mind. "We're meant to be running *with* the pack, not leading it."

"Fine," I grumbled, my maw letting out a frustrated whine. I slowed my pace slightly. I was sick of holding myself back, sick of making myself lesser than, to appeal to Ingrid. I hated how much Ingrid had us by the balls and how much I was contorting myself to appease her. Now, I even had to run differently.

"Soon we'll be running under the golden leaves of Olmdere again," my mate reassured me. "Soon."

"There will be no running through the forests of Olmdere if Ingrid doesn't agree to side with us." I shuddered at the thought. "What if she never makes a decision and stays neutral forever?"

"She's smart enough to know if she allows them to come for Olmdere, Taigos will be next."

"What if she brokers a deal and sides with Nero?"

"She won't." Grae's voice was thunder in my mind. "There's nothing that could be promised to her that couldn't just as easily be taken back. Nero has no loyalty to anyone but himself and Ingrid has just as much to lose as we do. More. We could cut off Olmdere from the rest of Aotreas far easier than Ingrid could, sharing two borders with enemy packs."

"She has mountains to protect her."

"And we have a treacherous stretch of sea and only one navigable port." Grae raced alongside me, so close I could feel his fur brush my own. "We could burn the port down. Close our borders, if we had to. There'd be lean times at first, but we could make it."

"Gods," I groaned, staring up at the moon. "Do you think it'll come to that?"

"I hope not, little fox."

My ears twitched as Briar's pained howl rent the air. A chill zipped down my spine that had nothing to do with the cold. I swiftly turned in her direction, trying to find her in my mind. "What is it? What happened?"

"Maez." Briar's voice was a broken cry. "She said . . . she said that . . ."

Hector practically bowled me over as we raced out onto a frozen clearing. "What happened?" he snapped. "Sadie? Is she okay?"

Briar appeared from the other side of the clearing, her golden fur glistening in the moonlight. Her ears were pinned back, her hackles raised.

"Briar." I bolted over to her. "What did Maez say?"

"Galen den' Mora was on the way to Upper Valta when they were hit by a sandstorm." Hector, Grae, and I paced anxiously around her as she spoke. "Navin and Sadie fell from the wagon."

We all froze.

"Fell?" Hector asked, searching between us. "How bad can a sandstorm be? Enough to . . ." He couldn't bring himself to say "kill" but a new kind of fear laced his lupine eyes.

"I don't know," Briar cried out as if she was being stabbed over and over, as if the pain Maez was feeling was manifesting throughout her entire body.

"Briar!" I shifted on instinct. "Briar, break the connection!" I dropped to my knees in the snow in front of her, so panicked I couldn't feel the sting of its cold. "Shift!"

At my command, she collapsed into the snow. I caught her in my arms as she shifted and writhed beneath me. I was only faintly aware of Grae barking orders at Hector and then fleeing back through the forest. Hector stood with his back to us, pacing, protecting us from any beasts that might be prowling the forest.

"Breathe, breathe," I commanded my twin as Briar shuddered in my arms, her fingers clawing at me and her legs flailing like a pup in slumber. "Open your eyes, Briar. Look at me."

Her blue eyes peeked open, her red hair strewn across the white snow. A sliver of moonlight beamed down onto us as her breathing steadied and then tears were spilling down her cheeks.

"They fell from the sky," she whispered, staring up at the moon as if she was reliving it anew. "I don't know how far. They disappeared into the storm."

Hector snarled and paced faster. A group of Ice Wolves skirted around the clearing, and with two snaps from Hector, they kept moving and didn't linger.

"Is Maez okay?" I asked.

"She got to Sankai-ed." Briar's chest heaved as she clung to me. "She went back down and searched for them after the storm . . . but she found no trace of them."

Hector whined again and I knew he feared the worst. Their bodies were probably buried in the storm. I tried to push the thought away. Sadie was the toughest Wolf I knew. If anyone could survive, it would be her. But Navin? There was no way he could have pulled through.

I tried to fight the pain blossoming in my chest. Then selfishly another thought popped into my mind, and I hated myself for it. "Did they uncover his secrets? Do they have any more answers?"

Hector's growl shook through me, making my whole body tremble. It was a shitty question. His sister might have just died, and I was still trying to uncover Navin's secret plot. His secrets had probably died with him.

And yet I was the Queen, and for all that it grieved me, part of my duty was to ask such shitty questions, so that others didn't have to. So I stared him down, and his ears flattened back in submission.

Now was *not* the time for division.

Grae reappeared through the trees in his human form dressed in a thick fur cloak. Whorls of steam escaped his mouth and billowed behind him, his breaths coming out in sharp pants. He carried an armful of clothing and two pairs of boots. He dropped the boots beside us and laid one fur cloak over Briar who I still cradled in my arms, then he wrapped the other cloak around my shoulders and crouched down beside me.

"We should get you two inside," he murmured gently, even though his face was tight with pain.

Briar didn't respond for a long time, but when she did, she said, "There's something else."

"Gods." The look in her eyes had my heart doubling pace. "What?"

Her throat bobbed. "Maez was so weakened by grief it slipped out of her mind. A memory. In this sandstone little border town . . ."

My eyes widened. "What was she keeping from you?"

"Sadie's father and uncles tried to capture her and take her to Rikesh."

"Rikesh?" I swept the hair from Briar's face. She wasn't making any sense. "Why?"

"Nero arranged her marriage to Prince Tadei."

Hector let out a piercing howl as Grae and I growled in unison. "He can't do that."

"He can." Briar's glassy gaze met mine. "At least, he believes he can, as does Tadei. And Sadie wasn't the only one Nero arranged a betrothal to."

"What? Who?"

"Me," she whispered, her voice cracking.

"But you have a mate!" My scream was so shrill it made Hector jolt. It was actually Briar who was calm this time.

"I know, Calla."

"Who did he promise you to?"

"Hemming's son," Briar said, glancing at Grae as she clutched the cloak tighter to her chest. His lip curled and a deep growl rumbled out of him. "His new heir, Evres." Briar's composure shattered once more, and she groaned and clutched her stomach, her body shaking with pain. "It hurts," she cried. "Maez hurts so badly." She tried to pull from my grip. "I need to go to her. I need to help her."

She tried to stand, and my arms banded around her tighter as Grae took a step between her and the edge of the clearing. "You're not going anywhere," I said. "Especially not now."

Briar battled against me, and I squeezed her tighter to me. She was strong, but I was stronger. I could feel her heartbreak radiating off her and couldn't imagine the pain of being forced to stay away from my mate. It was cruel. But losing her to Nero would be far crueler. She couldn't just go gallivanting off to Valta.

"Maez will return," I reassured her. "You'll be reunited soon. It's okay." Her battling arms weakened and she sagged in my grip. "It's okay."

Grae and I exchanged pained glances, and I knew he was imagining what it would be like to be separated from me, knowing I was in pain and being unable to reach me. Gods, he'd known that pain before. I couldn't hold his gaze, that sorrow suddenly fresh within me. I just held Briar tighter to my chest and rocked her until she went limp.

SADIE

I CAME TO WITH MY HANDS BOUND IN METAL SHACKLES BEHIND my back, too tight for me to break, even with my strength. Whoever had tied me up was either incredibly cunning or had detained Wolves before. With my arms in such a position, shifting would probably rip me in two. I'd seen it happen and the thought still made me sick to my stomach—a soldier panicked during a training exercise and had shifted, tearing a whole arm and part of their torso off in the process. No amount of shifting back healed him of that—even Wolves don't survive after losing a leg. He bled out in the forest of Highwick where we were training. I'd been thirteen at the time.

My feet were also shackled and a gag bit into the corners of my mouth. My head throbbed, an aching pain shooting out from behind my eyes, and I swore to the fucking Gods that if I passed out one more time, heads would roll.

I tried to focus my eyes and take in the room. It appeared to be an underground cave . . . probably a dungeon below the grand building above. The walls were all curving sandstone, the ground made of dark grit. The whole enclosed space was built along the natural rock formation apart from the iron bars at one end. No one guarded my cell. The *only* cell, it appeared . . . which told me this place didn't make a habit of taking prisoners, not enough to need a whole dungeon at least. There was still *a* cell in the basement, though, so they certainly weren't entirely benevolent either . . . and definitely not toward Wolves.

Sunlight shone from the long narrow stairwell up ahead, the only source of light. My snarl was muffled by my gag as I pulled my feet under me and tried to find a more comfortable position. I still only wore Navin's shirt, the V of the neckline gaping to the point one breast was almost spilling out of it. I could have cared less about that; if anything, I'd rather have been naked than wearing anything of his.

More than the shackles, Navin's shirt made me feel like I was actually trapped.

I heard a clank from up ahead and I honed my senses to the sound. Footsteps echoed on the stairs, the sunlight shadowed by the figure who descended the steps. My heartbeat picked up speed as I saw two leather sandals appear, then linen trousers, then a hand holding a skin of water. Those hands . . . I knew then who it was before his face even appeared.

I turned away from the bars, staring at the cave wall.

"Sadie?" Navin breathed, his voice cracking. His pace quickened and he ate up the distance between us. When he reached the grating, he paused and let out a whistle—two long notes punctuated by two short ones—and the door groaned, the rusty hinges swinging open.

What in the Gods' names was that? My heart leapt into my throat, my shoulders lifting in fear. Navin rushed to my side, spinning me to face him. His eyes were bloodshot and pleading as he untied my gag.

The second the gag left my mouth I spit in his face.

He frowned. "I guess I deserve that."

"You *guess*? You're married?" I barked. It was the wrong first question. There were so many other more important things I should've asked first: Who the fuck are you? What is this place? Why am I chained in a cell? But the words flew out of my mouth before I could rein them in.

"We were young," Navin said, shaking his head. "We were coming up in the guardianship together in Olmdere. Two boys who looked Valtan in a town of Olmderians. He was my only friend and . . . as we grew older, we fell for each other. But then life and work pulled us apart." He watched his hands as he uncapped the waterskin, seemingly unable to meet my eyes. "Our reunions became less frequent and less cherished until we realized we had grown into two people not meant for each other. That was many years ago."

"How quaint," I snarled as Navin lifted the skin to my lips. I turned my head away and he reached for my cheek. I jerked farther from his grasp. "Now untie me," I demanded.

"I can't yet, but I will find a way soon," he vowed. "I'll get you out of this. But first, here. Drink."

I snapped out at him, trying to bite his hand before he snatched it away with a bitter laugh. "Esh.

"You're going to bite me now?"

"*You* expect decorum from *me*?" I hissed. "How about I tie you up and leave you in a cell until you have sand caked in every fucking crevice and then you tell me if *I'm* being unreasonable." I kicked grit at him. "You're a liar." I tipped my chin to the bars. "And apparently a magic wielder of some sort. And you're married. Apologies if I don't believe you when you say you're going to get me out of this."

"I'm sorry I didn't tell you about him."

I hated that he heard the venom in the word "married." It made me almost want to laugh. I was a soldier and a Wolf; I was used to brutality. I knew being his captive was far more pressing than the fact he had a husband, and yet I couldn't let it go. Maez was right—I was the goddess of stubbornness.

"Humans aren't bound to marriages the way Wolves are," I growled. "You have choices. You could've ended things."

Navin shook his head. "I never had a reason to," he said quietly. "Rasil is the Head Guardian and I am one of Galen den' Mora. It looks good to the Songkeepers that we are united if only for show. All my other lovers were quick passing sparks. They never knew who I truly am."

Ah, there was the true question we were dancing around. I cocked my head, wishing I could gouge out his eyes and rip out his lying tongue. "And who are you, Navin Mourad? What is a Songkeeper?"

His eyes lifted to mine, and he whispered, "I am a keeper of the eternal songs."

"How cryptic. What does that even mean?" I glared at him. "I've never heard of such a sect."

"As well you shouldn't have. We worked very hard to make sure no Wolf had ever heard of us," he said. He frowned at the waterskin. "Please just drink and I promise I will tell you everything."

"I don't bargain with traitors. How long are you going to keep me here?" I demanded, ignoring the offering of water again. I didn't care that my throat was bone-dry. I wouldn't give him the satisfaction. "Are you planning on killing me?"

"No." His voice dropped an octave. He had the audacity to almost sound offended.

"It sure seems like your *husband* would like to kill me." I dealt him a bitter smile. "If he's concerned I'm your lover, you can assure him you've never been between my legs." My lip curled. "Nor shall you ever."

"He *will* free you, Sadie. I just need time to convince him."

I let out a rough bark. "Why should I believe anything you tell me?"

His eyes bracketed with pain. "Please," he said, lifting the water to my lips again. "Not everything between us was a lie."

"That only makes it worse then," I snapped. "How can you open doors with a *whistle*? How did you survive that fall? How did you get behind us when we were trailing you in Taigos?"

How the fuck could you do this to me?

He waited, his mouth tight, his hands still hovering, waiting for me to drink. I scowled and took a sip from the skin. I had half a mind to spit that water at him, too, but my mouth was so parched and the cool liquid revived me. My body refused to waste a single drop and I gulped it down. When I pulled away, I leaned back against the cave wall.

Navin reached out and adjusted the shirt to better cover me.

"How chivalrous," I said, and he pulled away. "Now tell me, how can you do all of those things?"

He rubbed the back of his neck, glancing again to the stairs as if afraid we might be overheard. "Magic."

My eyes flared. "Are you a sorcerer?"

"Gods no," he said, one cheek dimpling. "I am just as I told you—a musician. It's just that our magic is far more ancient than that of the sorcerers and monsters and even Wolves."

My brows pinched together. "Wolves roamed this land long before the humans."

He shook his head. "Your history has twisted the truth to suit your own beliefs."

"And how do you know that yours hasn't done the same?"

"I can take you to the library." He anxiously smoothed his hands down his trouser legs. "Once Rasil and his men are gone. I can explain everything."

"Will you untie me?" His eyes turned sad and I lifted my chin. "Ah. I see. You aren't allowed to unchain me, are you? Did your husband order that, too?"

"I will convince him to let you go. Believe me," he implored, inching closer to place his hands on my shoulders. Fury burned through my veins. How dare he try to comfort me! This lying piece of shit. How dare he act like my friend when he had just *imprisoned* me. "I will talk to Rasil. He will learn that you aren't a threat."

My lip curled and I flashed him a wicked smile. "That, Navin, is where you are very, *very* wrong," I said.

Before he could recoil, I lashed out, smashing my forehead into his nose. He let out a pained grunt as he toppled backward, and I followed, bowling him over as I rose to a stand. I planted one manacled foot on either side of his head, the chain crushing his windpipe. His eyes bugged as his hands scrambled for the chain at his neck. He scratched at my bare legs, trying to move me, his flailing growing weaker by the second.

I watched the panic and fear as his face turned bright red and his eyes rolled back, but I couldn't do it. Couldn't watch the life leave his eyes.

I ran through the still open door, leaving him gasping and sputtering in my wake. The chain between my feet was too short to get a good gait, but I stumbled and tripped my way up the stairs and into the open-air corridor. To my right, it led out into the heart of the heptagon to what appeared to be a tropical oasis, thin trails of waterfalls and lush greenery. To my left was the rolling desert and the road up to Sankai-ed. I bolted to the left, scrambling to keep my feet under me as I descended the steps and hit the burning sand.

Fuck it. I'd rather die being cooked on the hot sand than in the cell of this secret society. The second my feet hit the sand, however, two hands lurched up from below and grabbed my legs. I screamed as three more skinny bone-white hands appeared and pulled me downward. My shins disappeared into the hot earth as the hands pulled me under, grasping and groping their way up my body. I flailed and thrashed against the translucent fingers that clawed up my torso, the crushing sand rising to my hips.

"You see, my love?" Rasil's voice sounded behind me, and I twisted, spying him casually leaning in the tiled archway of the building just as he'd done the night before. Beside him stood a panting and bleeding Navin. Blood trailed from his nose, a bright bruising red line around his throat. "She's only a beast."

"She's a trapped animal—of course she ran! Besides, we need her alive, you fool," Navin spat, not even looking in my direction. My pulse quickened even further. I'm just an animal to him, aren't I? And what did that other part mean? Why did they need me alive? "Call off your samsavet."

Rasil rolled his eyes and lazily picked up the long whistle

hanging around his neck. He blew into it three short, shrill notes, and the hands released me. I wriggled out of the sand, falling face-first into the gritty ground, my hands still bound and unable to save me. I clambered to my feet and stood there, swaying, already dizzy from the heat as the two men stared at me from the shade.

"My samsavet patrols every corner of the guardianship border," Rasil said. "A mouse couldn't run across the sand without her knowing. There is no escaping here without *my* say-so. Remember that, Wolf." He said the word "Wolf" with such disgust, as if *I* were the abomination. I snarled back at him, and he only smiled and gave me a wink. "Now go back to your cage like a good little dog and we'll bring you a treat."

My eyes flared, and I was about to barrel headfirst into him, samsavet or no, when Navin cut him a sharp look and said, "Rasil, stop this. There's no need to be this cruel."

"Have you looked in the mirror, love?" Rasil smiled as he scanned Navin's brutalized face. "She just tried to kill you and you call *me* cruel?" He looked up to the cloudless sky and let out a deep, bellowing laugh. "Fine. Have your puppy love if you are so desperate to be killed by it. The Songkeepers leave for Allesdale in the morning. You will have two weeks with your pet to bring her to heel before we return."

He looked me over and inclined his head. "But the samsavet will have no master to recall her," he warned me. "So make sure you have chosen death before you step on this sand again."

SADIE

I REMAINED IN MY CELL FOR THE REST OF THE DAY. I DRIFTED in and out of consciousness, dreaming of monsters drowning me in burning sand and of the vengeance I would bring to my captors above, carving them open with the nearest sharp object, or maybe just my teeth—human or no.

I replayed every moment with Navin over and over in my mind, trying to relive every suspicion. How had I not seen this coming? How could he have lied so easily? Worst of all, how could he have used his twisted magic to ensnare my heart? That was the most egregious betrayal. He had magic. And he'd manipulated us all with it.

A stranger in traveling clothes and sun scarf came and untied me through the bars . . . bars too narrow to slip through even if I shifted. Smart. The relief of being able to move my arms again was huge, but I was still just as trapped. Even if I somehow breached my cell, I'd still have a sand monster to contend with. And if I somehow fought off the sand monster? In the night, there'd be a crishenem, and in the day, there'd be scorching sand between me and Sankai-ed. The stranger brought me a lump of stale bread and a skin of water, too. I sat there in Navin's browning tunic, wishing I hadn't been such a coward and had finished him when I had the chance. He deserved to die for everything he made me feel. Gods, why couldn't that sandstorm just have claimed us both?

I shifted to heal my injuries and regain some strength, but even belowground, the heat was too much for my furs. It was degrading putting Navin's shirt on after I shifted back, but I didn't want to be naked in front of these humans who already only saw me as a beast.

I stayed up long after the sun had faded from the sky, plotting how I might be able to end him, but knowing if I did, Rasil would kill me when he returned. Even in my Wolf form, I wouldn't be able to battle the samsavet, crishenem, and scorching sun and survive. I shuddered at the memory of those many hands pulling me under again.

Maybe Maez would come back for me? Would she even know where to look? Maybe she didn't survive the sandstorm . . . and if she did, she surely would think Navin and I had perished. Even if she did start looking, she'd never find this hidden place, nothing more than a mirage in the desert.

I tried to sing the notes that had opened my cell before, but no matter how many times I tried, the iron didn't budge. How did they wield the power of song? What made them special? How long had this secret group been working right under our noses?

I lay there turning over everything I learned in my head. There was a secret sect of humans who possessed magic . . . magic that was used through song. I knew Wolves possessed the magic to shift. Faeries possessed the magic to grant dying wishes. And sorcerers, they wielded death magic. But humans wielding a musical sort of magic? That I'd never heard of before.

It made me wonder how much more magic existed that I'd not heard of.

If Galen den' Mora was a part of this secret society, then why did they offer to give us a ride into Olmdere? They admitted to knowing full well we were Wolves. Weren't Wolves the enemies of these Songkeepers? I repositioned myself uncomfortably in my cell. From my reception, it certainly seemed so.

I scratched the grit from my ears. None of these choices made sense. Why did Ora and the others fight to put Calla on the throne? Were all the badge-wearing musicians who showed up that day part of these Songkeepers, too?

I was roused by the horses being readied long before the dawn, sleep eluding me as my many troubled thoughts ruminated. It sounded like a handful of people scuffling about above me—dishes clanging, feet shuffling, boisterous banter. As the whinny of horses faded into the distance, the sandaled feet appeared on the steps again.

"Is it broken?" I asked by way of greeting. "Your nose?"

"No," Navin said, squeezing the bridge of his nose as he stalked over to me. "But it still hurts if that makes you feel any better."

"It does a little," I grumbled.

"Are you still planning on killing me?" he asked as he rubbed one hand mindlessly across his swollen neck.

"Probably," I hedged. "But only once I'm free of this place. To kill you now, I'm sure Rasil would be delighted to end me in the cruelest way possible. Probably have his monster drown me in sand."

"Sadie—"

"You really had me fooled for a while there," I said bitterly. "The sweet musician. The human who just wanted to hold my hand and take me to dinner. Was that all part of some twisted joke?"

"No."

"Were you telling all of your Songkeeper friends in Galen den' Mora about how you were toying with the Wolf girl?"

"No," he said a little louder. His eyes filled with that strange anger, menace I'd never seen in him until the past few days. *So this was the real Navin, the one hiding under the mask.* "You liked that I was sweet back then. That I was different from the harshness and aggression of the Wolves." He folded his arms across his chest, seemingly growing another inch taller with the force of his personality alone. "I am still him, that human who wanted to hold your hand and take you to dinner and kiss you slowly in the rain." He inclined his head and stepped closer to the bars. "But there's another side of me, too. One that is a lot closer to who you are than you'd like to think. A darker part, one that is probably what really drew you to me in the first place."

I flashed my teeth at him, nipping the air. Being attracted to him had never made sense to me. A human. An artist. He seemed so sweet and gentle, and part of me was allured by that, yes. But another part of me knew all those things would never be enough, and yet he still pulled me into his orbit as if under a spell. Now, at least I understood a little more why. It had nothing to do with his so-called darkness.

It had to do with the fact that he cast his literal magic on me. No wonder my desire for him was so incongruous to any logic. It was just his power muddling my brain.

A memory flashed back to me. One I was only now willing to truly scrutinize. I'd been surprised the night the Silver Wolves tried to take Navin by how much of a fight he put up. He managed to hold his own against *three* Wolves for several minutes before they captured us and beat us into a bloody pulp. I had thought it had all been me, my strength and skill—or blind luck—but now I understood what had really happened. Navin was faster and stronger than he'd seemed. He'd been hiding his true skills from me all this time.

Yet he wanted me to trust him.

"Before we were attacked by that crishenem," I said, remembering the way he pinned me on that rock, the wanton look in his eyes. "It started to come out. The real you."

Navin paused at the bars, tossing a ball of plum fabric between his hands. "I want to explain this all to you. Everything," he said, his words rasping from the near-death choking I'd delivered the day before. "You're the first Wolf that has ever entered the refuge—"

"You call this place a refuge?" My eyebrows shot up. "It is a palace if ever I saw one. It is a grand citadel. *Refuge?*" I huffed, shaking my head at him.

Navin let out an exasperated sigh. "Rasil has granted me permission to tell you our histories in the hopes you'll agree to help us with something. That is an unprecedented honor—"

"I'm feeling *quite* honored," I cut in before he could continue. "But first I want to know why Rasil would agree to that in the first place. At what price?"

"A million gritas."

I gaped at him. "I'm sorry, I must have sand in my ears." My eyes narrowed. "I thought you just said a *million* gritas."

It looked like it pained Navin to speak the next words. "The bounty that Luo has placed on you."

"No." My cheeks flamed, and my heart thundered as the realization dawned on me. "I will not let you sell me to him. I will let that fucking monster drag me under the sand before—"

"It's a trade to get something of ours back. Rasil promises to let you go from here—"

"To sell me to another!" I shouted.

Navin shook his head. "We just need it back," he pleaded.

"What back?" It's not like I was going to entertain this lunacy, but I wanted to see what was so important that he'd betray me.

He ignored me. "Then I can help get you out of the palace. You don't have to stay in Rikesh, just help us get what we want and we can both run away."

"Together?" I laughed bitterly. "You can't be serious."

"Back to Olmdere," Navin said. "You can go back to your court. You will be safe. Just help us with this ruse."

"Just help you steal from the *King of Valta* by pretending to be his brother's fucking bride!" My voice scratched until I was as raspy as Navin. "How dare you say this to me like I have any choice!"

"You do," he said.

"And what choices are those?" I scoffed. "Die here, die in the desert, or help you steal from a king and die in his palace. And even if I manage to escape, what court will be left to return to? If I make enemies with Luo, he will help Nero destroy the Golden Court." Navin was silent and I let out a low growl. "Those are not choices at all. Those are just different kinds of death sentences."

"Fine," Navin said, dropping the bundle of fabric onto the sand at his feet. He turned and walked away, whistling the tune that opened my door. "I'll be in the library if you want answers."

AFTER STARING AT THE OPEN DOOR FOR WHAT FELT LIKE HOURS, hungry and thirsty, I decided I was a stubborn fool if I didn't walk through it. I hastily changed into the plum gown that Navin had brought. It was a light gauzy fabric, held together by golden clips at the shoulders and hips, and gathered with ribbons at the waist. I guessed the garment was some sort of musician's performance outfit, judging by the little musical notes embroidered down the plunging neckline. It was far too feminine for me and rather ridiculous looking on my warrior's body, but at least it wasn't a grungy stained shirt.

At least it wasn't *Navin's* shirt.

As I walked up the steps, the grand tiled hallway appeared again, but this time I turned toward the oasis instead of the desert and those many pale hands of the samsavet. I shuddered again, thinking of how it so easily pulled me into the sand. How many more monsters lurked beneath the desert surface, waiting to attack?

The roof opened up above me, the center of the building open to the sky. Seven tiled tunnels spilled into the oasis, each with its own unique tiled pattern and intricate swirling designs. Tall palm trees shaded the winding garden paths of cool river stones. Water trickled below my feet, stretching out to the many tropical fruit trees and shrubs. A well painted in sage green and ocean blue sat in the very center of thick greenery. A golden bucket hung from above the well and I paused to admire it. Clearly this well was something important, more of a statue than designed for practical use.

From each of the seven walls, a stream of water fell into a collection bowl that spilled over into the gardens. Rainbow-feathered birds twittered as they flew from tree to tree. Hummingbirds and butterflies pollinated the flowers and danced around the plants ripe with fruit, all moving as if in a choreographed dance. This place was amazing—clearly a dying wish teeming with magic. It had probably saved many lives from the scorching desert. I wanted to pause longer and take it all in, but the scratch of my dry throat overwhelmed me.

I rushed over to the nearest bowl, drinking from the falling water and splashing it over my face. I scrubbed the back of my neck and my bare arms, washing away the grit. My toes wriggled in the cool water spilling over the sides. I leaned my head back into the spray, uncaring as my dress got wet, too. The thin fabric would dry quickly in this heat. An impressive amount of sand washed from my hair as I untied my two braids and finger-combed out the many snarls. It felt incredible finally washing away the sand and sweat, finally feeling cool and clean.

As I wrung my hair out, I looked up to find Navin leaning against the far archway, barely visible through the trees.

He pushed off the wall and slowly curved around the outer path toward me. "If you wanted soap and bathing oils, you could just ask," he said mildly.

"I want my freedom."

"Not quite the same, and you know it."

He paused as he turned the corner, taking in the full sight of me, from my dripping hair spilling down my dress to the wet fabric hugging my curves and leaving nothing to the imagination.

"Then I will be clear: I want nothing from my captors," I said, wishing desperately I had my knives right then. Nothing made me feel more naked than being without my weapons. I supposed my teeth would have to do.

His expression darkened. "I am not your captor."

"Are you not?" My eyebrows lifted as I cut him a sarcastic look. "Are you saying I can walk out of here right now and not be drowned in the sand by the samsavet?" The muscle in his cheek flickered. "Exactly. *You* are my captor, Navin Mourad, whether you like it or not."

"This was never my plan," he said, taking another step toward me, his beseeching hands reaching out as I retreated, keeping the distance between us. I couldn't have him near, hated how his closeness always seemed to muddle my good sense. "I never intended to bring you here, only to take you to Rikesh just as we planned with Calla. I truly thought you could form an alliance with Valta and return to Olmdere without ever knowing about this place." He took another step. "But, Sadie, we can do all of that still."

"Except for the part about me offering myself to a prince in exchange for something that your band of humans wants. Something you won't even tell me what it is," I snarled. "You think once I'm in the clutches of the Onyx Wolves I'll be able to escape?"

"I will help you escape."

"I don't believe you." I laughed bitterly. "What reason have you given me to trust you?"

I looked all around me, studying the place and trying to ignore him. When I got a waft of fresh flatbread, I turned from him and started stalking toward the smell of food, my stomach rumbling. A trail of water droplets was left in my wake as I took the third tunnel down into a massive kitchen. Tables dotted the airy open space, covered in bowls of fruits and greens. Clay stoves and firepits lined one wall, one still smoking with a fresh plate of flatbread beside it. I hustled over, lifting the cloth that covered the plate and snatching a piece. I moaned as the garlic and oil flavors lit up my tongue, and I hungrily took another giant bite.

"Here," Navin offered, setting a bowl of red dipping spices beside me.

I kept my back to him and continued to eat, the need to fill my belly suddenly overwhelming. It was only once I'd eaten a whole piece of flatbread and was on to my second that I noticed a knife sitting at the edge of the table next to some chopped figs. I grabbed the knife and set it closer on the table beside me.

"Still thinking of killing me?" Navin asked from where he perched against the tabletop. "If you kill me, there'll be no getting out of this place, remember? I'd hoped that wouldn't be the only reason you'd want to keep me alive, but still," he mused, "it's worth mentioning."

I picked up the blade and flicked it back and forth in my hand. Not as satisfying as my own knives but still it felt good to have a weapon. "It would feel so good to drive this into your heart," I said quietly as I turned to look at him. I brushed crumbs from my nearly dry dress. "Maybe it would be worth it."

His eyes narrowed at me as one cheek dimpled. "But you won't."

"Why not?"

"Because you want to live," he said, his eyes scanning me up and down again. "And because even though you hate yourself for it, you still care for me."

I guffawed, crumbs flying from my mouth. "I absolutely do not."

Navin folded his arms across his chest. "It would be much easier if that was true, wouldn't it?" His lips curved, but his eyes were sad. "Come, I'll show you everything."

SADIE

SUNLIGHT FILTERED INTO THE GILDED LIBRARY. LIGHT WOOD shelves stretched up to where the roof began to slope with rolling golden ladders on either side of the aisles. A burgundy carpet bisected the room upon which sat tables strewn with giant tomes, scrolls, and maps. It looked more impressive than the temple of knowledge in Damrienn, more gilded than the castle of Olmdere, the frescoed ceilings more beautiful than any painting I'd ever seen before.

I walked through the space, taking it all in as Navin walked to the center table littered with books. Histories written in four of the Aotrean languages lay in front of me along with sheets and sheets of music. Navin's long fingers traced over one of the sheets. Blotted with ink, it seemed hastily scribbled by someone, the browning curled edges denoting its age.

"Long before the written word," he said, peeking up at me and then back down to the page, "there was song. Songs were the first magic in the world. Songs did far more than tell our people's stories. They mended and they moved. They created and they destroyed." His eyes flicked up to me and he said, "And then the Wolves came." I shuddered as he passed me another scroll, reading over the poem of the Wolves appearing from the sky.

"The Onyx Mountains?" I flipped over the page. "Is this . . . Valta?"

"Those mountains weren't always there in the sky," he said, passing me another piece of paper. One of the faded yellowing pages was a map, but where the telltale spots of floating mountains usually were was nothing but desert sand. "One day, as the songs go, the sun vanished from the sky. The whole world went dark. And when the light shone again, there were mountains in the sky and Wolves roamed the land."

I shook my head. "Our histories say the humans arrived on our shores, bringing their monsters along with them, begging the Wolves to rid them of the creatures."

Navin weighed his head side to side. "The humans did beg in the end," he said. "It was our own folly. When the Wolves came, they wanted our song magic, and not just the smaller tunes. They wanted the eternal songs—the ones that created and destroyed. When the humans denied them, the Wolves attacked." He passed me another sheet of music. "And so we did what we did best. We sang something new into creation." He twisted one of the heavy leather-bound tomes toward me, a painting of a juvleck battling an ostekke on the page.

I sucked in a breath. "Humans *created* the monsters?"

"They were meant to battle the Wolves, to protect us and our secrets." His throat bobbed and he nodded. "They were once within our control."

My mind spun so fast I thought I might topple over. "Like the way Rasil controls the samsavet?"

"Yes," Navin said. "Rasil's grandfather created that samsavet, and the beast is still controlled by his direct descendants through song and blood. But that creature's creation came at a great cost to the world."

"What about the other monsters? What happened to that control?"

"More and more were created, more hastily and by those who didn't possess a strong enough hold on their magic. This place was once a bastion for the Songkeepers. A refuge filled with hundreds of musicians who wielded the magical songs in the wars . . ." He shook his head, sorting through the stacks of paper and books. "The Songkeepers were dying in droves. If their magic didn't consume them, they died in the ancient wars. So few were left with the eternals songs to protect humankind . . . Our sect was almost entirely destroyed." His fingertips trailed delicately over the pages. "You'd think we'd have learned the cost of wielding such magic was too great, but they were desperate times and the War of Wolves demanded more and more power from us. But all magic comes at a price, a balance that the humans weren't respecting."

"Like the giving of one's soul for a dying wish," I murmured, studying a painting of a golden scale weighing two orbs—one golden, one emerald. The gold was the same shade that now scarred Calla's body, the emerald a perfect match to Sawyn's lightning bolts. My limbs felt light. My fingers tingled as I mindlessly turned through the pages.

"The creation of monsters needed a counterbalance. Their creation brought dark magic into the world." Navin continued on quicker as I whipped my head toward him. "That dark magic found the first hosts that would claim it. It turned some on both sides into the first sorcerers." I sucked in a sharp breath. "In the end, humans were so plagued by the beasts that they'd created, and the sorcerers that had turned to the darkness because of their creation, that they begged the Wolves to save them. Humans vowed they'd lay down their magic and never bring dark magic into the world again. They knelt to the Wolves, promised that they'd make them kings and Gods if they saved us." I gaped at the pages. "That is where our stories can agree at least."

"When Rasil's grandfather created that samsavet?" I whispered as my heartbeat thundered in my ears. "That created dark magic."

"At a terrible price. One he and I both paid for our whole lives along with the rest of our court." Navin's eyes glassed over. "The dark magic that samsavet created was claimed by Sawyn."

"By all the Gods." I braced my hands on the table to keep from toppling over. My cheeks flamed, my stomach clenched, and bile burned its way up my throat. "I thought sorcerers were created by death magic. I thought it was through their killing that the darkness took over."

"It is." Navin tilted his head, squinting, as if trying to figure out how to explain something so complicated to me. "But the killing is only the spark; without the creation of dark magic by the humans, there'd be no kindling for the flame. Without the creation of more monsters, there'd be no more dark magic in the ether for anyone to claim."

"You're saying if Rasil's grandfather hadn't conjured that monster, then Sawyn would've never existed? Olmdere would still be whole?"

"Yes."

"I feel like I'm going to be sick," I groaned, fanning myself with the music sheets. "And the Songkeepers?"

"There are so few of us left," Navin said. "There was a time when only one human in all of Aotreas still knew the eternal songs. Her name was Nahliel." He passed me a charcoal sketch and I recognized the shape instantly: Galen den' Mora.

"Ora's grandmother?"

"She made it her life's work to travel the continent and find those who still contained the spark of magic needed to wield songs. When she died, she wished for Galen den' Mora and her line still takes up the mantle of finding new Songkeepers all around the continent."

I scrutinized the sketch in my hands—a simple line drawing of Galen den' Mora high on a mountaintop. "How can you know who has this magic?"

"Little tests," he said. "Most of us never knew we possessed it. Most of us didn't even know such magic existed. We didn't realize the songs we'd sing for protection, for courage, for healing actually had power. I never knew my affinity for music was a gift from the Gods, nor did I know what I could do with it. There was a Songkeeper who rolled into our village, playing her music, and Rasil, my brother, and I all took to it straightaway. When I fled with my father, Rasil came with us. He took me to Valta, reunited us with grandparents he'd never known. It was here we found out Rasil came from a long line of Songkeepers. It was here that I met Ora." Navin stared down at his boots and rubbed the back of his neck. "If only my brother came with us."

I stiffened. "Your brother?" It dawned on me all at once. "This is the secret you wanted him to take to his grave."

Navin's eyebrow arched. "Could you imagine if Sawyn got her hands on this magic? If she could conjure new monsters at will? If she could control them? If she could create an army of fellow sorcerers?"

"She would've destroyed all of us," I said breathlessly. "So *you* can do all these things? You can create monsters?"

"I have the power to, though I don't know the specific song to conjure and control monsters. That song is kept in a *very* hard to access place so as not to tempt those who would use it for less than honorable reasons. It was hidden in plain sight, secreted away for safekeeping after what Rasil's grandfather did. I have never created a monster and will never try," Navin said decidedly. "I won't bring more dark magic into this world. I won't curse this land with more sorcerers." His eyes grew vacant again, and I knew he was going back to Olmdere as a child, reliving the tyranny of Sawyn all over again. "But I know where to find the eternal songs, yes."

"And Ora knows where to find them, too?" My eyes darted from one map to the other, landing on the detailed drawing of Damrienn. "Do you think the Silver Wolves know?"

"I think they know something. How much, I have no idea. If they know that the humans have a secret that could help them rule the entire continent if they could just unlock it," he said, "it would destroy the world."

"How many of you are there now?"

"You met most of them during the battle in Olmdere castle."

My eyes widened remembering the flurry of badges during the melee. "They were all Songkeepers?"

Navin nodded. "Ora had been summoning them every night since Calla set sights on Olmdere. Those songs Ora sang through the night were meant to call them home."

I racked my brain, remembering the tunes and ballads Ora would sing as we drifted off to sleep each night. I began to question every song I heard coming from them. What other powers could they wield? Was every moment with them an illusion? A manipulation?

"I just don't understand why?" I looked all around, scanning the ornate library. "That is one part I still can't comprehend. *Why* would Ora summon your entire order into battle to help a *Wolf*?"

Navin sighed, wandering from the table and dropping down into one of the upholstered leather chairs. "There is a divide amongst the Songkeepers now." He steepled his fingers and pressed them to his lips. "Those like Ora who want a world where Wolves and humans live side by side. Equals. Where we acknowledge that Wolves did save us long ago but that they hurt us now and perhaps there needs to be a balance, a harmony between us. No one bowing to the other anymore." His lips pursed and he looked at me. "And then there are those like Rasil and his grandfather."

"And what does Rasil want?"

Navin's eyes darkened. "To use whatever magic necessary for the world to revert back to a time when Wolves didn't exist here at all."

CALLA

BY THE THIRD DAY, BRIAR HAD STOPPED ASKING TO LEAVE Taigoska and go after Maez. According to Briar, Maez was dealing with her grief at the bottom of every available wine bottle in Sankai-ed. Sadie and Navin hadn't reappeared, and Maez didn't know how to get Galen den' Mora on the move again. The oxen apparently weren't budging. Briar had tried to encourage Maez to buy a horse and ride back to Taigos, but Maez wasn't responding well to her efforts. Leaving meant giving up hope that Sadie was still alive.

I felt devastated for my sister. Even as I mourned, at least I could do it with Grae by my side. My sister seemed desperate to comfort her mate, but now, with everything we knew about Briar's *engagement* to Evres, I wasn't letting my twin out of my sight. If Sadie's family was hunting for her, they'd be all too keen to snap up Briar, too.

I stared at my sister's reflection as she stood in front of the full-length mirror. I lounged on her bed, eating a bowl of candied almonds just like I had the day of her failed wedding to my now mate. Grae, Hector, and Mina played a Taigosi board game in the corner of Briar's suite—a game none of them seemed to fully understand the rules of.

"Shouldn't you be getting ready?" Briar asked the trio, as Hector knocked over a carved stone wolf from Mina's square.

Hector frowned down at his fighting leathers. "We are."

Briar smoothed down her sapphire satin dress that brought out the color of her eyes, her expression tight. "Grae, you at the very least can't be dressing like a soldier. You're the king consort of Olmdere."

"I'll put a crown on," he said as he moved his stone sword piece around the board.

Briar pinched the bridge of her nose. "At least put on a golden jacket or something!"

"I was joking, Briar," Grae said with a wink. "I'll go get dressed now." He passed a miniature glass orb to Mina and Hector, then threw his hands up in the air in a gesture I assumed meant he'd lost the game. Before leaving, Grae rounded the side of the bed, his hands bracketing on either side of me as he planted a long lavishing kiss on my lips. I knew that kiss. It was the "trying to goad me into bed" sort of kiss . . . not that I ever needed much convincing.

I started to rise off the bed when Briar commanded, "Calla, stay." Grae and I both frowned but I didn't move. "Grae, I trust you can go get changed on your own."

Grae gave my body a slow once-over that promised we would pick up where we left off soon and then he exited the room. I sighed and slumped back down on the pillow. Normally, I would've pushed back at Briar, but she needed this right now. Letting her take the lead with the Ingrid situation was the only thing keeping her from fleeing off to Valta to comfort Maez.

"You look gorgeous, Briar," I said, but that just made her look even more sad. "I promise to hold a ball in Olmdere as soon as Maez returns so she can see how beautiful her mate is." That seemed to perk her up a little.

"Don't get almond crumbs on your outfit," she scolded, but her eyes said, "thank you."

"What's your plan to charm Ingrid to our side now?"

"We need to stop thinking Ingrid will help us out of the goodness of her own heart," Briar said with a disappointed sigh. "She's too calculated for that. We need to beat her at her own game."

"And how are we going to do that?"

"Klaus," she said.

"Klaus?"

"I dance with him. I put some ideas in Ingrid's head," she said as if it was as easy as snapping her fingers. She held up two different teardrop earrings—one diamond, one sapphire—and scrutinized each one in her reflection.

"What *kind* of ideas are you planning on putting in Ingrid's head?"

"The kinds that involve Klaus and me."

An almond flew out of my mouth and across the room. "Excuse me?"

"Meanwhile," she continued as if we were discussing our favorite flavor of tea and not manipulating the Ice Wolf Queen, "you sidle up to Ingrid and make her think Klaus and I are hitting it off just as well as I'm going to make it *look* like we are. It will take barely a nudge, judging by her outburst in the greenhouse the other day. We'll put this idea in her head, one where *I* would make an excellent queen and that Klaus is very kingly himself."

"Are you trying to get me beheaded?" I glared openmouthed at her. "We need for her to help us, not slaughter us. You want me to make her think my twin is going to usurp her?"

"You will do it if you want her help," Briar insisted. "I've been watching the two of them since our arrival. I've seen how the pack responds to each of them, too. Ingrid needs Klaus's support. The Wolves instinctively flock toward him. Even Ingrid herself looks to him for his opinion, probably more than she should if you ask me. The night of our run, Klaus and Ingrid were both at the front of the pack, and I swear it felt like the others were following him."

"Patriarchal bullshit," I growled.

Mina tapped the table twice in a "here, here!" agreement. Hector rubbed his eyes in frustration as she moved a wolf across the board, clearly being beaten at another round of the game.

"If Ingrid thinks that such a relationship is even *remotely* a possibility, she will give you some soldiers and send us all on our merry ways at her earliest convenience," Briar said. "She'll need to get rid of us without rebuffing us now that I've delighted her court and ensnared her cousin's heart."

"Second cousin."

Briar shrugged. "No ensnaring will actually take place, of course," she said. "It just needs to appear that way to Ingrid for one perfect moment that rattles her enough to give in."

"I don't know, Briar," I muttered. "You have a way of melting every one of these Ice Wolves when they see you flouncing around."

She rolled her eyes. "If Valta and Damrienn are already questioning the validity of Ingrid's reign, she needs Klaus's support more than ever. If her pack starts to agree that they need a king more than a queen, it's all over for her. She'll want us out of her court and away from her pack, even if it means sacrificing a dozen of her best Wolves to help us rescue Ora."

I let out a low whistle. "For all your daintiness, Briar, Vellia has taught you well: you are actually an evil mastermind. I hope you know that."

She bowed to me in the mirror. "Thank you."

SADIE

I WANDERED THE HALLS, SEARCHING FOR A BED FOR THE NIGHT. I finally settled upon a room halfway down the third corridor, too tired to keep exploring the grounds. It was a simpler chamber than some of the more ostentatious stylings around the place, but everything from the bed to the wardrobe was made with fine materials and I liked how I could easily booby-trap the entrance to alert me to anyone entering . . . well, only one person.

I spent the evening pilfering through the drawers in the bedside table. My body was exhausted but my mind was still frantic. I lifted page after page of song sheets, ignoring them at first, but when I started to study the lyrics written between the bars, I realized—it wasn't a song at all but a letter.

I wondered if another secret message lay beneath the words, too. This note seemed to come from Taigos, the writer talking about performances and travel plans. I dropped the page and picked up another, my eyes widening at the name signed at the very bottom: Mina.

A knock sounded at the door and I jolted. Sweet Moon, I had reached that jittery kind of tired; I was practically swaying on my feet. But I needed to keep my wits about me in this place. Nothing was safe, especially not the person knocking on my door.

I debated not answering, just telling Navin to go away, but finally I relented and bitterly called, "Enter." As if I had any permission to give in this place. As if this wasn't just a prettier cell.

Navin peeked his head in, his eyes going from the lit candelabra to the dress hugging my figure and sandals on my feet. "Still awake."

"So perceptive." I folded my arms tight across my chest. "I don't suppose there's any point locking these doors when you can just whistle them open?"

Navin's pinched expression only enraged me further. Did he really think giving me some space over the course of a single day would sway me to see his side? Answers or no, he was my captor, my *enemy*.

"I can't open these locks," he assured me, gesturing to the door.

I hated the way that comforted me. It should be *him* locking his doors, *him* who was afraid that I'd prowl into his room at night and tear open his flesh with my teeth. Maybe I still would . . .

Navin nodded to the sheet music in my hand. "Planning on singing a tune before bed?"

"These are letters," I said, lifting the one in my hand.

"They are." Navin's eyebrows lifted, seemingly impressed.

I didn't want any of his validation. Even as he spoke, I was still plotting all the ways I could make him suffer once I was certain it wouldn't bring any suffering back onto me. That was a puzzle I still hadn't quite solved. Patience was never my strong suit. I wanted instant vengeance.

"So Mina is a Songkeeper." I shook my head. "I mean, I should've guessed. Everyone in Galen den' Mora was . . ." It felt so strange, people I thought I had a good read on, leading this completely different life.

"She's quite powerful in her own right," Navin said.

My eyes widened. I didn't know if it was the exhaustion or the litany of new information, but my mind instantly fled to the

Queen I'd left with a powerful magic wielder. I wondered if Mina was luring Hector in with her songs just as Navin was bespelling me. "Calla—"

"Calla is safe, even more so with Mina around," Navin said quickly. He held up a placating hand and I clenched my jaw at the sight of it. I didn't want his comfort. "I wished for Mina to return to Galen den' Mora with me, but she refused. She loves being a member of the Golden Court. She believes in what Calla is doing. You will never need to fear her disloyalty."

I huffed a bitter laugh. "I don't know." I looked him up and down. "I'm not so eager to start trusting sweet-natured musicians. I've been so, *so* wrong before."

"You aren't wrong about her." Navin leaned his head against the doorframe, the mottled bruises on his face shining in the candlelight. "I am so incredibly sorry, Sadie. But I will find a way to make it right."

I balled my hands into fists. Gods, it would feel good to smash his face in again. "You make this right by getting me out of here and then leaving me the fuck alone, you lying piece of shit."

I could tell he was trying to hide the hurt of my words. Or maybe it was just another act. Honestly, fuck him. I didn't need his sad little puppy dog eyes after he'd lied to me about *everything*. He'd locked me in a cell; he should be grateful he was only feeling the bite of my words and not my teeth.

"The way I see it, you have three choices," Navin said. "One: go along with my plan." He laughed mirthlessly. "Once we're out of here, you could easily overpower me if you still think I'm tricking you." I pursed my lips at that. Good. Let him not forget it. He lifted a second finger. "Two: kill me, try to best the samsavet, and flee. Or three: see if you can broker a better deal with Rasil when he returns."

"None of those sound particularly appealing."

"I know." He dusted his hands down his tunic, and it was only then I realized he had flour on them.

"Seems I'm not the only one who can't sleep."

"I'm making bhavi rolls," he said, watching me closely as the memory hit me.

I raised my eyebrows at that. He remembered. He'd taken me to dinner in Taigos, and we'd had these delicious little bread rolls stuffed with spices, honey, and glazed almonds. I'd joked I'd eat them every day if I could. I pinched off my heart from the many faces of this man: a baker, a songwriter, a magician, a liar. I couldn't wrap my brain around it. And I certainly wouldn't be lured back into trusting him with the promise of sweets of all things. I'd rather eat something bloody and raw anyway.

"I'm going to bed," I said instead, folding my arms. I'd sooner throw his baking in the sand than let him think he was winning me over.

"Okay." He lingered in the doorway. "Read the letters," he said, nodding to the song sheets in my hand. "You'll know I'm not lying about Mina's loyalty to Calla at least." I frowned and dropped onto the lumpy mattress. The whole bed creaked. "There are more comfortable bedrooms," Navin continued, as if he were finding any excuse not to leave me. "The one next door has the best mattress, I think."

I pinned him with a look as I stood and strode to the door. "I can sleep anywhere," I spat, gripping the door tighter. "After all, I'm just a dog, aren't I?" I slammed the door in his face before he could reply. I hoped Navin's heart sunk a little further with the snick of the lock.

I FLIPPED THROUGH A BOOK OF ANCIENT MAPS AS I PERCHED ON the kitchen table, eating my fourth bhavi roll. It wasn't until my stomach was painfully full that I licked the honey off my fingers and reached for the jug of freshly squeezed fruit juice.

I wondered if Navin had been up all night picking fruits and baking for me. Again, I had no sympathy for him. My forgiveness wasn't so easily won. I wouldn't be gently wooed into compliance. Not again.

But it was delicious . . .

No. That doesn't matter. Figuring out what is happening matters.

Now that Navin had steered me toward answers in the library, I was determined not to need him at all. I had a thousand questions right on the tip of my tongue—ones he could probably answer for me with no effort. But instead, I pored through tome after tome, searching for the answers the long way.

I'd stayed up most of the night reading Mina's letters to Ciara. Whoever this Ciara was, clearly the two of them were close friends. In letter after letter, Mina pleaded with Ciara to use any influence at their disposal to convince Rasil to support the Golden Court. It consoled me greatly to know Calla was safe with Mina; at least on that front, I hadn't entirely misjudged the musician.

I heard the scuffle of Navin's sandals long before he said, "I knew you'd like the juice."

He knew nothing about me.

I knocked the carafe off the table at that, knowing it made me petty, far more like a cat than a Wolf. The ceramic shattered, shards flying everywhere as juice splattered across the floor.

Navin, to my surprise, only let out a light laugh. "You'd saw off the branch you're sitting on just to watch it fall, hey?"

"Only if you were also on it. Goddess of stubbornness," I reminded him. "You think I'm only an animal, so I'm behaving like one."

"I said that so Rasil would leave you alone," he countered. "I thought he would retaliate after you nearly *choked me to death*," he added pointedly. A satisfied smile curved my lips at the memory. "I didn't want him to suspect how I truly feel."

I dramatically rolled my eyes at that. "If you felt anything at all, you would've been honest with me." I pressed my lips together, making a study of him. "The only thing I'm left to conclude is that I was some twisted obsession, a sick curiosity—"

"I would never think like that."

I picked up the book beside me and slid off the table. "Will you and your husband laugh about all this one day?" Chin high, I didn't meet Navin's eyes as I tried to walk past.

"Sadie—"

I knew before he even moved that he was going to reach out and try to grab me. I'd once been thrilled by the possessiveness of those hands, the confidence of his grip, but now . . . His hand had barely lifted when I moved, dropping the book I held and blindly reaching backward to grab the kitchen knife off the table behind me. My other hand grabbed Navin by the wrist and spun him, wrenching his arm until he barked out a cry. I slammed him into the wall. The tip of my blade was at his throat before he could even speak.

"You have a way of thinking you can just grab me whenever you like," I hissed, pushing my blade in for emphasis. "Let me make one thing abundantly clear, Navin Mourad." My nails bit into his wrist. "Every single time you touch me, it is only because *I* allow it." I threw the knife to the ground and released him, storming out the door as I said, "Remember that next time you think it's a good idea to stop me."

SADIE

WE NAVIGATED AROUND EACH OTHER THE NEXT FEW DAYS IN A wary dance, giving each other space. It wasn't exactly friendly, but the tension between us seemed to ease like a fatigued muscle. I couldn't hang on to that white-knuckled panic any longer. We were like two caged wild animals deciding to not kill each other. Begrudging allies at best. All I needed was to get out of there with my hands unbound and I'd be free. I'd find Maez and get the fuck out of the desert and back to the Golden Court. And if Navin was the ticket to that future, then so be it.

I was wandering aimlessly through a new part of the building when Navin turned the corner and startled, clearly surprised to find me there. My fingers traced over a mosaic of a bright green dragon, a juvleck in its talons. Navin paused and considered the mural beside me.

I thought about saying, "If only you had a dragon in the mines, maybe your father would still be alive." But I couldn't summon the will to be that cold.

I was still furious at him, leaving him messes to clean and punishing him with my silence, but even I wasn't that cruel. The silence was beginning to nag at me too, and I selfishly was considering breaking it just to have a conversation again. Besides, no amount of research in the library would give me all the answers that lay within Navin's mind. Only he could recount what the past few years had been like.

And that was only if I could believe him.

"This is why I need us to go along with this plan," he said.

"What?"

"This." He tipped his head to the mosaic. "No more monsters. No more sorcerers."

He said it like a prayer he'd voiced a thousand times before.

"And how is me helping you going to do that?"

He paused as if calculating how exactly to explain and I wondered, too, if he was calculating how much to refrain from sharing. "Remember how I told you an eternal song was in a very hard to reach place?" he asked. "Well, Rasil wants me to retrieve it for us."

"The last thing the world needs is Rasil wielding a weapon like that," I said tightly. "Look what his grandfather did with that power."

"Agreed."

The speed with which he said that surprised me. He didn't seem particularly fond of Rasil, but to be willing to go against the orders of the head of your pack—sect—whatever they called it, that was bold.

"Though as much as I don't want Rasil to possess such a song," I continued, "I don't know how I feel about it being in your possession, either."

"I don't plan on keeping it," he said. "It's too dangerous."

I stole a quick glance at Navin as he studied the dragon. "So what are you thinking?"

"I go to retrieve the eternal song under the guise of bringing it back to Rasil, and then we run and take it to Calla in Olmdere, hide it somewhere safe where no human nor Wolf is tempted to use it."

I scrutinized him. "How do I know you're not just saying this to convince me to help you?"

"You don't," he said plainly. "But I know you would stop me if you thought I wasn't keeping up my end of the deal."

"I would." I folded my arms across my chest. "So this song is what's in Rikesh? In King Luo's possession?"

Navin nodded. "It's carved on an ancient vase. The King believes it to be one of his many pretty relics and nothing more."

"This vase is what Rasil wants you to trade me to Prince Tadei for?" The look in Navin's eyes told me everything. "Me in exchange for a song powerful enough to destroy the world. Wonderful."

"It will only be for show," Navin pleaded. "I wouldn't actually leave you there."

"Oh no," I said sarcastically. "I can't think of any way this half-baked plan could go awry."

"Trust me—"

"But I *don't* trust you!" I erupted, taking a giant step away from him. Where was that kitchen knife when I needed it? "I don't trust you one whit and you shouldn't trust me, either. I'm still debating ripping out your throat with my teeth."

His gaze darkened. "Is killing me the only way you'll forgive me?"

That only enraged me further. "Perhaps."

"Shift then."

"What?"

"Shift," he said.

I glared at him in disbelief for a second before finally realizing he was serious. I huffed a bitter laugh. Fine. If he wanted to play with fire, then I'd happily burn him to ash.

In a blink, my body started morphing, bones twisting and sinews snapping, fur sprouting and teeth elongating. The light fabric of my dress easily shredded around me, and I shook off the remnants, keeping my lupine eyes fixed on the human in front of me.

A low growl rumbled through my barrel chest, and I sniffed

the air, taking in his scent of ink and resin-coated bowstrings. I would tear into him until he only smelled of the copper tang of blood.

My lips lifted, baring my teeth, and I stalked forward, hoping he'd run.

Instead, Navin yanked off his tunic, baring his vulnerable skin to me and dropping to his knees. "You are so beautiful," he whispered more to himself. "And powerful and terrifying and completely and utterly hypnotic. If anyone were to fell me, let it be you."

I paused, one paw hovering above the tile floor as Navin spread his arms wide in surrender. The action felt so familiar, like a Wolf displaying their belly to their pack leader, his way of showing me that despite everything, I was still in control. It relieved me and irked me in equal measure. I thought he'd have more fight.

Foolish, foolish human.

I stalked closer, watching his neck pulsing with every beat of his racing heart. I bet even his blood tasted sweet, still laced with juice and bhavi rolls. I got close enough it would take nothing to reach out and lick off the sweat beading across his chest, his limbs shaking in fear. How easily I could snap his neck.

"Do it," he said as I flashed my glinting canines again.

I snapped at the air and Navin squeezed his eyes shut but neither did he run nor cower nor beg.

"I'd rather die with your jaws around my throat than have you hate me forever."

I let out a disgusted huff. Killing him and hating him forever were not mutually exclusive. Mouth poised, maw open, I inched closer and his throat bobbed.

"But know this," he said, his voice growing deeper. "If you let me go now, I will never stop wanting you. I can't. I won't. Kill me now or I will keep fighting for this, for us. I'm yours, Sadie. I never lied about that."

There it was—the fight—I needed and craved it, that duality

of the soft and hard edges that melded into one. I needed the softest apologies and the fiercest promises and everything in between.

I froze, pulling my teeth away from his skin.

No. I didn't need anything from him. I shouldn't want him at all. Not after everything he'd done.

I didn't know what this was—this spell he'd put on me, this magic he cursed me with. How could I tell what was even real anymore? But it didn't matter, I knew, even without a monster lurking in the sand, I wouldn't be able to kill him. His soul had its hooks in me. So I simply turned and prowled away, losing my resolve with every step to go on hating him forever.

CALLA

THE ICE WOLVES CRAMMED INTO THE GIANT BALLROOM, THE crowd so tight it was nearly impossible to navigate through. Wolves, in all their splendor, danced and mingled in silver and diamond-studded attire—gossamer gowns as white as snow, shined silver boots the shade of moonlight, and enough jewelry that the room rattled with their movements, cutting over the music. The crowd was filled with a glittering lack of color, the ballroom overflowing onto the frozen balconies that looked out over the city. A ten-piece orchestra played for the ballroom and a lone violinist played for the balcony.

I hung close to Mina. She was wrapped head to toe in furs to keep warm. Meanwhile, I was overheated in my golden coat and tails, my thick hair in loose curls around my face making my cheeks hot. The warmth from the ballroom seeped out through the open windows, enough to fight off the winter's chill. It was nice out here away from the throng, but I knew I would eventually have to go in and participate in plan Manipulate the Ice Wolf Queen.

"I hate this," I signed to Mina and she smiled as she carried on playing. "You should be in a ball gown beside me right now."

She paused, tucking her violin and bow under her arm to sign, "I am a musician. Politics is your game." She gave me an incredulous look. "Let me perform." She paused for a moment as if debating herself before adding, "The music will help."

She carried on playing and the sound of her song did actually slow down my racing heart a little. I spotted Briar moving through the crowd, her fan fluttering to catch my attention. I locked eyes with her and nodded.

"See you in a bit," I said to Mina. She waved her bow at me and kept on playing.

Briar breezed through the crowd, and they all seemed to part for her. She was a beautiful blue beacon in a sea of white and silver. Klaus worked his way through the crowd toward her, and the two of them quickly struck up a lively conversation.

I found Grae next to Ingrid, chatting with similar joviality although the hoops of Ingrid's glittering ball gown were so wide that Grae stood beyond arm's reach.

"Ah, there you are." Grae's smile broadened as he reached out to me and pulled me into a lingering kiss. I wanted to tilt my head back and melt into him more, but I knew my crown would slip right off my head and clatter to the floor. Grae broke the kiss and wrapped his hand around my waist, pulling me into his side.

Ingrid watched us, a mixture of scrutiny and some kind of sadness, longing maybe, sketched across her face. I wondered if she had any lovers. I wondered if she ever got lonely on her frozen throne.

"Your sister is quite the charmer," she said, falling straight into Briar's trap.

I turned to find Briar and Klaus at the center of the ballroom. Briar's head was thrown back in laughter and Klaus beamed down at her. Judging by the look on his face, Briar's misguided attempt to only *appear* to ensnare Klaus's heart was most certainly failing. They twirled around the ballroom like something straight out of a storybook, drawing everyone's gazes.

"They certainly make quite the pair," I said, tilting my head and acting like I was admiring them. "Very regal."

Grae let out a little hum of agreement.

"Yes," Ingrid said with an air of boredom. "Such a shame your sister will never be a queen."

"Who knows." I shrugged, pretending to be just as casual about the tense topic. "Lines of succession change all the time. Who knows what will happen to either of us." Ingrid paused for such a brief moment that I almost missed it, but it was there. My words had landed their target. Now time for a hasty retreat. "Anyway," I said with a light laugh. I turned to Grae. "Shall we get another drink?"

We bowed our heads to Ingrid and she bowed back, the two of us skirting away before I could undo the work I'd done. Too heavy of a hand and Ingrid would be enraged, too light and she'd never consider it.

"Is she still looking at them?" I whispered to Grae. He twisted half back to steal a glance at Ingrid.

"She's staring daggers at Briar," Grae said and I pinched my lips together to keep from laughing. "Hector's talking to her now," Grae added and I had the urge to look back at our friend. I wondered why he would put himself in the line of Queen Ingrid's wrath, but maybe he was trying to stoke her suspicions as well.

"We're going to have to rescue Briar before the end of the night," I said. "I have a feeling she'd appreciate our help *detangling* from Klaus."

"He's a fool if he thinks those fluttering lashes are real," Grae said. We both looked over at the two of them, and Klaus had pulled Briar closer, the two of them dancing as if they were the only people in the room. "Maez is going to kill him," Grae muttered.

"She told Maez what she was doing, but . . . Maybe we should intervene?" I turned to move into the crowd of Ice Wolves when Grae's hand landed on the crook of my arm and he pulled me back.

"Give them a few more dances, little fox. She trained her whole life for this, remember?" he murmured as I let out a little whine, folding my arms across my chest. "And stop staring at them like that. Come on—let's go rub elbows, find ourselves some more allies." He paused, studying me. "You're going to have to stop glowering."

"I wasn't taught how to hide my feelings like you and Briar," I bit out. "I was taught how to use them to *kill* people."

Grae grimaced, sucking a breath through his teeth. "Okay, maybe we'll work up to the elbow rubbing." I tried to mold my expression into a hardened neutral one, but I was certain it was still far from pleasant. "Calla."

"I can't help it," I muttered, worrying my lip as I watched my sister swirl around the ballroom. "We need this. It's too important to fail."

"You staring at them won't do us any favors." Grae stepped in front of me, breaking my line of sight. "You need to relax. Let Briar work her magic."

I grabbed a flute of sparkling wine from a silver tray, swigged the whole thing back in one gulp, and set the glass back down before the server had time to zip past.

"That's not relaxed," Grae said from the corner of his mouth.

I was buzzing with nerves now, bouncing on the balls of my feet. "Distract me then."

Without missing a beat, Grae's lips landed on the shell of my ear, his warm breath making my skin tingle. "I hear the greenhouses are beautiful this time of evening."

I turned in his light hold and found his brow arched expectantly, his dark eyes hungry.

Touché, mate.

I bit the corner of my lip at that look and he reached out and tugged it free with his thumb, and Gods, I wished he'd done it with his own teeth.

Hunger curled low in my belly as I whispered, "Lead the way."

The words had barely escaped my lips before Grae's fingers threaded through mine and we practically ran out of the ballroom and down the quiet hall. I couldn't contain my giddy laughter.

Would it always be this way? Would I always feel so ravenous for him? My mate.

Gods, I hoped so.

His desire for me was clearly just as keen judging from the way he kicked the greenhouse door open and dragged me inside, my laughter pealing off the glass ceiling.

"Wait," he commanded. His hands frantically fumbled with his belt as he turned to the glass door.

"Slow down," I laughed.

"No—it's not like that. Although I don't have any interest in slowing down once I get started," and I nearly melted even as I squinted at him in confusion while he removed his belt until he started looping it through the door handles and tied them closed. I let out a surprised giggle as he turned around with a feral grin. "No interruptions," he rumbled, making my core clench.

He stormed toward me, not stopping as he stooped and hoisted me one-handed up and onto his shoulder. I let out a surprised squeak, holding my crown to my head, as we plunged deeper into the gardens. Broad leaves whacked into us like we were trekking through a jungle.

"Where are we—"

My words were silenced as Grae set me down against the back wall of the greenhouse. Behind the glass was a wall of glittering snow. In front of me was the thick foliage we'd just walked through, obscuring the path. We stood on a semicircle of white stones, cushions dotted around it. A beautiful space that looked designed for quiet contemplation, which was the furthest thing from my mind. Starlight beamed down from the glass roof, refracting and sending skitters of moonlight dancing across the plants as if we were floating in the middle of a constellation. It was magical, the perfect angle that could only be seen from this very spot.

"How did you know this place was here?" I asked.

"This used to be a favorite hiding spot when I'd visit Taigoska as a child," Grae said, his hands encircling me and pulling me against his chest as I reached out and rubbed a soft leaf between my thumb and forefinger. "I dreamed of showing you one day."

I released the plant and trailed my fingers up Grae's biceps and into his dark hair. "What else have you dreamed of showing me?"

My words unleashed him, and then we were a flurry of mouths and desperate hands. I loved this. The frenzy, the unending need for him.

I dropped my crown to the ground and carelessly knocked Grae's off as his tongue plundered my mouth. His fingers dug into my belt, frantically unbuckling it. I moaned into his mouth, and he snarled back, our Wolves howling to each other from inside our minds.

He yanked down my trousers as I hastily kicked off my boots, stripped bare from the waist down. Grae didn't waste a second, dropping to his knees before me. His hands kneaded the flesh of my ass as he pulled me toward him. My eyes fluttered closed as I felt his hot breath tickle through the hair between my legs. One single inhalation and then his tongue was licking up my folds and parting my flesh. I groaned, one hand fisting in his hair as my other slid across the slick glass behind me. Condensation beaded across the pane from our wildness. My palm mark squeaked across the wet glass as Grae's tongue circled my pulsing clit.

My moan echoed through the quiet space. Grae hitched one knee up over his shoulder and continued to feast on me. My head fell back, banging into the glass, the pleasure building tighter and higher like a hot coil ready to explode. My hand slipped again, squeaking across the glass, and I nearly toppled sideways. Grae clenched onto my hips tighter to keep me from falling face-first into the stones below as we both let out a chuckle.

"Grae." My voice came out all husky and raw as I steadied myself on his shoulders.

I dropped my foot back onto the stones below me and pushed

him backward until he was lying splayed across the ground. I straddled him, my hands frantically freeing his cock from his trousers, happy for a second reason he'd already taken off his belt. Grae's hooded eyes watched me with lust-laced heat as I guided him toward my dripping core. His fingernails dug into my hips as I lowered onto him, my head rolling back with the mounting pleasure. I didn't know how long I'd be able to hang on. I was already teetering on the edge of an orgasm. The stress and anxiety of the day just made my movements more feverish. I needed this, *we* needed this—this anchoring to something real and raw and so far from our fears.

I rode him with wanton abandon, relishing in the feeling of him filling me over and over again. Grae's hips bucked, bouncing me upward, matching each of his movements with my own.

"Fuck, that's good," he groaned, his breathing so jagged I knew he was trying to hold himself back. That only spurred me on, working him faster until his eyes were clenched closed and he sputtered, "Calla, I—"

My matching moan silenced him, my hands fisting in his jacket and holding on for dear life as my orgasm tore through me. My cries of pleasure bounced off the glass, echoing through the whole greenhouse as Grae erupted with me. He gripped me so tightly, plunging back into me as he released again and again, our orgasms burning so long and bright that I saw stars.

I collapsed on top of him and his arms banded around me, holding me to his heaving chest. I buried my face in his neck, breathing in his scent, listening to his heartbeat slow. I kissed his skin, tasting his salty sweat and wishing we could stay in this quiet little secret place in the world. But even as my release echoed through me, I knew I had to go save Briar from Klaus's overzealous advances. I had a Queen to convince I was worthy of her aid. I had a court that needed my protection and humans in Damrienn who needed saving.

"That is my favorite kind of distraction," I murmured against Grae's skin.

"Certainly clears the mind."

"Now let's go find ourselves some more allies." My mate grumbled as I forced myself to get up and regroup from that quick burst of passion, but he soon followed. We both knew we couldn't linger here.

In another life, Grae and I would stay all night, watching the stars and listening to each other's beating hearts. But that dream would only be a reality once I secured the future for us all.

SADIE

I WANDERED THROUGH THE GARDENS, PICKING AN AFTERNOON snack from the citrus trees on my way back to the library. The air was laced with the scent of blossoming tropical flowers and vanilla. The garden was truly magical, and I spent most of my waking hours there when I wasn't in the library combing through scrolls and stories.

It was a daunting task relearning and scrutinizing our ancient history through a completely different lens. Sometimes the Wolf and human stories aligned, sometimes they deviated entirely from each other, and I struggled to parse fact from fiction. Too many words, too many translations . . . When I closed my eyes, I still saw the words inked upon the page, felt the parchment rubbing across my fingertips, and heard pages being flicked like a shuffled deck of cards.

I took another breath, letting the heady jasmine and vanilla replace the dusty must of old tomes. I idled about the garden, taking another deep inhale, my scent superseding all my other senses. At the center of the garden, I found the tiled well and meandered over.

As I reached out for the golden bucket, Navin's voice said, "Don't."

Hand still hovering midair, I looked over my shoulder at him. "Why are you always lingering?"

Navin had been a constant shadow since the day I shifted, watching me from across the library as I flicked through every book I could get my hands on. Smart of him to keep his distance. Despite losing the resolve to kill him outright, I still was debating whether I could pull off a light stabbing. Of course, that wouldn't lend itself well to this ploy that Navin actually had control over me. If Rasil truly believed it when he returned, he was more of a bloody fool than I gave him credit for.

"Why are you hovering around like an annoying little gnat?" I asked again when Navin didn't immediately answer me.

He plucked a bright pink fruit from the branch above him, its soft flesh denting in his grip. "Because you're new to this place and you don't know its rules," he said, shining the fruit on his shirt before taking a bite.

"And one of the rules is don't touch the bucket?" I asked. "Is it magical?"

"Yes."

I look at him skeptically.

"It's a whispering well," he said through a mouthful of fruit. He wiped the back of his hand across his lips. "We use it to communicate with other Songkeepers, but if you don't know the right song, you might end up talking to the wrong well on the other end. It takes practice. I've accidentally scared a few farmers in my time."

I chuckled, imagining the frightened person hearing voices echoing up their well. That would certainly be a story to share around the fire. I lowered my hand and backed away from the well, turning instead toward a stone bench. I perched on the seat, staring up at the purple flowers that rambled over the archway.

"Could we contact Maez through the whispering well?"

"Does Maez often frequent wells? The Songkeepers know which ones to go to and when. If Maez even went to a well, the likelihood we'd synchronize our times seems improbable."

"Great," I muttered, dropping my head in my hands. What I'd give for a confirmation she was okay. But as the breeze blew through the trees and water trickled across the stones, I couldn't seem to summon the same panic I'd felt in the days preceding.

Navin hummed to himself as he ambled closer, and I wondered what magic he was casting. Did he ever hum just for mindless enjoyment? Was there always a reason? Was he controlling my emotions with his songs even now?

"You look tired," he said finally as he took another bite of food.

"I wonder why," I muttered. "I think I've read an entire shelf of books in your extensive library, and even then, I've only scratched the surface."

"I can tell you whatever you want to know."

"I don't want anything from you." I folded my arms across my chest to keep my hands from picking at my fingernails. Gods, I missed my knives. The kitchen ones just weren't the same.

"You need to rest."

"I need answers before Rasil returns," I countered.

"What answers?"

"All of them."

"Okay, well, let's start with one."

"I found another song sheet—a letter between you and Rasil—and the endings were all of the feminine neutral form?" The first question that popped into my mind was clearly not what Navin was expecting. "Why did Rasil call you that?"

Navin paused, then looked at me. "Are you familiar with the word 'avist'?"

"No."

"It's a Taigosi human word," he said with a shrug. "It means I'm indifferent to all genders. That's why Rasil called me that."

I blinked at him. This was just another way I didn't know Navin at all. "So when I call you *he* . . . ?"

"I don't care."

The wheels in my mind were turning so fast I couldn't keep up with them. "And if I called you *she*?"

"I also wouldn't care."

"But Rasil at least once called you she?"

"Which I'm also equally indifferent to." Navin leaned against a palm tree and flashed me a grin.

"But do you prefer one to the other?"

"No." His grin widened. "That's kind of the whole point."

"So you're like the Olmderian word 'nezaim' . . ."

"No."

"What do you mean 'no'?" I asked, my voice increasingly exasperated. Navin only laughed. "Speak!"

I was learning not only an entirely different language, but concepts that the Wolves had never welcomed. Everything was so rigid. There were men and women. Men were meant to lead and women meant to follow. Somewhere deep within me I'd always resented those notions but neither had I questioned changing them. As a warrior, I knew my power, but Wolf Kings would never even let women rule let alone embrace the concept of more than two genders like the humans did.

"Nezaim feel they belong in all of the other words and prefer for all the other words to be used for them."

"And you . . . just don't care?"

"I feel detached from the concept entirely." He shrugged. "When you travel to as many corners of the continent and learn as many new words and customs as I have, trying to encapsulate oneself with a single word seems too reductive. Call me what you will. I remain the same."

"But . . ."

He tried to hide his laughter as my mind raced. "You're looking at me like I just said I had dinner with an ostekke."

"I never knew about any of this! My world feels like it's exploding!" I barked, rising to a stand. "Until Calla ran off, I only ever knew that humans had different customs, and those were never elaborated upon nor were we ever encouraged to learn more about them. Gods, some things were outright forbidden." I waved a hand wildly between the two of us. "Then I learned in

Olmdere there were eight genders and learned what all of them meant and figured the other kingdoms would have some sort of amalgamation of them and now you're saying there's even more."

"There's infinite."

I clenched a fist to my gut. "My stomach hurts," I grumbled as I started to push past him and back toward the library. I needed some more boring old histories to calm down.

"I thought you hated me." Navin turned and tailed me like his normal lingering self. "Why are you so concerned with calling me the right thing?"

"I hate you for a lot of very good reasons. Imprisoning me against my will for instance." I turned to look at him one last time, my eyes promising my words. "But this, this isn't why I hate you. I'll call you by the right name as I slit a knife across your throat for lying to me."

Navin grinned. "There she is."

WE ATE DINNER IN THE GARDEN, UNDER THE OPEN SKY. I'D GIVEN up on my attempts to avoid Navin. The questions he had sparked in me never seemed to stop, and I didn't want to page through the whole library to get more answers.

There was a whole history, a whole system of magic, I had never known about. In the whirlwind of that thought, I'd almost forgotten everything that had transpired between us. Navin acted like we were allies, as if we were both thrown into this sordid arrangement together. But who knew what would happen once the others came back.

"I think my voice is growing hoarse." Navin chuckled and took a sip of his wine. "We still have one more day before Rasil returns. You can ask me more in the morning."

I yawned and stretched my arms above my head, my body finally feeling comfortable and well-fed. "Am I to go back to the dungeons tomorrow?" Navin cut me an incredulous look. "Do you have magic that can force me? Because you and I both know if it came to a hand-to-hand fight, I'd win."

His lips curved. "Agreed."

"Will they expect me to be bound and back in a cell when they return?"

Navin swallowed. "I want to get us out of here. If you can play their game a little longer, they will send us on our way with you as my prisoner."

I scoffed. "As if you could keep me on a leash."

He grinned. "Maybe I could," he goaded. "I have more tricks up my sleeve than you think."

"So I need to play the role for your husband until we leave this place?"

Navin's lips thinned at the word "husband" but he nodded. "Only in front of Rasil. Only until we can get out of here."

"Do you still love him?" The words tumbled out, and I frowned into my cup of wine for loosening my tongue.

"No," Navin said softer. "Not for a long time."

I rubbed the back of my neck, the silence between us eating away at me again. I still didn't know if I could trust Navin, but I knew I needed to get out of this place, and if letting the humans think they had the upper hand would do it, then I would play along. Once we got to Sankai-ed and found Maez, then she and I would decide together whether we helped retrieve this eternal song or left Navin in the dust.

"Do you think Maez is still alive?" I asked, my voice breaking a little thinking of her. She and I had been best friends since we were pups. The thought of anything happening to her made me ache.

"She's alive," Navin said with a nod. "Galen den' Mora is the safest place in all of Aotreas . . . once you're inside, that is."

"The songs written around the outside of the wagon?"

"You're catching on," he said. "They are wards and songs of protection."

"Can magical songs be written on objects to protect them?"

"No."

"But the wagon—"

"Galen den' Mora is a dying wish; it sings its own songs if you listen close enough." Navin sighed wistfully. "The magic must be felt, heard, or sung—even if it's only into our own minds, sometimes it's enough. But the louder it is, the more powerful."

I shook my head. "In Durid, when the Silver Wolves attacked us . . ."

"No song could've protected us from that many Wolves," he said. "I tried . . . tried to sing into my mind, tried to hold that protection for us. But remembering songs when fists are flying at your face isn't exactly easy. After that right hook from the big one, I could barely remember my own name let alone my magic."

I swallowed the lump that'd formed in my throat, remembering his bloodied, brutalized face. He bore some of the scars still—the nick in his eyebrow, the fading scar down his jaw. "You held your own for a while there."

"I tried not to," he countered. "But when I thought of them hurting you, I couldn't hide my fighting skills. You seemed too preoccupied to notice."

"Maybe I didn't want to notice. Maybe I wanted to consider myself the superior fighter."

"You are the superior fighter."

I huffed. "Fat lot of good it did us."

"They bound and gagged us," Navin reminded me. "But even without the gag, songs still don't heal as fast as a Wolf's shifting. Our lesser magic is only slightly faster than a normal, non-magical healer." He stared up at the cloudy sky above us. "I thought for certain we were going to die."

"We nearly did," I said, the guilt seeping from my pores, leaving an invisible sticky shame that only I could see. I'd carried that shame, that panic, for months, thinking that I had led Navin into the Silver Wolves' path, thinking that I was almost responsible for his death.

He leaned his shoulder into me. "You saved us." I dropped my head into my hands, pain rolling off me. The memories flashed through my mind like flashes of lightning. "Sadie?"

"I thought I had put you in the worst danger of your life. I thought you were this sweet musician and I felt responsible for your suffering. I was *sick* that I had done that to you, ruined someone so kind and pure. But you were never that, were you?" I stood too quickly. "I'm going to bed."

Navin caught my arm as I spun.

"Remember what I said about you grabbing me," I warned, but neither did I move.

Navin waited a breath before saying, "I'm sorry I didn't tell you who I was. When we met, you were pretending to be a human, too, remember? We thought we needed to keep our true selves from each other then, but whatever burden you carry for letting me get hurt, I absolve you of it." He touched a hand to his throat where I'd choked him. "And of the pain you've inflicted since," he added with a chuckle. "I've known danger, known pain, my whole life."

"I thought they were going to kill you," I whispered, choking on the words. "And I thought it was my fault."

"None of this is your fault," he said. "I chose this life."

"But you did not choose me!" My chest heaved, my heart cracking open as I laid it all bare for him. The truth echoed between us. He hadn't chosen me, just kept me on a too-long string, reeling me in again and again. I still felt gripped by a fear and shame that I never needed to feel because he was never the person I thought he was.

I cleared my throat and folded my arms tighter around myself, not wanting to face him anymore and all the feelings still being unearthed inside of me. All of it was just a manipulation. All of it was from his songs and secret power. All of it was a lie. "Just . . . I'm going to bed."

SADIE

THE CRACK OF A WHIP SOUNDED OVERHEAD, AND I SHOT UP from my bed. The satin sheets slid down my body and my pulse raced as the thunder rolled in. It was lightning. Just a storm. I let my breathing slow. I was safe.

Or as safe as a prisoner surrounded by monsters that would tear her to pieces the moment she stepped outside could be.

The skies seemed to open, and a deluge of rain poured down. The sound was deafening, torrents falling from the sky. I leapt out of bed and threw open my door. Both ends of the hall were obscured by waterfalls of rain. Navin's room was straight across the atrium, and I wondered if he lay awake in his own bed listening to water pour down from the roof.

My fingertips buzzed and I stalked toward that wall of water. Another rumble of thunder rolled in, echoing across the tiles. The reverberations shook through my body, and I braced myself against the wall. A flash of lightning lit up the whole space, and I saw the shadow of a figure on the other side of the water.

My chest rose and fell faster, knowing that exact silhouette. Was he coming for me? To check on me during the storm?

The deafening drum of thunder and clatter of rain was like a song all its own, pounding like a war drum and ratcheting up my pulse. I wondered if this storm song came with its own sort of magic, too. Time seemed to stand still, and I wondered if only for this moment the sounds could drown out my righteous anger, my wary heart. Maybe tonight I didn't need my weapons drawn. I could pick them back up with the rising sun.

I reached my hand to the waterfall and Navin did the same in mirror to my own. We stood there in this strange limbo, neither of us seemingly wanting to break the spell. Finally, I extended a hand out through the water, the coolness soothing my hot skin, and that hand grabbed mine and pulled me through.

I let out a surprised laugh as Navin yanked me into the rainstorm. I stretched out my hands in supplication, feeling the thousand little droplets dance across my skin. He smiled at me, his chest heaving in unison to my own as the rain washed over us.

"Rahm Bek Annataf," he said, closing his eyes and tilting his head skyward. "This storm comes only once a year." He had to shout to be heard over the rain. "Every plant and animal in Lower Valta lives and dies by this storm."

"Except for here," I said, spinning in a circle, my hair flying out behind me, spraying water as I spun. My feet slipped on the tiles and Navin's hand shot out and steadied my elbow. His laughter made my skin buzz along with the heavy rain massaging over my limbs.

"The rains of Rahm bless you," he said. "The Songkeepers believed they were magical. Many a song was written in their honor."

I could feel it. The magic consuming me, the storm seeming to wash everything else away.

Slicking my bangs out of my eyes, I paused to take in Navin's now soaked-through shirt. It clung to the lean muscles of his torso, creasing around his biceps and pecs in a way that made it hard to look away. I knew my nightdress, too, was similarly glued to my muscles and curves.

"Can your magic control the weather?" I asked.

Navin shook his head, water dripping from his brow, nose, and lips with every movement. "We thank Rahm in our songs, but I cannot summon storms. Even if it was possible, I think that would be greater magic, and I wouldn't want to pay that price."

"Like creating sorcerers," I said.

Navin wiped the rain out of his eyes. "Yes."

I walked slowly around the heptagonal space, my feet sliding across the slick tiles. Navin fell into stride beside me. "You hummed to keep that beast from attacking us," I said as we turned another side. My pulse raced as it all started to come together. All the things he hid from me. All the magic in plain sight.

"Yes," was his only response.

"You used your song to lose Maez and me in Taigos."

"Yes."

"You saved yourself from falling with magic."

"Yes."

I choked on the last words. "You made me fall in love with you."

His footsteps faltered and I kept walking, not knowing if the hot liquid on my cheeks was rain or tears. That's what this was after all, wasn't it? Love. There was no other explanation. He'd warped my mind, twisted and confused me into falling for him. Every ounce of logic in me told me he was a bad idea, but I couldn't stop thinking about him, couldn't stop *wanting* him, even when I knew he'd lied to me.

"Sadie," he said, reaching for me.

"It was all just magic," I muttered, easily maneuvering out of his hold.

As I rounded the next corner, he sidestepped me, his tall frame blocking my path. "You don't get to just say that and walk away from me," he panted, rain bucketing down upon us.

"Of course I do." I tried to duck under one of the palm leaves to move around him, but his hand splayed across my belly and pushed me back, turning me until I leaned against the slippery tiled walls.

Our eyes locked, and I knew he was thinking of that day I held a knife to his throat, knew he was remembering my threat:

know that every time you put your hands on me it is only because I've allowed you to.

When I didn't move, Navin pinned me to the wall with his chest, the wet fabric of our clothes meeting. I could've slipped from his hold, I could've twisted his arm or broken his wrist, but instead I stood stock-still, staring up into his eyes with hurt in my own. How dare he make me feel this way for him?

His hand reached out, sweeping wet strands of my hair behind my ear as he gently shook his head. "There is no magic in the world that can do that," he said, his hand bracketing my jaw as his thumb swept across my bottom lip. "And you, Sadie Rauxtide, would be the last person compelled to feel anything you did not want to. You're more stubborn than any magic."

I stared up into his dark eyes as they crinkled at the sides, a quick flash of a smile before his gaze drifted back to my mouth. I panted as though I'd been running, trying to catch a full breath as the skies poured down upon us.

"I shouldn't feel anything for you."

Navin's cheeks dimpled. "Nor I you," he said. "I spent my life vowing to protect humans from Wolves, not falling in love with them."

His words hit me all at once and my eyes flared. He loved me. *We* loved each other. I could still hate him, still guard my heart from this terrible, traitorous feeling, but there was no denying that feeling had a name. And it made no sense and it probably never should've been, but it was true.

"This was always a terrible idea," I said, half-heartedly shoving on his chest. "Even before I knew you had magic, we never made any sense."

I shoved him again, and Navin caught my wrists and held them to his chest as if he knew exactly how I needed him to fight with me, to show his backbone and not let me walk away.

"We make sense *because* of my magic," he said. "I don't know how, but you fell for the real me, not the ruse. Somewhere deep down you knew I was more than what I seemed. A guardian of magic and a Wolf soldier are not as dissimilar as you wish to believe." I pulled against his grip, testing him again, but he pulled me back into him, his ever-tightening hold making my lips part as his piercing eyes dropped to my mouth. "We both serve a higher purpose. We're both loyal to our chosen families. We've both fought and grieved and suffered to protect those we care about."

I scoffed. "You're no fighter."

A challenge. One my Wolf needed to see fulfilled: fight me, chase me. For once, Gods, let you be the predator and me your prey.

His eyes darkened, fueling my desire. "You still think that?" His grip tightened on my wrists, his large hands easily cuffing them like manacles, and my skin rippled with gooseflesh. "Then why do you think you fell for me? Not magic. The real answer."

My lips curved into a smile. Time to see how much he could really do. He thought he could immobilize me so easily? By simply *holding* my wrists? Fast as a snow snake, I twisted, driving my elbow into his sternum. He let out a grunt of air as I stomped on his foot and ripped my hands free. Except he was faster than I anticipated. His hands looped around my center, hoisting me into the air and dragging me back against him. I twisted in his hold, elbowing him in the ear and kicking out his knee. When he dropped, I hit the ground and ran through the nearest hallway, through the waterfall, spilling into the hallway on the other side. My feet slipped under me like I was running on ice, but I kept my balance.

Navin had caught up to me in two short strides. He grabbed me and I whirled, punching him in the side with a laugh. Dodging out of the next blow, he chuckled and spun me back into the wall. Before I could land another punch, his broad hand lifted my jaw and his lips landed on mine. All sense of battle vanished as I lifted on my toes, finally allowing the frenzy of fighting to morph into a frenzy of lust.

His tongue licked into my mouth, pulling a moan from me as his free hand skimmed up my wet body. I shoved him away, growling, one last fleeting attempt, but when he just stood there, waiting for me to decide if this is what I truly wanted, I knew I was done with these games. Panting, I reached for him, practically willing his body into mine. He found the clasps at my shoulders and pulled the pins free, pulling the wet fabric down my body without breaking our kiss. I stepped out of my wet dress, pulling open the V of his shirt and then ripping it the rest of the way.

He laughed against my mouth as his shirt hit the ground with a wet splat. He lifted me up by my ass, my back sliding up the tiles and my legs hooking around his hips. He unbuckled his belt and freed himself as I ground myself into his belly, writhing and desperate.

His hands found my hips and he stilled me. "I love you," he said, forcing me to meet his eyes. "Even if I shouldn't. Even if it makes no sense. I love you, Sadie. Every song in my soul sings your name."

My hands gripped Navin tighter, desperate for this feeling to deepen even further, knowing exactly how I wanted to take him. I still feared the truth of everything I was feeling, but I needed his body so desperately it was going to drive me mad.

"And you love me," Navin rumbled, the claiming in his voice making me ache with desire.

His cock was poised below me, waiting, and I couldn't bear the anticipation, needing all of him. I let out a snarl as I moved against him, wanting to be filled and hating him for his cursed patience. He'd wait all night for me to acknowledge his words just to torture me. I knew he would, knew he saw all the ways I still pushed him away.

"I hate you!" One last protest. One last vestige of strength but my grip was slipping.

"No. You don't." He rocked his hips, the tip of him rubbing against me, zapping me with such acute pleasure it felt like a lightning strike.

"Yes—"

"No," he said quietly, but with a strength like the rumbling thunder. If he put me down right now, my legs would not hold me. But he wasn't putting me down. He would do this forever. Hold me and tease me and get what he wanted from me. He'd told me he loved me and he knew I loved him back.

And I cursed him and thanked him in equal measure for making me say it, making me face the torrent of undeniable emotions inside. He and I both knew there would be no coming back from this moment. Might as well lay it all bare.

"Yes," I moaned, my hand finding his cock and positioning him at my entrance.

His eyes guttered, a groan pulling from his throat, but he didn't move. "Yes, what?"

I looked up at the tiled ceiling, droplets tracing down my skin between us, my chest heaving, and I prayed to the Moon Goddess to forgive me as I said, "Yes, I love you."

He thrust up into me, cutting off my words in a sharp moan. The pain that had been in my heart shattered as his claiming pulled me apart and put me back together. My head rolled back, leaning against the tiled wall, as I reveled in the sensation of him, so deep, so full. My thighs quivered around him. Gods, he felt so good. He pulled out slowly inch by inch and slid back in, stretching me each time in the most delicious way. I didn't think humans could fuck as good as Wolves, but I was very, *very* happy to be mistaken.

I let out a high-pitched whine and dug my fingernails into his back. Tilting my hips, riding him as he drove back into me. My breasts bounced with each thrust and Navin dropped his head to suck one hardened nipple into his mouth. I cried out, the feeling making everything happening between my legs even more heightened. My fingers delved into his wet hair and held him to my breast as he tested my nipple with his teeth and then sucked again.

"Yes," I panted, and his hips moved faster. I slid up and down the tiles, completely at his mercy as he impaled me onto him again and again. I clawed down his back, desperately hanging on as he drove harder and deeper, hitting that spot inside me that made my eyes cross and my moan catch in my throat.

"Sadie," he groaned against my breast, and I knew by the erratic movements of his hips he was close and just that thought alone pushed me higher toward my own release.

One hand strayed from my ass, shifting to my throbbing clit. One long finger snaked between us and he began circling me. The sensations were too much. I was practically scrambling up the wall away from the building power of my orgasm. I clawed up Navin's back as he pumped into me faster, that finger circling my swollen bud. With a broken cry, I came.

Lightning flashed outside, mirroring the bright lights shooting within me. My body clenched around Navin, pulling his own climax from him. He dropped his forehead to my shoulder and groaned even as his finger kept circling me, kept chasing my own rolling release. My body felt heavy and light, shattered and whole, everything in me pulling apart and mending back together as I came down from that euphoric high.

When my limbs fell limp to my sides and my head dropped to Navin's shoulder, he stepped away from the wall, cradling me to him while still inside me. His hand trailed down my back, his other cupping my ass as he carried me down the hall and into his bedroom.

All I kept thinking was *the rain is magic, the rain is magic, the rain is magic* . . .

SADIE

SUNLIGHT PEEKED THROUGH THE WINDOWS OF NAVIN'S ROOM. My head lay upon his bare chest as I listened to his steady, sleepy heartbeat. We lay across the couch built into the floor. It was positioned between a row of marble columns that propped up the frescoed ceiling. Behind us was a bed so large it could easily sleep five people, dotted with satin pillows and embroidered blankets. To think Navin spent most of his time sleeping in a cramped bunk in Galen den' Mora . . . This *refuge* looked built for a king.

Navin dropped a kiss to the top of my head, his hand trailing lazily up and down my bare back. I felt sated, smug, and more than a little confused. The sun had risen but I wasn't ready to pick back up my weapons. There were things we did, things we said, that we could never turn back from now. I didn't want to go back to pretending. It was too late to pull away, only forge ahead.

"Should I prepare the tea?" Navin asked as he idly explored my skin with his mouth and hands.

"Wolves don't need the tea," I said with a sigh, curling my toes and stretching my arms above my head. "We have our own ways of preventing unwanted pregnancies. The last thing either of us needs is a half-wolf running around."

"I'd never really thought about it before. Children," he corrected, "not half-wolves."

I chuckled. "Galen den' Mora doesn't seem like the most practical option."

"Nor does the life of a soldier," he said, and I bobbed my chin in agreement.

"But maybe one day," I mused to the ceiling. "When wars are done and kingdoms are saved and I put my knives down for good—"

"You'll never put your knives down for good."

"True." My smile broadened. "But maybe I'll use them more for whittling than stabbing by then."

"I like this future." Navin tugged me closer to him.

"If we survive to claim it," I said, meeting his eyes. He looked at me with such open adoration, and I knew in my bones this face he wore wasn't a mask. I shook my head. "You can't look at me like that when the Songkeepers return. Not until we're far clear of them."

His hands paused their roaming. "I'm sorry for what will happen today," he murmured into my hair. "I'm sorry for who I will have to be when Rasil returns. But if it means getting you out of here and safe from him . . ."

What had once been a simple diplomatic mission had now quickly spiraled into an elaborate plan. I had Silver Wolves wanting to capture me, Onyx Wolves wanting to marry me, humans wanting to use me, and a court that still needed me. I was attempting to trick people on all sides now, worst of all myself.

"It's nice to know I'm not the only one with a little bite," I said instead of voicing all my tangled thoughts. Navin's hand squeezed the flesh of my hip in acknowledgment. "I just wish I didn't have to pretend. I'd love nothing more than to carve that arrogant smile off your husband's face."

Navin coughed out a surprised laugh. "I don't think we'd get far past his samsavat if you did."

"Can't you control it?"

"Only the one who created it and his bloodline can," Navin said. "The song of control is meaningless without the song of creation—a song I don't possess. Besides, I don't make a habit of getting close to things that could eat me."

"And yet you fell for me," I murmured, my whole body shaking from his laughter.

"True," he said, warmth in his voice as he trailed a finger up my back. "Once we get to Sankai-ed and find Maez, we will get you new knives and you will feel much better."

I chuckled, twisting more to my side and hooking my knee over his thigh. "I feel naked without them."

"I prefer you naked." Navin's fingers trailed over the curve of my ass. "Does it feel different?" he mused, looking up at the ceiling. "Being with a human?"

"Not as much as I thought it would," I murmured. "This frenzy." My voice fell to a whisper. "I can't stop wanting you." Navin sleepily pulled me tighter against his bare chest and kissed up my neck. "I've only ever seen it in mates."

"Mates." Navin's lips paused and then he pulled his head back to stare deeply into my eyes.

"I know that's only a Wolf thing—"

"The Songkeepers believe in something similar," he said.

My eyes flared. "What?"

"It's when one soul sings to another." He swept his thumb across my lips, his eyes wandering from my mouth to meet my gaze. "I've wondered for a long time . . ." He swallowed as his voice grew thick. "My heart hears only your song."

We moved at the exact same time, our mouths colliding as we pulled each other closer until we were flush skin to skin. It didn't matter. Songs. Mates. Words were meaningless to this feeling, like he and I merged somewhere into one. My mouth claimed him along with my soul. No matter how unlikely, no matter how ludicrous, he was mine and I could never turn back from knowing it.

Navin's hand slid between us, and he started circling my clit, but his words, this knowledge of who we were to each other, it was too much. I pushed his hand away and he immediately moved it to my thigh, squeezing it as our mouths worked over each other.

I hitched my leg higher, angling my hips as I wrapped my hand around his silken hard cock. I lined him up to my entrance and he slowly pushed in. Each inch made my head fall back farther, my moan a broken rasp. It had only been one night, but Gods, I already loved when he was inside me. It was the most open and real we ever were with each other, our bodies always able to perfectly communicate in a language all their own.

Navin's hands kneaded my ass, pulling me farther onto his cock. He brushed my loose hair off my face, his hand sweeping around to the back of my neck and pulling my forehead to his. We moved in perfect unison, my hips rolling in time to his thrusts as our hooded gazes met. We paused, breathing each other in, feeling where we connected.

"We have enemies coming at us from every direction," Navin panted. "But I am always on your side, Sadie. Always." His fingers tightened their grip on me. "Even when you want to stab me."

My chuckle ended on a moan as he started moving again. "You're mine, Songkeeper," I groaned as he thrust into me deeper. "Always."

With those claiming words, we picked up the pace. My hips rocked, tilting into that perfect angle that I knew would make me come undone. The tip of Navin's cock grazed over the spot over and over, faster and faster, until our skin was slick and the air was filled with our carnal sounds.

With one final pump of his hips, we came together, my body clenching around him, pulling his release from him. Lightning skittered through my veins, my entire body fluttering as my orgasm roared through me. Wave after unending wave, I fell into that euphoric oblivion.

Navin's lips slowed as he breathed in my last panting breaths, our muscles finally releasing as we collapsed into the soft bed. I swept back my bangs clinging to my forehead with sweat as Navin traced circles over my belly and up the center of my chest.

When his fingertips circled my nipple, my pussy fluttered again. "Careful," I warned, rising onto my elbow and smiling at him. "Unless you're already prepared to go again?"

The whinny of horses in the distance signaled the return of Rasil and his crew.

Navin groaned at the sound. "They couldn't give us one more hour?"

"*I'm* the one who must return to the dungeon," I pointed out. "Yet you're the one moping."

He sighed and stood. As his eyes trailed over me, his impressive length hardened yet again after another round of lovemaking. He stretched his arms above his head and yawned and I rolled my eyes. How very Wolf-like indeed.

"You're insatiable," I said as I quickly grabbed the ball of discarded fabric in the corner and pulled one of his tattered sandy shirts back on. It had a terrible smell to it now and I wrinkled my nose.

Navin grabbed the shackles off his dresser and stooped, binding my feet. His hand trailed up my legs as he stood, leaving a trail of gooseflesh in its wake. Everything in me told me to fight, to rebel, but I knew the only way out of this place was to submit and I could no longer deny the thrill that came with him overpowering me, either. One more night of this charade and then we'd be on the road again.

Navin pulled my hands behind my back and bound them as he dropped his mouth to my ear. "I'm coming for you tonight."

I shuddered as he pulled on my bindings to check them, then his hand snaked around my front and he cupped my sex through his shirt. My head dropped back against his chest, and I took a shaky breath. How badly I wanted those fingers to push in, to begin circling me again. I'd be burning up the rest of the day with desire, thinking about when he'd come collect me that night. This feeling built in me wave after wave, completely inextinguishable.

I stepped out of his touch, practically stumbling forward with my bound feet. I turned to him and took a deep breath as my shoulders tensed. "Make it look good."

When I peeked my eyes open, Navin gaped at me. "What?"

"I can't go back to that cell looking all well-washed and well-fucked. You're supposed to be *taming* me, remember?" He smiled at me for a second, pure smug pride. I looked at him like he'd sprouted horns. Surely he knew this was coming. "You said we needed to play his game."

"Yes . . . ?"

"Well, then you're going to have to hit me."

Navin's eyes and nostrils flared like I'd just told him to slit my throat. "I'm not going to do that."

"A black eye at least," I insisted, tilting my face and offering out my cheek.

"No."

"Come on, show me that right hook," I goaded, dancing around in front of him. "Let's see how you stack up to the Wolves I've sparred with."

"Absolutely not."

"You're going to ruin this plan for both of us," I growled. "How will your husband believe you otherwise?"

"Husband in name only," he spat back. Good, maybe I could rile him up enough to relent. "And I never agreed I would hurt you."

"How did you think this was going to go? We need to show him you mean to deliver me to Rikesh as your *prisoner*," I said. "The only way we're getting out of here is if he thinks you can control me."

"I can't do that—"

"I will shift as soon as we're out of this shithole and the

wounds will heal and I'll be fine," I said, rolling my eyes. "Come on, you weak little bleeding-hearted musician, don't be pathetic. I'm a soldier, not a puppy, just fucking hit me!"

I KNEW THE BLOOMING BRUISE ALONG MY EYE WAS IMPRESSIVE. Navin wasn't the only one who knew all the right buttons to push. I smirked and my split lip stung, making me smile even more like a sadist. At least toying with the wound with my tongue gave me something to preoccupy my time.

It wasn't anywhere near the worst beatings I'd taken in the sparring rings. Sweet Moon, it probably didn't make the top one hundred, but I bet it looked magnificent still. Navin certainly knew how to use those big hands. My body still throbbed in the echoes of our passion, and despite being up all night, I wanted him more with every breath. Everything was suddenly driving me crazy with need. My toes wiggling in the sand of my cell, the brush of Navin's shirt across my nipples, the tickle of my hair down my neck. My entire oversensitive body was perpetually teetering on the edge, begging for Navin's body in a way that edged on madness. Our whole relationship felt like a fever dream—a foolish one.

I waited for hours, expecting Rasil to check on me right away, but the Songkeeper was clearly taking his time. One day, I'd find a way to return to this place just to punch him in his arrogant, beautiful face. The fact he thought I could be captured by any human was laughable let alone that I could be transported as a prisoner to Rikesh without a million opportunities to escape. I hated this ruse, hated how weak it made me look, but at least I was getting myself the fuck out of there.

When two sets of footsteps finally sounded on the stairs, the afternoon sun was low in the sky judging by the orange glow that filtered down behind them. I let out a long-suffering sigh and switched my position to cower in the corner, letting my mask of fear slip into place.

"Oh ho ho, Navin!" Rasil exclaimed delightedly as he sauntered over to the bars. I peeked up at him so he could get a good look at my face and then straight back down. "I didn't think you had it in you."

Rasil clapped Navin on the back with pride and Navin immediately stepped away.

"You always underestimate me," Navin said, his voice an octave lower than when I'd heard it last. He folded his arms across his chest. "I told you I had her under control." My stomach flipped at the sound, so dark and menacing.

Except this time, it didn't make me loathe him. I wondered if I could get him to use that voice again under much different circumstances.

"Clearly," Rasil said, holding a finger to his lips in contemplation as he studied me. "You will win us a treasure more precious than all the gold in Olmdere, Wolf." His grin was more feral than any Wolf. "I think I should send Ciara and Jaime with you."

"No," Navin cut him off a little too quickly, drawing Rasil's gaze. "They don't know the greater magics like us. They will just slow me down," he said a little slower.

"If only Mina were here," Rasil said, cocking his head. "Then there'd be at least two of you."

Navin hummed in agreement. "I thought it best she stay behind and keep a close eye on the Golden Court Queen," he said. "Mina is right in the Queen's pocket now, and with Damrienn and Olmdere both vying for Valta's armies in their brewing war, I thought it best that a Songkeeper stay close to her side."

"Always one step ahead of the rest." Rasil slid his hand from Navin's shoulder down his bicep in an affectionate, lingering touch that made me want to snarl. "And Kian. Is he still with us?"

Navin's shoulders tensed. "He is," Navin said carefully. "Though my brother is still recovering from his time as a Rook."

"When you return to Olmdere," Rasil said, "I expect Kian to face your judgment for his traitorous ways." Rasil actually expected Navin to punish his brother? What an absolute asshole.

Rasil looked back at me. "Now that I know you are up to the challenge, I will appoint you as our executioner. If only there was a song for death . . . Ah, well, the song we'll be acquiring is close enough." My head snapped up at that, my one good eye wide. "Do you have something to say, Wolf?" I cowered again and shook my head. "No, go on," Rasil taunted. "Tell me."

"You call us Wolves barbaric," I snarled. "Yet you'd send him to kill his own family."

"*I* am his family," Rasil said, his voice echoing off the cave wall. "The Songkeepers are his kin. Navin and the softhearted Ora seemed to have forgotten why we exist at all."

"I haven't forgotten," Navin cut in. "I will avenge us, and I will get our song back. Give me a horse and I'll take her now if you like. We'll be in Rikesh by the full moon."

"I like when you're eager to please me, love," Rasil said, rubbing a hand up Navin's arm again. "But you and I both know the crishenem will come for you after sunset."

Navin shrugged. "I will sing them away."

I silently begged him not to push Rasil any further. I knew he was trying to rescue me, but convincing Rasil of his intentions was walking a razor's edge.

Rasil shook his head. "Save your songs for Rikesh." He kicked sand at me and clicked his tongue when I flinched. "Let the little bitch have one more night in her cell to remind her not to mess with you. You'll leave at first light." He placed his hand on Navin's shoulder and steered him around. "Come, Bec is making dinner."

SADIE

IT WASN'T LONG INTO THE NIGHT BEFORE I HEARD THE SHUFFLE of sandaled feet coming down the steps. The Songkeepers who'd arrived during the day seemed to retire early after their travels. Navin swayed down the steps, wine seemingly loosening his limbs, and he whistled a low tune to open my cell door.

I leaned against the cave wall, using it to leverage my feet under me and rise to stand. I wandered over to him, his eyes filled with fire as I approached. Before I could open my mouth to speak, he bent down to kiss me. His tongue swept into my mouth, his hands pulled my hips into him, he breathed deeply as if he'd been waiting all day for this moment. My lip stung as his mouth worked over mine, but I couldn't stop, just as desperate for him.

"Come with me," he murmured against my lips. "I'll untie you once we're out of sight."

I followed him up the stairs, a little bounce in my step as I padded barefoot toward his room. I knew my glee was ridiculous given the circumstances, but all my good sense had vanished the day before. I was already on fire—I might as well dance in the flames.

We skirted through the atrium, the stars just beginning to twinkle overhead. "Is everyone asleep?" I whispered.

Navin's hand touched the small of my back, guiding me. "At least an hour ago," he whispered back.

"Impressive you could wait that long," I snarked.

"I was about to combust," he added with a chuckle.

We snuck down the hallway toward his bedroom when we heard a door shut.

"Shit," I hissed and bolted toward his room. The chains around my legs rattled as I awkwardly tried to tiptoe down the hall.

Navin whirled around as he shut the door behind me. I listened through the door as he removed a strand of keys from his pocket and jangled them around, covering my sound. The voices were muffled through the door, but I knew from the baritone rasp that it was Rasil.

Shit. Shit. Shit.

I darted into Navin's room and leapt over the back of his couch, falling hard on my shoulder as I rolled. I bit out a gasp as I inched to the column beside the couch and sat with my back to it, praying that Rasil wouldn't enter. But the Gods weren't listening, and the door rattled open after a ridiculous amount of fumbling from Navin. My chest rose and fell in giant heaves. If Rasil discovered me here it would ruin everything.

"I think that wine has gone straight to my head," Navin slurred.

"Whoa!" Rasil exclaimed with a chuckle. "How many glasses did you have?"

"Too many it seems," Navin said. Shuffling sounded as he stumbled around. "I should go to bed. Good night, Raz."

"I was thinking . . . ," Rasil hedged and I cringed.

Navin stumbled forward and dropped onto the couch right beside me. I knew the second he spotted me from his periphery, but he hid it well. His eyes widened ever so slightly as he put his arms over the back of the couch, his right hand so close it nearly skimmed my shoulder.

"I have a feeling I know what you're thinking, Raz," Navin said. "And the answer is always the same."

My shoulders bunched at the nickname, suddenly feeling like a voyeur to this intimate moment between husbands. Even if their history was long in the past, they still *had* a history.

"Things have changed," Rasil said from where he lingered in the doorway. I heard the careful snick of the door shutting, but I didn't hear his footsteps approach. "I've changed."

"You still seem like the same ambitious boy I once knew," Navin said. "Just with more facial hair."

Rasil chuckled. "You've certainly grown more confident, too," he said. "I think we make a better pair now than we ever did when we were young."

"I don't think that—"

"I know that there were others," Rasil cut in and I tensed. I couldn't believe he was saying this out loud. "I know we both indulged in other dalliances. But you're still mine, Navin."

Navin's hand dropped behind the couch, skimming over my collarbone, and it took everything in me not to jolt and rattle my chains. His finger trailed over my shoulder as he said, "I haven't been yours in a very long time, Raz." His hand drifted down, skimming over my chest, and I bit my lip as his thumb circled my nipple, rolling it into a peak.

"I could be," Rasil offered. "You still look at me with lust in your eyes."

Navin's hand dipped lower, down the plane of my belly, and bunched the fabric of my shirt in a fist. "That look in my eyes is exhaustion," he said. "I didn't get much sleep last night." He tugged up on the fabric until my whole lower half was bare.

My breathing hitched, and I thanked the Gods that Rasil couldn't hear as well as a Wolf. He'd probably be able to taste the current in the air, hear the pounding of my heart in my chest, know the pulsing that was building between my legs. All the wanton desire that had grown and grown over the course of the day all came to a head. Being touched by Navin, being nearly discovered, I was already wet and desperate for him.

"Why didn't you get much sleep last night?" Rasil asked carefully, and my pulse quickened even further.

"The bitch was yowling from her cell about her sore arms," Navin said without missing a beat. His fingers trailed up my leg, making my skin tingle. I wanted to spread my legs wider, wanted to shift and wriggle into his touch, but I knew one sound and I'd be found out. Maybe facing the samsavat would be worth it just to be touched by him again.

"Wolves," Rasil spat. "Are you sure you'll be all right to take her unaccompanied?"

"She's beaten and nearly starved," Navin said as his finger trailed up to my center and brushed through the dusting of hair between my legs. I bit down on my lip so hard I tasted blood. "And if she's shackled, she can't shift. She'll be a good dog for me." As he said the words, he trailed his finger down my folds and plunged into my wet heat.

I choked on air, my chin stretching skyward and toes curling as his fingers pushed inside of me and massaged my inner walls. I was already dripping for him. He slid his fingers out again and circled my clit, and I swore to all the Gods that my soul left my body as I tried not to moan. Let me just die here with his fingers inside me. I couldn't care beyond that.

"Will you please just do me a favor," Rasil said.

"It depends," Navin purred as his fingers slid in again, massaging me in tortuously slow movements.

"Will you think about us while you're in Rikesh," Rasil said. Navin's thumb circled my clit as his fingers pumped in and out. "Will you consider leaving Galen den' Mora and joining me here and being by my side?"

Navin's thumb pressed down harder on my throbbing bud, and I let out a short whine. He coughed, covering the sound. "Pardon me," he said, coughing a couple more times for good measure. "I will think about it, Raz," he said in a lazily bored tone that I knew was his attempt to curb his own lust. "But I think my conclusion will be the same as always."

"That's all I ask," Rasil said, and the door clicked as he opened it. "Good night, Navin."

"Good night." Navin circled me faster again.

He waited after the door was shut for a good few seconds to make sure Rasil was gone. Navin pulled his hands from my aching flesh and stood from the couch. He sidled over to his door, and I heard the lock click.

I let out a panting breath, resting my head against the cool column. When Navin turned around the column, he dropped into a crouch beside me.

"You're evil," I groaned, my cheeks and chest feeling flushed with heady desire.

He grinned, searching his pocket for his ring of keys to unchain me.

"Fuck me first," I said, my legs shaking as I balanced on the teetering edge, so close to coming. My orgasm was barely tethered down and begging to be unleashed.

Navin's smile turned to pure mischief as he flipped me so my chest landed on the ground, my bare ass up in the air. "You need me that bad, hmm?"

I heard the rustle of fabric, of buttons popping free, and then the head of his cock dragged down my wet sex. "Yes," I moaned. I tried to spread my knees wider but the cuffs bit into my ankles.

Navin slid his cock up and down my folds one more time, coating himself in my wetness before placing the head at my entrance again. Writhing, I tried to push back but I couldn't move. One hand landed on my shoulder, holding me in place as he slowly fed his cock into me. I groaned at the sensation, my pussy already fluttering around him.

"Esh," he rasped, the angle making my eyes roll back as he pushed deeper and deeper inside of me. "So tight like this."

When he was fully seated, his hand grabbed my hip and paused.

I let out a desperate, pleading whine. "I need you to move," I begged. "Now. Please."

Navin let out a dark chuckle and pulled out of me and slammed back in. I cried out, unable to contain the sound.

Navin tsked. "Last night I loved hearing all the ways I could make you scream," he said. "But tonight you need to be quiet."

"I can't," I heaved, pushing back to move him deeper.

"Here," Navin said, grabbing a cushion from the couch. "Bite this." I bit into the woven fabric as he commanded, frantic to do anything that would make him move again. "Good girl," he rasped, pulling out and thrusting into me again, and I moaned into the cushion. "That's right. Take it for me."

He slammed into me again and my vision spotted, a climax building and building inside me. He picked up a punishing pace, driving me hard into the tiled floor. My pussy was already clenching around him, the tension growing endlessly higher and higher as he rode me. With each thrust I cried out into the pillow, spurring him onward. The only sounds were my muffled cries and the wet slap of our flesh.

"Fuck, Sadie," Navin grunted as his fingernails dug into my hips. His finger trailed down between my cheeks, pressing the tip to my back entrance. I screamed, my orgasm tearing through me as his finger pushed into me.

My entire body spasmed as he fought my tight channel, battling his last thrusts into me until he was coming, spilling his heat into me as I clenched around his cock. He kept moving, kept pulling the ecstasy from me until my voice was hoarse and my limbs were spent.

Only once he sucked in his first deep breath did he remove the keys from his discarded pants and unbind my hands. My stiff shoulders barked as my hands were freed and came around to brace on the floor beside my head. His cock still twitched inside of me as his hands massaged up my arms and shoulders, soothing the sore muscles.

He pulled out of me, coating my legs in sticky heat as he unlocked my ankles. When I was freed, I collapsed onto the tiles and he picked me up in his arms and cradled me to his chest, the tenderness of the action so soft and gentle compared to the brutality of what we'd just done. He brushed a kiss to the top of my head, his hands soothing my aches. That small action made my eyes mist.

He was everything I never knew I wanted or needed. I was prepared to fight him, but now all I wanted to do was fight *for* him, fight for *us*. And the first step to doing that was getting the fuck out of this place.

CALLA

WE SAT BY THE FROZEN ICE FOUNTAIN IN THE HUMAN QUARTER. The pedestrians gave us a wide berth, making a giant ring around us. Klaus curled his lip at the humans and pulled his fur coat closer, but Queen Ingrid seemed mildly amused at least, even waving to a few onlookers.

"If you were so desperate for an outdoor venue, I could've suggested one," Klaus muttered to Briar who simply shrugged at him, clearly still having him on a tight leash.

"I like the colors," she said with a flutter of her lashes. I could easily see behind my sister's performance, but Sweet Moon was I impressed that she could still put it on, especially with someone as insufferable as Klaus.

Grae leaned into me and murmured, "This is where I first heard you sing."

My cheeks burned and not from the cold as I remembered singing "Sa Sortienna" with Ora in this very square. It felt like years ago and just yesterday all at once.

"This whole place reminds me of Ora," I said as I cradled the warm mug of cider in my hands. "Ora was the first person to help me put words to everything I was feeling inside. They are the one who helped me realize I was merem."

Ingrid immediately extricated herself from the conversation between Briar and Klaus to turn her icy gaze on me. "Merem?"

My pulse quickened. I hadn't thought she'd heard. Should I say she misheard me? Should I try and move the conversation along? Everything within me felt like it was shrinking smaller and smaller to appease her, and I didn't know if I could take it any longer.

I probably should've denied it—it would've been better for my court and our alliance—but instead my eyes narrowed at her above the steam curling from my mug. "Yes?"

"You use a *human* word to describe yourself? A Wolf Queen?" She looked at Grae for his reaction instead of me, as if my use of the word "merem" was an offense to *him*.

I blinked, trying to think of a more delicate response. The amount of contorting myself I had to do to stay on Ingrid's good side was already breaking me. I couldn't do it anymore. I couldn't perform this version of myself for her anymore. I had considered hiding my gender from her entirely, but I couldn't win. It hurt so deeply to not be who I truly was, but it hurt me even more to think of Ora and so many others who needed my help and I couldn't do it without Ingrid's allegiance.

"It doesn't have to be only a human word," I said tentatively as I worried my lip with my tooth. With a bit more strength, I added, "And I am not the Queen of just Wolves."

"You are so determined to get rid of all Wolf customs, aren't you?" Her slender brows lifted, her expression so sharp she could've sliced me in half. "When will it be enough?"

My brow furrowed. "Enough?"

"I agree that we need change," she said. "I thought you and I were aligned. We want Wolf Queens to be able to rule. We want equality for all Wolves. We want progress." She waved her hand around the square. "And want a good life for all of our citizens." She said it like it was an afterthought.

Grae let out a rough laugh. "Pickled fish and rotten vegetables is hardly the same as the things you grow in the greenhouses of your palace," he said. "Would you truly consider this equal?"

"Humans and Wolves equal?" She looked at him perplexed. "You can't compare the two. We both have such different strengths. We serve different purposes and occupy different spaces in the world. The humans *wanted* Wolves to rule." Ingrid pinned him with a look. "And the Taigosi humans have the best quality of life of *all* the courts of Aotreas."

I knew from the way she looked at me with the word "all" that she was implying the Olmdere humans had it worse than the Taigosi ones. It was true. I hoped for a better life for them, worked hard to help undo all the damage Sawyn's reign had done, but even so, the humans of Taigos were still better off.

For now.

If we weren't under the threat of Nero, the scales would've tipped in our favor even sooner. In my court, it would be the humans themselves who decided what a "good life" looked like as defined by and for themselves. And I'd do everything in my power to help them achieve it.

Grae seemed to read my mind as he tilted his head at Ingrid. "Have you asked your people?" He considered the space around us. "Have you asked them if this is the life they want? If there is any way it could be improved?"

It was a conversation I'd had many times with my people. What did they need? What did they want? I'd asked if they even wanted me to rule and was ready to step down if they said otherwise. But in every corner of Olmdere, they saw my golden scars and demanded I stay on my parents' throne. I'd wished for them to know peace with my dying breath, and they would hold me to account in fulfilling that promise.

Ingrid clicked her tongue and rolled her eyes at Grae. "I care about my people, Graemon, but you are seriously starting to sound like one of them. This isn't like you." She set down her mug and leaned into the frozen table, resting her hand on Grae's forearm. I forced myself not to lean forward and bite her wrist in half. "No matter your feelings, Wolves and humans are not the same. We are the shepherds and they the sheep." She released him and leaned back, finally asking me, "Are you a queen or a sheep?"

I wanted to shout, wanted to flip the table, wanted to rage at her, and judging by the growl escaping Grae, he wanted to do all those things, too, but Briar cleared her throat and let out a soft laugh.

"What have they put in this cider?" she tittered, trying to break the ice. I grimaced at her, and I knew she was internally cringing, too, even though her face was bright. But she pivoted to Queen Ingrid and smiled at her. "I hear that you have a herd of silver reindeer in Taigoska, Your Majesty," she quickly diverted the conversation.

Ingrid bristled as if shaking off my comments and then turned to Briar with a new light. "They are exquisite," she said. "Would you like to see them?"

"I'd be delighted," Briar said, leaving her mug and standing. She took off with Klaus and Ingrid, casting a glance over her shoulder at me that said, "Come on, let's go."

I let out a long sigh, trying to release the tension in me, but my hands were still balled into fists. Maybe this was all a mistake. Maybe I needed a better tactic. I was sick of bending to the whims of a flippant Queen. Life and death were happening just beyond her borders and she was ignoring it. Maybe I just needed to do it all myself.

My cheeks were white-hot as I battled back tears. I couldn't do it anymore. I couldn't keep shrinking myself down to appease Ingrid. Patience was beginning to feel a lot like weakness. I was drowning here and all the while Ora was probably being tortured in a cell. I remembered what I did the last time. When it was Maez in a cell and Briar under a curse, when I was told to be patient and tempered and just *wait*.

No more. No more sitting on my hands and politicking and being a good little dog. My tether had finally snapped.

I fled in the middle of the night back then, and Queen or no, I could do it again now.

I WAS HALFWAY OUT THE DOOR OF MY SUITE WHEN A MATCH struck to life in the hallway. My hand instinctively shot to the dagger on my hip, my years of fight training kicking in. But then that rainstorm scent swirled to me as a face I knew better than my own flickered in the burgeoning candlelight.

"You promised me never again, little fox." Grae's voice held a quiet menace, softness laced with poisoned anger.

As my eyes adjusted to the darkness, I noted that he was fully dressed. My mind spun. Had he really heard me tiptoe out of bed? Had he awoken and dressed while I packed my bag? Or had it been some sort of mate instinct, some sort of fear that I'd run off again?

"I need to get Ora," I said, my voice pleading. "I need to do something to help Damrienn. It's my fault they're suffering."

Grae's face softened but only for a split second before anger filled his expression again. He took one step, then another, and I found myself pacing backward into the room to keep the space between us. Grae shut the suite door behind him and lit the candelabra beside the door until the space was bright enough that his eyes were no longer cast in shadow.

"Wherever you go, I go, Calla," Grae said, echoing the words we'd promised each other so many moons ago. "To the ends of the world. To certain death. To the next life." He set the candle back in its holder on the entry table and took another prowling step closer, his hands coming up on either side of me as he backed me into the wall. "You and I are tied together, mate. You and I are *one*."

"I know," I whispered, my resolve breaking at that proclamation. "I just . . ." Grae searched my eyes. "I just can't do this anymore. I can't wait for Ingrid to understand me, if she *ever* will. I can't wait for her to help us." The words scratched out of me, and I hadn't realized how broken this whole visit had made me until right then. "I feel like I've been selfish." A tear slid down my cheek, and Grae brushed it away.

"Selfish? *You?*"

"I knew claiming the word 'merem' would be hard. I knew there would be people who wouldn't understand." I swallowed the burning knot forming in my throat. "But it made me feel seen. It made me feel like *me*, maybe for the first time ever and . . ." I heaved a shaking breath. "And claiming that word had been so euphoric, I thought that should be enough. But what if revealing who I am will hurt our people? What if being myself comes at too steep a price?"

Tears slipped down my cheeks faster than Grae could swipe them away, and he gave up trying, pulling me into a fierce hug instead. He buried his lips in my hair, his strong arms pulling me so tightly as if he could pull my pain into his own body.

"Fuck anyone who would ever make you feel less than," he said. "You deserve to be exactly who you are, unconditionally and without fear."

I sobbed as I remembered the way Ingrid looked at me in the square, the shock and disgust on her face that I would be so humanlike. It was as if I told her I hated being a Wolf. She looked at me like I'd betrayed her somehow. I felt it in that moment—her allegiance slipping through my fingers. I felt her backing away from me. And it broke me.

I sobbed harder, clinging to Grae's shoulders as he gently rubbed circles down my back.

"Maybe being who I am comes at too high a price," I cried again as I stained Grae's tunic with my tears.

"No." The word left his mouth before I even stopped talking. "Everything that you are, little fox—*everything*—is exactly as you are meant to be."

"But Ingrid—"

"Fuck Ingrid," Grae snarled. "We will find another way. We've been bending over backward for her and the Ice Wolves. Briar has faked her heart away to that idiot Klaus. But more than all that, I've been watching you shrink yourself smaller and smaller in her presence. I bit my tongue because I thought it's what you wanted, but I can't take it anymore, either. If they can't handle the brilliance with which you burn, Calla, then let them all catch fire. I'd rather be standing on top of their ashes than miss the brightness of your flame."

I let out a half laugh, half cry, my posture straightening as Grae's finger landed under my chin and he tilted my face up to meet his storming midnight eyes. He planted a kiss on my lips, the contact making my whole body sigh. He licked the salty tears from my bottom lip and coaxed my mouth to respond. The tightness in my chest eased as my mouth molded to his.

I knew he at least could handle all I was. All the Golden Court could. All the people I represented. All the people who *mattered* would never ask me to dull my shine or pretend to be something I'm not.

Grae's lips told me everything I couldn't find the words to say: there would be another way. We would find a new path. One that didn't break me in the process.

One that didn't ask me to forsake merem.

His hands slid up my arms to cup my cheeks, his kisses earnest and eager. The way he cradled my head was like he was focusing me in to only him, my guiding star, the one truth that would pull me back into myself. The tears ebbed as I kissed him deeper, the sorrow morphing into yearning.

A rumble of pleasure reverberated between our mouths as Grae stilled.

"We will fight this. Together," he murmured against my mouth. "But I swear to all the fucking Gods, little fox, if you try to leave me behind again, I won't be held responsible for destroying everything that stands between me and you." His hands trailed down from my cheeks, following the curve of my body and landing on the swell of my ass. His voice was dark and pleading. "Promise me." He rocked my hips into his hardening length, and I gasped with the power and possession in his demand.

"I promise," I said, and then again, my soul speaking directly to his. "I promise."

I was about to pull him into the bedroom when a knock sounded at the door.

"Grae?" Hector's sleepy voice was muffled by the door.

"It's always fucking Hector." Grae turned and leered at the door as I chuckled. "What do you want?" he barked.

"Queen Ingrid has heard from Nero," Hector called back, dousing ice on my burgeoning desire. "He's agreed to a trade for Ora."

I leaned past Grae, my heart leaping with the excitement before the dread cut it back down again. I stared at the shut door for a long time before asking, "In exchange for what?"

SADIE

WE RODE OUT WITH THE DAWN ON A SINGLE DAPPLED TAN MARE. My hands were once again bound behind my back as Rasil watched us leave. Navin's arms circled around me, keeping me from sliding off the horse's neck. I gripped the mare tightly with my thighs, wishing I had my hands free to hold on to her mane. At least my legs had been unchained, and they'd permitted me to wear some flimsy old breeches; otherwise the sores and chafing would've been unfathomable, even knowing I'd be able to shift once we'd put some distance between us and the refuge. Still, riding with bound hands was an exercise of misery.

"Just one more dune." Navin's warm breath skimmed the shell of my ear. "And then we'll be able to relax."

I kept having the urge to look back, but I knew we'd find no sign of the Songkeepers' sanctuary, only the slightest bend in the air where the glamour started, hidden amongst the waving heat lines.

I wore a bone-white scarf that wrapped around my nose and head, keeping the sunlight from burning my skin—Navin had convinced Rasil that no one wanted a red and peeling betrothed, and even then the asshole had barely relented. Meanwhile, Navin wore a chestnut, wide-brimmed hat that made him look more like a roguish pirate than a musician. I had zero qualms with that outfit, nor the way he roughly handled me onto the horse in front of Rasil. It felt good not always being the domineering one for once. I'd always been the instigator and commander of all my past trysts. I never thought it could be like this with anyone nor that I'd enjoy it, let alone with a human. And esh, this human, with his long fingers, and plundering tongue, and giant c—

I adjusted my seat and rolled my shoulders.

"Soon," Navin promised, mistaking my arousal for discomfort.

I cleared my throat but held my tongue. I didn't want to use it for speaking anyway—

Get it together, Sadie!

Soon, we wouldn't have to play this game anymore. Soon, we'd both be free. Maybe we could live in the Olmderian capital, or travel in the wagon, or just find *some way* to be together. Even if it didn't make any sense to either of us, maybe we could figure it out. I didn't know how but felt determined to try. Navin with his songs, me with my general propensity for debauchery— maybe we could carve out a place in the world that finally felt right.

Navin pulled on the horse's reins, slowing the mare to a stop. He pulled the keys from his saddlebag and unlocked my cuffs. I groaned as I pulled my hands in front of me and stretched my arms out. I rubbed my red, raw wrists.

"You could shift here," Navin offered. "Heal those bruises. No one will see."

"Except for your horse," I replied, patting the mare on her neck. "Who will definitely bolt off into the desert if she sees me." Sweat beaded on my brow and I blotted it with my scarf. "The Wolves' horses are trained *extensively* in Damrienn to not spook when they see one of us. I'm guessing the Songkeepers didn't prepare their horses for an enemy that looks like me." Navin sucked on his teeth at the word "enemy," and I'll admit to some frustration at that. Clearly, he wanted to forget all that it meant for him to be a human and me a Wolf. "Besides," I added, "the bruises and shackle marks will make our act more compelling. It worked on Rasil, after all."

Navin let out an unimpressed grunt and tightened one arm around me as he dropped the metal cuffs into his saddlebag. "I hate that I put them there."

"You put them there because I asked you to—and because I *let you*. And that's only after I screamed in your face and demanded that you do so," I chided. "Honestly, seeing me for five minutes in the sparring rings of Highwick would absolve you of your guilt. I don't mind a few hard-won bruises. Thank you for sparing me from having to smash my face into the wall or something."

"Even for a Wolf," he said with admiration, "you're the toughest person I know, recklessly so sometimes." By *sometimes*, we both knew he meant *most* of the time. "If we pass anyone on the road to Sankai-ed, just put your hands behind your back. If Galen den' Mora is still there, we won't need these." He tapped the saddlebag and it rattled. "But if we can't locate it straightaway, we'll find an inn and I'll put the cuffs back on until we get to our room."

Our room. I liked the sound of that. But instead, I nodded and said, "I hope Maez is still there."

"I hope she wasn't foolish enough to head to Rikesh without us."

"Have you met her?" I let out a derisive snort. "Without her mate around to temper her, our only hope is that she is still mourning us at the bottom of a wine barrel."

Navin's hand splayed across my belly, rising until his thumb skimmed the underside of my breast. A cough of surprise hacked out of my throat.

"Navin," I warned as his hand tugged up my grimy shirt and dipped under the fabric to slide up the same trail along my bare skin. "If you keep doing what you're doing, we're going to die of sun sickness fucking on the burning sand."

His laughter was a hot tickle in my ear. "That would certainly be a way to go." His hand rose higher to skim over my breast, my nipple hardening to his touch before he let out a frustrated grumble and pulled his hand away, taking the reins again. "Why must you be right this time?"

"I'm right *all* the time."

He chuckled, even as I felt him hard against my backside, and wondered if my hands were still bound what mischief they'd be making right now. Instead, I rubbed my hands down my sore thighs, knowing if I touched him now we'd both be doomed by our lust.

We rose up to the top of the next sand dune and finally spotted where the road to Sankai-ed joined the land. The onyx stones of the mountain glinted in the sunlight, casting rainbow spectrums onto the sand below. A donkey and cart ambled halfway up the road to the island, moving slowly up the rickety rope bridge.

Our horse kept her slow, steady pace as the sun lifted higher in the sky and the heat became scorching. I fanned out the sweaty shirt I wore, every point where Navin and I pressed together now slick with sweat. The constant wet rubbing chapped my skin and I found myself leaning forward, practically draping myself down the mare's neck to avoid the friction.

The heat baked us as the mare clip-clopped the first steps up the rope bridge into the cloudless sky. I yearned to whip the sweaty shirt off and just ride naked, but I knew the blistering sun would flay my skin off before we got to the tented shelters of Sankai-ed.

A sudden breeze picked up and I straightened, fear gripping me as I remembered plummeting from this road only a few days ago.

Navin's hand dropped to my hip and squeezed. "After the rains of Rahm, there will be no sandstorms for many moons," he assured me. "We are safe. Well . . ." He amended, "Safe as we can be on a mission like this."

"A mission I still think makes no sense. We will be losing the Onyx Wolves as an ally if I pull out of this marriage," I said, reveling in the breeze that tousled my hair. Each step higher into the air, the cooler we became, our sweaty clothes filling with wind like sails on a ship.

"I think you already lost them as an ally when King Nero offered you to Luo as a trade," Navin said bitterly. "But you rebuffing Prince Tadei will reflect badly on the Silver Wolf pack, too. They promised they could control you, and you are showing the Onyx pack that you are not owned by anyone."

I scowled. "And I'm not showing that by having you, a human, deliver me to them in chains?"

"It is a helpful deception. They will underestimate you at their own peril," he replied. "And make it all the easier for us to escape."

My shoulders tensed, my fingers curling in the breeze. "And what happens if we can't escape?"

Navin's arms tightened around me. "I will get you out," he said. "I promise I won't leave you there. I won't leave you," he murmured.

"You left me once," I whispered.

"And I regretted every day after the battle of Olmdere that I didn't turn back and make things right with you. I thought you'd never hear me out, and yet I should've stayed anyway, should've fought. I won't make that mistake again, love. Not now that I know what we mean to each other." One of Navin's hands dropped to my thigh, reminding me of the way he grabbed me the night before.

Desire bloomed in my core at the memory, but I pushed it aside once more, focusing on the ever-dwindling horizon below us. "You and I always felt impossible, nonsensical even, and yet somehow inescapable, too."

"Exactly." Navin dropped a kiss to the nape of my neck. "I knew somewhere deep in my soul that I loved you from the very first moment our eyes met in Nesra's Pass." His voice flushed with mirth as he added, "When you helped me bury those bodies."

"A morbid way to first fall for one another," I countered with a laugh. "Fitting in hindsight, I suppose. I thought falling for you would mean softer, sweeter things, things I didn't understand nor want. My life is dark and difficult."

"As is mine," Navin said.

I leaned into him in silent recognition. Knowing that truth changed things. Knowing that he walked as difficult a path as me made it easier to grapple with my feelings. Just *knowing* him, at least so much more than I did when he was lying to me, made all the difference. "Human or no," I murmured, "you and I are made of the same mettle. Even if my fur is different from your skin, you and I reflect each other in a way I never knew possible."

Navin didn't reply, only brushed another kiss to my neck. He lifted his head again, the mountain of Sankai-ed becoming clearer and more detailed with every breath. I wondered if some small part of him still held back from the truth of what I was. He said he was awed by my Wolf form, but . . . I still couldn't help but feel like he wished I was something else. How much easier our lives would be if that was true. I didn't dare scrutinize that seed of doubt further. I knew I wanted him and for now that would have to be enough. Whatever beasts lay ahead—human, Wolf, and monster alike—I wanted him there by my side, humming a tune meant only for my soul to hear.

CALLA

OUR STAGNANT LIVES OF PLAYING QUEEN INGRID'S GUESTS morphed into action at the arrival of Nero's message. I barely registered Hector's words of warning, only knowing we needed to get to the great hall and the messenger awaiting us. If Nero was willing to trade Ora, if there was a flicker of hope of getting my friend back, I'd have to take it.

"Easy," Grae said from a half step behind me, rushing to keep up with my eager pace. "You might have to say no, little fox. You don't know the conditions yet."

Hector grunted in agreement from the rear of our trio as we raced down the corridor.

"It's *Ora*," I said.

"Yes," Grae called out behind me. "And it's *Nero*."

Damn him for being so astute. Yet I didn't stop. Our footsteps echoed through the silent castle, slowing only when we entered the great hall where a lone Silver Wolf stood. A sliver of moonlight haloed the cloaked figure as it turned to face us.

Grae sniffed the air, thunder in his voice as he said, "Evres."

Hector hung back by the doorway, his grip tight on the hilt of his sword, as Grae and I moved closer. The sound of my boots clicking across the white tiles ricocheted off the austere and sparse expanse. I halted just before the silver carpet that ran the length of the room to the throne, placing it like a gleaming river between us and Evres. Grae appeared at my side, looking like he wanted to shred the person in front of us with his bare hands.

Evres pulled his hood back, a cold smile on his face as he tipped his chin to us. I thanked the Moon that Grae and I were both already dressed and armed.

I considered King Nero's new heir. Evres was just as tall as Grae, and despite him being leaner, his stance told me that he knew how to fight. The weapons on his hips were shined and gilded but used. His hair was shortly cropped, his features sharp, and his eyes were a shade of pewter that ringed his pupils like a shining eclipse. He was handsome in every sense, almost too much, an eerie mixture of pristine arrogance.

The perfect Silver Wolf, in other words.

Evres tilted his head, his fingers twitching by the hilt of his sword. "Graemon." His voice was a deep baritone that echoed through the shadowed hall.

"Nero doesn't seem too precious about his new heir if he sent you alone," I said, drawing Evres's silvery gaze.

Evres flashed a crooked smile. "Or perhaps he just has faith that you won't kill a messenger offering to give you your *friend* back." He had a pinched air of pretension in the way he spoke as if him becoming king one day had always been an inevitability.

"What is the meaning of this?" Ingrid blustered as she came in through a door behind the throne. "A midnight meeting between Olmdere and Damrienn conducted under *my* roof without me?"

"It is a simple message." Evres's eyes roved the Queen up and down in a way that would have any other man thrown in the dungeons. "I didn't want to interrupt your beauty sleep."

Ingrid's hair was tied up in ribbons atop her head, but she still looked regal in her fur-trimmed robe and satin slippers. She harrumphed at Evres's statement, clearly familiar with him enough not to take offense. She perched impatiently on her ornate throne as if it were a tavern barstool. "Evres." She covered her mouth as she yawned. "I'd ask to what do we owe this pleasure,

but my guards have roused me from my sleep due to the impru-
dent timing of your arrival so let's be frank: Why are you here?"

"I have a message from the King for Calla Marriel," Evres
said, lifting his dimpled chin and grinning. It clearly wasn't lost
on Queen Ingrid nor me that he said "the King" as if Nero was
ruler to us all. "Apologies, Ingrid"—again, the lack of title—"I
would have announced myself to you first, but I ran into an old
friend." He winked at Hector and Hector scowled back, crossing
his arms over his chest. Evres looked around the room and asked,
"And where is my betrothed?"

My mouth fell open for a split second in shock before the
rage kicked in. "She is not your anything—" I started to shout
but was silenced by Grae's hand on my forearm, preventing me
from drawing my sword and inciting a colossal incident. My
mate inched closer to me, and I knew he was preparing to hold
me back if necessary. Killing Evres would feel amazing for only
a second but would stoke the battle fires between our courts for
eternity.

"To my knowledge, the Crimson Princess is not yet betrothed," Evres said with a casual indifference that made my
blood boil. "Are you to tell me otherwise?"

"You are correct—in that she's most certainly not betrothed
to *you*. She is mated to Maez Claudius," I snapped.

"The Moon Goddess doesn't bless pack traitors," Evres shot
back. "Whatever they had is now defunct by our laws."

"Not by *mine*," I growled.

"This wolfish spat grows tiresome," Ingrid cut in. I glared at
her, her indifference, her pomposity—both of these two needed
someone to cut them down to size. I was imagining all the ways
I would tear Evres apart if ever we met on the battlefield when
Ingrid yawned again and asked, "What message has Nero sent?"

"His Majesty has agreed to return the human musician that
harbored the traitor Calla Marriel." Evres's predatory eyes darted
between us. "The one you're so fond of—"

"Their name is Ora," I hissed.

"A human is a human," Evres said with a shrug.

"What exactly does Nero want in exchange for the safe return of Ora?" Grae asked before I could retort, putting particular emphasis on the word "safe."

"Ten thousand crovers," Evres said.

"Done," I blurted out. We had ten times that much sitting under the castle—a trove the Silver Wolves clearly didn't know anything about. The ransom was a lot of coin but surprisingly reasonable. I wondered if Nero was truly so desperate for more gold that he'd make such a low offer. With trade cut off and humans fleeing, maybe Damrienn was falling apart.

"I wasn't finished," Evres replied with a chuckle. He cocked his patronizing head at me. "Ten thousand crovers *and* . . . your father's inauguration crown."

I gasped at the same time Grae snarled. Even Ingrid couldn't hide her surprise. There was no reason for Nero to want my father's crown except to gloat. I mostly wore my mother's crown, the size fitting my head better, but my father's crown sat atop a velvet pillow in the Olmdere grand hall. It was a symbol, a memory of my father, and a beautiful relic of my ancestors, and I knew Nero would use that symbol as a show of his power against us . . . but symbols weren't going to save Ora's life.

"Agreed," I muttered.

"Wait—" Grae said, but I shook my head. I'm sure Nero had a reason for wanting the crown, but it was a symbol, not the actual mandate to rule. Whatever he thought the crown meant was nothing compared to Ora.

Evres smiled. I didn't have a choice and he knew it. "Excellent."

Ingrid gestured between us. "And where exactly will this trade take place?"

"You wouldn't invite your Silver Wolf neighbors to Taigoska?" Evres mocked, his eyes dancing with delight as he watched Ingrid squirm. "No, we'll make the Olmderians do the traveling, hey, Ingrid?" The wink he gave Ingrid made a chill run down my spine. "Mount Achelon. Your castle there straddles the border of Taigos and Damrienn, does it not?"

"It does," Ingrid conceded. She seemed more than a little relieved at the location in the Stormcrest Ranges, so far from Taigoska. "Splendid idea. I will host the trade there on impartial territory."

Evres hummed. "Good." He looked at me, his moonlight eyes cutting straight through me. "If you send word now, a wagon of gold should be able to reach there in the next week." I didn't reply, just stared at him coldly. "I'll see you then, traitor."

"And we'll see *you*, whelp," Hector said.

But the insult—usually fighting words for Wolves—didn't faze Evres. "Whelp, eh?" As he turned, his body twisted and dropped, shifting with impressive speed into a Silver Wolf. He stepped forward and shook off the rest of the cloak. His silver fur matched the gleam of his eyes, his ears and snout tipped in midnight black, his paws nearly white as if dipped in snow. He was far more stout and muscular in his Wolf form. I made a note that he'd be much harder to outfight in our furs. I prayed to the Moon it wouldn't come to that. He gave us one final look from those bright crystalline eyes and then turned and ran out the far archway of the hall, leaving us all staring at each other with hesitant expressions.

No, definitely not a puppy. And I hated that Hector had spoken out of turn.

My stomach dropped as Evres howled in the distance. I turned to Hector. "Send word to Olmdere. Ten thousand crovers and my father's crown."

"Calla." Hector rocked back on his heels, his face strained. "Are you sure you want to—"

"Listen to your Queen." Grae pinned Hector with a vicious look, a quick sidelong glance to Ingrid indicating *not here*.

Hector's cheeks flushed as he bowed and left. I tried to ignore that little interaction, that slight crack in Hector's faith in me, the way he immediately obeyed Grae.

"Mount Achelon is a good location for a trade," Ingrid assured me. "The peak is too steep for a large force to attack. I'll send guards there now to be on lookout. We will only permit a single Damrienn carriage up the mountain."

"Regardless," I said. "I'm going to need more information on the mountain and schematics of your property there."

"Yes. Yes." Ingrid rose on weary legs and waved me off. "In the morning."

Her easy dismissal made me shrink another inch. I wished they would all respect me for the ruler I was, but more and more I was beginning to realize the only way to get through to Wolves was by force.

Well, if Briar had been raised for this aspect of politics, *I* was raised for force.

SADIE

THE RICH SCENT OF SPICES HUNG IN THE AIR AS WE RODE INTO the town of Sankai-ed. Every street and path was covered in tented tan linen, the entire city buried under fabric to keep cool from the sun. Already, the city was much less scorching than the deserts of Lower Valta, but it was still warm enough to make me sweat, especially with the throng of bodies.

Sankai-ed seemed like any other trader town, the markets lined with goods from every corner of Aotreas. Inns and taverns dotted the busy squares. Most people didn't even bother glancing up at us as we rode through the crowd, despite my bruised face and hands tucked behind my back.

"How could a wagon even navigate through this place?" I asked, craning my neck up to the labyrinth of thin fabric above us. People leaned out windows and shouted from rooftops. Smoke swirled in the air so thick it obscured some of the pathways. I was already completely turned around.

"The oxen know to keep to the outskirts," Navin said. "But it's faster through the center of town. Now to find Maez."

"Where is the seediest tavern in this place?" I asked, shouting to be heard over the music and banter. Despite my current predicament, it felt good to be in a city again. I missed the chaos and bustle after days in the desert.

Navin considered for a moment before saying, "The Sand Snake, but I don't think—"

"Take us there," I said, thinking of our days as new soldiers and all the decrepit holes-in-the-wall that we used to frequent. "If she's alive, that's where she'll be."

"You're so sure of your friend?"

"I've known her my whole life," I said, suddenly feeling the absence of Maez like a missing limb. "I left my entire family and pack to save her." I'd followed Grae, who was following Calla, yes, but Calla was going after Maez and I knew I needed to be a part of it. She was like another sibling to me, and I couldn't bear the thought of her locked up in a castle for the rest of her days. The fact that Nero hadn't even tried to save his niece still broke me. I was ashamed that it was the first time I truly questioned the pack leader . . . but once I did, I started to question everything. Now, with space and distance from Nero, I saw all the manipulation as clear as day and couldn't quite comprehend how I'd spent my whole life under Nero's thumb without feeling the way I did now.

We veered off the main street. The space grew quieter and more covered in shadow until we were in what was clearly the sordid underbelly of Sankai-ed. The decor and buildings might've been different, but it smelled the same as every other den of iniquity I'd frequented. People gambled down alleyways, drunks lay curled on stoops, and the sweet smell of spice was replaced by the stench of booze, bile, and piss. Crows of laughter pealed into the air, emanating from the one building lit with candlelight—the Sand Snake, I presumed.

"If we're keeping up this ruse," I said, as we drew nearer to the creaking doors, "you'll need to tie my hands."

Navin pulled the scarf from around his neck and started wrapping the fabric around my wrists. "Here."

"You know I can get out of this," I said, lowering my voice to a hiss as people watched us from the shadows with wary curiosity.

"I know that," he said. "But *they* won't unless you plan on sprouting fangs and fur. They think you're human." He tipped his chin to two shirtless humans pummeling their fists into each other while others threw coins into the gambling pot. "And if a brawl breaks out, I want you to be able to defend yourself."

I clenched my jaw as he pulled the fabric tighter and it burned into my skin. "I could take them with my hands tied behind my back."

"I know you could," Navin said, giving my leg one final squeeze before slowing the horse to a stop.

I glanced at him and then at the mare. "Maybe one of us should stay out here," I said, eyeing the mare. "Or I think your horse and saddlebags will be gone when you return."

"Fine," he said. "You stay with the horse; I'll go search for Maez. I have a feeling not many people will want to answer your questions dressed like that." He took a step in and then stopped himself, and I knew he'd wanted to kiss me. I grinned at him wickedly and he shook his head in equal frustration. "Don't get up to any mischief," he warned and then turned and pushed through the double doors into the tavern.

Unfortunately, this was the sort of place where mischief found you whether you were looking for it or not.

Three humans appeared from the alleyway almost instantly as Navin disappeared into the tavern. The front one cocked his head at me and looked me up and down.

"Why don't you run, girl?" he asked, adjusting the rough-spun wool of his vest that he wore around his barrel chest with nothing underneath. In my head I named them Vesty, Lanky, and Beardy, the three most useless-looking rapscallions I'd ever seen.

"Go on," Lanky said. "We won't tell 'im that you've run."

I narrowed my eyes at the three of them. "And then you can loot his saddlebags, hmm?"

"You'd protect your captor?" Beardy asked, the beads in his beard clinking as he shook his head. "Come on, girl—get gone."

"I am exactly where I want to be." I frowned at them. "Now why don't *you* fuck off. Or go fuck yourselves. Either way—"

"You got a mouth on you, don't you? We'll handle that. And we'll be taking that horse whether you like it or not," Vesty said, unsheathing a rusting blade from his worn leather belt. I threw my head back and laughed. That thing looked so blunted it probably couldn't slice a stick of warm butter.

"What's so funny?" Beardy gritted out, grabbing his own hand ax from his belt. It looked like an old carpentry tool, except the blade appeared dulled to no more than a blunt instrument. Still, with enough of a wallop, it could probably break a bone, but it wasn't quite the intimidation he probably thought it was.

I sized each of them up—their weapons, how they stood and maneuvered, the sides they leaned to, the hands they favored. It had been a while since I'd had any fight training; seemed a shame to waste the opportunity.

"Come on then," I goaded. They were lucky I didn't have my knives on me. "Let's see you try and take this horse."

I decided then and there I wasn't going to free my hands— I wanted it to at least be sporting for them.

The three of them exchanged bemused glances before they charged at me. I easily sidestepped Vesty and kicked out the back of his knee, sending him flying into a pile of horse dung. Lanky's fist glanced past my cheek, and I ducked under his rebounding blow. Bolting inward, I shouldered him backward, giving me just enough time to whirl on Beardy.

Short and stout, Beardy was a few inches shorter than me, which made him the perfect height for me to smash my forehead into his nose. I heard the crunch and then his scream as he dropped his ax and his hands flew up to his face. I kicked out, my boot colliding with Beardy's chin in a brutal uppercut that sent him toppling backward unconscious.

Lanky grabbed me by the hair, yanking my head back with a sharp jolt. Normally, I'd elbow him in the gut, and *technically*

I could still if I just ripped my hands free, but I still wanted to prove to myself I could do this without the use of my arms. My combat instructors would've been so proud. Perhaps it was a foolish move, but at least it made crushing them a little more fun.

I kicked for Lanky's knee but only landed on his shin, and he yanked my head back farther until my chin was pointed toward the sky. He had the audacity to laugh as his other hand wrapped around me and yanked me against him.

Good.

I forced all my weight into him, my momentum making him lose his footing, and we both stumbled backward into the glass window. I heard the shattering sound before I felt my stomach dip, and we tumbled through the window into the tavern. Luckily, Lanky made an excellent shield and I didn't feel a single cut as I landed back on top of him. I rolled off him toward a patch of bare floor that wasn't covered in scattered glass shards.

Lanky got to his feet first, but instead of turning back to where he could've easily pummeled me into the ground, he bolted out the door, whining, "Sallin's going to kill us when he sees what we did to his window!" He shouted to his comrades across the alley. "Come on, Bones—let's get out of here."

Grateful Lanky's broad boots had swept clear a path for my bare soles, I scrambled to my feet just in time to see Navin storming back through the crowd, gaping at me. The rest of the tavern carried on their drunken debauchery as if two people hadn't just crashed through their window.

"What did I say?" Navin gritted out, glancing over his shoulder before grabbing me by the arm and yanking me back out into the alleyway. "I told you not to cause any mischief."

I offered him a sheepish grin. "Would you call this mischief?"

"I know where Galen den' Mora is," he said, grabbing the horse's reins with one hand and holding my upper arm for show with the other. People cheered and toasted to Navin in the streets as if he caught himself a large deer and not an actual person.

They didn't even know I was a Wolf, which made their cheers all the more disturbing.

"And Maez?" I scanned the streets as if I might find her.

"They threw her out of here about an hour ago."

My body sagged in relief. "She's alive? She's safe?"

"She drank half the tavern dry."

"That sounds about right." Still, I bounced on the balls of my feet, adding gleefully, "I told you she'd be here."

"I don't know if I should be impressed or disturbed," he replied.

"Impressed, definitely," I teased. "But I should've known that she'd be nearly passed out before breakfast."

"The barman said she went back to the wagon to sleep it off, but he expected her back by dinnertime. Said she's practically lived in there the past two weeks."

Two weeks. Gods, it felt like a lifetime since that sandstorm, not simply a couple of weeks. Everything I knew about the person standing next to me had completely upended in that time.

"Well, I hate to break up her mourning," I said with a chuckle. "Let's go tell her we rose from the dead."

Navin nudged me with his shoulder. "Cruel."

I arched my brow. "You're just now realizing that?"

SADIE

WE FOUND GALEN DEN' MORA PARKED AT THE EDGE OF THE CITY where a few tussocks poked up from the sand and the oxen grazed. How they knew not to wander too close to the edge, I had no idea. The jagged cliffside seemed to appear out of nowhere, the sand on the mountain blurring into the sand far below. My legs felt shaky as we neared the edge, as if the entire mountain might plummet at any moment.

Despite being at the outskirts of the criminal part of town, Galen den' Mora looked as untouched as ever, not a single looter or ruffian nearby. I scrutinized the wagon with new eyes. The songs transcribed around the edges were branded into the wood like wards, no longer just merry tunes but actual protection from harm. All the paintings and symbols suddenly carried more weight. What I'd thought once to be fanciful decorations, now I could clearly see was the magic of this place.

A dozen new questions flooded into my mind. I wanted to know how it all worked. Was there more to Galen den' Mora's magic? What were the limits of it?

I heard the snoring before we even got to the door. I yanked my hands free of their binding and raced up the steps of the wagon, Navin at my back. When I peeled the curtain aside, I let out a giant sigh of relief.

Maez slept across one of the low couches, a bottle still dangling from her fingers and drool trailing down her cheek.

"Thank the Moon!" I exclaimed, rushing over to her and pulling her limp body into a hug.

"Wh—" Her hands shot out, holding me at arm's reach for a second and blinking the sleep from her eyes until she got a good look at my face. "Ostekke fucking gut me! I thought you were dead." She pulled me back into a crushing embrace. "What the fuck happened to you? You look like you went three rounds with a juvleck."

"Missed you, too," I murmured into her shoulder.

"And you," Maez barked as she looked at Navin. "How did *you* survive that fall?"

"That is a long, long story," I said, pulling her up to a seat beside me.

"Gods," she said glancing between us. She paused, her gaze snagging on me as her mouth split into a self-satisfied grin. "You two fucked, didn't you?"

I choked on nothing but air. "What?"

She guffawed, her words slurred with drink. "Oh, there is no point trying to deny it. I know you too well." She waved her hand in my face and grabbed my cheeks like I was a baby. "I know this face."

I shoved her arm away. "It's . . . uh, complicated," I hedged, cringing at Navin with an apologetic look. I'd told him he was effectively my mate, and now I called our relationship *complicated*? Great. *Really smooth, Sadie.* This is why I couldn't be trusted with relationships.

"Complicated. Clearly." Maez let out a derisive snort. "I mean, I already assumed you were off being a little skin chaser with him." I bared my teeth, and she held up her hands. "Don't get your tail in a twist," she said. "I meant it in a loving way."

"Joke or no," Navin said more quietly, "a relationship such as ours needs to be kept quiet in these parts. We don't want any Onyx Wolves catching on."

The conversation was cut short when I spotted my pack shoved under one of the low shelves. I squeaked as I dashed over and flung open the flap.

"What the fuck is she doing?" Maez asked from behind me.

"No clue," Navin replied.

Digging frantically, I threw all my clothes and belongings all over the floor until my hand landed on a hard leather bundle. I yanked it out and held it to my chest in the tightest hug. "My knives," I crooned, kissing each sheath one after the other. "My sweet, sweet knives."

"Of course," Maez said. "Your best friend gets a hug, but you're on the verge of tears for your knives. Thanks a lot, Stabby."

"I lost the others in the sandstorm," I said. "But I packed some backups." I rocked them back and forth, kissing them one more time, before whispering, "I'm never leaving you again."

I stood and rejoined Maez on the couch, still wiggling like a gleeful child. "Stop it," she muttered, rubbing her eyes. "You're already a blur."

Navin rolled up his sleeves. "I've got to go find somewhere to stable the horse. Then I'll get the oxen hitched up," he offered. "We should roll out of Sankai-ed as soon as possible." He paused, halfway out the doorway. "We can fill her in on our journey."

He got three steps out of the wagon before Maez turned to me and said, "So how big is he? Big, right? I've seen those hands—"

I cupped my palm over her lips. "I think we need to get you a very strong cup of tea before we have this conversation." She nodded and started to make her way to the kettle, but I remembered her attempts at the beverage.

"I'll make it."

TEA TURNED INTO A LEAN DINNER, WHICH TURNED INTO AFTER-dinner drinks. I was a bit surprised Maez would want more, but she just said, "Hair of the Wolf," and I couldn't help but nod—I'd been there.

Even long after the sun set, Maez still peppered me with questions. When the oxen started on the rope bridge to the next island up, Eshik, Navin came inside to join us. Maez hadn't kept the kitchen stocked and the provisions were sparse, but with a little ingenuity—and a lot of pickled vegetables—I managed to pull together a lentil stew that tasted good enough.

"So how come you're not just covered in song tattoos?" Maez asked, cocking her head at Navin.

I'd told her as much as I could about the Songkeepers. I could practically see her mind spinning in the exact same way I'd felt for days.

Navin pushed his empty bowl into the table and blotted his lips with a napkin. "Our magic must be sung or played—"

"But Galen den' Mora—" Maez countered.

"Is made of a dying wish. The songs protect the wagon, yes, but they are also there as a reminder for us to sing them. There's a lot of songs to remember."

"And not everyone has this song magic?"

Navin shook his head. "Only some possess the power to wield the song. It passes from one generation to the next. But many of those were lost to time. There might be some families out there that possess the magic and don't know it, like me and my brother."

"So what magic can you do specifically?"

"You ask better questions than me," I said, dipping the last of the stale bread into my stew. "It took me ages to get these answers."

Maez cut me a look. "That's because you were too busy playing prisoner . . . *and* getting fucked," she added under her breath. I stomped on her foot under the table. "What! Am I wrong?"

"You spoke of lesser and greater magics," I said, turning from Maez and ignoring her smug expression. "Can your magic unlock any door like you did in the cell?"

"Ooh, that's a good question." Maez went to prop her elbows

on the table but missed one and nearly smacked herself in the face. I moved her glass away from her.

"Only doors locked by our magic can be unlocked by them," Navin said. "But we can sing people to sleep and then nick the keys off of them, if that helps?"

Memories of Ora and Navin singing as we fell asleep in the wagon played over in my mind. I'd never slept as soundly nor fallen asleep as quickly as I had on Galen den' Mora. I'd thought maybe it was the rocking motion, but now it was clear it was their songs.

"And what if there's ten armed guards and not one?" I asked.

He stared at the ceiling, weighing the question before answering, "I don't know about ten. The greater the number of people, the harder it is."

"How many of you are strong enough to conjure monsters?" Maez asked.

Navin shook his head again. "The greater magics are forb—"

"I know, I know, conjuring monsters comes at a great cost," she said in a mocking tone. "*But* it could be powerful for us, too."

"Sawyn wasn't powerful for us. She was powerful against us," Navin said darkly.

"But what if the songs that control your monsters could control sorcerers, too?" Maez countered. "Has anyone ever tried?"

"It's not exactly something they could experiment on, Maez," I said. "It's an interesting theory though—controlling sorcerers, now maybe *that* could win a war."

"These ideas could get a lot of people hurt," Navin cut in.

"Or it could save them," I replied. "If King Nero discovers that Ora is more than just a meaningful person to Calla," I said. "If he learns that Ora possesses this knowledge, there'd be mountains of bodies . . ."

The three of us collectively shuddered.

Maez grabbed all the bowls and stacked them. "So *why* are we still going to Rikesh?"

"Because we are pretending to offer me to Tadei to steal the Onyx Wolves' treasure," I said.

Maez's tongue licked her back molar, confused. "*Because . . .*" Her eyes narrowed at me as she took a sip of the water I'd swapped for her drink.

I looked at Navin. "Because Navin promised his husband."

Water flew across the table, a giant spray of it coating the wood. "His *husband?*" Maez shouted and Navin pinched the bridge of his nose.

Maez moved to stand, and I grabbed her by the shoulder and roughly shoved her back into her chair. "Defend my honor another day," I snarled.

"You lying piece of shit," Maez snapped. "Was nothing you told us real?"

"Maez!" I shouted. She glared at me. "Do you think I didn't already go over all this?"

"But *I* didn't," she snapped.

"Three things I've told you were true," Navin said, answering her questions. "I am a musician. I travel the continent in Galen den' Mora." His warm eyes landed on me. "And I'm in love with your best friend."

Now was my turn to nearly spit my drink all over the table. I shoved my teacup away and rocked back in my chair, staring at him wide-eyed. "*When* did you tell her this?"

"In Taigos," Maez answered for him. "When you were sleeping."

My mouth fell open as I twisted back and forth between the two of them. "Maez knew before I did?" Without looking, I shifted my drink farther away as Maez grabbed for my cup.

She rolled her eyes, making her whole drunken body wobble, before she twirled an accusatory finger a little too close to my face. "Can we please circle back to how your human is *married?*"

I slapped her hand away. "Can we please circle back to how you didn't tell me he told you he *loved* me?"

Navin placed two placating hands on the table between us.

"Let's put this to the side for one second, okay? The real reason we need to go to Rikesh is not for the bounty."

Maez cocked her head at him like a confused pup. "It's not?"

"We need to go to Rikesh for a vase."

Maez's frown deepened. "And what is on this Rikeshi vase?"

"A song. *The* song," I said.

Navin grimaced, his words sputtering out as he grasped for an explanation. "Hidden amongst the carvings of the vase is the eternal song."

"And what exactly can this song do?"

He took a beat before finally replying, "It can conjure new monsters into the world." He glanced at me. "Our ancient predecessors gave the vase to the Wolves to keep us from using it. There was fear that using the song would destroy the world. My ancestors didn't expect the Wolves to treat us so badly. They never imagined we'd need it again."

Maez let out a groaning sigh. "Well, we sure could've used *that* power during Sawyn's reign."

"Sawyn's reign was because of that magic," Navin said. "Rasil's grandfather found the vase when he was performing at the palace and used the song to create his samsavat." Navin mimed the scuttling hands of the monster across the table. "That creation produced the dark magic that claimed Sawyn."

"What does that mean?"

"It means if anyone uses that song again, it will bring even more dark magic into the world." He scrubbed a hand down his face. No matter how many times I heard him explain it, the thought still made my stomach clench. "I don't want Rasil to have that vase, but I want the Onyx Wolves to possess it even less. If they know what it is they have . . ." He blew out a long concerned breath. "Every time the song is sung, a new sorcerer will be created."

"Fuck," Maez said, stringing out the word as she dropped her cheek into her hand. It was a relief she was handling this knowledge just as poorly as I had. "So using this power could create another Sawyn?" Navin nodded. "Curse all the fucking Gods. Why can't we just have one good thing?"

"This is why we wanted it protected," he said. "Somewhere where the Songkeepers would never be tempted to use it."

"And the Valtan King never learned of what he possesses?"

Navin shook his head. "He thinks it an ancient relic if he thinks about it at all. The Songkeepers never told him of what lies in his trove."

"And how do we get access to this trove?" Maez asked.

Navin held my gaze, and I already knew the answer.

"By pretending to be the King's new sister-in-law," I said.

"Oh, Gods no," she snapped. "You're seriously going through with this?"

I eyed her. "Damrienn has Ora. Valta has the vase. If either of them learn of the power of the Songkeepers, they'd be able to use it to crush the Golden Court," I said.

"This is far from a diplomatic mission now," Maez groaned. "I could handle enchanting a few Wolves to support the Golden Court, but this . . . this is a power that could destroy us all. And Wolf Kings are the least trustworthy with such power. They're the most hot-tempered, foolhardy of us all. They'd definitely try and use it."

"Exactly." I said. "Gods, I hope my father and uncles aren't in the palace. That will only complicate things further."

"They're not," Maez said matter-of-factly.

"*How* do you know that?"

She shrugged. "Drunks talk," she said. "Word spread of three Silver Wolves cutting across the desert and crossing the Stoneater back to Damrienn. Maybe they thought you died in that sandstorm. Guess they're going back to Nero with their tails between their legs."

I hoped Nero punished them in all the ways I imagined he would.

"Well, at least that's one less thing to worry about," I said. "Although it would've felt pretty good to see Navin take that bounty out from under them."

Maez rapped the table with her knuckles in front of Navin. When he lifted his gaze to hers, she pointed a finger at him. "Don't think I forgot about the husband thing," she said elbowing me. "You and I are going to have a little chat about that later."

"No fur. No fangs," I muttered to her.

"No fun," she replied.

SADIE

HALFWAY TO RIKESH, THE ROPE BRIDGE FORKED INTO TWO. Nestled between the V of the two paths upon a webbing of rope was a building. A creaking sign swung in the breeze about the splintering door: *Avan Vi Rikenna*—Don't Look Down.

I immediately looked down.

Wind blustered up from between the rickety slats of wood that led to the tavern door. The ground so far below my feet was just a blur of beige. In the distance, I could see the thin line of the Stoneater River that carved the border between Valta and Damrienn. Ostekke gut me, we were so high that clouds rushed by *below* us.

Merry music played and warm firelight flickered from the fogged windows, but my stomach was all the way in my feet as I walked down the last steps of Galen den' Mora.

"You know, when I said I could use a drink . . ." I hedged, wobbling on the last step that bounced with my weight.

"We need to pick up some supplies," Navin assured. He placed a hand on the small of my back and I leaned against it like a dog tugging on a tight leash, practically falling backward on my ass. "Trust me, you'll forget all about it once we're inside and have a couple pints."

"I very much doubt that, Nav," Maez said from behind us.

The wind whipped back the hood of my cloak—a terrible disguise if ever there was one. At least I wouldn't have to have my hands bound if I was hidden in the shadows of my garment. Maez in an act of solidarity donned a matching cloak, making us look more like temple acolytes than travel-weary passersby.

Navin stepped confidently onto the narrow boardwalk path that led to the tavern. I noted the way the slats bent and tilted under each of his footsteps. Acid rose up my throat. My limbs felt shaky and light, my appendages watery and out of control. It felt as if my body might fling me over the coarse rope barriers against my own will.

"Come on," Maez said, tugging me by the elbow. I clung to her arm like a hawk snatching a fish with its talons. "Seriously? Ouch," she grumbled, but I just dug my nails into her tighter.

There were times to be petulant and there were times to feign bravery and right now I gave absolutely zero fucks about how frightened I seemed, I was not letting go of her arm.

"I'm not falling from the fucking sky again, Maez," I muttered. My legs started trembling as we stepped onto the first board. My whole body braced as if the board would crack below my feet, my muscles tense and preparing for the plummet.

"Four more steps and we're in the doorway," Maez said, and I didn't know if she was trying to reassure herself or me. "Stop acting like a bunny and start acting like a soldier."

At that pointed comment, I moved. Better to just get it over with and stop drawing out my torment. I crossed the last four slats in a frantic scramble, dragging Maez along with me as we simultaneously yanked up our hoods. When we shut the tavern door behind us, my mind was left reeling at the disparity between one side of the threshold and the other. Inside, the tavern was warm and inviting, dimly lit by flickering candles atop each table and a roaring fire in the hearth along the far wall. Despite the sweltering climate of the floating mountains, the air around the tavern was rather cool with a draft of wind that made the fire pleasant rather than stifling.

Swallowing the lump in my throat, I tried to not think too much about the miles of air between me and the sand dunes far below.

Navin waved to the barmaid, miming a drink in his hand and mouthing the word "ale."

The tavern was nearly full to bursting, only a single barstool left unoccupied. The crowd didn't bother to look at us despite our dramatically frenetic entrance and shadowed hoods. Judging by the mishmash of patrons, the tavern was used to travelers from everywhere. A trio of musicians played from one corner, a rousing card game drawing a crowd from the other. People milled around the bar wearing everything from furs to lightweight linens, jewels to threadbare jackets, passing every type of coin over the bar top.

By the time I took the place in, Navin was already sitting at a booth beside the fire, having darted to claim the table that still carried the leftover dinner and half-finished drinks of the last patrons. Maez and I tiptoed over to him, cringing at every creak in the boards below our feet.

"You get used to it," Navin said as Maez and I shakily sat.

"After ten pints of ale perhaps," Maez muttered. "Ah," she said when the barmaid set three tall glasses of foaming golden liquid on the table. "Bless you, Goddess."

I couldn't quite fathom how, without even seeing Maez's face, the barmaid blushed and gave Maez a wink as she collected the dirty plates and glassware. I rolled my eyes. Like a sorcerer to the darkness, Maez seemed to draw in every living person in Aotreas. I chugged my drink, the liquid burning down my throat, and passed it back to the barmaid before she could even step away from the table.

I stifled a burp and dropped two golden gritas on her tray, saying, "Keep them coming."

Maez passed her now-empty glass over, too. "Agreed."

The barmaid's cheeks flushed a deeper shade of scarlet as Maez tossed another coin onto her tray. She gave a half curtsy and hustled back off toward the bar.

"You're mated," I reminded her.

"And Briar is lucky to have someone so desirable, no?"

Maez tugged her hood lower and turned her attention back to Navin. "So why exactly have you brought us to this death-defying interlude?"

"Look at this," he said, taking a crumpled sheet of paper from his pocket and unfurling it on the table. He placed the candlestick at one end and his glass of ale at the other to keep the paper from curling.

Maez and I leaned in, inspecting the rudimentary drawing. It appeared to be a floor plan.

"This," Navin said, circling his finger around the largest rectangular room, "is the grand hall. And here"—he moved his finger through a labyrinth of corridors to an oval room in the south corner—"this is the gallery where the vase is on display. The room is locked, though; we need to get Luo to open it."

We paused as the barmaid came back with more drinks, two for each of us, and Maez thumbed her an extra crover in appreciation. We waited until she disappeared into the throng again before Navin continued.

"Once Sadie and I announce ourselves at the gate, we will most likely be escorted through the grand hall to get an audience with the King," he said. "The King will want to make a spectacle of his brother's new bride."

My grip on my glass tightened. I knew this was the plan, but I didn't love hearing it stated out loud. "The only spectacles I like to make are in the sparring rings," I groused under my breath.

"Maez, you can go through the servants' passageway"—Navin pointed to a little doorway at the bottom of the page—"and wait by the door to the gallery. I will present Sadie and ask that instead of her hefty bounty I may select three pieces of art from his giant collection." Navin's grin widened. "He'll think me a foolish artist and agree. It's a better deal than parting with that much coin."

"And if he doesn't agree?" I asked.

"He will," Navin said. "I am highly doubtful that a King who loves gold as much as Luo wouldn't rather part with a few artifacts gifted to his family—by *human* artists no less. Luo agrees to hand over the vase, and then Maez can help you sneak out the back."

"Great," I muttered. "I'll just *sneak out the back,* shall I?"

"Wouldn't be the first time you had to jump out a bathing chamber window," Maez said with a laugh. "I doubt Prince Tadei will expect his bride to do that."

"Especially if we can make it look like your hands are bound when they aren't," Navin said. "They won't suspect you capable of running."

"How are we meant to fake shackles?" I asked, gulping down the rest of my drink. The warm buzz helped alleviate some of the terror swirling in my gut.

"She might have something." Navin nodded to an old woman who sat in the center of the room. She was knitting what looked to be a pair of mittens. A giant bag of yarn sat beside her, and the table was strewn with whorls of string.

Maez and I exchanged glances, ones that only our keen sight could see. She clearly was wondering if we were looking at the same woman, too. "How is she going to help us?"

"Let me worry about that," Navin hedged. "We should also prepare to create a distraction where Sadie can run back to the wagon that way if all else fails."

"That's going to have to be one epic distraction," I muttered.

"I have a few ideas," Maez said, propping her elbows on the table and grinning. "But how am I meant to just waltz into that doorway without a bunch of servants immediately questioning me?"

"As I said." Navin tipped the crown of his head toward the card game in the corner. "We came here to get supplies."

As the crowd parted, we spotted them. Two burly men in dented bronze armor covering tawny fighting leathers. Their chest plates bore the arcing symbols of the moon phases, and the hilts of their weapons were detailed with gold and gems like bursting miniature suns. Over the backs of their chairs, helmets hung by golden chin straps along with thigh-length tan military jackets covered in medals and badges denoting their rank.

Wolves. If the attire wasn't enough to give them away, the sharpness of their features and keen, wary eyes certainly did.

"What in the . . ."

"What are they doing all the way out here?" I leaned into the table and kept my voice low, not wanting the Wolves to hear us over the rabble. "Playing cards with humans no less?"

"Some of the Onyx Wolf pack live on the islands surrounding Rikesh," Navin said as he took another sip of ale.

Maez and I exchanged confused glances. "They don't all live in the city with their King?"

"I'm sure they convene frequently, but no," he said. "The pack is far more spread out than the Silver Wolves in Highwick."

I'd never really considered how much Nero wanted to keep us under his thumb. The rest of the Silver Wolf pack had lived in elaborate townhouses surrounding his castle no more than a stone's throw away. Soldiers were allowed to live slightly farther out for training, but we were all still right there in Highwick, where he could keep a watchful eye on everyone. King Luo seemed to have a far longer leash for his pack.

"I would've wagered a thousand crovers that no Wolves frequented this place," Maez said as she studied the two men.

"That's why they're here," Navin said with a shrug, waiting for us to piece the meaning of that statement together. When we only just stared back at him, he added, "Why do you think the Onyx Wolves come all the way out here?" He tipped his head to the table again as a human woman dropped into one of the Wolves' laps, cackling as she ripped off a bite of bread and fed it to him. The Wolf's hands were greedy and possessive as they fisted in her skirt and pulled her tighter. Her lust-filled grin matched his own. "They don't want anyone to see their *philandering*."

I dropped my gaze to scrutinize the table, afraid I might lock eyes with Navin. I knew by *philandering* he meant *skin chasing*, but he was trying to be diplomatic for my sake. I hated that I was ever made to feel like my attraction to Navin was taboo, that we were meant to be a secret, that people would speak of us in whispers. I hated more that I still felt shame creeping up my cheeks along with a burning blush.

I cleared my throat and steeled myself to look up again. "What supplies specifically are you planning on acquiring from them?"

"His uniform," Navin said matter-of-factly as the card game erupted into cheers. One of the Wolves dragged a pile of coins across the table. "None of the humans will bother Maez if she's dressed like a Wolf, and she will be very helpful in getting you back out of the palace again. No one will double-check Tadei's princess if she's moving with an Onyx Wolf guard."

I snorted into my drink, foam spraying across the table, as the human woman and the Onyx Wolf guard started sloppily kissing. "Looks like we've just got to give him a couple more minutes with her and nicking their clothes will be a piece of cake."

"For some reason he strikes me as the sort to keep his boots on," Maez added with a laugh. "Best you can hope for is he unbuckles his belt."

I chuckled back. "Point well made."

"I have a better idea anyway," Maez said, cheering the air and rising.

I tried to grab her elbow. "Maez, wait—"

But she was already swaggering over to the card table. She dropped a pouch of coins on the table and feigned a drunken stumble into the nearest chair. Her hood tipped back as she smiled with all the charm of a rich lord as she looked from one cardplayer to the next. "Who wants to make this game more interesting?"

SADIE

MAEZ WAS TRULY A CHARISMATIC MASTERMIND. I'D NEVER heard of the card game she proposed to the table, but it involved people removing items of clothing for every lost hand. By a dozen rounds in, Maez had only removed her boots, while the rest of the table was in various states of undress, one Wolf in only his undershorts. She made it look easy—and fun—just a human traveler with a penchant for debauchery.

After filling our bellies with greasy food—and washing it down with another few drinks—my anxiety finally eased. At some point, Navin's hand had found mine under the table. Our fingers skimmed over each other's, both of us wearing matching secret smiles. I wondered if he felt the freedom, the simple joy, of this little moment as much as I did. Here we were nameless. Just two people who wanted to hold each other's hands in a tavern at the edge of the world.

Navin tried to say something to me, but the roar of laughter from the card table was near deafening and the musicians were playing twice as loud to compete.

"It's too loud," I shouted as I stood from the table. Navin seemed to intuit what I said despite my words being drowned out by the clamor. I hooked my thumb at Maez who was now shirtless in only a black undervest and wearing an Onyx Wolf helmet askew on her head. "Let her play."

We sat on the steps of the wagon, the blustering wind now calming my flushed cheeks. The warm buzz of ale sang golden through my veins, and I stared out at the wisps of clouds dancing past us.

My whole body sighed along with each breath as Navin wrapped one arm around my shoulder and I leaned into him.

We stared at the dark underbelly of Rikesh floating in the distance as he said, "My father used to make up songs about the black rock mountains in the sky. I never thought one day I'd be floating in the air staring up at them, let alone frequenting them so often they start to feel . . . normal." I felt the lift of his cheek as he smiled against the top of my head.

"Was he a good man, your father?" I normally wouldn't have asked such a weighted question, but here with nothing but sky all around us and his arms encircling me, it felt safe to speak of such things.

Navin let out a little contemplative hum. "He was." His words were a whisper on the wind. "Parts of him are starting to fray in my memory like looking through a fogged window." I leaned in farther, loving the rhythm of his words, speaking in a way only a musician could. "The strangest things stand out: the way his eyes crinkled when he laughed, the timbre of his voice as he sang his larger-than-life stories, the way he would pick at his lute until the embers of our fire flickered out . . . but above all else, I remember one sound—the last sound he ever made." My breath caught in my throat, the moment so delicate I was afraid to speak or move. "It has haunted me these many years. I hear it on the storm wind and the swish of a broom and the whipping of sails. The sound of his last surprised gasp. One single breath. It wasn't a scream, no dramatic cry, just the tiniest inhalation, like a stolen breath between verses of a song, and then he vanished, pulled into the darkness of the gold mines."

My stomach roiled as I thought of the paintings I'd seen of juvlecks, of their whip-like tongues and long reptilian bodies. Grae had told me of his encounter with the beast deep within the mines of Sevelde. We'd never know the true number of how many people died fleeing from Sawyn's wrath through the Olmderian mines. But the vastness of loss could sometimes wash over me; the multitudes of faceless dead hurt less than the one—the father who always had a song, who died with a single gasp, leaving his son to flee the depths of the mines alone.

I cleared my throat, emotions constricting my windpipe.

"I've mourned him for so long," Navin said, his throaty words tight. "And yet sometimes it still doesn't feel real to have lost him. I never got to bury him. Never had but a carving on the mine's entrance of his initials to pray to."

"You deserve more than that," I said, wishing I could lift that invisible pain off him, the pain that made his shoulder slump and his head hang. "When we return to Olmdere, we will erect a proper memorial to your father so that whenever you travel through, you can visit him and say the prayers. We will mourn him in all the ways you never allowed yourself." I combed my fingers through Navin's hair as he sniffed. "We will mourn together."

"This is the cost of war. This feeling, this burning that is gnawing at my insides," he said. "This is what's at stake if we don't succeed tomorrow. This is the feeling I want to spare so many families from feeling. So many more could be lost to monsters if the Onyx Wolves find a way to harness those songs."

"We will get the vase," I reassured him. "And we will hide it where no human or Wolf can use it." Before this moment, I'd debated trying to convince Navin to use it, to see if we could use the songs to help us win this war. It felt . . . justifiable. But now, now I knew I never wanted to be responsible for the look on Navin's face. Now I knew I would do everything in my power to not let anyone drag one more scar across his heart. "One way or another. We will find a way to get Ora back, too—I promise you. There's enough grief in this world already."

"Sometimes I'm grateful in some strange little way for the suddenness with which I lost my father, for the finality of his death." Navin's guilty water-filled eyes finally lifted to mine. "Because I mourn my brother even as he still lives. I think you know that feeling all too well. You've lost your family, too, even though they are still alive."

My throat tightened further, tears pricking my eyes until they were as glassy as Navin's own. "I do." I whispered the tremulous words. "I wish I could just hate my father, wish it was as simple as that. But I grieve every good memory along with it. It wasn't all bad. It wasn't all evil. I don't know how to hang on to any of the good now; every moment of fondness feels like a betrayal. I've been reeling ever since we left. How do I reconcile two such disparate truths? How do we find where we belong outside of all that we were?"

Navin wiped one of my tears away with his knuckle, then palmed his cheeks to try to stop his matching tears from falling. "I found belonging with Galen den' Mora," he said. "But a part was always missing, too, like a melody without a final note. It wasn't home." He pulled me tighter to him and I slipped my arm around him back, needing his closeness.

"I doubted for so long if such a feeling was even real."

"I used to think that," he agreed. "But now I'm beginning to wonder." He sighed and looked up at the sparkling midnight above us. "Of all the places in Aotreas, why does *this moment* feel the most complete I've felt in a long, long time?" He threaded his fingers through my own and squeezed. "But I already knew the answer. It's already been written in all the old songs just waiting for me to recognize it: maybe home isn't a where but a who."

"Who?" I meant it as in questioning the premise, but his answer said it all.

"Only you, Sadie."

"Just me," I said, thinking about how he'd admitted as much to me in Taigos. How he'd wished I'd existed outside of anything else.

"No." Navin seemed to spot my train of thought. "Only you and all of you," he amended, dusting a soft kiss across my lips before pulling back again. "I want *everything* that you are— my stubborn, beautiful, recklessly brave Wolf."

More tears streaked down my cheeks as he said those words—*my* more than anything—as he claimed me for everything I was. I squeezed his hand back. I felt the truth in every syllable, recognized it reflecting back from within me. We'd battled monsters and fled attackers and fought each other until we were bloody, and yet I felt more steady in my soul than I ever had. I couldn't fight it any longer. Navin was my steadiness, my solitude, my home.

Maez kicked open the door to the tavern and swaggered out with a mountain of mismatching garments piled over her shoulder. "Let's get this show on the sky bridge before they come to their senses," she said, pausing as she noted the tears streaking our cheeks and the way we held each other. "I'm just going to . . . um." She skirted past us, tiptoeing up into the wagon. "I'll just be inside. When you're ready."

She awkwardly stumbled into Galen den' Mora, and Navin and I let out a unanimous laugh. I wiped the last of my tears, then stretched my arms skyward.

"We should probably go." I moved to stand when Navin's hand slid to the back of my neck and pulled my forehead back to his.

He brushed a featherlight kiss across my lips and whispered, "Thank you for asking me about him."

"I want to know, Navin. I want to know everything."

"Me, too."

I deepened our kiss, my hands threading through his mussed-up hair, wishing we could pause the world and take this time to be together, but knowing we needed to keep moving. I let my mouth tell him in all the ways my words failed me—stripped bare of all the rules and misbeliefs of Wolf life—I knew he and I fit together like the moon and the sun, and that was enough. Our love didn't need to make sense to anyone else but us.

CALLA

WE TRAVELED THROUGH NEAR WHITEOUT CONDITIONS. SEVERAL times I feared that our sleigh would get lost in the snow along with the sledge of gold that we towed behind us. Ingrid rode in the sleigh in front of us and another sleigh was packed with five of Ingrid's best guards in front of her. Despite her assurances to the contrary, I doubted if things went sideways, Ingrid's Wolf guards would bother to protect my court, especially the human ones.

When we arrived at the house at the top of the mountain, the air was so thin it was hard to take a deep enough breath. We'd passed through the other side of the storm clouds that clung to the craggy lower peaks. Up above the roiling frozen wind, the sky opened to twinkling golden stars. The constellations glittered so bright along with the half-moon that we could see the outline of the snow-covered peak and the mansion nestled into its side.

I lifted my chin to the Moon Goddess through the frosty window, hoping she protected us this night. My father's golden crown sat on my lap, and I gripped it so tightly I was sure I'd have an imprint of one of the giant rubies on my palm. All of Nero's calculations seemed intent on wounding me directly: taking Ora, demanding my father's crown . . . He was trying to win a war of spirits before he ever put one soldier on the advance.

But I wouldn't be broken by him, nor any Wolf, not even a King.

"I still don't think you should've come," Mina signed to Briar who kept nervously readjusting the white fur blanket over her lap.

"I still don't think *you* should've come," Hector cut in, looking at Mina. "What are you going to do if there's hostilities? Hit them with that?" He nodded to Mina's instrument case that rested against her shins. "If things go sour, you run, okay?"

Mina started to protest, but I held up my hands, halting the bickering. "I didn't want to bring any of you, but I also didn't want to leave any of you behind. So here we are." I let out a tense sigh between my clenched teeth and leaned back against the velvet seat. My breath streamed out in icy whorls as I spoke. "I don't trust leaving you in Taigoska without me," I said to Briar. "Because I fear you'd bolt to Valta to find Maez the second I take my eyes off you." Briar rolled her eyes. "And you," I said to Mina, "I want with me because the Wolves haven't treated you very well even with me watching. I don't like the idea of leaving you alone with them."

"I'm glad I'm here," she signed and nodded to her violin case. "Maybe a little music will help lighten the mood."

"We're going to need more than a merry tune to contend with Nero's soldiers," Grae said tightly.

"I'll take whatever I can get right now." I nudged him with my knee from under the fur blanket that covered our legs. "As soon as we get Ora and deliver this gold, we are turning this sleigh around and getting the fuck out of Taigos."

"Queens don't say fuck," Briar said.

"They do now." I gave my sister a frustrated look. I was done playing her version of a queen. "*I* do."

As we neared the house, we saw the chimneys already billowing with curling gray smoke. Five horses peeked from their stable stalls, already unhitched from the two carriages parked along the snow-covered building. Ingrid's mansion looked like a miniature version of her palace . . . perhaps miniature was a misnomer. It probably could easily house a hundred people.

Hector's knee bounced anxiously from where he sat between Mina and Briar. The action seemed to make Briar fiddle with her blanket more while Mina kept picking up her violin case and setting it back down again. I could practically taste the nerves hanging in the air between us. I had to reassure myself again we were on Ingrid's home turf. Between the two of us, we had several skilled guards not to mention our own fighting skills. Nero just wanted to humiliate me by taking my father's crown and demonstrating how easily he could manipulate me with Ora. But I would take the humiliation to get my friend back. That's all that mattered. I'd plan my revenge another day.

When the sleigh glided up to the mansion entrance, we didn't unpack our belongings, only stalked up the slippery, frozen steps. The tall wooden doors were wide open and warm light beckoned us through the fire and into the open expanse of the first floor. A fire roared in a gray stone fireplace, the chimney shooting straight up through the center of the room. Around it stood three Silver Wolves, and a fourth stood at the floor-to-ceiling windows that looked out over the mountainside and to the ocean beyond: Evres.

I scoured the room again. Apart from a few sparse cushioned chairs and a carved wooden table and chairs, the room was echoey and vacant, much like Ingrid's castle in the capital.

We heard the click-clack of the Ice Wolves' Queen's shoes climbing the stairs behind us, and then I caught her pausing in my periphery before gliding into the house and joining the Silver Wolves by the fire. She rubbed her hands together and stretched them toward the flames, such a casual act while her guards stood in rigid formation around her. Not a single cell in my body felt the cold, not as my heart raced in my chest and my hands gripped my father's crown tighter.

"No Nero?" I asked as I tentatively followed my guards into the space. Mina hummed as she wandered over to the bench and opened her violin case. She started playing with such haste as if she couldn't wait a single second for her music to begin, but it brought me little comfort as my stomach twisted into a knot. I tried to keep the fear out of my voice as I said, "I'd expected more of you."

"We're not here for a show of force," Evres said, twisting from the window to look back at me. His eyes danced with delight as they dropped to the crown in my grip. "We're here for a trade."

My eyes scanned over the room again. "Where's Ora?" Evres's smile widened. "We've brought your gold and crown, so where are they?"

"Come see this first." Evres beckoned with a hooked finger. "I want to show you our act of good faith."

Briar looped her arm through mine, clinging close to my side as my guards flanked me on either end. As I slowly paced over, I noted there were three doorways and two sets of windows through which we could flee. To my right, Ingrid and her guards lingered around the table by the archway that looked like it led into the rest of the house. To my left, the Silver Wolves lingered by the fire. On the far wall was a small door that looked like it led down into a cellar. Hector hung back close to the doorway out to the sleighs, protecting our exit.

Evres held a hand out to me, but I didn't take it as I approached.

"You are truly stunning," Evres murmured as his gaze slid up and down Briar.

I released Briar's arm and moved her behind me as Grae stepped between the two of them, blocking Briar from Evres's sight with his broad shoulders.

Evres let out a chuckle. "Forgive me," he said, holding up his hands and taking a step back. "It just seems such a pity that someone as regal as Briar Marriel isn't a queen. Damrienn still mourns the loss of the Crimson Princess."

"You mean the 'queen' Nero so easily pushed aside once he

realized she didn't have the power to give him what he wanted? You speak as if I'm dead, just as he did," Briar said, stepping around Grae. Clearly not cowed, her lips pinched into a tight frown. "I never wanted to be Queen. I only ever wanted a quiet life and a place to call home with my mate. Calla is more of a queen than I could've ever been. They are the Queen Olmdere needs and deserves."

She was looking directly at Evres, but I knew she was speaking solely to me. I wished we weren't in this crowded room of enemies and tentative allies. I wished I could spin around and hug her. Whenever I faltered, my twin somehow knew to instill that confidence back in me.

"A quiet life, hmm?" Evres's voice dipped, more contemplative as he ignored everything my sister said about me and my leadership. "Well, you'll always have a home with us in Damrienn, Princess. No matter what happens with Olmdere, you're part of the Silver Wolf pack."

"No," she said. "I'm a Golden Wolf. And this is my Queen."

"We'll see—"

"Enough." It was Klaus who cut him off. He took a pointed step toward Evres, the two Wolves sizing each other up as if ready to battle to claim Briar's hand.

I scrubbed a hand down my face, wanting to shout that she already has a mate. If Maez were here, there wouldn't be any of this peacocking. She'd probably have gutted a few of them by now.

"What is this act of good faith?" I asked, stalking the rest of the way to the windows and cutting off Evres and Klaus's staring contest.

At first, I couldn't see anything, simply seeing the reflections of ourselves and the firelight, but as I leaned closer, I started to make out the shadowed outline of the mountains and the waves distorting the moonlight on the water.

"Do you see them?" Evres leaned closer to the cool pane.

"See what?"

"On the water."

I narrowed my gaze further, making out tiny dots on the water. Initially, I thought they were waves, but then I recognized the outlines. "Are those . . ."

"Boats," Evres said.

Burning dread coiled tight in my stomach. Were they warships? Was Nero planning on attacking our shores? Were they luring us out here to leave Olmdere defenseless?

I tried to steady my breath. "And who is on those boats?"

"Humans," Evres said. I gave him a wary glance and he continued. "We gave them a choice. Stay in Damrienn and obey the Wolf laws, get rid of their ridiculous human words." He scanned me up and down, and I knew he was judging every inch of me, of who I was, of using the word "merem." "Or they can leave." I sucked in a sharp breath. "Any human who wishes to leave Damrienn has been granted safe passage to Olmderian shores. They are your problem now."

I watched through the window in disbelief until my breath fogged over the glass. There must be a hundred boats on the water fleeing to my shores. "Thank you," I whispered, my throat constricting with bitterness. "Thank you for at least letting them leave."

"Don't thank me yet," Evres said. Mina's music was a soft, slow tune that blanketed over the room as he spoke. "You will have to take care of all of them."

"I will," I vowed.

I'd make sure each and every one of them had a roof over their head and enough food to eat. I'd make a home for them better than any they ever had in Damrienn. I'd let them speak any language, pray to any Gods, and live the lives of their choosing. My hand drifted to my collarbone and the golden scar. I'd use every last piece of gold in my court and every ounce of magic from my dying wish to make it so.

Evres seemed disappointed, and I realized in this moment he thought this was supposed to upset me.

Yet another thing he and Nero clearly didn't understand about me. It made me stand just a bit straighter, knowing that Nero thought he had a bead on me, but was still the nearsighted, narrow-minded ruler. These people made my kingdom *stronger*. It may take time, but I would make sure of that.

I looked over at the three remaining Silver Wolves. "Now where's Ora?"

"Your father's crown first," Evres said, looking to the crown still in my clenched hand. He reached for it, and I threw it at his feet.

The sound of the metal clanging against the stone floor filled the room. I wondered if the same sound echoed through the hall of Olmdere when Sawyn killed my father. Which Nero did nothing about. One day I'd hear the sound of Nero's crown clattering to the floor—preferably with his head still attached. In the meantime, I'd make another crown in honor of my father's memory. Evres muttered under his breath but stooped to pick up the crown. He dusted it off with his velvet jacket sleeve and nodded to one of the other Silver Wolves.

The burly Wolf trudged down the three steps and banged on the cellar door behind him. A fifth Wolf appeared, and he shoved a person through the doorway.

"Ora!" I shouted, running over and catching Ora as they stumbled up the top step.

Their hands were bound in front of them, their mouth gagged, their eyes bloodshot and clothes crumpled, but they were alive and, from what I could tell, uninjured. I dropped to my knees in front of Ora, hugging them to me as they frantically muttered something through their gag.

"What?" I quickly reached for Ora's gag.

"It's a trap, Calla. Run!" they screamed as the *shing* of swords being unsheathed sounded behind me.

I stood and whirled, finding not only the three Silver Wolves and Evres with their swords drawn and pointed, but Ingrid's guards, too. We could fight, though. I was ready to fight. But then I stole a glance at the doorway and my heart plummeted.

Three men stalked up the steps, ones I recognized from Damrienn: Sadie and Hector's father and uncles. I thought Hector would whirl on them, fight them off, but instead his father walked right up to his son and clapped him on the shoulder with a smug smile.

Hector didn't meet my eyes as he lifted his sword and pointed it directly at us.

SADIE

WE ROLLED OVER THE REST OF THE ROPE BRIDGE, UP HIGHER where the railings disappeared and the wagon wheels were inches from the edge on either side. Maez and I clutched each other randomly at every rock and shake of the wagon, thinking we strayed a little too close to the edge and were falling. It probably didn't help that we were both impossibly hungover from the night of gambling that Maez had goaded me into once we left the tavern in the sky.

We were so high now I could barely make out the dots of the lagoons far, far below. Maez and I watched out the window as the sharp obsidian of the mountain's underbelly came into crystalline view. The jagged rocks looked almost carved like joinery fittings, and I wondered if there was another continent, another world where those puzzle work rocks fit like a lock to a key. The mystical nature of these floating mountains gave credence to the dusty old scrolls in the refuge library. Maybe Wolves truly weren't the first beings to inhabit this land. More and more, I believed the humans' histories and further doubted my own.

"One more bridge to go and we're in Rikesh," Navin said as he sipped the last of his tea at the kitchen table. Our two mugs sat cold across from him, our stomachs unable to manage more than pieces of the grease-fried bread Navin had whipped up for us.

"Another bridge," I groaned as Maez gripped my forearm. "Remind me never to return to this Gods-forsaken place."

"No wonder so few people make the journey to the Onyx Wolf kingdom," she quipped. She frowned at the last bite of bread pinched between her thumb and forefinger. "Why don't you have a song for curing hangovers?"

Navin chuckled and reached for my forsaken mug, helping himself. The Onyx guard's uniform was folded over the back of the chair next to him, looking freshly pressed now, along with a gauzy orange monstrosity that was apparently for me to wear. I didn't have the energy to complain, though. Maybe after another piece of bread . . .

As we entered the thick, teeming jungles of Eshik, the temperature morphed from the blistering dry heat of the desert to the far more humid kind. The wagon rocked again, rolling over the road covered in dried leaves and crawling vines. The verdant green surrounded us. Parrots squawked from the skies, black and golden monkeys climbed through the treetops, and striped snakes slithered off the road with the rumble of the wagon. The distinct smell hit me, too: not the spicy arid scent of Sankai-ed but now an earthy smell of leaves composting back into soil, damp foliage, and viscid air.

"It's beautiful," Maez said as she hooked her elbow out the window and admired the landscape.

"And shaded," I sighed as I poked my head out and looked up at the thick, flourishing canopy above us. The top of Galen den' Mora barely skirted through the arching space created from many traveling wagons, the trees trained up and around to create a tunnel through the forest.

"We'll need to keep our heads down in these parts," Navin said, grabbing me by the hips and tugging me back into my chair. "Both of you," he said, nodding at Maez. "You two will need to stay in the wagon until we reach the other side of the forest. No Wolves should be lurking out there."

"Makes sense," Maez says. She looked at me. "Are you going to be able to play along with this?"

"Of course."

I'd bathed and changed back into my own fighting leathers, my pack still waiting for me right where I'd left it the day of the sandstorm. Her eyes dropped to the butter knife I'd inadvertently picked up off the table and started flicking back and forth. I scowled and put the blunt knife back down.

"Of course? You know that means no violence, right? You need to seem under his control."

"Why does everybody keep treating me like I'm so prone to violence?" I spat, smacking the table and making the tableware clatter. Maez only raised her amused eyebrows at me. "Point taken. I only have to pretend for long enough for Navin to get the vase," I said.

Maez looked me up and down. "You should get her a veil in the next town. Present her as a little less feisty, more demure. No one would believe a human captured her looking like that." Maez held in a laugh. "Maybe that will buy us some time as well. Give Tadei some time to inspect his present—a little more pageantry might help sell it."

I mimicked gagging but said, "Fine, whatever." I pointed at Maez. "But you better be ready to make some moves. I've got about five smiles and fake laughs in me before I choke the life out of him." I stabbed my butter knife into the wood table, leaving only an amorphous dent.

Navin groaned. "Could you make your point without damaging the furniture, please?" I gave him a mischievous wink and he rolled his eyes.

"When we reach the other side of the forest, I should contact Briar," Maez said. "Last we spoke to Calla, we were here to make allies. Now we're going to steal from them."

"Surely Calla knew our chance at making allies disappeared

the moment Luo agreed to my marriage to Tadei without my consent?" I asked incredulously, and Maez snarled at the thought. "Exactly."

"The way these Wolf Kings think they can trade us around like sacks of grain without even our knowledge," Maez growled. "The Moon Goddess *herself* chose Briar for me and me for her. Why hasn't the pack risen up against Nero for this deal with Evres?"

"I don't know." I rubbed the back of my neck. "Fear of his retribution? If Nero says the Goddess made a mistake, who amongst the pack would lead the charge against him now that we're all gone?"

Maez's hands balled into fists. "I thought our families wouldn't be so cowardly."

I thought about my father and uncles, mourning the family I lost, one that I was just beginning to realize I never truly had to begin with. There was no loyalty to me. There was no loyalty even to the Gods. They only scrambled to save their own tails from Nero's wrath. They manipulated and abused to uphold the power of their King, and yet even the highest ranked among us lived and died by the whims of a system that was never designed to serve the many, but only the one.

"So Luo gets me, Nero gets Briar and a million Valtan gritas *and* an army of Onyx Wolves to help him take the rest of the continent," I said, craning my neck up to the high canvas ceilings as if searching for an answer.

"And I'm certain Nero promised to return Luo's money tenfold when they take Olmdere," Maez said. "Though I don't see the greedy bastard splitting his mines with Valta anytime soon. Maybe he'll cut them out entirely once he gets his hands on it."

"I would almost count on it. And Taigos?" I mused. "What will the country in the middle of all three do?"

"Survive. It depends if Calla is successful or not in persuading her, but I wouldn't be surprised if Queen Ingrid will do as she's always done," Maez observed. "Be impartial to protect her court.

Let whoever the strongest and baddest ruler is at the time dictate who enters her kingdom."

"Which is almost certainly not the Golden Wolves," I grumbled. "I know Calla is doing everything she can to rally Ingrid to her cause, but I don't think the Ice Wolf Queen has anything to give but empty promises."

"You'd think she'd at least try to protect herself from Valta," Maez said. "She was once promised to Luo, you know. He still feels jilted about not possessing Taigos if rumors are to be believed. With his alliance with Damrienn, he'll be able to take it from her."

"Too afraid to fight back until it's too late," I said. "Which is why we have to get this vase from them now." My gaze slid to Navin. "We can't let anyone possess such a powerful weapon, least of all our enemies."

"Only if you can pull off this ruse." Maez let out a sharp huff.

"How long does it take you to locate and steal a vase?"

Maez shrugged. "How long can you hold a smile without a knife in your hand?"

SADIE

"I LOOK LIKE A PUMPKIN," I GRUMBLED, STARING AT MYSELF IN the mirror. I wore a light flowing gown in a shade of deep orange that ruffled and cascaded down around my body doing nothing to accentuate my figure but rather hide it.

"Like a royal pumpkin," Maez countered as she finished tying my hair back in a matching orange scarf. "Besides, do you *want* to entice any of the Onyx Wolves? Here." She added the cream-colored veil over the top, the beads and lace obscuring my face. "This will buy us some time. Tadei will *love* the idea of being the first of his court to gaze upon your face."

"It's an archaic old Wolf custom," I muttered.

"So is selling off brides to the highest bidder. We're okay with playing that game, so let's be okay playing this one. It strokes his ego," Maez said. "And gives me more time to set up our escape plan. Navin will present you to the court and ask for his bounty. You *walk slowly*. Draw this thing out."

"I can barely see through this thing," I snarled as I pulled the veil off and set it on the kitchen table. "One belt of knives under the dress. Just one—"

"Nope," Maez said, holding up her hand. "You are a damsel in distress. Tadei is your knight in shining armor who is saving you from your human captor. Just follow the plan. Indulge the

King and his brother. You're the one who is so adamant this vase can't be in enemy hands."

I curled my lip. "Fine." I shimmied back out of the dress, stepping out into just my undergarments right as Navin walked through the curtains.

He froze, only his eyes moving to rove my figure for a split second before he cleared his throat and turned around. "Sorry," he said, "I have the rope to bind your hands with."

"Maez." I cut her a look. "Didn't you say you wanted to contact Briar?"

"I can't feel her in my mind," Maez muttered. "She's not in her Wolf form right now."

"Still," I pushed. "You should shift one more time anyway." I play-punched her in the arm. "We want you to be strong and ready."

"Stick to the eastern side of the jungle, though," Navin said, jutting his chin in the direction of the trees we were parked beside. "Stay in the thickest parts. If the trees start thinning, you're too close to the edge."

"Yeah, yeah." Maez looked at me and then Navin and then back at me before grumbling, "To be clear, Navin, you want me to go not too far, but far enough not to hear anything."

I glowered at her as both Navin and I blushed, but she just gave us a wink and wandered off.

When she was gone, Navin turned to me again, his eyes now hungry.

"Are you ready for this?" he asked, looking at the dress strewn across the table.

"As ready as I'll ever be." I tried to force confidence into my voice, but in truth my heart thundered in my chest. Finally, I relented and added, "There are so many ways tomorrow could go wrong. So many points at which it could all fall apart." Navin prowled closer. "And we need things to go our way at every turn to get out of there with our heads still attached to our bodies."

"I have faith," he said, approaching until we were toe to toe. "In you. In us. It will work out."

My gaze dropped to the silver rope in his hands. "It looks like metal," I said as I traced my hand over the painted fabric. The way the knots were woven made it appear almost like chain mail. At a distance they'd certainly be convincing.

"The platform is a good place for acquiring all manner of things." A thoughtful hum resonated through his pursed lips. "The Wolves will think you can't escape these bindings," he said, his warm breath whispering across my cheek. "But you will still be in control." He lifted the rope out of my touch, and I craned my neck up at him as he said, "Hold out your wrists." Breathlessly, I did as he commanded. "Like this." He tied the rope around my wrists, tucking the ends in the knot between, the glinting silver fabric looking like metal cuffs. "Good?" he asked.

My chest rose and fell faster as I nodded. "Good."

His other hand reached out and skimmed down my side before settling on my hip, leaving pinpricks in his wake. "I promise I'll get you out of there," he vowed. "I promise I'll keep us safe."

I looked up at him, holding those bronze storming eyes. "I know."

He bent down and ever so slowly kissed me. His warm lips moving over my own, the feeling making heat bloom low in my belly. His hands slid from my hips, up my torso, and to my arms, lifting them up until my bound hands stretched up above me. I arched my brow curiously as he backed me up a step and lifted the rope of my tied wrists to the coat hook behind me. It was just high enough that my heels lifted, and I had to stretch up onto the balls of my feet.

Navin smiled down at me, one hand still poised on the hook above me as he casually leaned over me. "This is just a taste of what's to come when we are free of this place," he murmured, dropping another lavishing kiss to my lips before stepping back and tugging my scarf down so it covered my eyes.

I gasped, suddenly more attuned to every sensation building in my body. My pulse thrummed through me as I waited, unseeing, wondering where he would touch next. As I teetered there on tiptoes, my ears strained to hear his breath, the sounds of him moving in front of me, the telltale thump of clothes hitting the floor.

I jumped when his two broad hands splayed across my outer thighs. Those hands moved up and down once before his fingers pressed in, squeezing my muscled flesh. I pressed my lips together, the anticipation already making me want to claw up a wall.

I felt his hot breath on my low belly, the air skittering down to the thin fabric between my legs. He pressed his lips to my mound and murmured, "You're already so wet for me, aren't you?"

"Yes," I whispered, my hips bucking to try to move that mouth lower.

His breathy chuckle danced across my flesh. He hooked a finger into my undergarments and pulled them down until they were pooled around my feet. I stepped out of them as those strong hands steadied my hips.

Lips trailed up my inner thigh. "Whatever happens in the palace tomorrow. Whatever Tadei says to you. I need you to remember one thing."

"What?" I asked breathlessly.

"You're mine, Sadie," Navin murmured, his breath tickling the hair between my legs. "No Wolf will ever claim you." My throat bobbed. "No mouth will ever taste you. No cock will ever fill you.

"Now tell me I'm yours."

His finger trailed down my folds and I shuddered, my head dropping back as he parted my flesh. His finger stilled, his breath hot on my pussy, waiting, and I let out a desperate groan.

"You're mine," I panted.

With a satisfied hum, he lowered his mouth and tasted me. I gasped, the sensation even more heightened with my eyes covered and my hands bound. He started in slow, leisurely licks that already had me climbing toward my climax. As he began moving faster, circling my clit, I let out a low moan. I squirmed against his mouth, needing something to hold on to, feeling like I might float away with the sensations building within me.

Reading my body, Navin hooked one of my knees over his shoulder and continued his wanton feast. His hand squeezed the flesh of my ass as I ground into him, leveraging the new angle to move him right where I wanted. Each circle of his tongue made my breath catch. My body was so sensitive to his touch as he played me better than any of his many instruments. He was my conductor, and my cries of pleasure were his song.

When Navin's other hand trailed up the inside of my thigh and his finger poised at my wet entrance, I shook my head.

"Wait," I moaned and his fingers stilled. "I want all of you."

His groan vibrated against my pussy, making my clit throb and pushing me closer toward an orgasm I knew was so close to the surface now. He released me, my breathing coming out in desperate heaves. I waited there, teetering so close to release, desperate to feel anchored by his touch again.

His hand lifted my bound wrists off the hook and looped my arms around his neck, leaving my eyes covered. My torso and belly brushed against his warm bare skin, the feeling electrifying. He lifted me by my ass, and I clung to him, unseeing, as he walked me down to the low couches and splayed me across the patchwork fabric.

I bit my lower lip at the feel of his hard length on my belly. Navin tugged up on the scarf, pulling it free, my hair spilling across the couch under me. His face hovered above mine, his eyes filled with heat. He pressed the tip of his cock to my entrance and my eyes fluttered closed.

"Look at me," he commanded, and my eyes opened again. He pushed into me an inch and my mouth dropped open into a perfect O. "I love you," he whispered as he pushed in farther. "I won't let anything happen to you tomorrow." His face was so open and raw as the feeling between my legs grew until he filled me to the hilt. "I swear it on my life. You are the bravest of warriors, but you can rely on me, too. I am stronger than you know. I will fight any human, Wolf, or monster who tries to tear us apart, Sadie."

Tears misted in my eyes, the emotion catching me by surprise. Normally it was me who did all the fighting. I was always the one vowing to slay my enemies and rain vengeance on loved ones' foes. Knowing I didn't always have to be the fighter, knowing in my deepest soul that Navin meant every word of love and protection, made a tear slide down my cheek.

"I love you," I said breathlessly, and Navin kissed that tear away. Just that slightest action made him move inside me and we both let out a unified moan. I relished the way we joined, never in my life feeling such a completion as when he and I were together.

He pulled out and pushed back in. Slow rolling thrusts that coaxed me back up toward the precipice I once teetered on. My bound hands threaded into his hair, pulling his lips to mine as he picked up speed again. I tilted my hips, meeting each of his pumps with a rocking of my own. He buried himself deep inside me, hitting a spot that made me cry out every time the tip of his cock grazed it. I was already so close, my thighs trembling as they tried to clench around his hips. Navin moved faster, his movements growing erratic as he grew closer to his own release.

"Yes," I moaned. "Gods, yes." He rode me faster, pushing me higher and higher.

"Sadie," he groaned, burying his face into the crook of my neck as he drove into me in deep, wild thrusts.

I tried to speak, tried to form words, but only a choked cry of ecstasy escaped my lips as my orgasm tore through me. My vision spotted, the force of it feeling like I was falling through the sky. My thighs gripped him tighter as my body clenched around him and he spilled into me. His fingernails clawed into my skin as his climax shattered him, until I couldn't tell where one moan ended and another began as wave after wave of pleasure coursed through me.

With a final breath Navin collapsed to my side and gathered me into his arms. And I knew then that this wasn't just to calm the anxiety we both felt for tomorrow, but also to remind us of all we had to fight for. Tomorrow would go well because it had to, because I needed hundreds of more nights in his arms, listening to our breathing slow and our heart rates steady. This moment was everything I wanted my future to be.

SADIE

THE CAPITAL CITY OF RIKESH WAS A VAST PYRAMID, SLOPING UP and up to the royal castle in the center that looked down on the domed rooftops, gilded spires, and waving pennants of the city below. When we departed the wagon, Maez gave my arm a quick squeeze. She cut an impressive figure in her stolen uniform. She'd had to cinch the Wolf's belt to the tightest hole, but otherwise the garments fit her surprisingly well. With the gilded chin strap and the low-brimmed helmet, her features were obscured enough that no human would question her. So long as a member of the pack didn't try to strike up a full-on conversation with her, she'd be fine.

"Be quick," I whispered to her as she adjusted her military jacket. I wanted to give her a hug. Her face told me she wanted to do the same. But there were too many eyes upon us now. Instead, I just gave her a swift pat on the shoulder like I'd done so many times before. "Good luck."

"We'll be laughing about this over a bottle of wine tonight. I promise you," she said in her usual cavalier way and dashed off through the crowd. The humans of Rikesh gave her a wide berth, darting out of her way like a school of fish scattering in the presence of a shark.

Navin tugged on my arm, and I adjusted my veil one more time. The bloody thing was itchy and sweltering. I could barely see the castle in the distance but up close was a blur and I was forced to rely on Navin to guide me through the crowd. We trudged uphill, Navin parading me through the streets to the towering castle gates. Everywhere around us dripped in opulence. Even the tall sandstone walls surrounding the castle were beautiful, adorned with intricate mosaics depicting the many monsters that the Onyx Wolves had driven out of Valta.

Now, all that history seemed tainted and warped somehow. The war with the humans was entirely left out of the legends depicted on the walls. The histories that wrapped around the Onyx Wolf palace were that of Wolf glory. The only humans amongst any of the mythical creatures and heroic figures were the ones kneeling and bowing to Wolf kings of old. Never once had I thought to question this art, this truth. Never once had I thought the Wolves were anything but the saviors of the humans despite how we treated them now in current times. How—*how*— could I have ever thought that? The fact that humans ever battled with Wolves was so diametrically opposed to everything I was raised to believe. But history forgets the losers. Only those who win wars get to dictate how that event is told, and in Wolf history, humans showed up on *our* shores, begging to be saved from monsters; we saved them and they made us Gods.

I wondered if, after all this, Calla or Nero would be the one writing our next phase of history.

My eyes trailed from the swirling murals along the walls to the lone guard who stood in front of the towering iron gates. I had to twist my head to the side to see him through my veil. The beads and lace made blotchy patches that obscured my view. Beyond him was a winding path that led up to the black and bronze steps of the giant castle, resplendent with seven gilded domes and glinting bronze parapets that glittered in the sunlight.

I imagined from all the way up there, they'd be in the clouds, watching the city below like a sea of ants. The grandiosity was even beyond that of the other court castles, and the imposing positioning made it very clear who the ruler was in this land: a King who lived at the tallest peak of the highest mountain.

"I need to speak with your King," Navin called to the guard who was clearly a Wolf. Even at several paces away, I could tell by the keenness in his eyes and that otherworldly stillness. As he swaggered closer, his image blurred, obscured by the beads and lace.

"And *why* would the King bother to see a human?" he asked with a rough chuckle. His assessing green eyes flickered toward me. I felt his gaze rove over my veil, down my ruffled gown, and to where my hands were bound in silver rope behind my back. "Who's she?"

Navin kept his grip on my upper arm as he took a step forward and leaned in—a universal sign of a secret to share—and the guard couldn't help but lean in, too. "Sadie Rauxtide," he whispered. "I have Tadei's bride here. I've come for my bounty."

The guard's eyes flared as he looked at me again. "Lift her veil," he commanded.

"And let you be the first to gaze upon her?" Navin had the gall to sound offended. I chewed on my lip to keep from smiling. He played this role too well, like so many others he played, but I saw beneath it now, saw to the core of him and all he so easily hid. "Let me ask you something: Do you know this Silver Wolf, Sadie Rauxtide, personally?" Navin asked, his voice heavy with skepticism. "Have you even seen her before or a painting of her likeness?"

"No," the guard spat. "But I know a *Wolf* when I see one. And I have a hard time believing a Silver Wolf could be caught by a single human."

"What about a hundred humans? My entire village was involved in her capture," Navin continued. "We have a vested interest in obtaining her bounty. Of course, now with her hands bound and the inability to shift, she's much more compliant, aren't you, dear?" He pulled me roughly forward, and I snarled at him as he shoved me into the bars of the gate. "Look her over, smell her, or whatever it is you Wolves do if you don't believe me. But if you touch the veil, I'll have to let Prince Tadei—and King Luo—know."

"You are rumpling my gown, you piece of shit," I gritted out.

Navin tsked and rolled his eyes, playing along as he said to the guard, "She'll certainly make a good princess, eh?"

The guard arched his brow, taking a step in toward me and sniffing the air. I tilted my head to get a better view as his pupils dilated and his lips curved. "She's a Wolf all right."

Navin bounced on his heels. "Excellent—"

"But who's to say she's the one King Nero promised my prince?"

"Who else could she possibly be?" Navin guffawed. "I thought Wolves didn't abandon their packs."

"Watch yourself, human," the guard growled, baring his teeth. "We *don't* leave our packs." His eyes landed on me again. "Not if we want to live."

"Then if she is a Silver Wolf, she can only be but one of two," Navin countered. "I followed her in the woods outside Sevelde before her capture, bright silver fur tipped in black. She's either Sadie Rauxtide or Maez Claudius, the only other woman to defect. Either way, you have Nero's niece or the King's future sister-in-law. I suspect he will want to know she's here regardless." Navin looked back behind him at the lingering crowd of onlookers. "You can inspect her as closely as you like inside, but let us in. I don't want one of these ruffians thinking of snatching my prize from me before I get my reward."

The guard paused for one more split second before relenting and unlocking the gates. Navin half-dragged me in and I put up a mild protest.

"Behave," he snapped at me, making the guard chuckle.

Our act seemed to encourage the guard more. "The King will

be overjoyed," he said. "To have his brother's bride here at last. Finally, there will be new royal pups. The people will rejoice. The line of Valtan succession will be secured when she whelps."

Normally, I would've pretended to dry heave at that sentiment, but I just kept walking. *Whelping.* They seriously thought they could just ship me off here and I'd be a good little bitch for these Onyx Wolf royals? Me? Of all people! Nero never knew me at all. Clearly, neither did my father. I hoped my father and uncles were rolled over, belly up in front of Nero's throne right now, begging for his forgiveness for not delivering me to Tadei.

My stomach soured, knowing Briar wasn't all that far off from living this life, too. She had been willing to go through with it when she was betrothed to Grae . . . and despite it making my stomach turn, I understood. It was all we'd ever known. No matter the ferocity of my female relatives, I came from a line of subservience and mind control that I was only beginning to unscramble. If it were me, would I have had the strength to deny King Nero's orders? Would I have said no?

But that hadn't happened. Instead, Nero was going to leave Maez to rot, and I *finally* had the courage to understand just how barbaric we could be as a people and rebel. Thank the Gods I did. Because maybe Nero had always planned on offering me to Tadei one day—a pawn in his games of power. Or if not this prince, some other Wolf not of my choosing. I shuddered, suddenly aware of how close I was to being trapped in a life like this.

As we entered into the spacious courtyard, I felt bolstered that I was a new person now—not a follower but a fighter in name *and* in action. The fragrant smell of flowers hit me as we crossed to the giant steps, radiating heat from their dark stones. Up here, the air was thinner and cooler than in the city below, and though the dark stones baked with heat, the castle still felt airy and fresh compared to the throng.

The guard scuttled ahead through the garden hedges to warn his comrades of my arrival. We followed the winding path through the gardens, curving through the lush flora until we reached those black and bronze steps.

The castle's interior was just as impressive as its exterior. The walls were covered in exquisite carvings, depicting scenes from ancient myths and stories of valor. The floors were covered with intricately patterned tiles, and the high domed ceilings were adorned with elaborately painted frescoes.

We wandered down the echoing space, Navin giving my arm an occasional squeeze as if to remind me that we were still here together. We'd find a way out. We just needed that vase and a hasty retreat.

When we entered the throne room, my heart skipped a beat. The space was enormous. Giant pennants of midnight draped from the ceilings all the way to the floor, swaying in the breeze like the forked tongue of a massive serpent.

We padded across the tiles to the empty dais ahead of us, each step bouncing around the empty room.

Courtiers hustled in from the doors lining the sides of the grand hall, whispering excitedly to each other. They wore light clothing in the most brilliant jewel tones, along with dented bronze and gemstone jewelry that displayed their clear wealth. Valta was one of the wealthiest courts in Aotreas, second only to Olmdere, and now with the Olmderian mines closed, Valta was poised to become the front-runner.

The throne itself was a masterpiece of craftsmanship, adorned with precious jewels and moon phase carvings. Two heralds rushed in, curling brass horns in hand, and they positioned themselves on either side of the dais as they waited for the King.

I stood before the first step up to the dais, Navin by my side. The crowds swarmed around our backs but kept at least two paces of distance as if they might catch something if they got too close. My stomach twisted into a burning knot. This was it.

The muffled whispers of the crowd were so quiet that the screech of the giant doors opening made me jolt. The room instantly silenced so that now the quiet was absolute, and my heart thundered so hard in my chest as a horde of guards entered, I wondered if others could hear it. Almost as a relief, horns bellowed a royal call as two figures clad in flowing black robes strode into the room. They wore elaborate headpieces, swirling atop their heads like antlers. The one at the front also wore a golden half-moon chest piece inlaid with red and blue gemstones. The one behind wore a smaller golden necklace depicting a bursting sun.

Their faces were stoic, yet their eyes bore a wary intensity as they stepped up onto the dais. King Luo, the one with a short gray beard and the more elaborate headpiece, carefully lowered himself onto his throne. He waited until Tadei moved to stand beside him before he spoke.

"So you found my brother's wayward bride?" His voice was a deep timbre that cut easily through the room, silencing the eager crowd.

Navin dropped into a low bow, placing his fist over his chest. "I have, Your Majesty," he answered in slightly garbled Valtan.

The King pressed one of his ringed fingers to his lips, intrigued. "Bring her forward." He lazily curled his fingers, beckoning us, and we approached the dais.

I didn't have to pretend to be panicked now. Fear wafted off me, enough to scent the air, and Tadei's mouth pinched as his frown lines deepened. I wouldn't be surprised if he could hear my eyes widening.

"Hello, wife," he purred, waiting for his brother to gesture with his hand before he approached me.

The snarl poised on my lips was silenced as Navin kicked my knee, forcing me to drop. "Bow for your King."

Tadei's delighted laugh grated against my skin. His eyes were alight with wicked intrigue, one that curdled my stomach. Oh, he clearly loved this, watching the way Navin manhandled me. The fucking sadist. I desperately wished for my knives.

As Tadei approached, he surveyed me with a cruel smirk that made a shiver of dread trail down my spine. Navin stiffened beside me.

"Why the veil?" Tadei asked Navin, dropping my hand to rub his thumb and forefinger across the fabric, but he didn't lift it.

"I thought you would want to be the first Rikeshi to see your bride's face," Navin said. "It's custom, isn't it, Your Highness?"

King Luo and Tadei flashed matching smiles. Clearly, they liked the thought of that as much as Maez had predicted. Tadei's fingers traced across the veil, lingering, seemingly enjoying the claim and possessiveness of it. This is what Wolf Kings did; they traded and sold us to consolidate their power. Bile rose up my throat at the thought. I knew they would delight in owning me, *breaking me*, another beautiful treasure for their mantel. How close was I to this becoming my life?

"The bounty," Navin pushed, looking past Tadei's lingering gaze on me and up to the King.

"Ah yes," King Luo said. "A million gritas, I believe. You will be a rich man—"

"I don't want it," Navin cut in, and the room broke out into frantic whispers. "Your Majesty," he added hastily. "I am a musician, an artist. I would rather possess some pieces of beauty than coin, relics I can show off on my travels. I know Your Majesty is quite the collector."

Luo arched his brow. "Relics, you say?" He didn't seem at all surprised, only vaguely amused. Dread pooled in my gut. Something about his reaction felt terribly wrong.

"If it pleases you, Your Majesty, I would like to pick three pieces of art from your gallery."

More murmurs of intrigue sounded behind us.

King Luo let out a long sigh and looked at his brother. "Artists," he said with a flippant roll of his eyes. He rose from his throne and waved a beckoning hand as if Navin were only a minor nuisance. "Fine. I agree to your request. Let's get it over with."

Tadei grabbed me by the upper arm and pulled me along, seemingly enjoying my discomfort as my arm tugged to the side. A prince who liked his betrothed's hands tied—that told me plenty about what kind of Wolf he was.

We followed Luo and Navin out the side door and into the hall, my eyes frantically searching for Maez. As soon as Navin got the vase, I wanted to get the fuck out of here.

Tadei squeezed me to his side with enough force to make a guttural warning escape my lips. That only made him grin.

"I like a bit of bite," he said, dropping his lips to the side of my veil. "It wouldn't be any fun otherwise." His foul breath wafted over to me, and I screwed my face up in disgust, wishing my veil was thicker.

"Someone's been licking their own asshole again," I muttered.

Tadei threw his head back in a hearty laugh while his fingers dug into my flesh so tightly I had to bite the inside of my cheek to keep from crying out in pain. "Come, bride, let me show you your new home," he said loud enough for everyone to hear. He lowered his voice just for me as he added, "I can't wait to see how many times I can snap these bones before shifting won't heal them."

I searched for Maez again as bile rose up my throat. Maybe I could kill this sick son of a bitch first, and then Maez could swoop in and escort me off the premises the second the vase was in Navin's hand. Someone really needed to kill this guy.

Each step down the long hallway made my stomach plummet further. Everything was going according to plan, I tried to reassure myself. Luo produced a key from around his neck and unlocked a set of heavy bronze doors. I could feel the excitement of the crowd behind me as the wood groaned and the doors opened.

We passed through an echoing atrium and into the gallery covered in floor-to-ceiling paintings and twin rows of pedestals bisecting the room upon which sat everything from golden plates to crowns and scepters.

The gaggle of onlookers followed close behind Tadei and me, whispering to each other about "the Silver Wolf bitch." I whipped my head around, though my glare was lost on them through the veil.

"You'll get used to it," Tadei said. "They'll respect you more once you've provided some sons for the crown."

It took everything within me not to give him a swift kick between the legs. Yeah, I couldn't let this prince live.

I found Navin up ahead, two paces behind King Luo, and tried to focus on their conversation rather than the malodorous beast beside me.

"This one?" Navin asked, gesturing to a landscape painting of the floating mountains of Upper Valta.

Luo shrugged. "I thought you'd pick something more . . . grand."

The crowd tittered as if he'd told a joke.

Navin nodded to one of the portraits on the far wall that was taller than me. "I'm afraid anything larger would be harder to travel with." He turned to the pedestals. "Perhaps something smaller." He paced down the row of precious relics, his footsteps slowing and then faltering as he reached the far wall. Then he halted.

In front of him was an empty pedestal.

"Looking for something in particular, human?" Luo asked, cocking his head at Navin in curiosity, but his smile filled my veins with ice.

Navin's eyes grew wider, and I prayed he kept his composure, even as I was itching to shift. I forced my Wolf back even as every alarm bell started ringing in my mind.

"I heard tell of a piece of art made by those in Lower Valta . . . It's a green stone vase, inlaid with gold . . ." Navin's words fell to silence as the door to the atrium opened again.

I twisted my veil to see who moved through the doorway as Tadei's hand regained its death grip on my arm. The green stone vase was proffered out. My entire body was doused in ice as my shaking gaze tracked from the beautiful vase up to the familiar eyes of the person holding it.

"You mean this vase, husband?"

CALLA

I DIDN'T SEE WHO MOVED FIRST. THE CLASHING OF SWORDS filled the air as the room erupted into chaos. Ingrid's guards made quick work cutting down my human ones. *Thud thud thud.* Their bodies smacked onto the stone floor before they even had a chance to scream.

Mina's frantic violin music filled the room as I shoved Ora behind me and took a step toward the outstretched blades of the Silver Wolves. I didn't have time to consider *why* she was playing at this moment; I shifted on instinct, Grae and Briar quickly following suit. Our clothes ripped and shredded, falling to the floor as we shook the remnants off us. Belt buckles and weaponry clattered to the ground. We were so vastly outnumbered that our attackers didn't even bother to shift and battle us in their furs. They circled us with ease as Briar, Grae, and I turned round, trying to decide where to attack first as the guards closed in.

Ingrid stepped up behind the circling guards, her cold eyes trained on Grae. "I'm sorry you were dragged into this by your wayward mate, Graemon," she said, her hands beseeching.

Grae snapped at the air in her direction but didn't lunge, not with the halo of sword tips pointed at us.

"Please, Ingrid. Don't be sorry," Evres said. "There's nothing wrong with choosing the winning side." He stooped into a crouch, his predatory smile glinting in the firelight as he stared at Briar. "You *will* be mine, Crimson Princess." I snarled, but when I tried to shoot forward, a sword hovered at my neck and I paused. Evres pointed to the spot beside him like recalling a dog. "Now, come to me, and I promise to let your twin and her mate flee back to Olmdere with their tails between their legs."

"Don't you fucking move," I snapped at Briar in my mind as the sword at my neck pressed deeper into my fur.

"I . . ." Briar's voice wobbled. Her eyes darted between me and Evres, whose eyes danced with the delight of victory. He clearly knew she had no other choice.

"Briar, don't. I already lost you once . . ."

"Which is why I can't lose you again."

A whine escaped my maw, my ears flattening as my twin padded across the floor and past the labyrinth of swords. Watching her walk through the wall of swords to Evres's side made my entire soul ache. I couldn't do this again, couldn't have her taken from me, not after I fought so hard to get her back. But I knew if I was in her position, I'd make the same exact choice.

Evres patted Briar's head. "Good girl." Her lip curled in a snarl, but he just laughed and rose to a stand.

A loud thud sounded to our right as two of Ingrid's guards hit the ground.

"What the . . ."

I hadn't noticed that Mina was still playing, nor that Ora now sat beside her with a short, tapered flute held between their bound hands. The two of them played a chaotic song that felt as panicked as my pounding heart. Another one of Ingrid's guards fell and then another. But they weren't dead . . . they were sleeping as if lulled under a magical spell—

I gaped, looking from Ora to the sleeping guards.

"You!" Ingrid shouted, pointing at Hector and flicking her gaze to the musicians. "Kill them!"

Hector, who stood closest to Mina and Ora, paused for a split second, holding up a hand to his father and uncles to let them know he could handle them. His father had the audacity to look proud. He must've convinced Hector to betray us, but when? I raked through every moment that Hector hung back or went off on his own over the past few weeks. How had he managed this deceit right under my nose? But as Hector's sword lifted toward the humans, advancing, I shoved the thoughts aside. I needed to take advantage of this distraction. In that split second, with everyone's attention focused on Hector, Grae and I shot forward and attacked.

I tore out the calf muscle of the closest guard with my teeth. Blood sprayed across the floor as screaming filled the air. My canines sliced deep into the thigh of the next Wolf before he could shift. The third was smart, one of the few guards not in armor so he could readily shift. He was already in his furs by the time I got to him. Chaos filled the room behind me as Grae attacked the guards on the other side, but all my energy was on reaching Mina and Ora and protecting my human friends from the traitor Wolf I had trusted.

Another Silver Wolf stood between me and the musicians, snapping out at my feet and then lunging at my shoulder, but I dodged him every time. I kept half my attention on him and half on Hector as he stormed up the stairs toward Mina and Ora.

Mina's violin halted but Ora kept going, and I knew from the crash onto the floor that another guard had fallen under their musical spell.

Instead of running away, though, Mina looked directly at Hector. Anger and hurt filled Mina's eyes as she dropped her violin and walked straight up to him.

"Don't," he murmured, his eyes filled with pain as she walked right up to him and placed the center of her chest at the tip of his sword.

"Go on," she signed.

He froze, utter devastation filling his face. He stole a glance backward as if afraid for his father to see, but his father and uncles were all swaying on their feet, being lulled under Ora's spell. Hector turned back to Mina, his face screwed up in anguish.

"Mina," he whispered, shaking his head, the tip of his sword lowering slightly. "Please. Step aside. Please. I'm sorry."

She didn't move, didn't sign, just stared him down, and I swore I could *feel* her heart breaking. Her eyes welled and Hector's eyes welled along with hers.

"It was the only way to save Sadie," Hector said, his words rapid and pleading. "It was the only way."

Mina leaned into Hector's blade now resting against her belly, and he instantly took a step back.

"Kill me," she signed. "Your bitch snow queen ordered it."

His eyes were glassed over as he shook his head. "I told you to run. Mina, please."

"You betray us, but use 'please'? How strange. But no, I won't let you hurt Ora." Mina advanced on him again and Hector took another step back. The normally quiet and shy Mina's eyes were filled with ferocity as she signed, "You'll have to kill me first, Hector. You can step over my dead body. I'm not stepping aside."

Hector froze for another second before lowering his sword. "I can't. I can't do it." Tears filled his eyes. "I can't hurt you."

"You already did."

He stole a glance at Ingrid and then turned and fled through the open doorway.

I was so distracted watching him run into the snowy night that I didn't notice the Silver Wolf's last lunge. I tried to duck but he bowled me over. Flailing, I quickly tried to right myself as his teeth sunk into my leg. I let out a piercing yowl as he tore and yanked, practically pulling my leg from the socket. I curled back on him, my tooth snagging on his ear and ripping it in two but still he yanked and tore.

This couldn't be it. This couldn't be how I died. Not after all I'd fought for, my dying wish still unfulfilled.

I screamed and realized it was my human lungs, blood spraying from my thigh. The air whizzed with static, and the Wolf finally released me, screaming with pain as he was dragged from me. I looked up to see Briar's golden fur matted in blood as she flipped him on his back and dug her teeth into his belly.

Evres and Klaus, still in their human skin, battled behind her. Both were blood spattered and looked exhausted, spinning round and round each other, both jockeying to get closest to Briar.

"You can't have her!" Klaus shouted, striking again and again, but Evres was faster and easily maneuvered out of each hit.

"Are you taking back our agreement?" Evres asked too casually for the bloodshed all around us.

"Let her go, Klaus!" Ingrid screamed in Taigosi. "Don't be a fool."

I scrambled to sit up, taking in the absolute carnage all around me. Pain radiated through my leg, so acute that I couldn't control the shift. I yearned to return to my furs and their healing magic, but the severity of my injury made it difficult to control.

I rolled to find Grae lying on his side pinned under Ingrid's boot, her sword at his throat and another Ice Wolf towering over him. Everything in me snapped at the sight of her sword against my mate's throat. I managed to stand on one wobbling leg and limped over, moving as fast as I could to barge into Ingrid's side. She barely budged as she shoved me back to the ground, but Grae managed to use the distraction to separate himself from Ingrid. He went after the other Ice Wolf as I circled Ingrid with a growl.

With her sword trained on me, she smiled. "It's politics, Calla, dear," she said with a shrug. Her crown was askew, her white dress caked in gore, but she still acted like she was hosting a morning tea. "I saw how attached my cousin was growing to your sister. We had to get rid of her."

My skin slipped across the blood-slick tiles as I moved backward toward the dead guards behind me. I needed a weapon. Ingrid smiled as I palmed a dagger that was kicked across the floor from Mina. She nodded to me and kept playing.

Ingrid chuckled as I rose on shaking legs. Her sword hand was steady, and I couldn't find a way past it.

"You've sacrificed everything you believe in," I spat. "Just to get rid of my sister? My *mated* sister? You and I could've taken Nero. We could've won. We could've made this world better."

Briar had miscalculated. She knew getting close to Klaus would make Ingrid want to send her away, but she hadn't bargained it would be into the hands of our enemies.

"I still believe in progress, you know," Ingrid said, bristling as if she was the one being insulted. "I believe in fighting for advancement. I believe in a world better than the one Nero has envisioned."

"And how are you going to bring that world about when you're under Nero's thumb?" My eyes dropped to her sword. "With all of your allies killed by *your* hands?" Her mouth pinched but she didn't speak. "You know Nero will promise Taigos to Valta?"

"I know no such thing," Ingrid sneered. "He promised we'd be left out of your squabbles if we gave him the Crimson Princess."

"And you *believed* him?" I let out a disgusted laugh. "I didn't realize you were so shortsighted.

"And now so alone."

Suddenly Grae was beside me, a sword in his hand, and Ingrid's eyes swept from him to the room behind us. Realization dawned on her face. We were the last two conscious warriors in the room, and we had our blades trained on her.

She immediately dropped to her knees. Her hands held up, pleading, but not to me, to Grae. I shook my head, a chuckle of surprise escaping my lips.

"Graemon, think about what you're doing," she besieged him. "I will make a deal with you. I will give you soldiers, please."

"You look to him even now?" I said, my voice dripping with disdain. "You beg *him*?" I stepped forward, grabbing her by the pale hair and yanking her neck back to meet my eyes. "You say you want a better world, but only for you," I seethed. "When it's all stripped bare, Ingrid, you don't even believe in your own words. You still seek out a man to beg. But no one puts a blade to my mate's throat." I dropped my mouth to her ear. "And no man will save you from my steel."

Her eyes flew wide a split second before I drove my dagger into her heart. She gaped unseeing at the sky as I twisted my blade deeper into her chest—the Queen who I'd tried so hard to please I'd nearly lost myself, the Queen who betrayed us anyway. Her eyes rolled back, and I snatched the crown off her head as her limp body fell to the ground with a sickening, wet *thunk*.

The room had gone quiet. Mina and Ora huddled together against the far wall, eyes wide and scanning the sea of bodies between us. I searched over the bodies, the silence making my heart beat faster and faster as I realized who was missing.

"Where's Briar?" I panted, suddenly running and flipping over bodies I knew weren't hers. Evres was gone and Briar along with him. "Briar!" I screamed, running to the window where I spotted a sleigh halfway down the road, disappearing into the darkness. "Briar!"

I bolted, ruined leg be damned. I felt the blood of each step gushing down my leg. I knew soon I would bleed out, but I didn't care. I had to get to her. She couldn't be captured. Not again. I wouldn't let them take her.

"Briar!" Her name shredded my throat as I screamed it again and again. "BRIAR!"

I didn't feel the sting of the snow on my feet as I bolted down the mountainside, trying to keep my feet under me as my wounded knee buckled with each step.

"Calla!" Grae shouted. I heard him bounding up behind me, knew with my injury that he would catch me, but I kept racing forward anyway.

Grae's bare arms banded around my torso, yanking me back as I flailed in his grip.

"No, no!" I wailed, fighting against him. "Briar!" Her name was a defeated sob now.

"You need to shift, Calla," Grae gritted out, tightening his grip on me to the point of pain. "She's too far gone now. You can try to connect with her that way, too. I promise—we *will* get her back, but first you need to shift, little fox, or you will kill us both."

At that, I stopped fighting. The reality of my brash actions slammed into me. I was willing to give up everything, my life even, to save my twin. But I could never hurt Grae, and if I died, he'd die, too. The thought finally cooled my panic just enough so I could find that magical thread to pull inside me, imagining the pain of muscles bending, the pop of bones crunching, and then I shifted.

Grae released me and I landed on all fours, howling to the moon a mournful cry. I couldn't feel Briar in my mind, knew she must be in her human form, and the thought of her trapped and naked in Evres's sleigh made me howl even louder. I walked over the mountain's edge, the sleigh already disappeared through the trees, too far even for my Wolf to catch. I knew I couldn't go after her alone, not into Damrienn.

Something to my right caught my eye, and what I saw made me collapse into the snow. The ocean was ablaze. The boats fleeing to Olmdere were all on fire. My stomach roiled as I took it in—such an unfathomable sight. It washed over me in waves of panic and sorrow. All those humans gone. Nero's message to them clear: try to run and you'll die. His message to me just as clear: try to fight me and more will die. I let out a broken howl as I stared out at the sea of golden flames, grieving the broken promise I made to those humans.

I turned to Grae and shifted back into my human form again, the wound on my thigh still raw but the bleeding stopped and the wound closed.

"We need to get out of Taigos. Now," I commanded, finally coming back to my senses enough to give direction. "Before we have a vengeful Ice Wolf pack on our tails." I darted back toward the mansion to get Ora and Mina.

"Breathe, Calla," Grae reminded me as I ran.

"Sweet Moon." I sucked in a breath through my teeth. "I think I've just started a war with Taigos."

SADIE

"RASIL," NAVIN CHOKED OUT. "WHAT HAVE YOU DONE?"

"You think I didn't know?" Rasil crooned. I tried to take a step away, but Tadei grabbed me by the upper arm and yanked me to his side. The Onyx Wolf pack growled at my back, and I felt dozens of hungry, murderous eyes trained on me, ready to strike. "I knew. I knew from the very first second you looked at her that you loved her, that you wouldn't do what you must. I came here the very next day to warn the King."

"Raz," Navin whispered. "You've betrayed our people, our cause—"

"*You* betrayed our people with her," Rasil hissed. "*I* am keeping us safe. Our songs were meant to be sung, Navin. You were always too cowardly to see it."

"Your Majesty," Navin implored the King. "Whatever allegiance he promises to you, his goal is to exterminate Wolfkind—"

Rasil whirled to Luo and bowed deeply. "Your Majesty, his lies are just as I warned you. We live to serve our kings, our *Gods*," he said, lifting a finger and pointing it accusatorially at me. "Sadie Rauxtide is not only a defector of the Silver Wolf pack, she is also a skin chaser." He held the vase aloft to the room. "And Navin Mourad is trying to steal something very precious from you."

"You think you can fool the Onyx Wolves?" King Luo seethed at me and Navin. "Bring me the brand." From the forges burning beyond the doorway, one of the guards pulled a hot metal poker, the end shaped into a paw print.

"No!" Navin screamed as two guards grabbed him by either arm. He thrashed against their grip, headbutting one before the other landed a right hook square to Navin's jaw and he dropped to his knees. "Sadie!"

I gave Navin one last look, knowing it might be the last time I locked eyes with him, and he nodded back. "I'll find you in the next life, love," he whispered. "Listen for my song."

I kept that smile plastered on my face as I turned back to Tadei. "Let's at least go out singing," I said to no one but Navin.

"Go ahead," Tadei murmured to me, dropping his mouth to my ear in a sinister curl. "Try to shift like that and see what happens."

He kicked me to my knees beside Navin and I let out a deep, mocking laugh. Tadei's eyes flared, darting between me and Navin with sudden alarm. Maybe he expected tears or pleading, but certainly not laughter.

Tadei's hands balled into fists. "What's so funny?"

I watched his face fall as I yanked, ripping the silver rope free from behind my back. "My hands were never bound."

In a single breath, I shifted.

A cacophony of sound exploded through the room as my glorious Wolf form ripped my dress and I dropped onto all fours. I snapped out at Tadei's leg, and my teeth managed to sink into his flesh before he screamed and shifted on instinct.

From behind me, I was vaguely aware of Navin breaking free from the guards and charging toward Rasil. But the crowd seemed to shift in unison, prepared to die to save their King. The room turned into a sea of obsidian fur, tatters of shredding clothing being tossed up into the air and jewelry thunking to the ground.

I spotted Maez rushing through an open doorway and barreling into the crowd. She battled a dozen Wolves from every angle, her silver fur already coated in blood. Tadei was pushed backward, the pack moving in front of him to protect their prince. I drove into the nearest Wolf's side, flipping them onto their back and tearing out their throat with my teeth. Quick, efficient, merciless. I needed to take down as many as I could as quickly as possible if we were to somehow make it out of here alive. Blood misted the air as the Wolves around me snapped and snarled. One took a chunk out of my side, and I yowled as another's teeth sunk into my tail, dragging me backward.

So much black fur and blood surrounded me, I couldn't see. Pain stabbed through me in a million different directions, and I wondered if I was being pulled apart right there on the floor. How many sets of teeth were digging into me? How many had I taken down first? There were too many of them now. There would be no stopping the onslaught of biting and shredding teeth. I let out a mournful howl, thinking of Navin and Maez and how far we'd come on this quest only to fail. Would the others even know how we died?

A sharp crack sounded as brilliant green lightning flashed above me. Suddenly Wolves were being ripped off me by sharpened gold talons. I gasped as I stared up into the bloodstained, chewing mouth of a flying winged creature. It had golden leathery wings, a body of scaled glittering burgundy, and dual lines of spiked ventral scales that ran from its head to the tip of its tail like jagged teeth.

A dragon.

It batted its wings in annoyance, its wingspan so large it could barely fit in the room. Its dark amber eyes narrowed at me before moving beyond me to snatch up its next Onyx Wolf meal.

Gore flew across my face as the monster crunched its next victim in two. Bile burned up my throat and I rolled just in time to vomit. Blood and stomach acid splattered back at me.

I rose up on my haunches, so coated in blood and viscera that I couldn't see the silver of my fur. I looked up to find Navin, vase clutched in his hand, a guttural war song escaping his lips.

His eyes were transfixed on the dragon as he controlled it with his song. Blood trailed from his temple and nose, his clothes shredded and bloody, his muscles straining with the concentration it took to command the beast. Eerie green clouds hung in the air around him—dark magic waiting to find its host.

The dragon easily tore through the Onyx Wolf crowd, devouring them in a horrific circle of sawlike, shredding teeth. I searched the carnage for Rasil's cream-colored robes and spotted just the faintest trail of fabric as he fled out the side hallway. Tadei hustled out the door behind him along with a handful of guards. A fiery rage blossomed within me, and I was about to charge after him when I heard Maez's howl.

I turned toward Maez at the other end of the room, who limped as she still battled off three more Wolves.

I ran, my limbs screaming at me with each movement as I bowled the Wolf biting her back over and off her. My teeth sunk into the Wolf's belly, the coppery tang of blood coating my tongue as I ripped out their innards, their keening screams filling the air. I turned back to Maez, blood dripping from my maw, but Maez's Wolf eyes were now hooked on something behind me.

I whirled to the sight and found Navin kneeling with a dagger to his throat. King Luo stood there, his robes hanging loosely around him, his skin speckled with blood.

I shifted back into my human form on instinct, my howl morphing into a cry as my knees cracked into the hard tiles slick with blood. "Don't!"

"Call off your beast," Luo snarled. Navin muttered five words, the low hypnotic song making the dragon halt mid-strike. "Good."

Luo pried the vase from Navin's grip. Maez shifted forms beside me, her body so covered head to toe in the carnage of blood and fur that I couldn't see her skin.

"I will be taking this vase," Luo said. "And your life, human, for what you've done to my pack."

"Luo, stop!" I screamed and the King looked up at me with a curl of his lip.

"Or what, little skin chaser?" he bellowed. "What will you do without your Songkeeper and your beasts? Your pathetic Queen's court will belong to Damrienn soon enough. And Taigos will be mine. We've given you females too much power for too long."

"You will never have Olmdere," I hissed.

The remainder of the pack converged around us, and my stomach dropped. We'd killed so many between us and the dragon, but it wasn't enough to destroy the entire pack, and now with the beast called off, we didn't stand a chance.

"And who is there to protect Olmdere?" Luo balked. "I had a pigeon arrive just this morning, telling me of how well that little meeting in the Stormcrest Ranges went." Luo's eyes darkened and he sneered as he turned his gaze to Maez. "Your mate, the Crimson Princess, is already on her way home with her new betrothed, Prince Evres."

"No." Maez's voice was the ghost of a whisper. "I heard her calling to me in my mind, but . . . that . . . that can't be."

"She's gone," Luo said with smug satisfaction.

"That can't be!" Maez barked, her voice filled with panic.

"She's already across the Damrienn border," Luo said with a laugh. "I know she'll take a strong hand to break in, but I'm sure Evres is up to the task."

"No!" Maez screamed, the sound piercing through the space. Her hands flew skyward. "I will kill you all for this!" she roared and lightning flashed again.

I watched in horror as the green cloud above Navin's head flew across the room, shoving its magical smoke down Maez's throat.

"Maez, stop!" I shouted, but my voice was drowned out over the howling wind.

When Maez opened her eyes again, they were an eerie, violent green. A wicked smile stretched across her lips, and I could see the dark magic churning beneath her skin.

She was the sorceress conjuring the dragon had made.

SADIE

THE SCREAMS WERE CUT OFF IN A FLASH OF BLINDING EMERALD light. I cowered, shielding my eyes from the brilliant green, and when I opened them, I was surrounded by a mountain of bodies. Wolves and humans alike lay stacked one atop the other all around me, their lifeless charred bodies still sizzling from the bolts of lightning. The smell of cooking flesh turned my stomach again as I took in the utter carnage and shocking silence. I'd seen this magic before, watched as Sawyn's bolts of magic carved up Calla, but this . . . this was an unfathomable amount of slaughter and it all happened in a single flash.

I blinked, swatting away the smoke circling my head to take in more of the room, but Maez was nowhere to be seen.

Rising onto shaking feet, I stumbled forward across the piles of bodies. I slipped across the sticky, wet tiles, and when the smoke cleared enough to take in the whole room, I spotted Navin lying limp upon the dais.

I screamed his name, running toward him in the unsettling quiet. Hundreds of bodies and not a single sound except for the slap of my bare feet on the tiled ground. I slid the last few paces to him and dropped to my knees.

I searched his body for burn holes, my eyes roving over him, but he was completely unscarred. The cut at his temple was gone, the trail of blood down his nose was now dried, the nick of a dagger cut at his neck had disappeared. I pulled him up to my chest, sobbing as I cried out his name.

His arms twitched beside me, and then his hands lifted, circling around me and pulling me farther into him.

"I'm okay," he groaned, pushing us up into a seated position. He cupped my cheeks, wiping my frantic tears with his thumbs as he leaned his forehead against my own. "I'm alive."

"Wh-what happened?" My voice trembled as I held him tighter. "The vase?"

He shook his head, refusing to let me go as I tried to search the gory space. "It's gone. She took it. I . . ." His voice cracked and tears misted his eyes. "I'm so sorry, Sadie."

"Stop," I croaked. "You saved us. You saved my life."

"It's my fault she's a sorceress." More of my tears fell at his confirmation as if I could've denied what had truly happened a little longer, but now that he said it, I knew it was true. "It's why I wanted to get the vase away—so that it couldn't be used to do exactly what I did. It's my fault that dark magic was conjured. It's my fault. All of this. I didn't know what else to do." His words flew from his mouth. "I thought they were going to kill you and—"

I silenced him with a kiss, tasting the salt of my tears on his lips. I kissed him slowly and deeply, needing that anchor for myself from the shock as much as for Navin himself. I felt my pounding heart slow, my trembling hands steady, as my lips molded to his own. His fingertips pressed into my blood-slick bare skin. He pulled me flush against his chest, his whole body shaking so violently that his teeth chattered.

"Okay." I took a steeling breath. "Okay. We need to . . ." My mind reeled as I pressed my forehead to his again. "Panic later. We need to get out of here. Now."

Navin cleared his throat, swallowing back more tears as he rose on wobbling feet. "My injuries," he said, looking down at his tattered clothes streaked in red. "They're gone. H-how?"

"Panic and answers later," I reminded him as I stooped and snatched the flowing black robes from Luo's dead body and hastily wrapped them around myself. "Tadei will surely return with more soldiers," I said. "You told me that there were Wolves who lived on all of the surrounding islands, too. The pack hasn't been wholly destroyed, and the fact that we had a hand in their King's demise means we're enemy number one. We need to run before they come after us."

Navin's hands clenched into fists. "I'd like to see them try." He let out a low resonant whistle, and the dragon reared up on its hind legs again.

My mouth dropped open as I sized up the creature. It was beautiful and terrifying in equal measure. "Gods," I breathed, staring as I laced the inner belt together until the obsidian fabric drowned my body. "How long will you be able to control it?"

"Long enough to get Galen den' Mora out of this place," Navin vowed. "Hopefully long enough to get us back to Olmdere. However long it takes."

"You remember the song from the vase?" I asked.

"Only parts, only some," he considered, wrapping his arm around my side and holding me to him as he descended the dais. "But enough for now. Let's go."

We stalked through the carnage of the room, Navin muttering ancient words under his breath, half song, half chant, and the dragon followed behind us, each stomp making the ground rattle. I shuddered at the sound of it settling its wings back against its body like the flap of a sail.

The halls were empty as we walked back down toward the courtyard. In the city far below, people were still screaming and fleeing. A fireball hovered in midair over the golden domes of the palace, its green flames licking high toward the sky and spreading out across the land like swirling emerald ink. People scattered in every direction, leaving a path of chaos in their wake, as we walked swiftly toward the wagon. No one paid us any notice as they ran. I looked back one last time, stealing a final glance at the palace and thinking of all the bodies that lay inside. If a war had been brewing before, now it had well and truly begun. The massacre of Rikesh would never be forgotten as long as the Onyx Wolf pack lived. Nor, I thought, the birth of a new sorcerer. My eyes fell to the tiled murals along the palace wall, imagining the story fitting in amongst the tales of triumph.

A cloud of shimmering green ashes glittered through the sky, heading in the direction across the far river toward Damrienn. I prayed that trail of dark magic meant Maez was heading to Highwick to rescue her mate, but also worried she was only going to bring more death and destruction. Would she even care about Briar now that she'd given over her soul to that dark power?

As we navigated through the crowds, panicked tears slipped down my cheeks. I couldn't reconcile what had just happened. In a flash, she was just simply gone. There was no coming back from such magic. As more tears fell, I knew I'd lost Maez to it. I'd lost my best friend forever.

WE ROLLED THROUGH ESHIK WITHOUT A SINGLE FOLLOWER. No one peeked out windows and no one watched us flee. Galen den' Mora rolled onward like a lone carriage at a funeral procession. Even long after the dragon flew off ahead of us, roaming the skies out toward the Stoneater River, we were met with silence. Did the people know the driver of this wagon had the power to conjure monsters? Did they know a sorceress was on the loose? Either the news of the palace battle had preceded us, or the sight of the flying monster had everyone so afraid that they'd locked down their cities.

The creak of our wagon wheels sounded foreboding in the darkness of the night from one unwelcome island to another. Not a single candle flickered on a windowsill. No songs were sung from rooftops. No celebrations in the town square. Not even the seediest taverns had their doors open. The streets suddenly seemed too wide, the city too big.

As we hit the road to Sankai-ed, I began to feel so hollow; I wondered if any of it had been real. It felt like waking from a nightmare. As the adrenaline wore off, the haunting silence mocked me. No matter how I scrubbed in the waters of Galen den' Mora's bathing spigot, I couldn't seem to wash off the blood. It lingered, as if I was limned in pink, and the smell . . .

I was a soldier; I'd killed before. I thought I was immune to the scent of death and the sight of gore. But never, *never*, had I been in such a melee, not even when we raided Sawyn's celebration in Olmdere. The Rooks had laid down their weapons then. They had surrendered . . . but that was probably because they were human.

Wolves never surrendered when their pack leader was under threat. They would've never stopped coming for us. We probably only escaped Eshik because the Wolves hadn't regrouped to the orders of their new King, Tadei. Tadei and his guards were seemingly the only ones willing to leave Luo to his fate. That chaos and confusion had probably saved us. But a war half-won was not won at all, and the fact that some Onyx Wolves remained alive meant there were plenty who would be wanting to avenge their pack and family.

And now we were without Maez and with only half the vase's song.

My panic eased only slightly as we crossed to the other side of Sankai-ed, still waiting for the Onyx Wolves to appear and chase us. Navin stayed out in the front of the wagon for the first several hours, making sure the oxen found the right way. But as the oxen ventured onto the rope bridge to Lower Valta, Navin finally came back through the window, finding me pacing back and forth. I felt like a Wolf chasing my own tail, the anxiety still strong even though exhaustion was taking hold. I didn't know if I needed to vomit or cry or stab something. I couldn't pin down a single shot as sickening images flashed one after another through my mind.

"Sadie." Navin walked over to me and pulled me into his

arms. "Breathe," he said like he'd commanded so many times before. It wasn't until my cheek pressed against his chest that I felt its wetness. I hadn't even realized I'd been crying. "We're safe in Galen den' Mora," he reassured me. "No one breaches this wagon without our welcome." I trembled in his arms. "You're so cold," he said, lifting my still wet hair off the loose fabric of my vest.

"I feel hot," I replied even as I trembled more. Everything in my body felt upended, the turmoil inside of me bringing the strangest reactions forward.

"We're safe," Navin said again, stroking a hand down my back as he folded himself around me, clearly trying to warm me up. "We made it out."

"But so many didn't," I said, my voice choppy and breathing erratic. I pulled back. "Rasil, he—"

Navin swept his thumb over my bottom lip. "He will pay for what he has done. The Songkeepers will destroy him for conspiring with the Onyx Wolves."

"I can't believe he betrayed you like that," I whispered.

"I can." Navin's eyes darkened. "I should've fought him ages ago. I should've ousted him from his position for his violent aspirations. I knew he was jealous and petty, but even I didn't know he'd go this far."

"But—but he wanted a world without Wolves?" I searched Navin's face, trying to understand.

"And if he's memorized the vase's songs like his grandfather once did, he will have it," he said. "The Onyx Wolves don't know what dark dealings they've entered into by letting him simply read it. Rasil probably promised Luo to use the magic for him, and the Wolf King probably couldn't fathom a human turning such magic against him."

"Do you think Rasil remembers all the songs on that vase?" I asked. "How much do you remember?"

"If there's one thing Rasil was good at, it was sight-reading.

I wouldn't be surprised if he has it all now—especially if he had even an hour with the vase. As for me, I know enough to be a danger to everyone around us," Navin said, his eyes bracketing with pain. "I remember enough to do more harm just like I did with Maez." He swallowed thickly as he continued rubbing my arms up and down. "But there was something on that vase I hadn't expected," he added. "Etched into the stone was a song that . . . I think . . . I think there might be a way to control monsters like I did the dragon without conjuring new ones."

My eyes widened. "Without bringing more dark magic into the world?"

"Yes."

"Control others' monsters?"

He thought on it. "Yes. I may have to play with some of the notes to make sure I have it right, but I know the melodies and the tempo of the song . . ."

My body still shook, but my senses began to sharpen from their whirling panic to more focused intention. "So we could go around collecting an army of monsters to join this war? To fight on our side? Without bringing more dark magic into the world?"

Navin's brow dropped low over his eyes, clearly unhappy with my train of thought. "Possibly," he hedged.

"Possibly," I echoed. "I know you find this repugnant, but we're past the point of musical theory, Navin. Our list of enemies is growing by the minute. We have to find a way to fight them, and this might be it."

It took him a while to say anything. I could see how much the idea of that—of using the song where it might hurt people— devastated him. And with the aftermath of what he'd just sung, I understood his hesitancy. This was where we differed, he and I. He was, at heart, an artist.

I was the warrior.

And because of that, it was up to me to remind him how warriors thought. How Nero thought.

"It might be our only hope," I said softly.

"There might be more answers in the library at the refuge," Navin said.

"We can't go back there." I shook my head. "What if Rasil returns? Is there anywhere else? Anywhere we can get answers but wouldn't be found?"

Navin considered me and I could see the wheels in his mind spinning. "There's a ruin south of Allesdale, deep in the woods. It used to be a temple of knowledge. Ora and I found it from an old Songkeeper's map we discovered in the bottom of a drawer." Navin smoothed a hand down my arm. "No one knows it's there but us."

"Damrienn?" I balked. "You want us to go to Damrienn?"

"No Wolf has set foot that far south in centuries," Navin said confidently. "There's barely a human around those parts. It might be the safest place for us and give us time to figure out this magic. While the Silver Wolves are looking north, we move south."

I pulled from his grip, my senses honing further as my brain moved beyond shock and started to formulate a plan. "An excellent direction to attack from, too." I could tell this response made Navin uneasy, but again, I was the warrior. And now was surely a time of war. "Does this place have a whispering well?"

"It does." His lips curved into a frown. "But there are closer ones on the trail there, too."

"We need to update Calla on everything that's happened." I nodded. "And we search the temple of knowledge for answers on reversing dark magic, too. There must be a way."

"Sadie," Navin pleaded. "I don't think that's possible. I don't know that we can save Maez."

"We will!" I shouted, the panic rising in me again. "We will save her. We *have to* save her."

Navin slowly slid his hands down my bare arms, letting out a soothing shush. "We will get to the temple soon," he assured me.

"And all of those questions we will begin to find answers to. There is nothing we can do in the meantime but wait and rest."

I shook my head. "I can't do that," I said, another tear spilling down my cheek. "I can't just sit here. Can't just sleep. Not when Maez is gone. I need to come up with a plan. I need a strategy. I need to come up with answers somehow—"

Navin's lips dropped to my cheek in a soft kiss and skimmed up to my ear. "There are no answers in this wagon," he murmured. "We almost just died. Please," he begged. "Let me hold you. Let me feel you. Let me make sure you will be all right. Let's start with getting you out of these wet clothes."

I let out a rough breath as his hands skimmed up my sides and found the hem of my shirt. He pulled it up over my head and dropped it to the floor. I met his eyes and his hands stilled for a second as I said, "I almost lost you today."

"I thought I'd lost you, too," he said, tugging his shirt off from over his head. He pulled me back into him, both of us stripped bare from the waist up. The feeling of my skin against his made warmth spread up from my belly, stretching out across my limbs in pinpricks.

"I'm here," Navin whispered again. "*We're* here. We survived."

"We're here," I said, stretching up on my tiptoes, relief flooding through me as my muscles finally relaxed. As my lips met his, I surrendered to this moment, to the comfort I knew only his body would bring me.

I needed him in so many ways in that moment. Needed his comfort, his reassurance, his warmth, his love; needed to feel like I wasn't free-falling through the sky but firmly planted on solid ground.

As his warm hand splayed across the small of my back, he crushed me tighter into him. I let out a soft moan. His tongue licked into my mouth, caressing my own, luring me back to life, reeling me back into myself. My fingers trailed down his hot torso, landing on his belt buckle. He unbuttoned my wide-legged trousers without breaking our kiss. The fabric dropped to my feet, and I stepped out of it, kicking it aside. In my panic, I hadn't bothered with undergarments and was now justly rewarded for it as his hands trailed up my backside and squeezed.

I finally worked his belt open and hooked my fingers in both his trousers and undershorts, yanking them down and freeing his erection. I stretched up to kiss him again, my skin burning at every point we touched. I backed him up until the backs of his legs hit the kitchen table behind him, and I leaned into him until he sat.

"We're going to have to burn this table," he said with a laugh as I nipped at his bottom lip.

I shoved him back farther, his hands steadying me as I put one knee up on one side of him, climbing onto his lap. He gripped my ass tighter, holding me there poised above his hard cock.

"We survived," I whispered, holding his gaze as I stroked him from base to tip. His eyes guttered as I positioned him at my entrance, my mouth parting on a shaky breath as I began to lower myself onto him.

"We survived," he groaned, his hands tensing as I lowered farther until I was fully seated and every point of us joined.

I kissed him, reveling in the fullness, feeling for the first time since the battle anchored in a way that I so desperately needed. This was a promise only our bodies could make. We were here. Together. Tomorrow would bring with it a myriad of sorrows. I steeled my heart for all the pain I knew was to come, but there, with him, for one split second, everything felt safe and warm and right.

CALLA

WE STOPPED ON THE OUTSKIRTS OF DURID, RIGHT BEFORE THE border with Olmdere. I'd wanted to keep going, to get back to my home court, feeling like an army of Ice Wolves was on our tail the whole ride, but Mina and Ora had both insisted that we could contact Sadie from here, and so we stopped.

Ora had tried to explain what had just happened over and over on the ride, but no words seemed to permeate the barriers erected in my mind. I wanted to feel hurt, betrayed even, by their lack of faith in me. They had secrets that they never shared, magic that they'd never used, or at least if they had, I hadn't been aware of it. I'd shown Ora the quietest and rarest parts of my soul, and they had seen and accepted me for them. But still, I knew there was so much of their life I had barely scratched the surface of. Of course, the mysterious musicians of Galen den' Mora had their secrets, and from what I'd seen, clearly ones that should be kept from Wolves. It made sense, and yet I couldn't seize hold of that information, couldn't turn it around in my mind and inspect it the way I wanted to. I heard the words: Songkeepers, magic, Sawyn . . . but they meant nothing. Ora went on and on, and I barely moved, barely reacted. At some point I'd need to figure out how to use everything they'd told me to help with this war, but first I needed to find a way to get the horrific memories out of the way.

All I could think about was Briar, the echoes of my screams, the rush of blood from my wounded leg. Briar was so much a part of me, the other side to my coin, and Sawyn had stolen her from me, my only family or friend at the time. I'd fought through three kingdoms to get her back, *died* to save her, and now she was gone again. The loss felt like a missing piece of me, so numb and hollow without her.

Where did they take her? Was she hurting? Was she locked up in a room like the one Nero had left her in that dreamless slumber? Forgotten?

I wished with everything in me that I could turn around and race to Damrienn, sword in hand. I hated, too, the way I felt tugged in a million different directions now: Queen and sister, warrior and diplomat. I wanted to slaughter every single Wolf who stood between me and my twin, and yet I was going in the opposite direction, preparing to protect my people. I knew Briar would tell me to do as much, and still, I loathed myself for it, because it meant I was still weak, still able to be threatened with the people I loved.

The sun shone high above, warming the chill that filled my body. Grae had to guide me like a dog herding sheep as we disembarked from the carriage. My legs moved, my arms swung, but my mind was stuck reliving Briar's abduction over and over. Ora had acquired us some clothing from a washing line on our journey northward. My velvet robes waved in the breeze, flapping like the sound of a crow's wings.

Tears carved lines down my ruddy cheeks as I stared at my vacant reflection in the gleam of my golden bracelet. Everything in me felt both numbed and heightened, the strangest senses being pulled to the forefront—the smell of limescale and blood, the soft squish of the loamy earth below my feet, the rustle of the pine trees . . .

When we arrived at a crumbling stone well, I tried to pull

some of my worries back into myself, tried to meet Ora's gaze and speak some wooden words.

"Why are we here?" My words were scratchy and foreign to my ears.

"To contact Navin and Sadie," Ora said, leaning their elbow onto the tumbledown wall. "It's a whispering well. Around the continent we speak through these wells when the sun is highest in the sky. If Navin's near one, he will hear it."

Ora let out a long, trilling whistle, the song echoing down the cavernous well and ricocheting back up again until it morphed into a sound unlike the one Ora had originally created. This new song was lower, more throaty and slow.

Ora held out a hand to me and beckoned me over. Their eyes bracketed with sympathy as I stumbled over the patchy muck and leaned over the well. I opened my mouth to speak, and my treacherous bottom lip wobbled. If Sadie was on the other side, I'd have to tell her. I'd have to tell her that I killed the Queen of Taigos, that Briar was taken, and that her brother was a part of her abduction.

More warm tears streamed down my cheeks, and I cleared my throat. Grae strode over to me, his warm broad hand on the small of my back, reassuring me that I could do this. That I must. That hand told me he'd hold me together even if this shattered me into a thousand pieces. But I had to keep going, had to push forward, had to lead even as it broke me.

I leaned my elbows onto the well, my skin pinching where the jagged stone dug into my still-raw skin. I couldn't tell if it was the wind cupping my ears or I was imagining it, but I swore I heard a shaking breath rise up the well and bounce off the stones.

I swallowed and said, "Sadie?"

SADIE

ALL THE RESOLVE I THOUGHT I'D REGAINED OVER THE LAST two days vanished when I heard Calla croak, "Sadie?"

"Calla." The name lodged in my throat, and it was all I could say for a moment. Not even the soft hum of Navin beside me could soothe me now.

We'd made it to a half caved-in well in the middle of nowhere, far from the road south. The Stoneater River was a thin line on the horizon.

I crumpled beside the whispering well, Navin's hands shooting out and catching me as my knees buckled. I clung to the well as he held me, resting my cheek on the rough stone. Brief flashes of shade covered us from the scalding sun as the red-and-gold dragon flew overhead like a circling vulture.

I pushed down on my tears enough to let the stream of words echo down the sonorous hollow: Luo was dead along with many others. Tadei was still alive having fled the carnage. I told Calla about the Songkeepers and the vase and the dragon and then . . .

Harried tears dripped off my nose and lips as I told Calla that Maez had taken hold of the dark magic, slaughtered most of the Onyx Wolf pack, and disappeared. We'd lost her. She was gone.

A long resounding silence followed before Calla asked, "You said her magic trailed off toward the Stoneater? Do you think she's going after Briar?" The words were both desperate and hopeful, as if Calla secretly wanted for Maez to be using her magic to get their twin back.

I wasn't sure, but I think I secretly hoped that, too.

"I don't know," I said. "It's unprecedented. A mated sorceress? I don't know if mating bonds can survive through such darkness." Navin shook his head beside me. "There's not a single book on it that either of us knows of."

"I have to believe that it could," Calla said, though their words were strained. "I have to believe Maez is on her way to rescue Briar. Just thinking about what she must be going through—" Calla's words died on a sob, and I heard the comforting whispers of Grae echo up through the well. I knew he was holding Calla together as much as Navin was for me in that moment.

"There's something else, Sadie," Grae said, taking over for his mate. His words came out so slowly that dread trickled down my spine.

"What is it?"

"It's Hector."

My whole body seized, weightless, my mind spinning like being tumbled in a giant wave. I couldn't lose Hector. He couldn't be gone, too. Somewhere deep within me, I thought I'd always know if something ever happened to my older brother. Like some sudden strike of pain and knowing, even if we were separated. We'd always been so connected even as we fought and bickered that I thought I'd instinctively feel his loss somehow. "Is he—"

"He's alive," Grae said quickly, and my shoulders sagged. I clenched my fist to my gut at the relief. "For all we know."

"For all you know?" I searched around me, my thoughts spinning so fast I thought I might vomit. "What do you mean, for all you know? He's not with you? Did Nero take him, too? Is he hurt? Where is he?"

"He . . ." Grae battled to get the words out, which only stoked my fears further. "Sadie, he betrayed us."

"No." The sound barely escaped my lips. "He—he couldn't

have done that. You must've gotten it wrong. He is loyal. He's loyal to us. He's loyal to *me*."

"I think he did it for you. To save you from Tadei, maybe. Who knows what Nero and your father promised him."

"My father?"

"He and your uncles were there. They must've gotten to Hector. He attacked us, Sadie. Sold us out. I'm not mistaken." Grae spoke clearly and plainly as if debriefing a soldier after an attack. "He pointed his sword at us and blocked our exits. He gave us up to Nero. He worked with Ingrid to lure us into a trap."

"No."

"I'm sorry, Sadie. He fled before they took Briar and his paw prints lead toward Nesra's Pass."

A broken sob escaped my lips. First Maez, now Hector. Navin's arms banded tighter around me and crushed me into his chest as if protecting me from the blow of those words. Still, they landed like a poisoned arrow straight to my sternum.

My true family. Betrayed. Gone.

Hector had been spying on the Golden Court for King Nero? How had my father and uncles wormed their way back into his life? Had they given him an ultimatum like they'd tried to do with me? Was he their first port of call to getting their lives and reputations back after I evaded them?

I shook my head, shoving out of Navin's grip, trying to battle the very notion that Hector had it in him. I stormed toward the wagon and let out a sharp scream that ricocheted across the bare desert. Balling my hands into fists, I shrieked my vengeance and cursed the Goddess in the sky. I unsheathed a knife from my thigh belt and stabbed it into the metal spoke in front of me, again and again, not even denting the magical wagon wheel. I attacked unseeing, my eyes welling with tears faster than I could blink them away. What had happened to us? To all of the people I called family?

My hand slipped down the blade, cutting my palm open, and I dropped it to the sand, punching the wheel with my bare knuckles instead. Every ounce of pain exploded though me as my knuckles crunched on the hard wood. Maez. Briar. Hector. All those Onyx Wolf bodies. All the citizens suffering in Damrienn. All the people, human and Wolf alike, who would die still. The carnage would be so vast it would never end. This war would raze the entire continent.

Navin's arms banded around me, hauling me off my feet and fusing me against him. I screamed and thrashed in his grip, blind with rage, but he didn't let go as he began humming a tune to me. Each deep note vibrated into my back, making my movements slow until my limbs and eyelids were heavy.

"You bastard!" I screamed as Navin continued his deep, slow song. Blood from my sliced hand splattered across the tiles and smeared down his arms as I struggled. "Don't you dare use your magic on me! Let me go!"

He stopped singing, and I wondered if his songs were a gut instinct rather than intentional. I knew he would never use magic on me without my permission ever again. But when he loosened his grip on me, I felt like a kite with its strings cut. Floating, lost, rudderless. The grief instantly became unbearable again.

"Make it stop," I cried, wrapping his arms back around me. "Please!"

Navin's grip tightened again, and he resumed his song. I thrashed one more time, my whole body feeling weighed down with lead. I opened my mouth to scream my anguish again, but the will to do so slowly ebbed, my anger morphing into exhaustion and exhaustion into sleep. Anger was foreign to me now, rage unable to be summoned. My body went limp as Navin scooped me up into his arms.

"*Save your rage, my love, my goddess,*" he sang, carrying on the tune that was pulling me under. "*Save your wrath for the enemies growing like the flames. Save your wrath for the monsters, and traitors, and war games. This broken world I promise you . . ."*

His words faded away into nothingness as I slipped into a deep dreamless sleep.

THE FOLLOWING DAY WAS A BLUR OF SLEEP AND SONG, AND IT was evening before I finally roused enough to open my eyes. I took in the canvas ceiling of Galen den' Mora first as the remnants of sleep dissipated from my mind. The tight grip of sleep loosened, and my mind started to pull into the present moment. My body felt calm, my hands running across the smooth sheets below me, no twinges of cuts or pain radiating from them. My bloody palms and knuckles were healed. I must've shifted in my sleep, but I had no recollection of it.

From my periphery, I saw Navin perched at the edge of my bunk humming a familiar little song—the same song he'd sung as we'd rode through the Sevelde Forest what felt like a lifetime ago. His singing halted as I rolled to my side.

"Is it a magical song?" I mused, wiping the grit of sleep from my eyes. The sky through the window was awash with soft pinks and burnt oranges. I didn't know if it was dawn or dusk, my body still boneless and disoriented from the power of Navin's song.

"All songs are magic, whether they're spells or not." Calloused fingers slid over the dip of my waist and up to rest on my thigh. "But yes, it's a protection song," he said, his voice scratchy, and I wondered how many hours he'd been singing. "I hadn't realized I was singing it, must've been instinct." His eyes shined like molten copper as they lifted to mine. "I hum when I'm worried."

I imagined him and his father singing the same song as they traversed the shadowed caverns of the Sevelde mines—of his lone song carrying on after his father had died. A sorrowful pain bloomed in my chest, thinking of him nervously singing it still as we rolled through the golden trees. I was glad now that I'd chosen to sit there and hold his hand, letting him know this time he didn't have to be brave alone.

"I can't believe you have a song powerful enough to make me sleep when I was in such a state." I'd intended the statement to sound accusatory, but it lacked my intended bite.

"You were about to shatter every bone in your hands," he said, his thumb sweeping across my now-healed knuckles and lifting my hand to kiss them. "Even if you could heal yourself, I couldn't bear to watch you destroy yourself. I hate watching you suffer."

"Maybe I needed to suffer," I said as all the horror of the past few days washed through me again. It had always been my coping strategy—to excise the pain within my heart by inflicting it upon others or even within my own physical body. I didn't know any other way to release it and now it festered there still even after shifting and rest.

"No one needs to suffer. Not even your enemies," Navin said, letting out a disapproving grunt. I wanted to argue with him, to tell him exactly who I thought needed to suffer, but I knew he was right. Kill, yes—there were people who needed to die by my teeth and claws. But suffer? No—that wasn't the warrior way. I was still trying to figure out exactly what being a warrior in this brand-new world meant, but I knew, deep down, that *had* to be part of it if I was going to retain any bit of my true self.

He tugged my hand, pulling me onto his lap. He brushed the disheveled hair from my eyes, holding my gaze for a moment, before rising to stand and lifting me along with him.

"Come," he said. "I made something while you were sleeping."

I stretched and followed him, combing my fingers through my hair as we moved through the galley and out onto the back steps of Galen den' Mora. The evening air was cool and fragrant as Navin led me toward a rock formation of pale stone. The dip of a rock created a little alcove of striated rock, and upon the ledge . . . was an altar. A sage silk stole was held in place by a bowl of silver coins, along with a smattering of ivory candles— one already lit. A string of auspicious silver moons hung between the two rock walls, the metal gleaming in the flicker of candle-light. I knew what this was, had seen it in the castle of Damrienn during the full moon ceremonies when we were called by the moon priests to pray. I couldn't remember the last time I'd lined up to light a candle. When was the last time I'd begged the God-dess to hear my prayers?

My brows knitted as I stared at the moon altar. "Wh—"

"I thought you might like to light a candle," Navin whis-pered, kissing my temple. "It's how the Wolves pray, is it not?"

My traitorous eyes welled at the sight, my emotions still adrift after all that had transpired. "You built me an altar so that I can pray?"

"It's the full moon tonight," he offered, looking up at the swollen moon hanging low in the sky. "I thought you might want to commune with your Goddess." When I didn't reply, he shuffled his weight uncomfortably, clearly thinking he'd made a misstep.

I cleared my throat, so overcome with emotions I'd forgot-ten to speak. I'd never felt more deeply seen or embraced nor did I realize how desperately I needed a funnel through which to grieve—one that wouldn't shatter bones and leave the walls bloody. But Navin knew.

"I love it." I threaded my fingers with his, and his shoulders eased in relief as he pulled me into his side. "Definitely beats breaking my hands."

He knowingly laughed, rustling my loose hair as he dusted another kiss to my temple. "Do you want me to go or stay?"

"Stay." The word instantly left my lips as quickly as I could think it. I wanted him here, holding this space for me, my heart finally willing to admit how much I needed him.

I selected the single glowing candle and lifted my chin to the sky, letting the sight of the full moon wash through me as I murmured my prayers.

"Moon Goddess, hear me this night," I said.

My voice wobbled and I couldn't get the words out, my prayer morphing into one of raw emotions instead of words. Navin shuffled closer until I could feel the heat of his chest at my back. I wanted to ask the Goddess to forgive me for all who'd died by my hands, to usher all the fallen souls into the afterlife. I wanted to ask her to guide my next steps and to watch over me for another moon. More hot tears streamed down my face and dripped off my chin. I wanted to ask her to find a way to reckon with my brother and to bring Maez back to me.

But instead, I just cried and trusted that she knew everything unfurling from my heart. These tears felt different than all the ones I'd shed before, neither panicked nor breaking but rather healing like the gentleness of falling asleep, like the whole world sighing. The tears cleansed me of all the fear and rage. The pain was still there but lessened, pulling from me like the smoke from the flame. The moonlight mended me back together along with the hand clenching my own.

I set the candle back down and turned into Navin, his arms ready to envelop me. "Thank you," I whispered into his tear-stained tunic.

When I released him, I grabbed a candle and passed it to him. "Let's pray for your family, too."

His throat bobbed as he took the candle from me, and I saw all the emotions in his expression that he would never be able to put words to, not even a song. Lighting the candle felt like a vow between the two of us, standing at the altar of moonlight.

I watched the flickering candles through watery eyes as we reckoned with all we'd lost together. I knew it would take many moons, maybe a lifetime, to fully heal, but the moon was still in the sky and Navin was still by my side and right then I knew I had to make that count for more than the fear of what comes next.

CALLA

THE HALLS OF OLMDERE WERE BLEAK NOW WITH SO MANY gone. A somber shadow blanketed my court. Briar, Maez . . . I felt Sadie's absence so acutely, wishing she could be here with us to reconcile everything that had just happened to us. I even grieved Hector. I wanted to dream of skewering him through like I had Ingrid, but instead I dreamed of cornering him and demanding to know just one thing: Why? After all we'd been through, how could he turn his weapons on us, not just me but Grae, his oldest friend.

I shoved it aside. He was Sadie's kill now. I'd let her deal with him. If only hate could be a singular emotion. If only the others didn't crowd it out and temper its blaze. If only my mind could stop reliving every moment with Hector in Taigos wondering when—*when*—had he turned on us? How had Nero gotten his claws into him and Ingrid from so far away?

Ora's palm gently settled atop my hand, and I realized I'd been picking at my fingernails until they bled. I'd shift and they'd be gone, and I'd pick them all over again and gnaw at the inside of my cheek until I tasted copper.

The evening air carried a slight chill that raised the hairs on my arms. We sat around the firepit on the upper terrace of the palace, overlooking the lively western quarter of the city. Sadie and Maez should be down there now, jigging to a fiddle player and besting the patrons at a game of darts. My gaze flickered to the woods beyond, where no swirl of smoke arose from the lone cabin, no windows afire with the light of a warm hearth. The secret dream Briar had never whispered even to me, the one she finally got to live, now sat cold and joyless on the shadowed horizon.

I took in our group huddled around the firepit. Grae, Ora, Mina, and myself. So few. Too few.

Sadie and Navin were still in Lower Valta on their way to southern Damrienn. Their harebrained plan to turn monsters into weapons of war was underway, but even with a legion of beasts under their control, I felt that hopelessness creeping in. Was this my only choice? Would I have to order monsters to slaughter every Wolf who didn't bend the knee to me? All of Aotreas would be at war with us by the time the sun rose. Nero was spreading his campaign of hatred far and wide; soon Taigos would be infected and humans everywhere would suffer. I could see no path forward except for one of bloodshed.

Ora's hand squeezed my arm. "Hope isn't lost yet," they said as if reading my thoughts.

"Taigos is too busy with ranking and infighting to be a threat," Grae said, though that did little to comfort me. "Whatever is left of Valta will try to take Taigos while they are without a ruler. Which means the Ice Wolves will be too preoccupied with protecting their southern borders to orchestrate an attack on us."

"But they would attack us, *will* attack us, once they get organized." I shook my head. "We are worse off than when we started. We don't have a single ally on the entire continent now."

"*Wolf* ally," Ora corrected. "We won't find our allies with the Wolves right now. Once they see your strength, maybe, but right now we'll find our allies with the humans. I think they'll be more inclined than ever to support your cause, too."

Mina knocked on the arm of her chair and I lifted my head. "You are the only ruler left defending the humans now," she signed. "People will rally to you. Galen den' Mora will come to your aid once more."

I remembered the battle in the grand hall just below out feet. "All those badges," I whispered, thinking of the sea of musicians who attacked Sawyn's Rooks and the little embroidered badges hidden amongst the crowd.

"I've sent the songs down the wells," Ora said with a slow nod. "They will come."

I slid my gaze to them. "Do they all have magic like yours?"

"Some have more potential for magic than others." Ora pursed their painted red lips, debating for a second before nodding. "I suppose there should be no more secrets between members of the Golden Court. I don't know if they all will be able to control beasts, if that's what you're asking, but many might prove useful in times of war—healing the wounded, calming the frightened. Gods, even just helping an unsettled court sleep."

"We should send the Songkeepers to Valta," Mina signed. "Have them train with Navin. He can teach them the songs and weed out the ones with the most potential."

"They were once called officers in the Songkeepers army," Ora mused, contemplatively scratching the scruff on their chin. "I never thought I'd live to see the rise of such an army again. But you're right. It's time."

Grae reached over and threaded his fingers through my own. "One person controlling a monster would be an advantage, but hundreds?" He offered me a half-smile, one cheek dimpling. "If it can be done—"

"That is a big if," I cut in, unwilling to let in even a sliver of hope.

"*If* it can be done," Grae continued, squeezing my hand, "it might be enough to win a war."

Ora chuckled, light and lilting. "How my ancestors would roll in their graves to see us now," they said. "The Songkeepers working with Wolves."

Mina snorted. "To help the Wolves save humans, no less."

"It might be enough," I murmured. "It has to be enough."

Soon, I'd need to address the people of Olmdere. I'd need to tell my people what had happened in Taigos and give speeches rallying soldiers in a land that had barely known a season's peace since the death of Sawyn. It was beyond cruel, pulling them from tyranny and thrusting them into another war. Soon, I'd need to be the strong Queen who held my head high and spoke with a reassuring confidence I didn't feel inside.

Soon.

But now, alone with my most trusted friends and mate, I could be uncertain, defeated, afraid. They'd hold me together for this one night and then I'd need to lead again.

"Maybe we'll have more luck on our side than we think," Grae said, tipping his chin to the sky.

My eyes trailed over the constellations, down, down, down to the point that just skimmed over the horizon: Damrienn. There the stars twinkled with a brilliant emerald light, reflecting the eerie green magic that I'd once seen Sawyn wield. Sorcerer's magic. *Maez's* magic.

My pulse thrummed in my ears as I stared up at the emerald stars filling the distant sky. "Sweet Moon, I hope she's going to rescue Briar. Please, by all the Gods, be going to protect her." My windpipe squeezed as I added, "But she could be just as likely going there to kill my sister and everyone else in that palace. Death magic only sees enemies. She might not care who dies for her purposes any more than Sawyn did."

"Perhaps the magic of their mating bond still lives on even with all of that violent magic inside her," Ora said. "It won't be easy, but maybe she can fight that darkness, maybe she can find a way back to herself through that connection . . . or harness it at least to help her mate. Maybe their love is stronger than the darkness."

The world took on a glassy sheen as my eyes welled, my cheeks heating as I remembered that sleigh disappearing down the mountain. Still, I was plagued by the ghosts of my screams. I subconsciously rubbed my hand down my thigh where I still bore the scar from the attack. The pain and fear echoed in me, resurfacing again and again. I prayed to any god that would listen, prayed that Ora was right, that Maez could fight with her sorceress magic *for* us instead of against us.

"Come on, Maez," I whispered to those twinkling distant stars. "Bring Briar back."

"My cousin is stubborn. I have faith." Grae kissed my temple. "You're stubborn, too, little fox." His calloused palm trailed over the bolt of golden lighting across my collarbone. "You've battled a sorceress before and won. I have faith in us, in *you*. You will fight and you will win and you will bring peace to this land just as you wished with your dying breath."

My hand reached up and covered his. I closed my eyes, mapping the trail of my scars in my mind. It gave me a little strength knowing I had that golden magic still singing through my veins. My family was stolen from me through fear of this power, for the allegiances I had to every person in my court. Grae was right. There were so many people in the shadows that stretched out over the horizon, people like me who wanted to claim their life, their destinies with two hands, just as Vellia had once told me to do. I couldn't shrink myself down like I had in Taigos anymore. I needed to live bigger, louder, until my people believed they could, too. I knew being merem might never get easier, but I would get stronger until every single person in my court never felt the shame of trying to contort themselves into a box that never fit. I would make this court better than the one I inherited even if I had to die all over again trying.

"We're going to the council chamber." I stood with a new-found resoluteness. I'd indulged my doubts; now I needed to rule. "We will mourn while we plan. Nero has started a war on humans." I looked back up to the distant emerald sky. "And we will make sure he lives to regret that choice before we end him."

SADIE

I STARED OUT AT THE WOBBLING ROPE BRIDGE WAITING FOR US to cross the Stoneater River. I dipped a toe into the burning sand and quickly pulled it out again. I was ready for a change in weather.

Navin plucked at the strings of his lastar, the dragon arcing through the sky—up and down—flying rhythmically to the music. To our right, heat waves warped the horizon, the brightness of the sun leaching the world of color as I squinted. To our left, a shoreline of river grasses morphed into a rolling pine forest. Damrienn. My homeland.

The week had been a slow process of weaving my soul back together. There were edges that would always be frayed, questions that kept me on tenterhooks, but at least through practice and sheer determination I could keep going. Navin had helped spool me back in, the comfort of his body calling me home like a lover's song. His love sustained me in the wreckage of a world come undone.

As the dragon moved, I scribbled onto a piece of parchment our findings. The monster didn't turn my stomach like it used to, having gazed upon it enough times to morph from dread to curiosity to an almost begrudging respect. It would make a fearsome ally if Navin could harness its strength. There was still so much more we needed to test, though.

How long could he control this creature? Did the vase's song only work on this dragon? When Navin needed to sleep and his songs were interrupted, the dragon would return to the sky and hunt for creatures in the distant dunes. When the dragon had returned one morning still chewing a crishenem leg in its mouth, I knew we had a formidable weapon in this war.

I began to wonder how long after Navin's songs played was the dragon still within his control. It seemed to know to return to Galen den' Mora after a night's hunt. Would it stay close without any songs at all?

I lifted the hem of my tunic and dabbed the sweat on my brow. Squinting at the horizon, I asked, "No sign of anyone?"

Navin paused, dropping his lastar and sitting in the shade of the steps. He was slick with sweat, clearly exhausted from his hours of singing. We needed more people desperately if we were going to make this work. One Songkeeper couldn't conduct a beast through an hours-long battle.

"They've been contacted," Navin panted, whipping his tunic over his head to wipe his face. My eyes trailed down his lean torso, a familiar hunger building in me again. The fact we got any work done at all was a miracle. "But I don't know how many heard, nor how many will come. The Songkeepers have truly fractured now—Rasil's gone rogue and others will join him. Who knows if any will stand with Galen den' Mora anymore."

I held a hand over my brow and stared off in the direction of the Stormcrest Ranges so far in the distance I'd lose them on the horizon if I stared too long. I wanted to return to Olmdere, wanted to hold Calla as she grieved, wanted to rally with the others to her cause, but this . . . this could win us the war. I wouldn't let my stubbornness win out. We'd find a way to control these beasts and bring them into her army.

"That was good," I said, finishing jotting down my notes and tucking the booklet back in my pocket.

Navin braced his hands on his knees and sucked in deep frenzied breaths. "Just good?"

"We'll try to find an ostekke at sunset."

"You're evil." Navin tossed his balled-up tunic at me. "I never thought I would ever be seeking out monsters."

"We need to try," I opposed. "Or we can summon more—"

"I'll do everything I can," he said tightly, clearly exhausted but adamant. The guilt of his conjuring gnawed at him. Nightmares pulled him from the depths of sleep. Maez still hadn't been found. For all we knew, Briar was still in Nero's control, too. And my brother . . . there had been no word from my brother, and I prayed that he was somewhere dead in the snow. Because if he was alive, I would kill him.

"I'm glad it is you with the power now and not me," I said finally, stepping out of Navin's touch. As the dragon disappeared over the pine forest, I picked up his lastar and patted him on the shoulder. "You should go again. I'm going to keep translating that songbook we found under Ora's pillow."

Navin grabbed the instrument from my hand and gently propped it back against the wall. He leaned his bare chest into me, his half-mast eyes dropping to my mouth. "I'll join you."

"No."

His hands skimmed up my sides. "Why not?"

"Because when you *join me*, we never get any work done," I said, playfully shoving at him as his hands tightened on my waist.

We'd been poring over every dusty old tome and song sheet we could find in Galen den' Mora, translating so many ancient scrolls that my skin bore the permanent scent of old parchment. But still, we'd found no answers to how to reverse the effects of dark magic. I hoped the temple of knowledge might have more answers. Surely if there was a way to conjure it into the world, there was a way of pulling it back out again?

Navin let out a hungry protestation as he nipped at my earlobe. "I like the way we work."

My hands trailed up his back as he kissed his way down my neck. "Don't think I don't know what you're doing, distracting me."

He laughed against my shoulder. "So long as it's working."

A high whistle sang out over the desert. We lifted our heads, finding a tall figure cresting the nearest dune, a trail of a dozen others following him.

"I think you've had this place all to yourself for too long, Navin," the tall one called. The man had a smooth, honeyed baritone, his eyes a matching bronze to Navin's own. His gaze slid to me. "We meet again, Wolf."

Recognition alighted my expression. I'd seen this man before. Behind him the others gathered, all of them wearing little badges on their lapels: the Songkeepers of Galen den' Mora. They'd come to our aid once more.

But the tall one—the one I'd nearly cut down with my sword only a few moons ago—the one Navin stopped me from killing. I glowered back at him. Of all the people to answer Ora's call . . .

The group as one crossed fists over their chests and dropped into a bow.

"What is this, Kian?" Navin asked.

"We heard Ora's song. We're the new officers of your army, General." Navin's brother rose and smiled. "We're here to train some monsters."

DRAMATIS PERSONAE

Calla Marriel: Gold Wolf, twin to Briar, child of the late King
  and Queen of Olmdere
Briar Marriel: Gold Wolf, twin to Calla, Crown Princess, child
  of the late King and Queen of Olmdere
Grae Claudius: Silver Wolf, Crown Prince of Damrienn
Nero Claudius: Silver Wolf, King of Damrienn
Maez Claudius: Silver Wolf, cousin to Grae and niece to the King,
  one of Grae's royal guard
Sadie Rauxtide: Silver Wolf, sister to Hector, one of Grae's royal
  guard
Hector Rauxtide: Silver Wolf, brother to Sadie, one of Grae's
  royal guard
Ora: human, leader of Galen den' Mora musical troupe
Navin: human, part of Galen den' Mora
Mina: human, twin to Malou, part of Galen den' Mora
Malou: human, twin to Mina, part of Galen den' Mora, deceased
  in battle of Olmdere
Sawyn: sorceress who killed the King and Queen of Olmdere and
  now controls the kingdom
Rooks: soldiers of Sawyn's army
Ingrid Engdahl: Queen of the Ice Wolves
Klaus: Queen Ingrid's cousin

Luo Yassine: King of the Onyx Wolves, older brother to Taidei

Taidei Yassine: Prince of the Onyx Wolves, younger brother to Luo

Rasil: Head Guardian of the Songkeepers

Aubron and Pilus: Lord Rauxtide's brothers, Sadie's uncles

COURTS

Olmdere (capital: Olmdere City): home to humans and the Gold Wolf pack

Damrienn (capital: Highwick): home to humans and the Silver Wolf pack

Taigos (capital: Taigoska): home to humans and the Ice Wolf pack

Valta (capital: Rikesh): home to humans and the Onyx Wolf pack

ACKNOWLEDGMENTS

THANK YOU TO MY MOUNTAINEERS FOR CELEBRATING MY BOOKS both online and out in the world. You are the most amazing group of readers and I'm honored to share these stories with you! *The best mountains to climb are fictional ones xx.*

Thank you to all my amazing patrons! A very special thank you to my Fae, Royal, and Goddess patrons: Samantha, Abigail, Val, Lindsay, Bri, Divya, Kat, Stacy, JeNaya, Lauren, Latham, Audrey, Mandy, Leigh, Jaime, Kelly, Hannah, Sarah, Amy, Marissa, Ciara, Linda, Katie, and Virginia! Your support means so much to me! I can't wait to take you on more fantasy adventures!

Thank you to my book wifey and cozy co-author, Kate, for all of your support and for the amazing job you do formatting my gorgeous rom-coms, designing merch, and running the A.K. shop! Thank you to my assistant extraordinaire, Treece, for keeping Team A.K. going. I so appreciate all the work you do!

Thank you to my amazing agent, Jessica Watterson at SDLA, for championing my stories and for supporting me through this wild journey of publishing. I love being represented by you and look forward to many more bookish adventures in the future!

Thank you to the whole Harper Voyager team all over the world. It has been a pleasure working with you all. Thank you to my amazing team for championing this book and supporting diverse stories. A big thank you to my editor, David Pomerico, for helping shape this story into the best it can be and making me a better writer!

Thank you to my family for supporting me and encouraging me to pursue the career of my dreams. I adore the life we've built together and love you endlessly. To my kids, thank you for having imaginations bigger than the sky and for giving me *many* fantastical words and ideas through our play together!

Lastly, thank you to my fur babies, Ziggy, Bruno, and Timmy, for being furry weighted blankets who support me to finish these books.

ABOUT THE AUTHOR

A.K. MULFORD is a bestselling fantasy author and former wildlife biologist who swapped rehabilitating monkeys for writing novels. She/they are inspired to create diverse stories that transport readers to new realms, making them fall in love with fantasy for the first time, or all over again. She now lives in Australia with her husband and two young human primates, creating lovable fantasy characters and making ridiculous TikToks.